## IN A PIRATE'S CLUTCHES

The old adversarial habit eclipsed their flirtatious banter, but Felicity didn't want to lose the ground she'd gained by her change of tactics. That was the only reason she wished to hear the huskiness in his voice return. "My father would be horrified if he knew half the things I know about you."

Her gentle barb recalled Drew's slow grin. He closed the short distance between them until they stood mere inches from each other. She tensed, thinking he might kiss her.

His warm breath caressed her cheek. "Do go on, Felicity."

The deepness of his softly spoken dare gave her the courage to continue.

"How do I know you're a pirate yourself?"

Drew's focus dropped to her mouth and lingered there. "You don't."

She was out of her element. She'd pushed the game to the brink and waited for him to seal her fate with a kiss, but he didn't even flinch.

"I suppose the fact that you haven't ravaged me accounts for something."

"I'm considering it."

Other *Leisure* books by Cheryl Howe:
**AFTER THE ASHES**

# *The Pirate &*
# THE PURITAN

## CHERYL HOWE

LEISURE BOOKS  NEW YORK CITY

A LEISURE BOOK®

September 2003

Published by

Dorchester Publishing Co., Inc.
200 Madison Avenue
New York, NY 10016

ISBN 0-8439-5274-1

The name "Leisure Books" and the stylized "L" with design are
trademarks of Dorchester Publishing Co., Inc.

Printed in the United States of America.

Visit us on the web at www.dorchesterpub.com.

*To Cid and Orlando Stephenson and Ella Fleming, my first fans. Thank you for loving my books and always wanting to read the next manuscript.*

*And to Lorelle Marinello, my friend, critique partner and shoulder to cry on. Thank you for your genuine support and encouragement.*

# The Pirate &
# THE PURITAN

# Chapter One

*Barbados, The British West Indies, 1721*

Felicity Kendall fumbled beneath her collar to unbutton the high neck of her wool bodice. Escape from the floating torture chamber that had carried her from Boston hadn't eased her discomfort in the least; the solid ground under her feet continued to lurch. She used the flat of her hand to shield her eyes against the unrelenting sun, feeling as vulnerable as if she'd been set down in the center of Babylon instead of the British West Indies.

"You all right, mistress?"

Felicity jerked her gaze from the shifting cobblestones. A woman with skin the color of roasted pecans and a purple silk umbrella over her head leaned in closer and mercifully blocked the rays of searing heat.

"Thank you, mistress," Felicity replied. "I just needed to catch my breath." She offered the woman a weak smile while trying not to gawk at her odd mode of dress. Shiny material of gold, crimson and hunter green plaid draped

1

carelessly across the Barbadian's hips and knotted in a manner that exposed her from mid-shin to bare feet. Her bodice consisted of nothing more than a corset dyed the same purple as her parasol.

"You're going to have to shed some of those clothes if you want to stay on your feet. Here, you take this." The woman tried to hand over her umbrella. Jewel-encrusted rings of gold and silver adorned her every finger.

Felicity sucked in a breath and stepped back. "I couldn't. Thank you for your kindness. I'm fine now."

The woman shrugged and sauntered off.

Felicity let out her breath. Immediately, she wished she could recall the Barbadian, but the woman had already melted back into the colorful throng crowding the wharf. The humid air she inhaled too quickly almost forced Felicity to her knees. She pulled the prickly, damp wool of her bodice from her skin, willing herself not to faint. In such dire circumstances, accepting a beautiful silk parasol from a well-meaning woman could hardly be categorized as the sin of vanity.

Not that Felicity had yet noticed anyone who seemed concerned with excessive dress one way or the other. Apparently Barbados hadn't adopted anything remotely resembling the code adhered to by most Bostonians. Woe to her weak-willed father. Truly, her arrival would be fortuitous for them both. And, if she kept telling herself so, she might actually manage to convince him—unless, of course, she located him after the captain of the *Queen Elizabeth*.

Desperation forced Felicity to trudge on, despite the fact that the ground still swayed with each step. She carefully rounded the growing pile of her father's unloaded cargo.

A sailor she recognized from her voyage hoisted another large crate onto the stack. He'd removed his shirt, and Felicity turned away. The idea that she'd underestimated the ease with which she'd fit into her new home unsettled her stomach all over again. No one had ever mentioned that seasickness lasted beyond the confines of the sea.

"Excuse me, sir," she called to the sailor over her shoulder, her face averted. "Is my father's bookkeeper about?" Someone should be recording the stock. They'd be able to escort her to her father.

"That'd be Master Marley, but I don't see him." The sailor stepped onto a crate and scanned the crowd. "Over there. Captain McCulla, he works for your father. He'll help ya."

She nodded, grateful for his assistance, though she had no doubt he only obliged her because he wanted her gone as much as his captain.

After taking a deep breath and clutching her black leather valise close to her body, Felicity plowed past half-dressed natives selling fruit, equally disrobed women selling themselves, and a horde of unwashed sailors. Under the eaves of a brick warehouse, she found a portly man asleep in a barrel-backed chair. A dirty boy crouched at his feet.

"Captain McCulla?" She tapped her foot. Explaining why she'd traveled across an ocean uninvited appeared less of a problem by the moment. Her father needed her organizational skills desperately. She couldn't believe Richard Marley, her father's longtime partner in his shipping interest, would let things slide so severely—even if he did have a new young wife.

"Captain McCulla!"

The boy jumped to his feet. "Can I help you, miss?"

"I'm Benjamin Kendall's daughter and I'm looking for my father."

The boy's hazel eyes widened and a smile lit his dirty face. "Gosh, Miss Felicity, you look full-grown. I thought you was a girl." Just as suddenly as it had come, the smile collapsed into a frown. "Did one of your kin die?"

"Oh, no, that's not why I'm here." Though Felicity had

renewed hope that her father might also assume her unexpected arrival was spurred by tragedy. Perhaps he'd be so relieved to discover all was well in Boston, he'd be happy to see her after all. At least he'd spoken of her to these people.

"Then why are you dressed all in black? You don't have to lie to me just 'cause I'm a kid. I know a lot about dying." The boy's red brows drew together in an expression much too old for his age.

Felicity forced a smile she'd never normally give to a stranger, not even a child. "I'm of the Puritan faith. We don't believe in excess of dress or mannerisms. It's godly to be somber, but I'm not in mourning. Truly."

The furrows in the boy's brow grew deeper, assuring Felicity she'd only confused him further. She didn't fool him any more than she did herself. "Perhaps you should take me to find my father."

"Yes, miss. This way." The barefoot boy skipped down the street. "I'm Tanner," he called over his shoulder.

Felicity hesitated. "Does *he* need help?" She scanned the red-faced man who slumped in the chair for signs of life. An enormous black fly landed on his bulbous nose and he reflexively slapped it away.

"He's always like that. Come on."

Felicity followed Tanner up the cobblestoned road marked Broad Street. Rows of planked buildings painted bright pink and greenish-blue shaded their way. The fragrance of magnolias drifted on a soft breeze, mercifully diminishing the stink from the dock. Felicity took a deep breath through her nose. Babylon or not, she hoped she could finally find peace in this strange, vibrant place.

Tanner suddenly turned and walked backward. "My folks were Scottish. I'm glad they weren't Puritan, because you look awful hot. Is your father a Puritan?"

"No. Definitely not." Felicity grinned again, pleased to be amused. Her father had always supported her mother

4

in shoving the children into the Puritan faith, but no one had ever maintained the notion of bringing jovial Benjamin Kendall into the fold. As affable as he was, the man had never been prudent, pious or thrifty a day in his life.

"I didn't think so. Your father's a fine man. He gave Captain McCulla work 'cause nobody else would. The captain's not my papa. He just takes care of me 'cause I don't have nobody else, neither."

Felicity gazed over the boy's head. A team of horses pulling an overstuffed wagon careened onto the narrow street. "Look where you're going before you get hurt," she warned.

Tanner blushed at her concern, as if she had just paid him a compliment. "Aw, I'm fine." He pranced forward a few feet, then turned to face her again. "Your father gives me boiled sweets whenever I want. And Lord Christian's gonna give me one of his coats when I'm big enough. He's got one in every color. Even orange."

Felicity herded Tanner to the side of the street before the wagon rattled past. "Who might this Lord Christian be?"

"He's one of them haughty nobles. That's what Captain McCulla says. Lord Christian and the captain don't like each other much, on account of Lord Christian wanting to give the captain the boot and find me another place to live. I told Lord Christian I didn't want to have to live with somebody new again, so he gave up. We're still friends, though."

"And Master Marley, how is he faring?"

Tanner's grin slid from his face along with its color. His freckles stood out in bold contrast. He abruptly turned and ran ahead, forcing Felicity to raise the hem of her skirts to keep up. She reassured herself that she'd arrived in the nick of time. Her father's tendency to trust the wrong sort had obviously flared up again.

How soon he'd apparently forgotten the last nobleman

with connections who had promised the New England Trading Company a special charter to trade if only they'd cross the right palms with enough gold! By the time Marley had discovered that the aristocrat had no real influence, their coffers were practically empty. Her father and Marley had been forced to sell all but one ship, the very one that took them to Barbados to start over again.

No doubt her father and Marley had had another falling out over her father's impulsive business practices. Whoever this Lord Christian might be, he'd have to go.

They reached a tall white building with the NEW ENGLAND TRADING COMPANY carved into a wood plaque overhead, and Tanner burst through the door. Felicity caught up a few moments later, but paused to wipe the sweat from her brow. She needed to be calm and confident when she faced her father, not wilted and unnerved. She plastered a smile on her face before stepping inside.

Her father stood over a paper-strewn desk, frozen in the motion of handing Tanner something wrapped in pink-and-gold paper. Seeing the way her father's plump figure had swelled, Felicity would have guessed it was a sugar-plum—his favorite—even if Tanner hadn't already given him away.

Tanner glanced at her, then back to her father. "I forgot to tell you I brought Miss Felicity."

The expression of sheer horror on her father's face told her she'd beaten the *Queen Elizabeth*'s captain with news of her arrival. Even so, her father seemed indisputably displeased. Felicity strained to keep her smile in place. The fact that he didn't want her either hurt more than she dared dwell on at the moment.

Heavy boots dropping to the brick floor drew Felicity's attention to a man seated behind an adjacent desk. He had an excessively powdered face and hair a ghoulish shade of white. His painted, cherry-red lips and cheeks added to his inhuman countenance. To the further detriment of his appearance, he sported a suit of vibrant blue satin of a shade that would force even a peacock to blush. He seemed more a caricature of an aristocrat than an aristocrat. How could her father be taken in by this man?

The garish stranger stalked in her direction. He was too large, too tall, to be wearing such effeminate dress. She stiffened, not about to be intimidated.

He smiled, but it looked more like a sneer, then bowed at the waist. "Lord Christian Andrews at your service. May I be of assistance?"

His sea-green gaze snared hers, and she had the physical sensation of being grabbed despite the fact that no one had moved. Ruthlessness lurked beneath the man's bland expression.

"Dear God!"

Felicity's attention darted back to her father in time to see him barrel around the desk. "Felicity, what are you doing here?"

"Father, hold your tongue. The door is wide open. Someone could overhear."

No wonder Master Marley hid himself. A man who took the Lord's name in vain had had a hot poker plunged through his tongue the week before she left Boston. If her father continued on this path, he'd have more than the damnation of his eternal soul to fear.

"You're no longer in New England," her father said, taking her hands in his. Despite the midday heat, they were cold. "There are worse things that can happen on Barbados. You shouldn't be here."

She looked pointedly at Lord Christian, then met her father's frightened eyes. "Well, I *am* here, and I can help you." She lowered her voice. "Are you in debt to him?"

"It's nothing like that. You're the one I'm worried about."

"Ben, are you going to introduce us?" Lord Christian's tone was mild, unworried. No doubt he'd swindled her father in some way and thought he'd gotten away with his misdeeds.

"Lord Christian, this is my daughter Felicity. Felicity, my business partner, Lord Christian Andrews."

Lord Christian bowed again. In response, Felicity folded her arms over her chest and begrudgingly offered a nod of acknowledgment. He probably expected some ceremonial pomp due his birth, but he wouldn't get it from her.

Ignoring Lord Christian, she addressed her father. "What happened to Master Marley?"

"Tanner," boomed Lord Christian.

The boy jumped to his feet in a shower of candy wrappers. Both cheeks swelled with sugarplums.

Lord Christian tossed the boy a coin, a Spanish piece of eight judging by its size. "Go find yourself something solid to eat. Don't show McCulla what I gave you. And don't tell anyone about Ben's daughter, either. All right?"

Felicity withheld her approval for his generosity. The coin no doubt belonged to her father.

The boy's enthusiastic nod sent a hank of copper hair into his eyes. "Thank you, milord." He brushed past and ran from the room like a gust off the ocean.

Lord Christian turned his commanding gaze on her. Apparently he wasn't finished giving orders. "How did you get here and who else did you speak to?"

"Father!" She refused to be interrogated by this overgrown fop.

Her father ran his fingers through the tufts of his thinning white hair. "It's no use. She undoubtedly arrived on our ship. The *Queen Elizabeth* docked well over an hour ago. Her crew's probably overrun every tavern along Carlisle Bay. We can't keep her a secret."

Heat rose to Felicity's cheeks. She suspected her father might be upset with her uninvited arrival, but to be treated like a cargo of blankets infected with yellow fever was too much.

8

"Why would you want to keep me a secret? Am I something to be ashamed of?"

Her father gently squeezed her shoulders and studied her as if seeing her for the first time. "How could I be ashamed? Look how you've become a woman. You look so much like your mother did when—"

"We might not be able to keep her a secret, but we can return her to Boston before anyone can do anything about it." Lord Christian strode toward the door. "You keep her here while I arrange passage for her on the next ship raising anchor."

Felicity jerked from her father's grasp and raced to block the aristocrat's exit. "I'm not going anywhere. I don't know who you think you are, but you're not ridding yourself of me."

He easily beat her to the door. She had to come to a stumbling halt or risk collision. But that didn't mean she had any intention of giving up. She had to stay in Barbados. "I don't know how you worked your way into my father's interests, but it won't continue."

Lord Christian gripped the front doorknob with enough force to turn his knuckles as white as his powdered hair. "Miss Kendall, you'll do as we say. Truly, we only have your best interests at heart."

"You have your own best interest at heart, sir. Don't think I don't see that." She turned to her father. "I've traveled a great distance and I'd like to lie down. Please take me home."

Her father frowned. "You look like you've lost weight, daughter. Was your voyage unpleasant?"

"She doesn't leave this office. Keep her here while I see to her passage to Boston."

"I'm sorry, Felicity. You have to stay here."

The fact that her father succumbed to the other man's demands like a child infuriated Felicity all over again.

Hands on hips, she whirled around to confront Lord Christian herself. "I intend to lie down."

The man took a step forward and, without wanting to, Felicity slunk back. Andrew's green eyes narrowed, and she noticed he had a strong jaw and what looked like a once-broken nose. Underneath all that paint he had the face of a man used to violence. He was nothing like the English aristocrats fluttering around Boston.

"Sit down. I'd hate to have to tie you to that chair for the remainder of your stay in our 'Little England,' Miss Kendall."

He slipped into the more formal tones of a gentleman at the end of his threat, but the effect was chilling rather than polite.

Felicity plopped into the chair facing her father's desk and showed the man her back. She might look compliant, but she was dismissing him—whether he realized it or not. Antagonizing him further would get her nowhere. Despite the thudding of her heart, he didn't intimidate her. She was just being sensible, changing her tactics when the necessity arose.

The door slammed, and she knew by the relief sagging her shoulders that he'd left. After a cursory glance around the room, she started devising a way to send Lord Christian Andrews packing rather than herself.

"What in God's name brings you here, Felicity?"

Her father's question jerked her from her scheming. The confrontation she'd dreaded loomed before her like a dark, thunderous cloud.

Her father eased behind the desk while Felicity continued to scan the small office instead of answering his question. Two well-used desks, a few straight-backed chairs and a scarred bench comprised the room's furnishings. Yellowed maps decorated the crumbling plaster walls, with only a single gilded mirror for ornamentation—surely an addition of Lord Christian's. She'd have to start thinking of him by his surname. Thinking of him as Lord anything, especially Christian, was blasphemous.

"Felicity, I mean it. You have some explaining to do."

Her gaze finally landed on her father, the smile that crept to her face genuine. They had had several conversations over the years beginning with that same demand. Surely he hadn't changed so much that this confrontation would be different. He'd always forgiven her anything.

"I came to help you."

"Help with what?"

"By the number of goods you've been shipping to the Boston warehouse, I couldn't help but notice how your business has grown. Surely you and Master Marley could use some help."

Her father paled, then averted his gaze to the scars in his mahogany desk.

Felicity rushed on. "Has this, this . . . Master Andrews caused a rift between you and Master Marley?"

Her father lifted his head, his soft brown eyes sterner than she'd ever seen them. "You weren't to bother yourself with the business in Boston. I was wrong to ever let you help me with my financial affairs. Mistress Bishop was right: Trade with men is no place for a young woman."

"But I'm no longer a young woman." Felicity had hoped she wouldn't have to confront this argument again. Didn't her father see that spinsterhood had settled around her like a wool shawl? "Mistress Bishop meant well, but as you can see, learning to knit hasn't made me any more desirable to a prospective husband."

Her father's eyes softened to the color of milk-sweetened coffee. "How can you say that? With your rosy cheeks and sturdy frame—"

She held up her hand to stop her father. Next he'd say something about her strong white teeth. "I've seen twenty-nine years, Father, too many to be taken seriously as a wife. No one wants me, so why can't I stay here and be with you? I enjoy the work. It makes me feel useful." Felicity swallowed the emotion that had crept into her voice. He'd forced her to be blunt and it was only half as humiliating as she'd expected.

"Your brother needs you. Your place is in Boston with him."

"Jonathon's to be married soon. Isn't that wonderful?"

Her father continued to frown.

She leaned forward and grabbed his hand across the wide desk. "He's grown up since you've been away. He deserves to start a new life with his young bride. They don't want me underfoot."

"I don't believe that."

Felicity studied the planked floor. Fine white sand crept in from the bay like spilt sugar. How much of her desperation would she have to admit to make him see reason?

She forced her gaze back to her father's. "Jonathon would never cast me out. Mother willed him the house to raise a family of his own. I won't deny him that."

Her father rubbed his forehead. "Still, you didn't have to leave Boston."

She swallowed what little pride she had left. "Mistress Bishop said I was a pariah. A burden to Jonathon. An unwanted thorn in God's eye. In her view, my only hope of redemption was in marrying one of the two men she'd chosen. One was old enough to be my grandfather, the other a bitter widower with five children. Both needed nursemaids."

Her father lifted his head. "Love can grow in the strangest places, Felicity. You should give marriage a chance."

She could never marry. Her own impulsive actions had ensured that. "I hoped to be more than some man's cheap source of labor."

His eyes glazed with a sorrow he tried to blink away. She hated hurting him like this. It wasn't his fault she had ruined her life so thoroughly.

"There are things here you don't know about. Something awful has happened."

As her father paused for breath, Lord Christian Andrews blew back through the door like a bad omen. He strode past them without a word, then leaned against the adjacent desk and folded his arms over his chest. Felicity had the distinct impression he was furious, with her of all things.

"Excuse me, sir, but my father and I are having a private conversation."

Her father cleared the slight tremble from his throat. "That's quite all right. Lord Christian can better explain what's happened here."

"I'd rather hear it from you." She didn't know what *it* was, but she knew she'd get nowhere with Master Andrews. He had his own agenda, which she would vow had nothing to do with her best interests or her father's.

Andrews cocked his head as if to admire her. "Why didn't you tell me your daughter was so charming, Ben? She certainly won the heart of the *Queen Elizabeth*'s captain."

Her father frowned. She hated how quickly he realized Andrews was being sarcastic.

"She actually threatened to demote him to cook if he didn't bring her to Barbados."

Felicity closed her eyes. She'd intended to tell her father about her relationship with his employees once he'd warmed to the idea of having her around.

"Father." She leaned forward, trying to snare his attention away from Andrews. "I wanted to tell you that—"

"That she booted out your man and runs the New England Trading Company's Boston office." Andrews pushed away from the desk, grabbed the back of her chair and whipped her around to face him. "Do you have any idea how stupid that was?"

She gripped the smooth wood seat to keep from falling

13

out of it. For the first time in her life, all she could do was turn a pleading gaze on her father.

He leaned his head into his hand, his thick fingers covering his eyes. "How could you do something like this, Felicity?"

The hurt in his question urged her to his side, but Andrews's hulking form blocked her from even standing. "The man you hired was incompetent. You should be thanking me."

Andrews squared his shoulders, straining the frills on his shirt. "You are a huge problem, woman."

Felicity rose to her full height, hoping he'd have the good sense to step out of her way. She was no wisp of a woman, yet he towered over her. He probably donned those high heels vain men found so fashionable. She refused to lower her gaze to check. But meeting his assault directly was a mistake. He stared at her with such single-minded intensity that she instantly wanted to dart her gaze away like a silly girl. How in the world did this ruffian pass himself off as anything other than a common thug?

"Where is Master Marley?"

She had some satisfaction when he flinched, however slightly.

"That's why we're so upset at your arrival." Her father's voice sounded near to breaking. "There's been a terrible tragedy."

She nailed Andrews with her best glare. His nearness made her all too aware of the fact that he was a man, and she a woman. She'd vowed no other man would be allowed to effect her that way, make her vulnerable and wanting and entirely too breathless. When he still wouldn't budge, she had no choice but to brush past.

He caught her wrist. "You're not listening to us."

She gasped in outrage. "Who do you think you are?"

"Someone you don't want to know."

She tried to jerk her arm away, but he held her tight,

increasing the pressure. He wanted her to cower. Instead, she challenged his scalding stare with her own, unflinching under the will he tried to exert on her. And then something in him softened; he loosened his grip and dropped his gaze to her mouth. His breathing changed, deepened. The rhythm lulled her head back, forced her lips to part slightly. She caught herself before she licked them in invitation. His change in tactics couldn't have been any more diabolical.

"Please, Drew. Manhandling Felicity won't erase what happened to Beatrice."

Her father's reprimand met with instant success. Drew, as her father called him, released her and stepped back, blinking as if he'd just been abruptly awakened.

"She's going to get herself killed," the man mumbled to himself.

Felicity turned to her father, rubbing her wrist. The name Drew reminded her of a gangly boy she'd known as a child who'd had too much confidence for his own good. This man wasn't any different. And she might have been able to believe that if the heat from his long fingers didn't linger upon her skin, disrupting her breath and her equilibrium. A slight flutter in her woman's heart warned this was a rake as well as a thief.

She turned her ire on her father. "How can you associate with such a person? What did he do to Marley's wife?" No doubt it had something to do with his effect on the supposedly weaker sex. The beast.

Her father gripped the edge of his cluttered desk. "*He* didn't do anything. He's just trying to make you understand the seriousness of what's happened. The danger you're in."

Felicity flung a glance over her shoulder. Drew—the man with more bluff than bluster, which was how she decided to think of him from then on—retreated to the far side of the small office. His head remained lowered and his fists were shoved in his pockets. His true character tore a hole in his fancy velvet exterior, and they both knew it.

She only hoped her own inherent wantonness hadn't been as obvious. "The only danger I'm in is from your new partner."

Her father shook his head. When she opened her mouth to elaborate on Drew's bad behavior, her father held up a hand to stop her.

"Marley's been murdered. Beatrice, too."

"Murdered?" Felicity slid back into her chair, her courage punctured. Marley and his wife killed? She glanced at Drew, unable to imagine him the culprit. Swindler, yes; murderer, no. "Who would want to hurt Master Marley?"

"Pirates. At least that is the rumor." Her father's glance at Drew warned her he knew more than he was saying.

"I don't understand. Was Master Marley on one of your ships? As I remember, he hated to be under sail." Felicity studied her father's new business partner for hints at the demise of his predecessor. The way he kept his head lowered and stared at the jewel-studded buckles on his shoes added credence to Felicity's growing suspicions. Surely, he hadn't committed the crimes, but they had something to do with him.

Her father shuffled the papers on his desk. "Marley and his wife were murdered in their home. He'd recently purchased a large house on an isolated cove for Beatrice. I warned him against flaunting our good fortune. You see now why you must return to Boston."

"If these pirates are bold enough to attack on land, they certainly wouldn't hesitate to pluck one of your ships at sea." Though Felicity would never admit it aloud, in light of the murders, the idea of her sailing around Barbados gave her the queasiest feeling in the pit of her stomach.

Drew straightened. "I've already booked your passage on another merchant's ship."

"But as you pointed out, Lord Christian"—she practically choked on the courtesy title, but the way she said it let him know she wasn't convinced of its validity—"my association with the New England Trading Company is widely known. If the pirates are looking for ransom . . . I'd be a lamb sent to the slaughter."

Her father stood. "That can't happen. I won't let that happen. And after what befell Beatrice . . . Drew, you have to do something."

Drew moved toward them. "The Royal Navy makes rounds through the English colonies. We'll find her passage on the first ship scheduled for Boston."

Felicity closed her mouth, refusing to argue. She was staying, whether they knew it or not. She'd use her time wisely, and Drew would be the one leaving with the Royal Navy—in chains, if she had her way.

He stopped in front of her chair. "I expect you to lie low while you're here."

She smiled at him. "But of course. In fact, I can just tidy Father's ledgers. I'm sure you won't mind if I have a look at the New England Trading Company's books."

"By all means, keep yourself busy." He bowed at the waist. "Just don't overstep your place again. Even in paradise the snakes are poisonous."

He exited through the door, leaving with that last word. Felicity wasn't sure if she'd been threatened or warned. Either way, she had a mystery to unravel. What lay beneath Lord Christian Andrews's powdered facade was the first loose string.

# Chapter Two

Samantha Linley's breath tickled Drew's ear. "Christian, you must meet me later. It's been too long."

Piles of coarse black hair, with only a snail's trail of silvery-gray to hint at the age of its owner, irritated his cheek, leaving him with the urge to swat her away like a fly. He stared at the ripple of moonlight riding the waves, doing his best to ignore her.

In an attempt to escape Linley Hall's brightly lit drawing room, he had slipped out onto the back terrace overlooking the sea. Unfortunately, his departure had not gone unnoticed.

The heavy scent of wild jasmine struggled above the cloying perfume worn by his hostess, reminding Drew that the Linleys' attempt to overpower the indigenous vegetation with English roses had failed miserably. The idea made him smile.

Samantha's right hand strayed brazenly low in its measuring of his torso. He grabbed her wrists and placed them by her side. "Sam, darling, it's good to see you haven't lost your bravado. Philip must find you endlessly amusing."

He released her then. The memory of his confrontation with Felicity still haunted him. Pleasuring women with his touch remained one of his greatest joys, but he wanted nothing more than to throttle Felicity Kendall. Well, that wasn't exactly true. A glimpse of her full mouth had jolted him out of his anger and on to a much more dangerous emotion. But he couldn't afford to be attracted to the young woman. And if he forgot again, he'd force himself to remember Beatrice Marley. Even if there was no solid evidence that Marley and his wife had been killed because of their association with him, the rumors insinuating that El Diablo had taken a hand in the occurrence made it almost a certainty.

Samantha stuck out her lower lip in an exaggerated pout, regaining his attention. "How can you mention my husband when you know it's you I want to amuse? It's cruel of you to ignore me for so long. Where have you been hiding, Lord Christian?"

Drew longed for the persona of Lord Christian to disappear. If he had a choice, he'd be free of this place, chasing the tail of the moon across the water. His role as the wayward youngest son of an English duke had lost its ironic appeal.

Unfortunately, the character he'd created to account for the goods he'd been stealing rather than importing from England saved his bloody neck at the moment.

Drew shrugged. "All that business with my partner's murder put a damper on my social schedule. I didn't want to be the center of another scandal before poor Richard's ashes cooled."

"You're concerned over social improprieties? I thought you thrived on scandal." Samantha's hands rested on her hips in a mock display of temper.

He suspected she orchestrated the position to allow him a better view of her plunging décolletage. He feared if she

19

moved too quickly her entire nipple would be in plain view, but knowing Samantha, that was her intention.

Turning away from the ocean, he leaned against the stone wall surrounding the terrace. It would be an easy thing for him to escape this party and follow the hidden trail that led from the plantation to the beach. He no doubt knew the house and lands better than its current owners. Revealing he'd spent his youth slaving away on this very plantation would almost be worth the look of horror on Sam's face.

Drew forced himself to take a deep breath and let it out again. To even consider such thoughts at a time like this warned he was slipping. When a warm breeze caressed his thigh instead of Samantha's overheated hand, Drew tried to relax.

"Things have changed. I'm not the man I used to be."

Sam placed her palm on the front of his sedate brown jacket and began again her slow exploration of his body. This time she paced herself, veering her hand up toward his shoulder in correction of her earlier indiscretion. "I see this new somberness extends to your wardrobe, too. I hope you're still the same decadent man in bed. I'd be eternally heartbroken if that changed. This godforsaken island would be unbearable without my little amusements."

Staring up at the fat three-quarter moon allowed him to avoid her heavily painted face. Funny, he couldn't recall why he'd ever found her remotely attractive.

Bedding the mistress of the plantation where he'd been an indentured servant represented a twisted sort of justice, he supposed. The change in proprietorship hadn't mattered. Now he could consider himself truly equal to those he mocked. The sudden realization ruined any satisfaction he'd gained from his licentious affair with Samantha Linley.

She balled his velvet lapel in her clenched fist. "Who is she?"

Movement from the doorway caught Drew's attention. Felicity Kendall appeared on the edge of the terrace, light spilling from behind her. Shadows hid her face, but he recognized the erect posture of the avenging angel.

He could only guess how much she'd witnessed. No matter. He was certain she'd already formed an opinion and waited anxiously to flog him with it. Maybe that jolt of attraction which had kept him awake these last few nights had been nothing more than a much needed antidote to the sameness he'd begun to find in every woman he met, or perhaps it was something more. As disastrous as it would be, he longed for something more.

Samantha followed his gaze, then quickly put a respectable distance between them. Felicity charged in their direction, and Drew acknowledged the real reason he'd accepted the Linleys' invitation: He'd wanted to see this woman again.

From the moment she laid eyes on him, she'd treated him like a common criminal. True as it was, he didn't like it. Nor did he like the behavior to which she reduced him. Treating the gentler sex gently was one of the few moral codes he still honored. He'd always been able to charm them into anything—from goodwill to bed. Even if he wouldn't follow through with the act, he wanted Felicity as well as himself to know he could have her at any time.

Philip Linley and Ben followed Felicity through the open terrace doors. Drew stood away from the waist-high wall, bracing himself for the confrontation to come.

"There's my lovely wife." Philip's tight smile failed to reach his eyes. "I was just giving Miss Kendall a tour of our home."

Everyone exchanged stiff greetings except for Ben, who was incapable of being anything other than friendly. Felicity refused to speak. She acknowledged her introduction to Samantha Linley with a curt nod. Drew received no such courtesy, just a fiery glare.

In light of Felicity's witness to the spectacle with Samantha, he'd wasted his effort in toning down Lord Christian's flamboyant wardrobe. And Felicity would never be charmed by his notorious good looks alone, no matter how he packaged himself. She behaved unlike any woman he had ever come across. He wouldn't forget that again.

Cool suffocating silence settled over the small gathering like a blanket of snow. Samantha cracked under the strain first. She excused herself and gracefully retreated.

"Benjamin, how about a nip of rum before dinner? It makes the food easier to digest," suggested Philip.

Ben nodded. "Felicity, come along and I'll find you a fan and a cool place to sit. You look flushed."

"I'd rather stay out here. The breeze seems to lighten the air."

Ben's gaze bounced between Drew and Felicity. It appeared he didn't want to leave them alone. Not that Drew could blame him. "Lord Christian, care to join us?"

"No. Thank you."

Linley's pinched features relaxed. Ben, on the other hand, yanked his fingers through his remaining tufts of hair. He leaned toward Felicity. "Remember your promise."

Felicity nodded, but her dusky inferno of a gaze never left Drew.

With one last backward glance, Ben disappeared into the buzzing houseful of guests with Philip Linley.

"You are even more despicable than I imagined! That woman is our host's wife," snapped Felicity the moment the tall French doors closed.

"May I say you look lovely tonight, Miss Kendall? Black suits you."

"Don't mock me. I'm not taken with your presence, as is Mistress Linley. I see you for the snake you are."

Felicity laced her fingers in front of her to keep from

self-consciously smoothing her drab skirts. That there would be a complete absence of Puritan morality on the island was something she hadn't anticipated. She wore the identical garment she'd had on at their first meeting. Not even a trace of embroidery adorned her plain white collar. For the first time since she'd wholeheartedly embraced the protective armor of her mother's religion, she experienced shame. She felt as if she should be serving the guests rather than being one of them.

He lounged against the stone railing, smiling at her taunt. "Yet you didn't heed my warning or you wouldn't be here."

"Yes. The snakes are poisonous. I remember from our last meeting. You've no need to worry. I don't intend to get close enough to feel your bite. The only reason I'm here is because my father insisted. Word of my arrival spread over the island and Master Linley wanted to meet me."

"I meant out here. Alone with me. Maybe you're jealous."

She choked on her anger, having to gasp for breath before she could speak. "Your immoral habits are no concern of mine, except when they involve my father. Seducing the wife of a man you trade with is not the act of a gentleman. I refuse to stand by while you taint my father's good name."

A couple dressed in shades of lime green and flame orange strolled out onto the terrace. They paused against the railing a few yards away. Though they entwined their bewigged heads in an intimate conversation, their presence was as loud and unsettling as the cries of the vibrant-colored parrots that inhabited the island.

Drew's glance casually swept over the couple before resting on Felicity again. "Since you've taken it upon yourself to chastise me for all my shortcomings, I suggest you move closer. We wouldn't want to scare the other guests with your shrill lecture."

She inched toward the wall, where he draped himself like a sultan awaiting his every whim to be fulfilled. Pretending to admire the sea saved her from looking at him. His appeal as a man agitated her as much as his arrogant nature. She clasped her hands to stop their slight tremble, refusing to let him know he unnerved her. To calm herself, she tried to slow her rapid breathing to the rhythmic sound of the waves lapping against the beach below.

He straightened, then made a great show of trying to catch a glimpse of her face. "What did you promise your father?"

Felicity ignored his efforts. "To behave."

"I make you misbehave? Mmm, I like that." His tone assured her a wicked smile still tugged at his mouth.

She turned to him, her arms wrapped protectively in front of her. "The only thing you do is disgust me. My father was referring to any comments I might make about the Linleys' slaves. I abhor slavery, as any God-fearing soul should."

"That leaves me out."

"My thoughts exactly."

His grin showed he found her denunciation of his character amusing. "You've also thrown every white inhabitant of Barbados among the soulless. You won't be popular."

"I know that. I don't want my father's interests hurt, but slavery's not right. Our own Samuel Sewall, a prominent Puritan," she added, sure he had no knowledge of her faith's great scholars, "published a pamphlet on the inherent sinfulness of slavery. Perhaps I should locate a copy for you."

"Oh, do." He leaned in closer, and she suspected he was testing to see if she would move away. "I must say, I'm relieved to know you have another monster to fight besides me."

She tilted her chin to meet his gaze. When she'd walked out on the terrace, she'd checked. He didn't wear high heels. "You're my first."

"Then move closer and let's get on with it. I promise not to sink my fangs in your soft white skin."

To prove to him that she could, she closed the distance between them until they were as close as the lovers on the opposite end of the terrace. Her promise to her father had included avoiding an incident with Drew as well as her opinions on slavery. The aristocrat's behavior with Mistress Linley proved he relished public spectacles, and she'd not give him another one by scolding him in front of the other guests.

"Don't waste your time saving Samantha," he guessed. When he spoke, she felt the warmth of his breath on her cheek. "I've already seduced her. You can move on to the next of my sins."

"As you have, I've no doubt." She wanted to flinch at his callousness but refused to show any signs his words disturbed her beyond anger. "I find your behavior cruel and despicable. Do you think of women only in terms of seduction?"

"Usually, but since you're Ben's daughter I was going to let you go unvarnished. Unless you'd rather I not. If that's the case, you should call me Christian."

"I certainly will not call you by that name. It's blasphemous. Your mother must regret choosing something so inappropriate."

The masculine scent of musk and brandy battled the strangling smell of roses. His choice of cologne didn't disguise his smoldering aggression any better than his velvet suit.

" 'Felicity,' " he said. "I believe that means great happiness. From what I know of you, your name doesn't seem to fit you either."

She stared at the shadowed waves disturbing the black

25

surface of the sea, refusing to let him know how close his jabs came to the truth. He must be the devil himself to be so handsome, yet possess such an ungodly soul.

"I didn't stay out here to trade insults with you. I came to warn you: I've discovered your secret." Her bluff aimed at penetrating his armor as his teasing did hers. His silence gave her the courage to turn and look at him.

He studied her openly. "I love secrets. Tell me what you think mine is."

Unfortunately, she'd discovered nothing amiss in the records of the New England Trading Company. According to her father, Lord Christian's family influence in England had saved the small company from bankruptcy. Everyone knew that without a champion in the right circles, gaining a royal charter to trade was impossible. And without a charter, one would be considered no more than a common criminal—or worse, a pirate.

The figures confirmed that the beleaguered New England Trading Company was finally in the black, but Felicity speculated on the method. Her instincts told her Christian Andrews was not the son of a duke, much less an honest merchant. The thought that her father might have unwittingly become a front for someone's illicit activities forced Felicity's hand. She latched on to the one curious notation in the ledgers:

"*General goods.*"

He grinned. "Shocking."

"There's more." When the smirk spread to his eyes, she grew more determined to wipe it from his face. Her suspicions were vague and unsubstantiated, but she had no other clue.

"Go on, Felicity. Tell me what goes on inside that head of yours."

"Master Marley meticulously recorded all the exports from the island. Only the imports are marked *general goods*.

26

Whatever the items are, they bring more money than even sugar."

The amused sparkle in his eyes dulled, but he still showed his teeth. "Providing valuable merchandise isn't a sin. The transplanted English like their luxury goods, and sugar gives them money to buy whatever they desire."

"Whether or not it's a sin depends on what those goods are and where they came from."

His smile faded. "I have nothing to do with the ledgers. Marley labeled the merchandise as he saw fit."

His reaction turned Felicity's speculation into certainty. "No? But I believe we both know what 'general goods' is politely hiding."

The cool mask he wore on their first meeting returned. He would reveal nothing else until provoked.

She sensed her tactic's success and guessed wildly. "Slavery."

"What?" He moved away from the wall.

"I believe you're dealing in slaves and using 'general goods' to hide your horrid deeds from my father."

Her confidence sagged with his laughter. "I see. I am evil . . . and clever, too. Did I fool Marley, or was he involved as well?"

"I don't know the details."

"Have you told Ben of your discovery?"

"No, and I don't want you to say anything to him. Knowing that his ships promoted slavery would hurt him deeply. I'll be satisfied if you leave Barbados and never bother my father again."

"Slavery is not illegal."

"It should be. It's immoral, and immorality is something at which you excel. My guess is, you're an expert at using other human beings for your own self-interests."

All traces of humor evaporated from his face. "Why do you hate me?" he asked.

"Because you're manipulating my father. You're hiding

behind your fancy clothes and powdered wig. I don't know why, but I'll find out."

"And what are you hiding from? You have a luscious mouth, but all you use it for is to screech like a shrew. Unbind your hair and smile, and you could be beautiful. Why aren't you married? Would none of your Puritan men let you be on top? I would."

She suspected he wanted to shock her, but his lusty innuendo was nothing but a cruel quip at her expense. "I prefer men who smell less like a rosebush and more like a man. You can stop trying to sway me with your sexual prowess. I find you revolting. Leave Barbados before I expose you for the fraud you are."

When she turned to leave, he grabbed her elbow.

"I'm afraid I can't do that, Felicity. Someone has taken a dislike to the owners of the New England Trading Company. If I don't discover the identity of Marley's killer, who knows who might be next?"

She yanked her arm away, but instead of leaving, she stood toe-to-toe with him. "Are you threatening me?"

He squared his shoulders like a bull ready to charge. "I'm stating a fact."

"The Linleys' guests seem to think a pirate called El Diablo killed Marley and his wife. Perhaps you've come to another conclusion because you were involved in the murders."

The sharp angles of his jaw became more pronounced as he ground his teeth. "It's stupid to make accusations you can't substantiate."

They stared at each other, neither willing to back down. Finally, he shook his head and turned away.

"You don't have to believe me, but I don't want to see Ben hurt either. If you're so intent on using your keen mind to castrate me, go ahead. Just think before you do something that will cause your father any more grief." He bowed over the railing. "Go inside, Felicity, before you make me do something else I'll regret."

She uncurled her fists and caught her breath. Of all the commandments, murder remained the only one she had not suspected him of breaking. The same instinct that assured her he was a fraud kept her from believing him a cold-blooded killer. She'd not leave until she knew for sure.

"I have to calm down first. My father will know I've been arguing with you, and he made me promise not to."

Drew chuckled, but his laugh rang hollow. "How did mild-mannered Ben Kendall wind up with a daughter like you?"

She edged beside him and flattened her palms on the cool stone railing. The way he stared out at the sea seemed to relax him. She would be wise to keep him off guard until she found the answers she wanted.

"I've always had a mind of my own, if that's what you're referring to. It didn't bother my mother and father—though the congregation of our church had quite a lot to say about it. They wanted my parents to break my spirit, with force if necessary. As you know, force doesn't work."

He glanced down at her wrist, bared below her cuff. "Did I leave a bruise?" He lifted her hand with reverence.

"No, but it still pains me," she lied, not sure if he were truly concerned or just toying with her again. Hopefully, the fib explained her slight shudder at his touch.

"I'm sorry."

The sharp retort his insincerity deserved melted on her tongue. She became entranced by his concern-softened features. He bent down and placed a light kiss on the throbbing pulse point below her palm. The intimacy of the touch weakened her knees. Her lips parted as the flick of his tongue caressed her skin.

She yanked her hand away before she moaned. But even the wind conspired to seduce her. A soft breeze licked the wet spot left by his mouth. Felicity shivered, but instead of chilled, she felt feverish. Being civil to him had been a mistake. He used her own weakness against her.

She contorted her features into the pinched countenance of the matrons of the Puritan church. "That won't secure my silence. I have no proof yet, but I will."

"I've no doubt you'll find evidence to convict me of whatever misdeed you choose." The humor in his voice gave no sign that her threat concerned him.

"If you'll excuse me, I've had enough of your company." She was tired of being a source of amusement. Worse, knowing he was a cad didn't stop her body from tingling in all the wrong places.

She turned to go, but Drew touched her arm. She spun around to face him, her eyes wide with indignation. Only a fool would fall into that trap again.

He held up his hands in a gesture of surrender. "Just one thing. I was wrong when I assumed your marital status was due to the lack of a man. I've no doubt that if you made up your mind to marry, married you would be, and the man of your choosing would have little to say about it."

She couldn't tell if he meant his words to be compliment or insult. "I'm sure you're also used to getting exactly what you want. It seems we've each met our match."

He genuinely laughed. Its rawness was melodic. "No, Felicity. You're no match for me. I don't usually get what I want; I only get what I can." Then he shook off his moment of melancholy. "I'm curious; why have you chosen to remain a spinster?"

If she hadn't been scrutinizing every subtle change in his expression, she would have missed the flash of vulnerability.

"I succumbed to a handsome rogue exactly like you

when I was still young and naive. I believed his empty flattery and paid dearly for it. He bested me. You won't."

Without further explanation, she turned and left him alone on the terrace.

# Chapter Three

The Linleys' decadent feast was wasted on Drew. He picked at the shrimp-stuffed snapper and disregarded the suckling pig fresh from the roasting pit. Digging into Felicity Kendall appealed to him much more than any entrée weighting the lace-draped table.

Under the glow of candlelight, amber streaks rippled through her restrained hair, hinting at unruly curls. Subduing the thick mass in the severe knot at her nape appeared painful. How the disobedience of her hair must gall her. Drew wiped his mouth with a napkin to hide his smile.

His position at the long dining table forced him to be obvious in his ogling. Visions of her hair, free from its prison of pins, toyed with his imagination. Her puritanical fortress ensconced a unique beauty. He'd had women in all shapes and sizes, but none that spit sparks from her eyes and turned each conversation into a battle of wills.

As if to confirm his insight, Felicity sneaked a glance in his direction. An elusive flare of green darted beneath her large, almond-shaped lids. He'd thought her eyes dull brown. In the soft light, they shone a misty hazel, a murky pond pierced by a ray of sunlight. Drew didn't bother to hide his fascination; he just smiled suggestively until she returned to scrutinizing the crab spilling over her gold-rimmed plate.

Miss Kendall provided a mystery in need of unraveling. Why she went to great lengths to disguise attributes most women would flaunt stoked Drew's imagination. He'd love to know what else she concealed under her yards of black wool.

"Why are you gawking at Benjamin Kendall's very boring daughter?" whispered Samantha, who had indiscreetly arranged to be seated on his right.

Drew downed the remainder of his wine. Whenever he attended a social gathering of the self-appointed aristocracy of Barbados, he tried to be quite intoxicated by this point in the evening. He attributed his relative sobriety to finally finding something interesting at Linley Hall.

"I've never seen a Puritan before."

"How surprising! They're all over the American colonies. I thought you spent a great deal of time there during your long absences."

"I don't frequent their circles, Sam." He ignored her powdered breasts thrust over his dinner plate and gestured for a servant to pour him more wine.

Beneath the table, Samantha placed her hand on his thigh. "I despise it when you use that insipid nickname as if I were one of your chums. I believe I've given you too many liberties with my affection, Lord Christian. If that girl was not such a mouse, I would actually be jealous."

Drew gazed down at Samantha without the slightest show of interest. She removed her hand, not waiting to be asked.

"She is a woman, not a girl, and she is anything but a mouse."

"You don't say. Lucky for me I keep a full stable." Samantha winked, then turned away from him and began a conversation with the red-coated British officer seated across from her, undoubtedly Drew's replacement. She probably kept them close together in the hopes of some excitement. Felicity's unusual appeal escaped Samantha no more than it did him, or he doubted she would have given up on her plans so easily. He wondered how many others Felicity's prudish facade fooled. Suddenly, the hastily mentioned rogue in her past developed erotic dimensions. The idea that another lech had discovered the pearl clamped in Felicity's calcified shell annoyed him.

Drew returned his gaze to the woman in question, searching for a clue to confirm his suspicions, only to find her fierce scrutiny poured in his direction. She must have noticed the exchange between he and Samantha. He raised his glass in a silent toast. She looked away, ignoring the gesture.

His grin deepened. Bedding her would be a challenge, and he loved a challenge. Especially when his reward would be unleashing the passions of a repressed wanton. The way his body responded when she tried to wither him with her fire-and-brimstone stares assured him that her heat came from more than moral outrage. He'd actually be providing Felicity a great service. Puritan or not, her foul temper was the cry of a female in dire need of seduction. And he was just the man to answer that call.

Out on the terrace, he'd thought she'd had him by the ballocks when she mentioned general goods. Luckily, her wrong turn in the labyrinth of truth led her nowhere. As long as she lost herself in the maze she'd created, his secret would be secure.

He lowered his wineglass and stopped smiling. Who was he to think of bedding Ben's daughter? Not only was Benjamin his friend, but if Beatrice's murderer suspected he cared a whit about Felicity Kendall, she might be the next victim.

Felicity watched Drew turn his lazy observance of the dinner party inward. As he stared into his cut-crystal glass, filled to the brim with deep red wine, a brooding veil settled over his features. Felicity welcomed the sudden droop of his high spirits. He'd been toying with her like a cat with a wounded mouse.

Not for a moment did she believe his flirtatious glances sincere. Never should she have hinted at the real reason she'd been forced to remain a spinster. Though the irony in his attempt to seduce her should have amused her, it didn't.

His conceit explained his choice of tactics. It had nothing to do with her weakness for rakes. Using his masculine prowess to melt her hostility came as naturally to him as breathing. If he assumed she would succumb to the charms of a well-practiced flirt twice, he underestimated her.

She dragged her gaze away from Drew and stared at the picked-over remains of her meal. Removing him from her sight didn't ease the pain flowing from the wound he'd reopened. A handsome man would not have the opportunity for another slice of her soul.

Pressure on her shoulder shattered her thoughts. A large ruby winking from a gaudy ring captured her gaze. She followed the length of a brown velvet sleeve to find its owner.

"Daydreaming? I would have wagered the very serious Miss Kendall didn't indulge in such a luxury. Is that allowed in the Puritan handbook, or shall we consult another of Samuel Sewall's pamphlets?"

Her scrutiny traveled no farther. She knew exactly to whom the dark satin voice belonged. And he'd come to harrass her again.

"Leave me alone."

He dragged her chair away from the table. In answer to

35

his unwanted gallantry, she glared at him over her shoulder.

He smiled and extended his hand. "May I escort you to the music room for sherry with the ladies, or would you prefer a stroll on the beach?"

At his audacity, her anger turned to disbelief. Surely her father hadn't expected her to tolerate such abuse. She glanced around the large dining hall, seeking his help. Several servants busily cleared away dishes. All of the other guests had deserted the crimson-padded room. Without acknowledging Drew, Felicity stood and walked past him.

Muffled chatter buzzed from the adjoining drawing room. She intended to find her father and put an end to the evening.

Drew caught her by hooking his arm with hers, oblivious to her rebuke. He lowered his head to whisper intimately in her ear. "I think I'd rather be flailed by your vicious temper than ignored."

Once they passed under the mahogany archway carved in a pattern of shells and vines, satin-clad ladies and bejeweled men surrounded them in a sea of bold color. She couldn't yank her arm away without notice. Large gilded mirrors, mounted atop the plum-and-cream-striped wall covering, artfully captured the guests' reflections. Women, who had stopped their conversation when Drew escorted her into the room, stared enviously. The image of Drew bending down to her in attentive intimacy increased the beating of her heart.

Part of Felicity longed to cling to her unwanted escort. The other part, the coward, urged her to run from the room. Next to Drew and the other guests, she appeared the black raincloud hovering over a spring carnival. Instead of shrinking, she invoked her callused pride and tried once more to separate herself from the man at her side.

The firmness underneath his plush coat confirmed the strength of his presence was not merely an illusion created by padding his shoulders. His arm entwined with hers felt hard and unyielding. The ruby ring appeared awkward on his large, rough fingers. His hand overpowered the feminine adornment. Drew didn't possess the hand of a nobleman. He possessed the hand of a laborer.

"Do all aristocrats work with their hands, or is that a peculiarity to you?"

He smiled down at her. "That's more like it. I wondered how long you could remain silent."

"Let go. I must find my father." Her need to escape him overwhelmed her desire for discretion. She tugged against his hold with all her strength.

He hardly flexed a muscle in his restraint. "The fire is back. How easily you ignite. Perhaps I should show you rather than tell you the skills I've perfected with my hands."

"Save your demonstrations for Mistress Linley."

Drew's eyebrows rose suggestively. "For a virgin, you are far from naive. Do Puritans instruct their unmarried women in something I should know? I might have a religious conversion on the spot."

Lowering her face hid her flushed cheeks. He seemed to read through her every word. She needed to find her father and leave at once.

Determinedly, she yanked her arm away from his. Lack of resistance left her stumbling, but she quickly regained her balance. Fists on her hips, she had every intention of laying into him with a detailed inventory of his horrid behavior, until she noticed he looked past her.

Her father followed Master Linley and another man she vaguely recognized into the room through doors that led from the entry hall. A hush descended on the disconnected chatter of the guests. When she finally placed Captain McCulla, the concern tightening her father's features brought goose flesh to her skin like a winter wind.

Drew pulled a gold watch from the fob pocket of his

breeches and casually glanced at the time. "McCulla, what tears you away from the Hare and the Hound . . . and so close to the witching hour?"

Captain McCulla, the man Felicity had seen in a stupor at the dock, blanched. He straightened his ill-fitting dark blue coat, losing the intensity of purpose with which he had burst into the room. Felicity's initial impulse urged her to go to her father, but she hung back when the crowd formed a semicircle around the three men. Mistress Linley stared covetously at Drew across the space.

With her vibrant blue eyes and petite figure emphasized by her tight-waisted gown, Samantha Linley garnered secret glances from every virile man in the room except one. But for that reason Felicity suddenly found comfort in Drew's constant attention. It set her apart, even if Drew did it only to bait her. Mistress Linley didn't know that. Felicity not only held her ground at Drew's side but edged closer.

When it became obvious McCulla had lost his bravado, Master Linley spoke up. "You might wish to recant that slur against your man, Lord Christian. McCulla's brought news of the Marleys' murderer."

"Aye. This broadsheet showed up at the Hare and . . ." McCulla's flushed face turned redder than it already was. "It doesn't matter where it came from. I knew Master Kendall would want to see it straightaway. So here I am. It was El Diablo who did the deed, just as everyone's been saying."

Drew's sardonic smirk drooped. "How do you know it was El Diablo? Is there proof?"

McCulla waved the broadsheet. "Must be. This price on his head doesn't leave room for doubt. I know twenty men right now ready to sign on to look for the bastard."

Drew appeared to recover in the breath of McCulla's response, replacing his watch with languid motions. He showed no more concern than if they were discussing the weather. "We'll see if their enthusiasm outlasts their ale," he guessed. "I heard this El Diablo character is rather elusive."

Her father stepped between Drew and McCulla to grab the handbill. "Who's offering this reward?" He scanned the paper. "It doesn't say. And this picture is awfully vague. I wonder if this El Diablo even exists. This might be a hoax."

"He exists, all right," McCulla said. Then, with all ears straining to hear his words, he continued in wide-eyed drama. "Heard stories about a Spanish merchanter he took. The crew saw his black ship bearing down on them, and when he raised his flag—a white devil skewering a bleeding heart—they knew they was doomed. They tossed down their weapons and begged to be put ashore. He set them all adrift in their skiff and told them to thank El Diablo for their lives."

Drew dismissed McCulla's tale with a shrug. "That could have been his idea of irony, not a declaration of his name. Besides, I heard the same story, and the crew had plenty of food and water to make it to shore. The man hardly sounds like a bloodthirsty murderer."

"You, Lord Christian, are the only one I know with such a twisted sense of humor," said Master Linley. "If he killed the Marleys, El Diablo has obviously gone mad. Now that those vermin of the seas are being hunted by His Majesty's Navy, they're all running scared and destroying everything in their wake. Show him the handbill, Benjamin."

Felicity's father shook his head. "You can't tell anything from this sketch. And I question the reward. If it's from the crown, I wonder why the governor didn't notify me. I was Marley's partner. I think this handbill was printed just to scare us—probably by the Marleys' real killer." Gesturing with the paper as he spoke, he came too close to one of the tall, iron candelabra flanking the double doors. Luckily, his flailing only resulted in extinguishing two of the candles rather than setting the broadsheet aflame.

"Let me see that." Drew strode over and snatched the handbill. He silently studied the rumpled piece of paper, apparently oblivious to the wave of whispers that began to break in the room.

Felicity moved behind him, glancing around his stiff shoulder to view the face of the infamous devil pirate.

"All I know is what it says. And for a thousand pounds, I'd find my way to hell and bring back the real devil," McCulla bragged. He tugged on the lapels of his jacket. "What do you say, Master Kendall? The boys and I are ready to leave tonight. Give me a ship and we'll bring you the Marleys' killer."

Drew absently passed the handbill to Felicity. In a strange gesture, he touched his cheek, then his hair. He glanced at his fingertips before wiping them on his breeches, leaving a white smudge of powder marring the crisp velvet. He didn't seem to notice, nor did anyone else as they crowded around, anxious to view the sketch of El Diablo.

Master Linley slapped McCulla on the back. "Good work, man. I want this marauder brought to justice as much as Benjamin, here. Decent people can't sleep at night knowing a pirate who will murder them in their beds is on the loose. If Ben supplies the ship, I'll purchase the provisions."

Ben looked unconvinced. "Let's not panic. I think we should have a clear head before we act. I don't want to risk injury to my employees." He glanced at Drew, apparently for support, but Drew was too busy glaring at McCulla with an expression that promised retribution rather than gratitude.

McCulla didn't seem to notice. "That bloody pirate's no match for me. Give me a chance and I'll show you Harold McCulla is worth his salt."

Someone crowded behind Felicity to see the broadsheet,

distracting her from the strange interplay and forcing her to focus on the crude drawing lest she lose it. The etching revealed the sharp features of a man who would be considered handsome if it weren't for his eyes. For a brief moment, she thought she recognized him, but quickly changed her mind. El Diablo's eyes were cold, devoid of life, though he smiled. The man had no soul and no remorse.

Passing the etching to the next eager pair of hands, she looked beyond the throng of guests to find Drew. She wondered if his subdued behavior had anything to do with fear. Perhaps he suspected he was next on El Diablo's list, and the broadsheet confirmed his worst fears. Drew seemed too arrogant to respect an obvious threat, but she had no other explanation for his reaction.

She found Drew and her father tucked in a dark corner away from the other guests. At her approach, they fell silent. Drew ignored her, while her father embraced her as if she might disappear.

"Felicity, I'd like to accompany Lord Christian to the Hare and the Hound to see if we can discover more about this mysterious broadsheet. Would you like to stay here, or should I have my driver see you home?" What Drew hid expertly overflowed from every one of her father's pores. He practically shook with fright.

Felicity hooked her arm through his. "I wish to come with you."

"No." Drew's curt command held no hint of the polished aristocrat.

"Lord Christian's right. It'll be no place for a woman." Her father disengaged from her grasp. He held her hand, patting the back of it.

Felicity straightened, trying to appear taller than he. "I knew Master Marley since I was a child. I'm just as anxious to find the killer as you."

"Not this time, Felicity," Drew said. "For once in your

41

life, you'll do as you're told." He stepped toward her, apparently forgetting to be indifferent.

"I was speaking to my father." She held her position at the edge of the plush carpet, despite the urge to melt back into the throng of guests still gathered around Captain McCulla and Master Linley.

"Don't argue with me about this."

Her father cut off Drew's advance. "She's only trying to help. I won't have you bullying her."

Drew's narrowed gaze instantly dropped. He raised his hands as if he intended to rake his fingers through his hair, but lowered his arms when he made contact with his ridiculous wig. It appeared he wasn't used to the fancy dress of an aristocrat after all—not that Felicity was terribly surprised.

When her father gripped her hand, his cold, wet palms pulled her back to the problem at hand. "Though I disagree with his high-handed manner, I agree with Drew. I must insist that Avery see you home."

Her father's obvious agitation forced her to hold her tongue—not the fact that Drew's tight jaw warned arguing would be useless.

"Ben, you need to take Felicity home yourself. She shouldn't be left in the care of a driver," Drew instructed.

Her father shoved his hands into the pockets of his knee-length coat. "I don't want you dealing with this alone. Now, more than ever, we need to stay together."

Drew glanced at Felicity as if she were an unwanted piece of baggage. "I won't be alone. Besides, it's more important to keep Felicity safe and away from the docks."

"You're right." Her father nodded, but the sagging of his shoulders proved he didn't like his choice. "I must think of Felicity first." Her father clasped her hand again. "Come along, daughter. I'm sure our hosts will understand our early departure."

She followed him, slightly shaken by Drew's curt dismissal. Lord, but he was good. He could turn the charm off and on as he pleased, could become demanding and powerful in the blink of an eye. Despite knowing better, she had actually started to believe his flirtatious glances over dinner.

In the cool marble foyer, the threesome exchanged a hasty farewell with Philip and Samantha Linley. Felicity couldn't help but notice Samantha's desperate attempt to pull Drew away from the group with whispered pleas. Her irritated scowl at his rebuke left Felicity with unjustified satisfaction. But it was short-lived as Mistress Linley swung around to stare at her.

After a head-to-toe perusal, the older woman dismissed her with a smirk. Apparently, Mistress Linley found no threat to her relationship with Drew. Not that Felicity could blame her. Even the gout-ridden merchant who had sat next to her during dinner had stared past Felicity to marvel at Samantha Linley's classic beauty.

After her fall from grace had ensured her she'd never be any man's wife, Felicity assumed she'd accepted the fact that the male population only gazed upon her in a sisterly fashion. It was what she'd told herself she wanted. But bluff or not, Drew's decidedly heated attention proved how wrong she'd been.

Without conscious thought, Felicity slipped her arm through his. He only gave her a brief curious glance before he guided her out the door. A quick glimpse over her shoulder rewarded Felicity with the droop of Mistress Linley's smile.

Felicity allowed herself to be meekly led to the waiting carriage, then climbed in, grateful that Drew let her action go without comment. Tactfully, she'd decided to wait for her father's seclusion from Drew before she convinced him to take them in the direction of the Hare and the Hound. Drew's change from fop to bully might subdue her father, but it wouldn't stop her. Not until she found out what upset him enough to crack his gentlemanly guise.

"Just a moment, Felicity. I'd like a word with Lord Christian." Ben closed the carriage's heavy door on his daughter before she could voice her obvious objections. With her out of the way, the man began again the conversation she had interrupted. "Are you sure leaving Barbados is the right thing to do, Drew?"

He glanced across the brick drive to assure himself the nickname had not been overheard. Torches guarded the polished stone steps to Linley Hall with silent uniformity, casting ominous shadows but revealing no curious ears.

Motioning to Ben, Drew receded into a nook shaded by an overgrown bougainvillea whose bloodred petals fell in a dark pool at the driveway's edge. Secluding himself with his remaining business partner might appear suspicious, but better that than to have Felicity or anyone overhear their conversation.

"You saw the sketch. First the rumors that El Diablo killed Marley and Beatrice, and now this. I need to leave Barbados. Maybe if I'd left earlier Marley and Beatrice would still be alive."

Ben reached out and squeezed his shoulder. "I don't blame you. You know that, so stop blaming yourself. Marley and I both knew the risk of selling pirated goods. We're in this together, Drew."

Drew folded his arms over his chest and casually disengaged Ben's grip. "I don't think Marley would have agreed."

"Lord Christian kept Marley out of debtors's prison. And purchased him his house on the hill and the love of a woman who wouldn't have looked twice at him before. And Lord Christian can protect you now. Don't leave."

Drew shook his head. "We always knew our charade would come to an end. It was only a matter of time before someone discovered 'Lord Christian' wasn't whom he claimed. We should have quit the moment King George started his crusade against piracy."

Ben straightened and narrowed his gaze. "That was my decision as well as yours. And Marley's. I don't remember Richard complaining until pirates and the merchants who bought from them started being hanged from the docks on a regular basis."

"It's not as simple as selling pirate contraband under the guise of a legitimate charter anymore. King George's edicts aren't all we have to contend with. Someone calling himself El Diablo is killing people associated with our venture." His voice was full of import. "You might be willing to take responsibility for your part in our plan, but what about Felicity? She's involved now. It's clear I must leave."

Ben cut his gaze to the deep shadows in the foliage. Drew suspected Ben knew he was right but was too good a friend to send him out on his own—which was more than Drew deserved. What would Ben think if he knew that after Drew's horror over Beatrice's death had faded, his first reaction to Marley's murder was relief?

"But what about you? You won't be safe on the open sea. I didn't save your life to watch you throw it away," Ben said. But the conviction in his voice was clearly gone.

"That's the last thing I'm doing. Now that there's a king's ransom on El Diablo's head, I'm no safer on Barbados than at sea. Besides, I want to find the bastard who is ruining my life."

"Just send word that you're safe."

"No contact. I'll leave on the *Sea Mistress* tonight and you won't see me again until I find Marley and Beatrice's killer."

Drew extended his hand. Ben ignored it, opting to hug him instead. With little choice, Drew accepted the embrace, not really minding at all.

As they walked back to the black coach perched atop red

wheels, Ben hung his head and sighed. The man did a poor job of hiding his emotions. Drew never should have suggested he involve himself in this illicit profession. The irony was, at the time Drew thought he was doing Ben a favor, neatly paying off a debt.

Drew stopped his friend before he opened the carriage door. Through the window, in the confines of the dark interior, Felicity's pale face glowed like the moon. The way she stared straight ahead, ignoring their approach, warned she'd been straining to hear their conversation. He'd been a fool to think her taking his arm and allowing him to guide her down the Linleys' front steps had been some sort of truce; no doubt she'd considered the fact that dew had gathered on the marble, and she'd needed something to cushion her fall if she slipped.

Drew, leaning on the window's edge, saw a secret smile play on the young woman's full lips. If Ben hadn't been hovering nearby, he might risk stealing a kiss good-bye. The resounding slap he'd no doubt earn for his efforts would surely be worth it.

"Miss Kendall, I'll bid you goodnight. It's always a pleasure," he said.

She turned to him, her gaze smoldering with satisfaction. He'd love to see that look on her face for reasons other than his imminent departure.

"I'm glad you're so easily amused. Personally, I find talk of murderous pirates anything but pleasant. But I suppose therein lies our difference."

Drew straightened. Lord, but her thorns were sharp. She'd surely make a man bleed before he reached her soft petals. "As always, you're absolutely right. What would I do without your guidance?"

"Burn in hell, which I'm sure you'll do with or without me."

Drew cleared his throat. His usually thick charm evaporated on his tongue. The truth of her words—something he'd always known and sometimes prided himself on—suddenly raised a chill on his hot skin. He turned away. Perhaps Felicity was a challenge he'd not be able to overcome. He hoped it wasn't a sign that there'd soon be others.

"Keep an eye on that daughter of yours," he said to Ben. "You have enough to worry about with her underfoot."

His friend nodded, then slipped into the carriage. He settled across from Felicity, and Drew tried not to notice the grooves that marred the man's face. Ben had aged ten years since Marley's death; Drew feared his own might add another ten. But better that than Ben dying himself.

The carriage slipped off into the night and Drew said a silent farewell. He'd keep his vow to destroy El Diablo, and he'd never see Ben or his daughter again.

With great effort, Felicity pretended she hadn't overheard the whispered voices carried on the heated breeze like the thick smell of tropical flowers. She studied the coach's fleurs-de-lis–embossed walls and red leather seats, only slightly curious how her father had come by such a monstrosity. She was sure Drew arranged the purchase—as he'd no doubt hired the musket-toting driver who'd worried her on the ride to the Linleys'—but at the moment her sole interest lay in her father's conversation with Drew.

An oppressive silence settled around her and her father, the only noise between them the carriage's rattle and the rhythm of the horses' hooves. She drew a breath with the intention of casually interrogating him, then swallowed her words. His usually plump cheeks drooped with the weight that bent his shoulders.

"Father, are you ill?" Her concern momentarily replaced her excitement in discovering Drew planned to leave Barbados.

"It's nothing, daughter. Talk of the murders has upset me all over again."

Her father's distress at the brutal deaths was genuine,

but she sensed his grieving went deeper. Drew's impending departure upset him. If she only had proof of the rogue's misdeeds, her father would be grateful instead of suffering unjustified sorrow.

She patted his knee. "It was a senseless act carried out by brutal men with no apparent conscience, so please stop blaming yourself. It isn't good for you."

"I am far more responsible than I have the courage to admit."

Helpless to stop her father's self-imposed guilt, she settled against the padded seat in a squeak of rich leather. He blamed himself when responsibility for the murders belonged to Drew. In the snippets of conversation she'd overheard, Drew had admitted it. If she had to guess, she'd say he had some unscrupulous dealings involving pirates. After they'd been swindled, they probably wanted their due, and Marley and his wife had paid with their lives.

In a way, Drew had seduced her father just as he had intended to seduce her. The realization conjured a surge of anger for her own weakness as much as Drew's actions. She couldn't deny the unwanted desires he had spawned any more than she could deny her relief that he would soon be gone.

With each plodding step of the horses, their slick black carriage was carried farther from the docks. Her opportunity to change her father's mind about visiting the Hare and the Hound and finding out more about El Diablo faded with the distant lights of Bridgetown. Guilt at playing on her father's remorse held her silent.

Drew and his abrupt change of plans were the principal culprits in her father's dour mood. She stared at the passing scenery. Murky green shadows tangled in a tunnel of foliage. The contradictions in Drew's behavior disturbed her. He was leaving Barbados, but he had told her earlier that evening the seas were not safe for him. Had Drew become strange after McCulla confirmed El Diablo's responsibility for the murders, or had he realized, during their conversation on the terrace, that Felicity knew too much?

She sat up abruptly. Perhaps his departure would hurt her father in the end. One glance at his frowning features and she knew his troubles with that aristocratic fraud were far from over. If Drew fled to allow her father to take the blame for his misdeeds, his betrayal would compound the man's current misery. Felicity had personal experience with abandonment. She'd not let her father be duped as she had been.

On the long ride home, Felicity furiously devised a plan. A plan that would be carried out tonight.

# Chapter Four

The *Sea Mistress!* Even if the ship had not been listed as Lord Christian Andrews's personal vessel in the records of the New England Trading Company, her ownership would not be hard to guess. All the other ships held by the partnership bore names of ports of call or English royalty. Drew's christening of his vessel flagrantly declared his taste for debauchery. What else would he call one of his harem of females but a mistress?

Felicity gripped the varnished railing and carefully edged her foot to the next step. The glow of a single candle ensconced in a rusty lantern allowed her to see no farther than the length of her arm. Her descent into the belly of the *Sea Mistress* reminded her of Jonah being swallowed by the whale.

Like a thief she crept down the narrow corridor. If she didn't find evidence to discredit Drew, she'd be considered just that. When her attempt to pick the lock barring her from the decks below failed, she splintered the wooden hatch with a heavy crank handle. Though she instantly regretted the extreme act, her curiosity and determination compelled her to continue. Justification for damaging Drew's property depended on finding proof that he'd enraged a pirate and inadvertently caused Marley's death.

The stagnant smell of the sea clung to the interior of the ship, vividly reminding Felicity of her last and only voyage. She paused to let the twinge of nausea pass before continuing her exploration. Raising her lantern to examine the walls from top to bottom revealed everything to be as ordinary as on the *Queen Elizabeth*. The stars pressed into her tin lantern danced across a smooth, varnished hull. Not even a decorative grove cluttered the ship's spare insides.

She opened the utilitarian portals lining the passageway. A galley with a long wooden table and a large cabin supplied with canvas hammocks were her only reward. She'd been to Puritan homes with more knickknacks. Though she hadn't expected to find a chest overflowing with jewels and gold doubloons, a skull and crossbones emblazoned on its lid, the *Sea Mistress*'s lack of luxury proved an unexpected disappointment. But she'd already sneaked from her father's single-gabled home while he slept, stole through the streets leading to the docks, dodging harlots and drunken sailors alike and, last but not least, vandalized private property. She'd come too far to falter.

An ornately carved door at the stern buoyed her spirits. The portal stuck, then screeched in protest when she opened it with a forceful kick—the resulting bang against the wall echoing through the deserted ship like a dinner gong. Once her lantern light fell upon the treasure she'd uncovered, Felicity knew her extreme actions had been worth the effort. Finally, she'd uncovered Lord Christian Andrews's lair.

An enormous satin tester dominated a corner of the cabin, screaming decadence. A trek to the oversized bed nestled under the gold-and-peach canopy was muffled by thick carpet. Felicity lowered her lantern to examine the

Persian rug that devoured a large portion of the deck. The furnishings in this cabin alone cost as much as her father earned in a year.

Felicity lifted the lantern and swept the cabin with her gaze. Lord Christian's "mistress" appeared just as she'd imagined when she discovered the ship's existence in the ledgers. She didn't have to close her eyes to picture Drew lounging on the mound of silk pillows. Without warning, Samantha Linley joined the fray, crawling over Drew's lean body like the wild bougainvillea that crowded the island.

As quickly as it came, Felicity banished the disturbing image as absurd. Not that Mistress Linley would repulse the opportunity to act wanton, but the slick satin coverlet didn't show a hint of a wrinkle, even in the weak light. The bed appeared as if it had never even been laid upon. In fact, the whole room looked as if it had never been used. A stale smell of dye and wood polish bolstered her assumption. The cabin's cold elegance didn't betray the raw masculinity she'd begun to associate with Drew; it hid his secrets better than he did himself.

But not for long. A quick study of the room told Felicity the armoire of cherrywood hovering against the far wall would be the best place to start her unmasking. A turn of the latch revealed its double doors unlocked, but the hollow interior doused her premature flicker of excitement. Not a single article of clothing hung in the empty space. Then she stuck the lantern into the dark cavern, and a wooden box on a high narrow shelf greeted her with a pleasant surprise. She stood on her toes to retrieve her prize, then whisked it to the round table in the center of the room for a better look. Lifting the lid, Felicity found an overflow of papers and mementos that made her giddy.

Before she plundered her find, she let her hands glide across the box's oiled surface. She noted the nicks and scratches with the sensitive pads of her fingertips, wondering if something this simple and well worn could possibly be valued by the seemingly shallow Drew. A dried spray of lilac kindled doubt that the box belonged to him at all.

But below that, a piece of paper less aged than the other keepsakes held some promise. Glancing it over, Felicity found her breath hitched in her throat. It was a bill of sale—something she'd seen plenty of in her life—but never one that listed a human being as its commodity. A man named Drew Crawford was listed as the buyer.

Confirmation of her worst suspicions regarding Lord Christian Andrews unfurled a sense of betrayal in her Felicity hadn't expected. But there was no other explanation. "Drew Crawford" suited the honey-tongued rake with the laborer's hands better than Lord Christian Andrews.

Yet, even with written proof of his deception, Felicity found herself not wanting to believe him genuinely evil. Despite their verbal dueling and her firm belief he was nothing more than a lusty cad, she found herself fascinated by him. And yes, she'd been waylaid by his charm as effectively as every other woman at the Linleys' dinner party. If she was honest with herself, she'd admit she wanted to believe he could find her half as fascinating as he claimed.

Still, she'd long ago traded trusting her feelings for respectability—and that was a good thing, considering she still hadn't learned her lesson.

She smoothed the bill of sale against the table with the base of her palm, erasing the wrinkles created by the pressure of her grasp. Her father would never know of Drew Crawford's crimes. He'd be crushed to learn that the company he'd spent his life building profited from slavery. If Drew dared to return to Barbados, she'd confront him alone, but this time with evidence he could not disguise with a flippant remark or a wink of his seductive eye. Seeking him out before he left would prove even better, ensuring he'd simply never show his face again.

Felicity found no satisfaction in her success. She picked

up an identical piece of paper lying directly under the one she had just removed. An acrid taste coated her tongue. The commodity purchased was a boy of three. Drew Crawford had arrogantly scrawled his name across the bottom of the page.

Muffled voices startled Felicity from her horrified stupor. Immediately, she blew out the candle and sat frozen in blue-black shadows. A familiar creak penetrated the silence. She recognized the protesting sound of the heavy door. Scooping up her plunder along with her lantern and the box, she rushed to the open arms of the armoire. She flung the box and lantern on the top shelf, then squeezed herself and her heavy wool skirts into the cavity below.

Silently congratulating herself on successfully swinging the doors shut, she pressed her ear against the thick wood and listened. Silence greeted her. The outer door had not budged without noise enough to wake the devil, and she doubted anyone could open it without her hearing them, but minutes of agonized waiting passed before she convinced herself the man whose voice she'd heard never entered the cabin. To be sure, she intended to crack the door only enough to let in light thrown off by a candle before opening it wide enough for her to crawl out.

She glided her hand along the slick wood of the armoire, looking for a handle to open the door. Finding none, her predicament dawned on her. She pushed on the solid panels to no avail. An attempt to wedge her fingers in the tight closure of the ornate doors rewarded her with a torn nail. In between berating herself for her stupidity in trapping herself inside the armoire and sucking on her injured finger, she weighed her options. Preparation for the ship's impending voyage would eventually bring a servant to load the empty piece of furniture with Drew's riotous wardrobe. If she were lucky, she could convince her rescuer not to speak of her presence on board his employer's vessel.

As the minutes passed, her surroundings closed in on

her like a sealed coffin. Being discovered by the man outside the cabin became more appealing. Desperation finally persuaded her to beat against the armoire. The sound echoed in the tiny space, drowning out any noise from outside. Explanations for her current predicament became less important as her fists grew sore and no one came to her rescue.

Sudden motion threw her against the front of the armoire. It surprised her as thoroughly as the burst of pain on the back of her head. Her world went black just before she realized the *Sea Mistress* was moving.

On the deck above, the pattering of rain increased to a steady roar, dashing Drew Crawford's hope that the storm had passed. With a mumbled curse, he returned his attention to the charts he'd spread out across the cherrywood dinning table.

The bloody tropical storm had blown the *Sea Mistress* dangerously off course. He couldn't depend on the noonday sun to struggle through the gray, boiling sky to verify his longitude. His best guess placed them a day and a half sail to the safety of his island refuge. He consulted his compass and navigation ruler, hoping that the break in the clouds didn't find them anywhere near the Spanish Main. The scars from his last unscheduled visit to Spanish territory had faded from his skin but not his memory.

As the deluge pounded his ship like a kettledrum, Drew counted the one blessing in his favor: The downpour had washed his hair and face clean of the sticky white powder he wore in the persona of Lord Christian. He ran his fingers across his scalp and through his wet hair. Thanks to Marley's murderer, he would never have to bother with the ridiculous disguise again. He might have even been grateful if the culprit's plan had not included murdering a defenseless man and an innocent woman.

Not that the pirate had single-handedly ruined his formerly carefree lifestyle; Felicity Kendall also wanted a pound of his flesh. But it was his willingness to oblige her with more than that which created the true problem. Leaving Barbados provided the only solution to both dilemmas. His strange attraction to the little Puritan left him exposed.

He noticed the drops spreading across his map and shook his head over the overpriced carpet instead, creating a shower of water. The last thing he needed was a misguided woman clouding his thoughts with morality.

A hard thud sounded above the drumming rain. Startled, Drew juggled the compass he'd just picked up to prevent it from tumbling to the deck. An angry lurch of the ship conspired to toss him from his chair along with the delicate instrument.

God, but he was jumpy. Too long a time in civilization frayed his nerves, as it must have his crew. He would have thought securing the mainmast and working the pumps on the pitching deck would have drained their stores of energy. A second thud resounded against his cabin and stretched the limits of his patience.

"Save your bloody fighting for the bastard who murdered Beatrice and Marley," he yelled.

Instead of being followed by immediate compliance, Drew's command provoked a frantic onslaught of pounding. When he realized the racket came from the armoire, he shot to his feet.

If the storm had not thrown them off course, requiring him to find a dry place to unfurl his charts, the doxy one of his men had stuffed in the oversized piece of furniture would have remained undiscovered. The man responsible for spiriting away this favorite whore would rue the day he went against his captain's orders of strict discretion. Now more than ever Drew couldn't afford to have his true identity or the location of his island sanctuary revealed.

Before violently yanking open the ornate door, Drew caught himself and paused with his hand tightly gripped around the brass handle. He'd not unleash his frustration on the innocent woman trapped inside.

As he eased open the door, the tangle of black skirts and wild curls that slid from the interior forced him to reconsider. He'd considered *the storm* bad luck? The roguish smile he'd thought to use to charm his stowaway slipped into a frown. What had he done to deserve this?

Felicity Kendall lifted her head from the puddle of black wool she'd formed on the carpet. Her face shone a translucent white through a waterfall of light brown hair. For the first time in their acquaintance, her glazed expression lacked hostility . . . or even recognition. Drew couldn't conjure a witty remark, much less form a coherent thought. Once again Felicity had got the best of him, and she'd yet to utter a word. He just stood there, stunned and speechless.

She struggled to lift herself off the floor. Once she braced herself on hands and knees, she paused to pant like a wounded pup.

"Take me back to shore," she commanded the Persian rug.

Unbelievable. Drew recovered enough to know that, in this case, he did indeed have the upper hand with Miss Kendall. Not only that, she was aboard his ship, subject to his domain. The question of what the hell she was doing on board his ship still beat a frantic refrain in his head. But that truly didn't matter. He'd be the one giving orders, not the other way around.

"Sorry I can't oblige your request. Seems we're in the grips of a nasty . . ."

She emptied the contents of her stomach onto the plush carpet, splattering his boots in the process, and Drew forgot what else he'd intended to say.

As if to remind them of the tempest, the ship lurched to its side, then just as abruptly righted itself, banging the armoire doors closed. Drew absorbed the motion by balancing his weight on his splayed legs. Felicity was thrown to her side, where she remained unmoving. In fact, she lay so still, her eyes glazed and unfocused, he feared her dead. He bent down and lifted a clump of hair from her face. At his touch, she curled into a ball, her hands clutched to her stomach.

"Maybe some fresh air wouldn't be such a bad idea after all." He crouched, waiting for her reaction.

If her unusual silence wasn't hint enough, the perspiration that beaded her upper lip along with her chalky pallor warned she'd soon be retching again. He scooped her into his arms. "Come on, sweeting. You'll feel better with a little water splashed on your face." Or a lot, as the case might be.

Drew carried his bundle through the narrow passageway, marveling at her meekness. Her cheek nestled against his damp shirt, and the contact seared him all the way to his thudding heart. Having Felicity on board his ship was enough to fray his nerves; having her cradled in his arms sped his pulse to the rhythm of the constant rain. Dread and forbidden lust formed a heady aphrodisiac.

Two faces squeezed between the galley's entrance gaped at his progress. Drew turned Felicity's face into his chest. "Avery, clean up the mess in the great cabin."

"Aye, Captain." Avery Sneed only blinked once before he followed Drew's orders. Red, the other crewman, slunk back into the galley—probably to save himself from helping Avery.

Turning his back on the men, Drew ascended the stairs that led to the main deck. Let them think what they would as long as they didn't recognize Felicity. He doubted they'd appreciate having an unscheduled passenger who could identify them. Avery had been Ben's driver, Red his cook.

When Drew stepped into the hissing storm with his limp bundle, the deck careened with what seemed like malicious intent to knock him to his knees. The rolling waves sounded like an army of furious tigers trapped in a hollow cave. He almost changed his mind about bringing Felicity on deck, but the ship righted itself and the rain slowed to a tolerable shower instead of a pelting fury.

A glimpse at the sky showed a patch of illuminated gray passing overhead, but black beasts were on its tail. Drew strode to the protection of the mainmast. Felicity could gulp a few lungfuls of fresh air before she'd have to be trapped below for God knows how long. He eased her down the length of his body until her feet touched the deck. Her stiff demeanor had tricked him into believing her more solidly built, but her dead weight hardly caused him to strain.

She leaned against him, drowning in the heavy black material of her dress as much as the rain. Though she clenched her fist around his shirt, she'd have sunk to her knees if his arm wasn't wrapped securely around her waist. With his free hand, he pulled the wild strands of hair plastered across her face out of her eyes. Before he leaned down to kiss the top of her head, he caught himself.

He shook off the foolish impulse, questioning his sanity. To remind himself who she was, he lifted her chin so he could look into her face. Purple circles ringed her dark eyes. The rush of empathy that had almost prompted a kiss returned.

"This will pass, love. Is the air helping at all?"

"I don't feel well," she croaked.

Drew swallowed a chuckle but didn't bother to hide his grin. "That's obvious." Never could he have imagined Felicity Kendall at a loss for words so blatantly apparent.

"No"—she paused to gasp for breath before she could finish the sentence she seemed desperate to get out—"I don't feel well right now."

Her words prompted Drew into immediate action. He pried her fingers off his shirt and lowered her to her knees, then kneeled behind her, holding her steady, while she braced herself on all fours. Having her lean over the side of the ship would have gotten them both washed overboard. Between the miserable dry coughs that sliced through the pounding waves, he heard her soft sobs. Both tore at his hardened heart.

Drew reached for the thick rope of hair that hung across her face and spilled onto the deck. He held the mass out of her way with one hand. With his other arm, he circled her waist and held her rump steadfastly against his hip. His knees planted firmly on the deck absorbed the continued rolls of the ship and anchored both their weights.

When her heavy breathing was the only sound that could be heard above the rain and wind, he realized the awkwardness of their positions. Of course he'd been in similar positions with women before, but never in his wildest dreams had he pictured Felicity and himself in such circumstances. And never had the women been getting sick.

A nasty wave crawled over the deck and forced him to flex his thighs to maintain their balance. Despite the storm that howled its return, his traitorous body interpreted the movement as something else entirely. With his blood eagerly rushing to places it had no business being, he reached underneath Felicity's arms and pulled her up with him as he stood. "Your stomach is empty, love, so I'm going to have to take you below."

He lifted her in his arms, and she sagged against his chest like a broken doll, succumbing to his will without an ounce of protest. The drastic change in her personality worried Drew all over again. Once he entered the protected deck below, he studied her closed eyes and gave in to his earlier urge: He placed an almost invisible kiss on the top of her head.

Drew returned to the luxurious great cabin, the only chamber on the *Sea Mistress* furnished for the needs of a woman. He planned on getting rid of the ship after this voyage. Too much attention had been attracted to it and to his true identity. He laid Felicity on the silk comforter, realizing she would have put all the clues together, anyway. Her unscheduled trip on the *Sea Mistress* had only hastened the process.

Her docile demeanor wouldn't last, but that didn't stop Drew's desire to hasten her recovery. He hated seeing her so weak. A dark halo spread around her as the ivory bedding absorbed the water from her drenched clothing and hair. Drew sat beside her, unbuttoning the high neck of her heavy gown. Her lack of protest when he began to undress her sounded an alarm. He touched her cheeks, finding her skin chilled. Banishing his guilt and ignoring his slight glee, he peeled off the black casing Felicity used to shield herself from the world.

He dropped the gown to the floor and attacked the fastening of her stiff corset. His hands stilled as he stared at the lushness he uncovered. Apparently no one had ever instructed Felicity in the wearing of the things. The feminine undergarment concealed, almost strangled, what it should have accentuated. Miss Kendall had a figure to rival Venus. Her breasts were full, large and appeared enticingly firm. Her white cotton chemise escaped the drenching of her dress, keeping her somewhat concealed and teasing his imagination with what lay beneath. He tore his gaze away before he burned a hole in the cotton. If he wanted to adhere to the integrity of his role as nursemaid, he'd better move on to a less challenging duty.

Underskirts entwined around Felicity's legs, hiding those appendages from the world. Drew reached down to remove the black boots peeking out beneath. Even with his gaze focused on nothing but the laces of her shoes, he felt like a lecher taking advantage of a helpless female.

Fortifying himself with the innocence of his intent and ignoring his not so virtuous urges, he pulled off layers of muslin petticoats, refusing to touch the knee-length chemise. He brushed his fingers along Felicity's calf. Her stockings remained thankfully dry. Reaching under her chemise to remove them would have sorely tested his endurance.

He got up from the bed to search for something to dry her hair. When she regained her strength, something he assured himself would happen, she'd be livid to find he of all people had undressed her. He doubted she'd be satisfied with the fact that he had no choice, or appeased by the knowledge that his skill in the area of undressing women allowed him to do so quickly. Yet having a crewmember do the job was out of the question. His men were self-confessed cutthroats, not gentlemen who would respect a lady—no matter how angelic she might look at the moment. He pulled his hot gaze away from where her light cotton chemise clung to the apex of her thighs. He wasn't much better.

When he turned to the armoire, hoping to find a towel, he noticed the wooden box that had spilled out with Felicity. Seeing the tattered remnants of his life scattered across the floor confirmed his worst suspicions: The little witch had been spying on him.

He gathered the fragile items he'd sworn to toss overboard a dozen times. A yellowed, returned and unopened letter his mother had written to his father lay among the pile. The parchment's neat folds looked as if they hadn't been disturbed. Drew had never had the courage to read the last letter his mother had written, and the thought of Felicity doing so irritated Drew enough to chide himself for his compassion. If he'd decided to strip her naked and tie her to the bed until the storm passed instead of taking such precious care with her, he'd be justified.

He scooped up the sprig of purple lilac, a few more of whose tiny petals had fallen off. He sniffed it, though he knew the fragrance was long gone. He should just throw it away. Instead, he gently returned the letter and the sprig to the security of the tattered wooden box, the only baggage he'd brought with him from England.

With the heirloom tucked under his arm, he stalked over to the bed. He searched the features of the tranquil figure in white for the conniving shrew who'd broken onto his ship and ransacked his belongings.

After he studied her still face to assure himself her extreme condition wasn't a ploy, he placed his palm against the side of her cheek and traced her lips with his thumb. With his other hand, he brushed her hair away from her face. He let his fingers stray until they were enveloped in the golden brown torrent spilling over the pillow. Her placid features tightened in pain when his caress found a lump the size of an egg protruding from the back of her skull. He gingerly removed his hands from her hair and reached for the box. No new scratch marred the sturdy wood to discern whether she had found the heavy object or it found her.

Whether she'd managed to examine the contents of the box before it hit her on the head mattered not. Felicity Kendall was finally at his mercy. She would answer his many questions, not the other way around. God help them both.

# Chapter Five

Felicity shook herself from a deep sleep. Even before she could pry open her eyes, she knew he was gone. How long she'd drifted in and out of an endless nightmare of pain, her head throbbing, her stomach pitching, provided as great a mystery as who *he* was. Strong fingers massaging her temples and a deep voice coaxing her from her misery remained the only tangible evidence that her savior had been flesh and blood instead of a figment of her desperate imagination.

But even her tangled memories conspired to confuse her. Who could possibly be so kind, stay beside her bed the entire night, hold back her hair through bouts of intense nausea that wouldn't cease even after her stomach had long been empty?

She blinked, trying to clear her vision. Instead of the whitewashed ceiling of her bedroom, uniform planks, varnished and shiny, loomed over her head. Sunlight filled the room with a hazy afternoon glow. She must be seriously ill to sleep so far past dawn. Sleeping late was a sin.

Though not serious enough to earn a whipping, a reprimand in front of the congregation would be in order. She let her eyes drift shut again, relishing her last moments of decadence. As miserable as she felt, lying abed until late morning felt oh so good. No wonder it was a sin.

Reluctantly, she stretched, and discovered her stockings glided over what had to be silk. Not that she had much experience with the expensive material. The most she'd ever seen had been in the cabin. . . . .

Tattered glimpses of how she'd come to be lying between silk sheets on a moving ship trickled to the forefront of her thinking like an unwanted fever. Her imprisonment in the armoire had turned from a slight inconvenience to the incarnation of hell as she woke to the mad pitching of the ship. Even inside the armoire she'd fully expected to be her tomb, she could hear the crashing waves and the howling wind. Thankfully, the sudden increased pounding in her head prevented her from remembering much else.

Except for that man. Now that she had somewhat returned to her senses, she could assure herself he wasn't Drew. The idea that she could still think he had any redeeming qualities was humiliating.

She took a deep, shuddering breath, grateful to be alive, and realized her gown had been removed, along with her corset. How she'd come to be without them presented another mystery she must solve. She flung out her hand and groped for a pillow to cover her face. If she could just go back to sleep until the throbbing in her head subsided, she could figure out her predicament later.

The feather-stuffed silk shut out the light but didn't squelch the rapid flood of her returning memory. She was on Lord Christian Andrews's ship. Under full sail no less.

She removed the pillow and listened. The motion of the ship had steadied and waves lapped against the hull instead of beating the sides like fists. No one else seemed to be in the cabin she occupied. To be sure of that, she forced herself to sit up. As soon as she lifted her heavy head off the pillow, splintering pain tossed bright fragments of light in front of her eyes. She squeezed her eyelids shut against the explosion.

Just as a sob tightened her throat, a loud screech announced the opening of the rusty portal.

The sound delivered another unbearable slice of pain. Knowing someone entered the room forced Felicity to open her eyes in a squint. For the first time, she caught a clear glimpse of the man who had played her nurse. She quickly darted her gaze away before she had to meet his eyes. Good lord, *he'd* undressed her.

Even with her focus firmly fixed on the silk coverlet, his image burned into her mind's eye. He bore a tray in his hands, but that didn't hinder his swagger in the least. His hair fell in thick brown waves just past his broad shoulders and stood starkly against the white cambric shirt he'd not bothered to lace. His close-fitting black breeches tapered into scuffed boots that began below his knees. A blush crept to Felicity's cheeks as she remembered her first glimpse of those boots and the powerful legs attached to them.

"I owe you heartfelt thanks, sir, and my apologies," she whispered, cringing against the sound of her own voice.

She closed her eyes briefly, struggling with the reality of her flesh-and-blood rescuer. He appeared to be pure muscle under his rumpled clothes. It was hard to believe he was the same man who had touched her with such gentleness.

Images of his body pressed intimately against hers came back with enough force to turn her cheeks hot. Though she believed his actions innocent and her condition kept her from any say in the matter, his unexpected virility washed her in guilt, as if they had intentionally participated in some type of lascivious behavior. When his boots echoed across the wooden floor, then drifted onto the carpet, she yanked the bedcovers to her neck.

His weight sagged the mattress as he brazenly sank down next to her. Maybe if she pretended she was asleep, he'd go away. Usually she wasn't so cowardly, but usually she wasn't practically naked in the company of a stranger—a stranger she was forced to rely upon.

He brushed strands of hair from her face and cupped her cheek, then her forehead. His touch was gentle, but she couldn't stop herself from stiffening. She should tell him to leave. He'd taken too many liberties already. Though she appreciated his kind intent, he was a man and she a woman and the devil lurked in such innocent situations. At least she'd been told so enough times to make her think of it now.

To her shock, she enjoyed his touch. She needed the warmth of his physical support, his help. She needed him. Unaccustomed tears stung her eyes. She turned her face against her pillow, confused by her weakness. Instead of pulling away, he caressed her cheek. His thumb captured the tear clinging to her lashes.

"Please, don't," she whispered hoarsely. She couldn't remember the last time she had wept. To have someone wipe away her tears had been an eternity.

He removed his hands obediently at her croaked command.

"I'm sorry. You've been so kind." She wiped her tears and sniffed. Even in her worst bouts of seasickness aboard the *Queen Elizabeth*, she'd not felt this awful. "What's wrong with me?"

She forced herself to finally look at him and instantly wished she hadn't. His face was tanned and rough, yet undeniably appealing. Eyes the color of warm tropical waters simmered in angular contours. Against her will she had the urge to compare her rescuer to Drew. She urgently pushed the thought away. This was a kind stranger, not another handsome man for her to ogle. What was wrong with her? Was she being tested? The good Lord should have known by now she'd surely fail.

He stared at her in sincere confusion, as if she spoke a language foreign to him. "You hit your head."

His voice sounded peppered with loose gravel, not like the smooth, comforting tone she remembered from her blurred hours of semiconsciousness. Felicity studied his features. As he met her gaze without the slightest wavering, she was forced to look away to stop the heat that crept up her neck.

"How did I hit my head? I recall being trapped in the armoire. . . ." She let her words trail off. The awkwardness of her position rattled her all over again. She tensed, but couldn't sit up even if an armed assassin had marched through the door. Her very presence proved she'd been lurking where she shouldn't. And then there was the box. If Lord Christian Andrews dealt in slaves—as she now knew he did—perhaps he would sell her as well. She'd heard of such things, and it would suit him nicely to have her out of the way forever. This sailor could be nursing her back to health on his orders.

"My father is Benjamin Kendall. Perhaps he's your employer?" When he continued to stare without expression, she rushed to fill up the space left by his apparent desire not to reveal himself to her. "My presence here was a mistake. I assure you, it's not what you might think."

Trying to figure out what he might think while coming up with a plausible excuse for it proved too much for her. Her thoughts became more muddled than they were already. She again gave up the struggle with her eyelids, bringing up her hand to gently massage her temples. What had hit her on the head? The only other thing in the armoire was the box. The box . . . it was too much to think about with the excessive hammering in her brain.

She slid her hand into her hair to find the source of her

pain. Her fingers grazed an enormous knot. Examining its size was too painful, but she imagined it swelled the better part of her skull. Blasted box.

"Rest," her benefactor commanded in his previous half-growl. When he removed himself from her bed, Felicity had to force herself to be relieved.

"You should eat," he said. "I brought you some broth and crackers." He enunciated every word slowly and carefully, as if it strained him. His perfect English led her to believe the language was not foreign to him.

A whiff of what he'd brought on his tray reached her nose.

"No. I don't want anything." She covered her mouth. The idea alone almost made her retch.

"I'll feed you. You won't have to lift your head." He answered more easily and smoothly this time, and his voice grew more familiar, like the soft words from last night. Though she had no idea what Drew looked like without wig and makeup, and she didn't even know the color of his hair, she tried to assure herself this stranger wasn't he.

She strained to look at him from the corner of her eye. Something about his appearance triggered her memory, but she refused to believe it was her fancy from last night.

"What's your name? I owe you so much."

He turned his back on her in answer to her question, proving he was purposely avoiding her request for information. She truly was grateful, but she'd need more from him than he had already given. He was her only ally at the moment.

Before she realized what he had tucked in his hand, he lifted a brown chipped mug to her lips. "Drink. We'll talk later."

"No!" Her sharp answer startled both of them. The closer he brought the concoction to her nose, the more violently her stomach reacted. "Please, I'd rather sleep."

He nodded, then disappeared from her view again.

When his boots sounded his return, she forced her eyes open. Before she could return to the sleep she desperately needed, she had to have the answer to the question that had haunted her since she came to her senses:

"Does your employer know I'm here?"

He shrugged. "Of course."

Felicity bolted to a sitting position. Splinters of pain penetrated the back of her eyes and the room spun, but she refused to give in to her weakness or her fear.

If this man was Drew devoid of powdered hair and skin, surely he'd not miss the opportunity to gloat at her misfortune. She forced herself to study his features with all the intensity her fuzzy mind could muster. Unfortunately, the effort brought another wave of wicked nausea.

"I'm the captain of this ship," the man said. "I answer only to myself, and you've nothing to fear from me."

His words swept away some of her panic, but confusion swiftly followed Felicity's moment of relief. Had she sneaked aboard the wrong ship?

"Sleep," her benefactor commanded. A smirk tugged at the corners of his mouth. "I'll make you eat some soup if you don't slow that mischievous mind of yours."

She pretended to follow his request, but his crooked grin burned behind her eyelids. Another face danced through the misty meadow separating dream and reality. A brass gong banged beside her aching head couldn't have been more unpleasantly shocking. The unusual color of his eyes, the lean, tall build, even the arrogant smirk—they were hauntingly similar. Yet it couldn't be. Even if they were twins, the sheer kindness, the long hours of unselfish caring starkly separated the two men. This was not Drew. She refused to believe otherwise or she'd go mad.

Calmed by her rationalization, she allowed her eyes to flutter shut. A healing sleep crawled over her and swept her away in spite of the man lingering in the half-open doorway.

\* \* \*

Drew indulged his desire to watch Felicity sleep.

When she'd failed to instantly recognize him, he'd almost believed that his bad luck had turned; but the calculating gleam in her suddenly wide eyes had dashed any hope he could whisk her back to Barbados without her knowing his identity. Her gratitude shocked him. Her vulnerability unnerved him, even more so with her fully awake. The hissing wet cat he'd faced on every other meeting protected a childlike heart, raw and ripe for the plucking. Her prickly facade hid what she thought of as weakness. She craved the touch of another human being, just like everyone else.

Of course, acting on his attraction for her could only cause them both harm. He turned and left the room, denying himself the pleasure of pressing his palm against her cheek. Checking for fever could no longer be used as an excuse to touch her.

He climbed the steps to the main deck to relieve the helmsman. Much of his time had been spent nursing Felicity, leaving his small crew exhausted. The severity of her condition had justified his actions. Her return to consciousness stole his excuse to linger by her side. Besides, now that she could, she'd probably slap him for the liberties he'd taken.

At Drew's approach, Smythe relinquished the wheel without a word and stumbled below in a bleary-eyed daze. The rhythmic sloshing of the calm sea warned Drew the simple act of steering the ship would not serve as the distraction he needed. Thoughts of his uninvited guest would consume him.

Felicity's frosty exterior protected a woman eager to burn with her pent-up desire, he realized. She was powder waiting to be ignited. Yet, no matter how much he'd like to see her burn with lust, he'd have to settle for only setting ablaze her anger. He wished curtailing his appetite had been one of his virtues.

Drew forcibly reminded himself that Felicity was a friend's daughter and normally not a woman easily dabbled with. She'd see him hang if she knew who he was and had the chance. Yet despite her past animosity toward him, he must continue to act as her protector—even if it meant taming a shrew while playing the tedious part of gentleman. How ironic that that was the one disguise he'd never truly mastered.

The morning sun awakened the old Felicity. Drew walked into his cabin to find her poised in front of the armoire, balanced on her tiptoes, searching the top shelf for something that wasn't there.

Last night he'd oiled the squeaky door, partly out of an inherent need for stealth and partly for her comfort. As always, his devious nature proved advantageous. A tray bearing a breakfast of weak broth, rainwater flavored with a pinch of tea, and a few crackers occupied his hands, forcing him to kick the door shut with a resounding boom.

Felicity's gaze jerked over her shoulder. She froze in her guilty pose, like a child caught misbehaving. Drew also found himself taken by surprise, staring as wide-eyed as she. His reaction, however, had more to do with the transparency of her chemise in the morning light than the discovery of her snooping.

Recovering first, Drew sauntered across the room and set down the tray. He faced her, arms folded across his chest, feet braced. "Looking for something?"

Felicity thawed from her position, her arms slowly melting to hang by her sides. Waves of wild curls shimmered with a hint of gold in the sun spilling from the cabin's window. His gaze drifted hungrily from her hair to the veil of her chemise. The white garment left her arms bare and exposed her legs, knee to feet. What it did to her ample curves forced him to drag his perusal back to the glint in her green-brown eyes.

He corrected his earlier observation: Ice appropriately described Miss Kendall at their first meeting, but flame came to mind at the moment. The annoying ache in his empty stomach slithered lower due to hunger pains of a different kind.

"I . . ." began Felicity. Her explanation appeared to evaporate with the questions that drifted across her features. Her eyes narrowed into feral aggression. The answers she found on her own obviously stirred her temper. The meek and mild Felicity of the night before transformed into the adversary he'd come to admire.

"You!" she said in a whispered curse.

"I'm so pleased you're feeling better." With the shrew back in his helpless patient, he allowed the desire coiled in his belly to claw its way into his gaze. His vow to protect the vulnerability he'd discovered in her two nights before wavered when faced with her venom-filled glare.

But alas, his little Puritan didn't appear to notice her state of undress or the wanting in his warning leer.

Shoulders back, she boldly stalked him, thrusting her breasts against the thin white cotton of her chemise. When she planted her hands on her well-rounded hips, perfect rose nipples strained against the thin material.

"What is your game?"

As always, the woman's audacity pushed Drew past his good intentions. He erased the space between them. His towering stance forced her to turn her face up to his. He wanted her to feel his presence, his dominance. The veneer of civility no longer held him in check and she needed to understand that right from the start.

"Felicity." He curled her name around his tongue like a sugar-dipped confection. "No game, love." He placed a finger underneath her chin, forcing her to tilt her head even farther, laying open her soft, pale throat. "But I will be needing an explanation for *your* presence aboard *my* ship."

She slapped away his hand. Her glare declared her refusal to be intimidated as much as her physical blow. "I insist you take me back to Barbados this instant. I know you're a fraud, so don't even attempt to taunt me."

He wanted to laugh at her audacity and wring her arrogant neck at the same time. "That's right, Felicity. I'm no aristocrat. I'm not even considered a gentleman. I'm just a lowly commoner they would cross the street to avoid."

His sarcastic comment pricked at his own raw wound he'd sworn had closed. No matter what he did or became, or how much money he accumulated, the truth in the statement always haunted him when he least expected it.

"Don't flatter yourself. You sully the name of good common men by lumping yourself with them. You're nothing but a criminal."

As she vehemently flung her insult, she discreetly backed away from him. He closed the gap in two determined strides.

"My point exactly, though you express it more eloquently. You are in no position to make demands." With the pad of his index finger, he caressed her shoulder to elbow. "I'll be the one doing the demanding."

Instead of betraying the slightest alarm at his blatant sexual threat, her pupils flared with indignant rage. She jerked away from him, but out of obvious disgust rather than distress.

"Please stop this charade. Your interest in me is as transparent as your fraudulent name. If you continue, you'll send me into another bout of nausea."

Her distaste insulted him more than a slap might have. Women loved him. Men feared him. Felicity seemed to think him a joke. The fact that his flicker of attraction for this vicious piece of Puritan baggage had raged into an inferno annoyed him even more at her rebuke.

In what he hoped was a convincing sign of indifference, he shrugged and hid behind an amused observance. She wasn't about to witness the effect she had on him a moment longer. Her heart might be soft and fragile deep down, but its fortress was laced with broken glass.

"Are you going to take me back to Barbados or not?" Felicity folded her arms over her chest, making Drew wonder if she had finally realized her chemise had become enticingly transparent.

"No." He enunciated the single word with immense satisfaction.

He thought her confidence wavered slightly when she paused to gape at him, but her screech banished the notion. "No? I demand to know what you plan to do with me."

"If you haven't noticed, we're not moving. We're drifting. Maybe if you demanded the wind blow, it would cooperate. I know I would."

"So, you are going to return me to Barbados eventually?"

"I'm afraid I've worn out my welcome on that particular island. But not to worry; I'll get you home somehow. Nagging sea hags are notoriously bad luck."

Her stunned expression proved he'd hit a nerve. She recovered quickly, baring her teeth for a counterattack.

"Oh, yes. I haven't forgotten your cowardly retreat, Lord Christian. Or should I call you Master Crawford?"

His grin, or sneer to be more accurate, confirmed her shaky aim. He could tell by her satisfied smirk that she'd not known for sure her stab at the truth would be accurate. The little fool had no idea that a man would be in serious danger for knowing less about him.

"So, what else do you know, my pretty spy? Perhaps you might not be going home after all."

The long-awaited show of panic that knitted her brow

hardly pricked his conscience. He'd used to enjoy the thinness of the veil separating his criminal activities from his true identity. Now that the curtain separating him from the hangman's noose had begun to unravel, he found no humor or irony in any of his secrets.

"You wouldn't dare hurt me," she said. "My father would figure out what happened to me. He would discover your deceit as easily as I have." The cracking of her voice when she mentioned her father destroyed the bluster of her threat.

"I suppose Ben might be inclined to sail off to your rescue. Not to worry. I'll be ready for him." Drew retrieved the pistol tucked in the waistband of his breeches and watched her remaining composure slip away.

"Don't you dare lay a hand on my father. You've caused enough damage to his life. If you've left him to take the blame for your wrongdoings—"

"You'll what? I have the gun, Felicity." He waved the weapon to make his point. "And I'm bigger than you." He found it amazing and ridiculous that she couldn't keep her sharp tongue in check. He had to be the one to stop the insane drift of their conversation before she realized he was bluffing or, worse, she forced him to do something he would regret just to save face. "I don't want to hurt you or Ben."

He lowered the gun. Her wide eyes followed the weapon.

"It's not even primed." He tossed the pistol on the bed to prove it harmless. But that didn't stop her from backing against the far wall.

His success in finally intimidating her made him feel like a bully for the second time in their short relationship. "Come sit down, Felicity. Eat the food I brought you."

She watched him warily. "Why should I believe you or anything you say?"

He sat in one of the high-backed chairs crowding the

table, hoping she'd follow his lead. "You threw up on my boots. If I didn't toss you overboard after that greeting, I don't know what else I can do to prove you're safe on this ship."

Apprehension drained from her face, replaced by a flush that colored her cheeks. "You *would* have to remind me of that. I suppose any shred of manners you possessed went out the window with your fancy clothes." She warily approached the table. After making a show of examining the stale crackers and pottery mugs, she sat across from him. "I did thank you, you know."

Their gazes collided and held. In the momentary lull in their animosity, a sharp jolt of sexual awareness shot down the length of him. He would have sworn the same emotion turned her cool brown eyes to warm hazel, but she looked away before he knew for sure.

"It was the least I could do." He continued as if the moment never happened. "But now we have a problem. Don't we?"

"I know who you are and that you deal in slaves, among other things. Is that the problem you're speaking of?" Felicity stopped sniffing the mug of tea she held and gazed over its glazed rim as if she'd just delivered a mortal blow.

"You know my name, but you don't know much else." She opened her mouth to refute his statement, but he fended her off with a raised hand. "I picked up the contents of my chest that were scattered on the floor. I assumed you looked through it. Those things were personal, by the way."

"But I saw the documents. You bought slaves under a different name. Drew Crawford, I believe. Not very clever, *Drew*."

"Slavery is not illegal, *Felicity*." He drawled her name as she did his. In spite of the circumstances, he liked the sound of his name on her lips. "All you really know is that I was impersonating nobility."

"Your actions are reprehensible, legal or not. My father would be horrified."

"Yes, he would. I don't think you want that. And if you spread the news of your discovery, who knows how many of my other reprehensible acts will turn up? Guilt by association is an unfair practice, but all too common. Men have hanged for less."

"You said you didn't want to hurt my father. Do you actually believe I could sit by and let you continue your treachery against his good name?"

Her color rose with her pitch, but she managed to keep her anger under control. He could only assume she had more common sense when her father was in jeopardy rather than herself.

"No, Felicity. I have a proposition I think we can both live with, and I mean that figuratively, of course." He couldn't resist giving her one of his most wicked smiles. "You'll keep your beautiful mouth shut and I'll never try to contact your father again. I'll stay out of his life completely and relinquish all claims to the New England Trading Company."

She sat straighter in her chair. He could only imagine how she'd longed to hear those precise words roll off his tongue. She'd probably prefer him on his knees, but this was the best she would get.

In her eagerness, she scooted to the edge of her seat. "You'll sign a statement to that effect?"

"If you want. What name would you like me to use?"

She drew her brows together and assessed him from the corner of one eye.

He shrugged. "It really doesn't matter if I sign a document or not. I don't want my true name revealed in Barbados any more than you want your father associated with my horrid deeds. If I were you, I wouldn't even tell Ben. It would only hurt him. But that's entirely up to you."

She studied the sleek tabletop. The tightness around her

full lips hinted at her inward battle. When she finally met his gaze, her brown eyes were clear and sure. To his surprise, she reached out her hand to him. "You stay away from my father and I'll keep your secrets."

He grasped her hand, giving it a firm squeeze, then a shake, unable to resist holding her longer than necessary. This was the first time she'd voluntarily touched him skin to skin. It signified a beginning, but of what he didn't dare dwell on. A slight tug on her part won her instant release.

Felicity returned her concentration to the contents of her cup, but he noticed her shiver. The temperature in the cabin sweltered. The tropical sun heated everything that had been drenched by the rain to an unbearable intensity. Perhaps the heat only affected him, and for reasons other than the humidity.

"Are you feeling all right? You're not chilled?" He stood to leave, reminding himself of his many duties, like getting his ship to their home port before his men started to eat the sails, or worse, each other.

"I'm fine." After an extended examination, she sipped the tea, then winced. "You can take this. I'm not all that hungry." She nudged the tray in his direction.

He pushed it back, rattling the cup and bowl. "If I take it away, someone will eat it. Probably me. I want it all gone before I come back."

"But I'm not hungry and it doesn't smell very good."

"You will be before the day is over, and that's all the food we have. Your unscheduled passage has left me at a loss. I didn't have the foresight to bring her highness's favorite dishes."

"I didn't ask for special treatment."

"No, you just demanded it. Nothing like a sick woman in your bed to get your attention."

"Please, I've thanked you already." Her pinched expression wavered between annoyance and embarrassment. She pushed the tray toward him a second time. "Here. You eat it. I can wait until you take me home."

"Felicity, you haven't eaten in two days. If the wind doesn't pick up, it might be two more." He walked toward the door without the tray.

"Two days? I've been here for two days?" Her head sank into her hands. He stopped and watched her struggle to account for the lost time.

"I'll get you home as soon as I can. Get some rest. That bump on your head must still hurt." He wrestled with the urge to comfort her. His struggle ended with the realization that conscious, she wasn't nearly as pliable. To force her to rest, he'd probably have to wrestle her into bed. With that all too enticing thought, he strode to the door.

"Drew?"

Her call stopped him before he could slip into the hall. When she said his name again, the same shiver of pleasure crawled up his spine.

He grinned. "You must have begun to like me a little. You're calling me by my first name."

"I don't like you at all. It's just that I'm not used to your real name, and Drew is what my father called you." The way she avoided his gaze while she stumbled over her words gave him the impression she did care for him more than she let on.

Maybe she wouldn't mind being wrestled into bed. He had to get out of the cabin before the idea took root.

Before he could escape, he caught her striding toward the door. The thin cloth of her chemise clung to her thighs and molded against the curve of her hips. He had no choice but to stare like the hungry letch he was.

She brought her arms across her chest. "Where are the rest of my clothes?"

She was aware of her state of undress after all. Apparently, she wore masks as expertly as he.

"I'm sorry, Felicity. Your clothes were ruined. I tossed

them overboard. You were sick all over everything. I tried—"

"I understand." She stopped him before he could go into further detail. "You'll need to find something else for me to wear when I leave the ship. What I have on is fine for now"—she tugged on the scooped neckline of her chemise and turned away from him—"as it's miserable in here."

His smile widened at her attempt to reduce her flimsy attire as having no consequence except in practical terms. Could she truly be blind to her blatant seductiveness in the thin chemise? Just in case, he decided to remind her.

"Don't leave this cabin. Believe it or not, there are worse fiends walking this ship than myself. They might find your attire appealing for reasons besides its suitability for this cabin's heat."

She nodded, then turned away. He paused before closing the door to savor the enticing outline that view provided. Oh, but she did have curves!

In the companionway leading to the main deck, he whistled. As he passed the galley, he ignored the grumbling of his crew and the hunger gnawing at his own belly. The tightness in his breeches was something he couldn't ignore. Confrontations with Felicity Kendall had left him exhilarated from their first meeting. This encounter proved to be no exception. Even when she was at his mercy, she came out fighting. But his opponent had lost one of her defenses.

His emergence from the deck below surrounded him with white-hot sunshine. He shielded his gaze and studied the brilliant blue cloudless sky. Not a single breeze disturbed the grandeur of the steamy tropical day. A sailor's curse. Drew snatched the black bundle of cloth drying over a mast. As he threw the garments into the calm turquoise sea, he thought his luck might have changed after all.

# Chapter Six

Felicity clutched together the lapels of the wool jacket she wore over her chemise and sank onto the silk cushions banking the panel of windows at the stern. The single ship that bobbed in the turquoise cove appeared to be the small island's only resident. She tried to quell her rising panic at the fact that they'd not arrived in Barbados.

When she'd awoken to find dawn creeping across her bed, she noticed the man's jacket draped at her feet and assumed she would be eating breakfast at her father's table. As the day grew hotter and her hunger stronger, she could do nothing but lie on the big bed and question her fate. She was dealing with a criminal, after all.

Still, she found it difficult to reconcile Drew Crawford with Lord Christian Andrews. Somehow, the polished persona of Lord Christian had worried her more than the rough, self-admitted charlatan who had undressed her and been her nursemaid. She fingered her coat's frayed lapel, turning it up to bury her nose in its masculine fragrance of musk, sea and untamable wind. The garment had to belong to Drew. His presence stormed her senses and sent ripples of awareness across her skin.

The *Sea Mistress* glided deeper into the hidden cove's green-sloped arms. Sunlight turned the water's surface a living carpet of molten gold. Palm trees sprung from a pristine white beach. The clear blue water turned pale green, then liquid crystal as it caressed the shores with rhythmic whispers. The island's sensual beauty threatened to seduce her as effectively as a whiff from Drew's jacket. Realizing the danger she was in, Felicity stood and paced the confines of the cabin instead.

What did Drew plan on doing with her? He had mentioned his need for discretion. Perhaps he planned to persuade one of his disreputable associates, the owner of the lone ship, to return her to Barbados. The thought chilled her. Drew might be no better than a common criminal, but he was a known evil. Harm to her virtue might not be the greatest threat she might have to face, after all.

She fingered the frayed coat's lapel while she tried to reconcile exactly what she did know about the man who had her at his mercy. Rough and well worn, the plain wool would have never found a place in Lord Christian's wardrobe. But Lord Christian didn't exist. A completely new man had taken his place—a man wrapped in as many mysteries and contradictions as the two personalities he'd presented to her.

She returned to the padded bench in front of the window. The sinking sun threw its last powerful rays across the water, dropping a burnished gold veil over the cove. But the idyllic sunset she braced herself against changed to something altogether more frightening: Men filed onto the virgin beach, looming like wild beasts in the orange glow. Finding the island deserted would have disturbed her less than the decidedly uncivilized inhabitants ruining the sand's white luster.

The ship's steady slide to shore brought sword-wielding

ruffians, worse than any of the usual harbor rats she'd seen before, into heart-stopping clarity. Through the tangles of their unkempt hair, an occasional gold earring caught the light.

Answering jeers and shouts drifted from the deck above. Scathing taunts from Drew's crew blistered Felicity's ears but sounded unmistakably friendly. Clanking metal and scurrying footsteps drowned out some of the overly descriptive greetings.

Lest they spot her, she backed away from the large window. Confidence in her situation faded with the men's appearance on the beach and the character of Drew's unseen crew. If Drew thought for a moment she would allow those barbarians to take her back to Barbados, he was delirious.

In the purple haze between dusk and dark, the light of a lantern guided a launch to shore. She crept back to the window in time to recognize Drew in the front of the small boat. Torches had been lit on the beach and the throng of beastlike men awaited his arrival. When he reached the shore, they surrounded him. He took command, his broad back straight and forbidding against the wild licking flames that outlined him in an unearthly haze.

His tangled, shoulder-length mane enhanced his role as leader of the pack. If he peeled off his shirt he'd be one of them. No, he wouldn't be one of them; he'd still be their captain or king or whatever he was to these fiends. Which meant he was more dangerous than the most savage of the unruly lot.

A hollow silence drifted down from the decks above. She'd been abandoned on the empty ship. A dull headache wrapped around her skull. She attributed it to hunger and couldn't help wondering whether Drew and his clan planned an exotically hedonistic feast. Perhaps they'd sacrifice a virgin. For once, she found the bright side of her little indiscretion. She paced the room, allowing anger as a welcome replacement to her anxiety.

Drew had never mentioned she was to be his prisoner. To ensure he knew that, she wouldn't await his instructions like a helpless captive. She slipped her arms through Drew's coat and secured its two buttons. The garment, designed to fall to the top of a man's knees, covered her to mid-shin. Decently shielded from lecherous eyes, she strode intently, if not altogether confidently, to the door.

She stopped after one tentative step into the companionway. A knocking against the ship's side muffled the distinctive splashing of water. She listened intently, almost convincing herself it was nothing but a loose rigging, but at the same time finding it hard to breathe.

The noise began to inch its way up the ship's side. She darted back into the cabin. After she yanked the portal shut, she frantically looked for a weapon or a place to hide. The wardrobe in the corner mocked her as she glanced its way. She wouldn't use that option again.

Heavy footfalls approached the cabin in a rhythm she didn't recognize as Drew's. The easy opening of the cabin's door silenced her frantic thoughts. A dark shadow slipped into the room, whisking away any hope of escape.

Unfortunately, it wasn't Drew. The stranger was not as tall, but wider, thicker. He stood as solid as a tree stump. She strained to make him out in the darkness. If she saw even a glimmer of gold near his ear, she'd scream.

"Miss Kendall, do not be afraid. My name is Solomon. The captain sent me to take you to the other ship," said the shadow.

"I'm not afraid," responded Felicity before she'd decided whether she was or not. Solomon's voice resounded deep and rich like molasses. His crisp pronunciation went a long way to dispel the picture of the beastly creatures crowding her mind.

"You should be afraid, Miss Kendall. Take my hand. We must hurry."

"I'd like to speak to the captain, please." She hoped she

sounded stern but polite. Crisp pronunciation or not, she wasn't going anywhere with this new threat.

Warm fingers wrapped around her wrist, followed by a tug that pulled her forward, proved he had other plans. "I don't have time to accommodate your insolence. I've been ordered to move you to the other ship before the others come aboard."

Solomon dragged her through the portal and down the passageway. In light of his revelation, she agreed with his decision to leave. When the thugs lurking on the island overran this ship, she wanted to be on the other vessel. Though she didn't like his manner, common sense urged that she follow quietly.

Solomon helped her up the steps leading to the main deck, touching her as stiffly as if she were covered in wet varnish. Why had Drew sent this rude man to take her onboard the other ship? Did he find her as inconvenient as Solomon obviously did? The fact that the very idea hurt her feelings warned her all over again that she mustn't let Drew slide further past her defenses than he already had.

When she reached the open deck, she took her first breath of fresh air in what seemed like an eternity. A warm breeze brushed her cheek and rustled her hair. She shuddered, drinking in the sweet summer air. With the men and torches gone from the beach, the night-enshrouded island rivaled the golden seductiveness of late afternoon. Stars dusted the tropical paradise with a soft white glow. The reflection in the water shimmered with the illusion of a thousand fallen celestial bodies. A large sliver of moon draped an incandescent path across the lagoon.

She wrapped her arms around herself and turned up her face to the sky, bathing in rays of silver light. Her hand absently caressed her arm though the wool of Drew's jacket. Bursts of liquid sensation spread though her body, pooling in her most private recesses.

She turned to find Solomon, needing conversation to

distract herself from the euphoria conjured by this mystical place. Her every nerve ending tingled. Fingers of sea breeze slithered under Drew's long jacket and crawled up the backs of her legs, intimately touching places she'd forgotten existed. She would have believed Drew had cast a spell on her if she didn't already know her own secret weaknesses were boiling too close to the surface.

"Solomon?" She heard the taut edge of panic in her own voice.

Solomon had been bent over, untangling something on the deck. When he stood to face her, she saw him clearly for the first time. Even with the infusion of light from the star-strewn sky, his features receded into the night. The dark blue of his silk brocade jacket and vest were a few shades lighter than his skin. Black pants covered his stocky legs and his black boots were well polished, catching bits of soft starlight.

"We'll wrap you in this and I'll lower you to the launch." Solomon held up a net. He began to walk toward her with the obvious intention of throwing the dirty mesh over her head. If his approach had not distracted her from her gawking, she would have been bagged like an oversized fish.

"That is a terrible idea. The net might break." She hoped her logic dissuaded him.

The only dark-skinned people she knew were slaves. She'd seen the written proof of Drew's inhumane practices, but flesh-and-blood evidence shocked her all over again. Drew had to know she'd be furious if he sent a slave to do his bidding. Surely he hadn't forgotten their conversation at Linley Hall. Obviously, her opinion of him didn't matter. His caring had only gone as far as her physical illness, and she'd been fool enough to interpret it as more than what it was.

"You're a slave."

He stiffened, and she realized the insensitivity of her

comment. She meant the censor in her voice for Drew's actions, not to demean Solomon.

"I'm the quartermaster of this ship." Thinly veiled hostility replaced his cool politeness.

He stepped toward her and grabbed her waist. Before Felicity thought to pull away, he swung her impersonally over his shoulder like a sack of flour. He strode to the side of the ship, and for a moment she had the unsettling notion he meant to toss her overboard.

"This was my second choice." He climbed over the ship's side and made his way down a rope ladder. She squirmed, trying to get him to put her down. He halted his swift and sure-footed descent. "Please stay still. If I drop you, the captain will not be pleased."

The white foam lapping at the ship looked less crystalline and more deep and murky from her view several feet above the water. Blood rushed to her head, making it pound all over again. Breath squeezed from her lungs with Solomon's every movement. Putting a poultice on his animosity for her reigned in her mind.

"I wouldn't let anything happen to you, Solomon," she squeaked. "Maybe I can help." Speaking proved difficult in her undignified position. His indignant grunt stopped further commentary.

"It seems to me you're the one in need of help. I think you'd fare far better in our company if you would remember that."

Silence followed the rest of their descent to the rowboat waiting at the waterline. Solomon set Felicity on her feet, and the small craft lurched violently. She clutched his shoulders, suddenly thankful one of her childhood demands had involved learning to swim with her brother. That battle she'd won.

When they both settled into the boat, Solomon took up the oars and guided them out to sea. Felicity blamed herself for the strain with him. The man's careful speech should have warned her of his pride and struggle to disassociate himself from the typical assumptions made because of his skin color. Her thoughtless words had sounded like an accusation.

By the reverence with which he spoke of being quartermaster, she surmised Drew had given him a position of importance on the ship. Though Solomon had avoided her tactless comment, she guessed he was a slave despite the title. Solomon was the name inscribed on one of documents she'd found among Drew's possessions. She was almost sure of it.

Just because Drew appeared to treat his slaves decently shouldn't lessen her indignation over his behavior. She knew her initial outrage had melted and it worried her. She had to force herself not to trust Drew no matter what swayed her to the contrary. Unfortunately, his presence robbed her of all common sense.

If she could make a friend out of Solomon, her position would be strengthened. She needed someone to trust on the ship. With Drew, she couldn't even trust herself.

They slid along the side of the other ship. Shadowed red letters hugged the black hull. When the first rung of a flimsy rope ladder came within her reach, deciphering the name of the vessel was forgotten. She pulled herself up while Solomon remained occupied securing the small rowboat. Once he realized her plan, he grabbed for her ankle and succeeded in halting her progress.

"You'll make me fall," she called over her shoulder.

He released her, then hurried up behind. Upon reaching the top, she discovered hurling her body over the side was harder than she'd anticipated. Stuck with one leg over the railing and the other groping for a foothold, Solomon came up behind her, sending her over the top with a shove. As she stood up from her collision with the deck, she noticed a glint of satisfaction in his eyes.

She started to scold him for his overzealous help, but he beat her to it.

"I am responsible for your well-being. If you act without waiting for my instruction again, I'll have to restrain you. I do this only for your own safety."

He turned and walked away before she could comment on his provisions for her safety. The bruise on her backside said otherwise. If he would only soften his attitude toward her, maybe they could help each other.

He lit a lantern at the portal leading belowdeck. "Follow me to your quarters. And don't touch anything." He disappeared down the companionway without waiting for her.

The ship's interior reflected the polished simplicity of its exterior. Every line seemed built for speed and maneuverability. Solomon unlocked a portal at the end of the passageway, and Felicity discovered the exception. A room not nearly as large as the cabin on the *Sea Mistress*, but stuffed with twice as many furnishings, appeared through the door Solomon pushed open.

He stepped aside and, with a wave of his hand, gestured for her to enter. "These will be your accommodations for the rest of your stay with us. The captain wishes you to make yourself comfortable."

She hesitantly entered the room, wary of what she might find. Color overwhelmed her senses. Deep reds, burgundies, purples and greens vied for attention. More subtle hues of gold, yellow and soft brown blended in exotic prints on tossed cushions and heavy swaths of material hanging from the walls, creating a tentlike atmosphere.

An oak four-poster bed was crowded into the corner, a mound of pillows hiding the headboard. The chaotic decor represented a multitude of cultures. Where the main cabin on the *Sea Mistress* stood untouchable in its elegant perfection, this room invited relaxation like an overstuffed feather bed.

The smell of strong cheese drifted from a round pedestal

table. A silver platter loaded with a variety of cheeses, breads and fruits rested atop a silk scarf of burnt orange and red. Next to the food sat a silver decanter inlaid with flat, dull stones. Felicity's awe at her surroundings waned as her hunger increased.

Solomon nodded curtly toward the table. "The captain will be joining you for a late dinner, but he asked that a light meal be prepared to satisfy you until then. If you'll excuse me, I'll bring the water for your bath."

At Solomon's mention of it, Felicity noticed the bronze tub set in another corner of the cabin. Clawed feet supported a large oval bath more inviting than any apple. All the temptations a devil could muster beckoned her primal desires.

The lavish bath, as did the rest of Drew's quarters, reeked of ill-gotten gains. Such luxury could have tempted a saint. And experience had taught Felicity she was no saint. Turning away from the decadence required all the rigidity she had perfected in the last ten years of her life.

"Tell your master I can't accept his offerings, nor do I wish to share a meal with him. My only desire is to be taken to Barbados as quickly as possible." She wrapped her arms around her abdomen to keep her stomach from grumbling in protest of her decision.

Solomon's shoulders squared. The smooth molasses in his voice froze hard and brittle. "I call no man my master."

"I'm sorry." She stumbled over the apology. Part of her reason for denying the ill-gotten luxury was her fear that it came from the sweat and tears of men like him. "I wouldn't have assumed by your manner you were anything, but a free and educated man. I saw documents with your name on them and—"

The tight lines around his mouth warned her she'd just insulted him further. "I heard of your trespassing. Instead of receiving the punishment you deserve, the captain offered you his hospitality. You have the arrogance to refuse it?"

"I don't deserve to be punished. I haven't committed any crime." She straightened and almost equaled Solomon's height, but his bulk proved she was no match to him physically.

"Your presence is a crime. Women are not allowed on this ship. As quartermaster, it is my job to see the rules are adhered to. The generosity of the captain is the only thing keeping me from carrying out my duty."

"You're the one who brought me onboard. But if it soothes your conscience, punish me. I didn't ask to be treated like a royal guest."

Confinement to a small, spare hold was more than likely the punishment Solomon had in mind, and it would solve two problems. He'd be satisfied, and she'd be protected from her own dark desires.

"Death is the punishment for anyone who breaks the rules of this ship, Miss Kendall. The captain's hospitality is the only thing keeping you from that fate. Do you still wish to refuse it?"

She shook her head, for once having the sense to keep her mouth shut. Death? He couldn't be serious. But his stern expression gave no indication that he'd ever jested in his life.

He turned to leave the room, but she called to him before he disappeared through the portal. "Does Drew—I mean, the captain—He's allowed to disregard your... rules?"

"Apparently. Though he would be better served to follow them like every other man on this ship. My friendship for Drew makes me respect his feelings where you're concerned, not because he's the captain. Don't make either of us regret our decision, Miss Kendall."

She hardly noticed Solomon's departure or the click of the lock that pronounced her a prisoner. Apparently she owed Drew more than she'd first imagined. Gratitude and lust mingled in a dangerous combination. Also apparently, Drew had feelings for her as well—feelings that had prompted him to go against the rules of his own ship and the approval of his friend. Yet what those feeling were, she dared not imagine.

# Chapter Seven

A spiced halo lured Felicity deeper into its fragrant arms. She'd only used a few drops of the amber oil that sat among the array of glass bottles Solomon placed beside the tub, but the aromatic mixture of roses and sweet wood wafted from the bath like a thick, drugging smoke. She slid down the brass side until the warm water licked the tops of her breasts. With her eyes closed, she leaned her head on the tub's rim and surrendered to lush sensation. Even Drew's selection of soap was decadent.

Her mind drifted hazily between images: Drew as Lord Christian. Drew as her enemy. Drew as her savior. All clouded together, merging into one clear picture: Drew the man. She grew light-headed, blaming it on the wine she didn't have the courage to refuse. Visions of Drew's warm gaze touched her physically, like a finger drawn up her spine. The bathwater became a living thing, kissing her in places she'd never before considered. Her stiff knees relaxed and fell to the sides of the tub. Her entire body grew limp and pliant.

He boldly stood at the edge of the tub, every inch of his body bare. With sun-bronzed arms, he scooped her out of the water and molded her against him. Her nipples strained against the hard muscles of his chest. Sensation too intoxicating to resist weakened her limbs, and all she could do was let her head fall back as he lavished kisses on her neck. She thought she would surely burst into flames for wanting him so desperately. Finally, he rubbed the potent evidence of his desire between her . . .

Felicity sat up abruptly, sloshing water over the sides of the tub. She blinked several times in a frantic attempt to dispel the vision. To assure her guilty conscience that she was indeed alone, she swept the room with her gaze. She stood and reached for the thick towel resting by the oils and soaps. With the key to the cabin wrapped in her palm before Solomon had exited the room, she assumed it would be safe to indulge in the steaming bath. When she had stripped off Drew's coat and her foul-smelling chemise, she'd had no idea the danger to her tarnished virtue stepped into the bath with her.

She rubbed her skin with the rough cloth until it hurt, hoping the sting would obliterate the ache coiled between her legs. Over the years, she'd managed to curb her carnal cravings. And when they did seize her in the dark of night, urging her to do things she couldn't even admit to herself the next morning, she would force herself to recall Sally Bishop.

The poor girl had been caught in an intimate embrace with a young British soldier in the alley beside her parents' house. Being the minister's daughter, her parents had been especially harsh, taking it upon themselves to punish her—as an example to other young girls who might be tempted by Boston's ever-increasing secular population. Sally had been locked in the stockade for a full twenty-four hours. Every time Felicity passed that stockade on her way to church, she counted herself lucky. Her indiscretion would have rewarded her with a visit to the whipping post instead. But there was neither whipping post nor stockade to be found in Drew's lush den.

After securing the oversized towel around her chest, Felicity retrieved her discarded chemise. If only her encounter with temptation had been unpleasant, she wouldn't need such extreme reminders to keep her from sin. Even a flash of Erik's hand clutched in her hair and his hot breath on her neck as he slid between her thighs touched her in places that ached at the mere memory. She'd come to the conclusion years ago that the devil had a firm hold on her in the guise of her womanhood. Women weren't supposed to have the base urges Felicity had. Truly, if anyone from the congregation knew of her secret thoughts, a whipping wouldn't suffice; she'd have been burned at the stake.

Unable to talk herself into dragging the stained garment over her head, she dropped the chemise and turned to the large trunk Solomon had left in the middle of the cabin. He'd informed her that the trunk contained women's clothing for her use. At the time, she'd found the idea reprehensible and insulting. She would rather wear a sailor's uniform than the clothes of one of Drew's mistresses. Of course, she'd not mentioned a word of her rejection to Solomon. He'd made his position clear.

With her skin saturated with scent so decadent she couldn't even name it, and flushed from wine, heat and her own wicked thoughts, she had no choice but to make use of the clothing in the trunk. Remaining nude and tingling was out of the question, even if Drew's arrival wasn't soon expected. An immediate need to be dressed in several layers of thick, rough cloth pushed aside all objections to pillaging the trunk. She lifted the lid while clutching the towel tightly over her full breasts. The clothes probably wouldn't fit. A man like Drew would have a petite mistress.

A tangle of richly colored garments, none of them black,

filled the trunk. She dug past the first layer of lace-trimmed undergarments, looking for something more suitable. When her hand brushed raw silk, her fingers closed around the cool cloth of their own volition.

A bloodred robe absorbed the soft light from the candles. A breathless sound of wonder escaped her parted lips. In the cabin's shadows, the fabric's deep color danced between black and red. She carried the robe closer to the glass globes mounted on either side of the four-poster bed, banishing the hint of black she had come to despise and allowing the pure ruby to shimmer and gleam.

She dropped the towel and slipped into the robe before her nagging conscience intervened. Wearing silk had been grounds for arrest in her mother's day and still garnered condemnation in her own circle. The cabin's seclusion and the separation of an ocean ensured her safety against prying eyes and wagging tongues. She caressed the lustrous fabric covering her arms as she glided over to a large gold-framed mirror mounted across from the oak bed. The prospect of seeing herself in something other than black enthralled her.

A stranger approached the looking glass, giving her the brief sensation that someone else had entered the room. Her eyes widened at the sight of the dark-eyed temptress staring back at her. She tugged at her tightly knotted bun, letting her hair escape down her back. Willful curls softened the pale face she'd always considered too long and angular. The robe's color complimented the mouth she'd thought too wide. A woman she'd never seen before effortlessly grinned back at her from the mirror.

Oh, but she had seen that face before! Yet as a girl, never a woman. Tears burned the back of her eyes when she recognized her old friend, the Felicity before the fall.

A hesitant knock at the door distracted her temporarily but could not tear her away from the discovery that something lush and untamed still thrived behind the tangle of thorns she'd grown to protect herself. The sound of a key in the lock before the door was thrust open did.

Drew stood in the open portal, unguarded surprise dropping his jaw. He devoured her with a gaze that swept the length of her body. Hunger mingling with shock sparkled in the stormy blue-green of his eyes. His blatant awareness of her as a woman bore no resemblance to his calculating flirtations of the past. Perhaps Drew also witnessed what Felicity had in the mirror's reflection.

To play at being the young woman who still believed she could catch and hold a man's attention with the sway of her hips was too tempting. After all, who would know? "Did you get all dressed up for me, Drew?" Felicity asked. "I believe you have me at a disadvantage."

She softened her voice seductively, seduction being a game she'd only dared play once before. Her one experience in those untried waters had left her the loser before she'd even known the rules. She sauntered toward Drew, feeling the ruby silk cling to her thighs.

He followed her every movement with a transfixed stare. For the first time in their acquaintance, he seemed unaware of his powerful presence and staggered by hers. In this particular match, the odds appeared to be in her favor.

He closed the door behind him. "I thought you'd have finished your bath. I didn't want to keep you waiting."

She tried to imitate the lazy grin of a well-fed cat, a gesture she'd seen him wield with perfection. "How considerate. I can hardly imagine what other surprises you have in store."

She hooded her gaze, unable to maintain eye contact in the aftermath of her suggestive remark. What had gotten into her? The silk robe must have cast some sort of wicked spell. Her only consolation was that Drew seemed more disconcerted by the turn of events than she.

Under the shelter of her lowered lashes, she examined him with her eyes. He wore fawn-colored breeches that were clean and freshly pressed. An exotic embroidered vest in hues of cinnamon and jade covered a white shirt left open from the throat to the top of his tanned chest. Even his boots appeared recently polished.

His clean-shaven face and neatly tied-back hair confirmed he had indeed taken care with his appearance. She realized the effort had been for her approval. Before she'd donned the robe, she never would have guessed his vanity had anything to do with her. The realization multiplied the effect his good looks had on her weakened defenses. The robe's magic wrapped itself more tightly around her.

As her senses reeled, he appeared to compose himself.

"I assume my appearance meets your standards. I didn't want you to think you'd left civilization behind." Despite his casual explanation, his bright stare burned a hole through her silk robe.

She took a deep breath to calm herself. "Are you referring to those men on the island?"

He linked his hands behind his back and took a tentative step forward. "Or the island itself. I imagined you found it rather deserted at our approach. Maybe you even thought I went back on our bargain."

He paused at the table to pour himself some wine. He refilled the pewter goblet she'd used earlier and offered it to her.

Determined not to become the prey in this game she'd initiated, she moved to the opposite edge of the table and took the wine from his hand. When their fingers brushed, the predatory hunger in his eyes flared.

She sipped the wine in order to quell the nervous bubble that tightened her throat. "The island doesn't concern me nearly as much as the men inhabiting it. Who are they?"

He placed his palms flat on the table and leaned his weight on them, bringing his face closer to hers. "My crew."

"I was afraid you were going to say that."

She met his direct gaze, which only seemed to encourage him to drop his eyes to the gathering of her robe. The small expanse of exposed skin suddenly made Felicity feel bare to the waist, though the silk clinging to her breasts assured her she was still decently covered. With so much attention in their direction, her nipples started to strain against the thin material. She abruptly crossed her arms over her chest and played with a loose strand of hair. In what she thought was a flirtatious gesture, she bit her lip. Her pretense felt a little foolish and altogether contrived, but she refused to turn back into a mouse as long as she held his fascination.

"Must you hire such dangerous men? I found them terribly frightening."

He raised his eyebrows and smirked. She cringed inwardly at his sign of disbelief in her sudden feminine fears.

"Dangerous men sail the waters of the Caribbean. I would be a fool not to fight fire with fire. But don't worry. I'll protect you." His declaration mocked her with its condescension.

"Do you trade with pirates?"

He genuinely smiled at her question. "In a way."

Her efforts to be alluring were forgotten. She strode around the table to confront him. "I knew you were up to something illegal. Or are you going to tell me buying pirate contraband is legal in the Caribbean? My father—"

"Doesn't know of my illegal activities," finished Drew. His teasing tone faded with his smile.

"Of course he doesn't." She forced a tight laugh. The old adversarial habit eclipsed their flirtatious banter, but she didn't want to lose the ground she'd gained by her change of tactics. That was the only reason she wished to hear the huskiness in his voice return.

"My father would be horrified if he knew half the things I know about you."

Her gentle barb recalled his slow grin. He closed the

short distance between them until they stood mere inches from each other. She tensed, thinking he might kiss her.

His warm breath caressed her cheek. "Do go on, Felicity."

The deepness of his softly spoken dare gave her the courage to continue.

"How do I know you're not a pirate yourself?"

Drew's focus dropped to her mouth and lingered there. "You don't."

She was out of her element. She'd pushed the game to the brink and waited for him to seal her fate with a kiss, but he didn't even flinch.

"I suppose the fact that you haven't ravaged me counts for something."

"I'm considering it." He swept her hair off her shoulders.

She clutched the robe to her neck. Was he teasing her? She turned away before he could laugh at her sudden dismay. Whether she was more horrified by the fact that men and women actually spoke of such things aloud or by the instant wanting his words evoked, she couldn't say. The image of Mistress Bishop, her face twisted in puritanical outrage, tried to lecture Felicity on the cost of giving in to temptation. Unfortunately, a primal yearning spoke louder. Felicity was more depraved than she'd even suspected.

"I should change. If you would leave the room for a moment, I'll find something more appropriate to wear." Her voice sounded hesitant even to her own ears, but she had to say something in response to his lewd comment. If she didn't, he might suspect she'd fall into his arms as easily as every other woman he'd come across.

She dared a glance over her shoulder to find him studying her with a curious tilt of his head. Lord, but what would she do if he kissed her? She feared she already knew the answer.

\*    \*    \*

"You're fine as you are," Drew said. "Solomon will be bringing our dinner shortly." Composed and polite, he stepped to the table Felicity had put between them. He pulled out her chair and gestured for her to sit.

He hoped his struggle for control didn't show on his face. He'd probably scared the hell out of her with his leering. Her effort to keep the clinging robe closed distracted her from the white-knuckled grip he had on the back of the chair. When he released his hold, he was surprised to find that he hadn't left imprints in the wood.

He took the seat opposite her and curled his fingers around his wine goblet. Before he drained the glass as he longed to, he nudged her goblet in front of her. She tipped her cup and gulped the contents. He set down his wine without touching it. What had gotten into her? More to the point, what had gotten into him?

He'd walked into the room and found her wrapped in nothing but liquid ruby, and he'd temporarily lost the ability to breathe. Then, the way she had talked to him . . . Perhaps his lust-clouded brain had imagined the seductive tone and double-meaning of every word leaving her luscious mouth. For a moment, he'd believed her mention of ravishment an invitation—and God help him, he'd almost taken her up on it. A fierce arousal began to throb with the idea.

She'd been flirting with him; he was sure of that. Her attempt at seduction resembled that of a young girl testing her charms for the first time. Unfortunately, her caressing purrs fell from the lips of a voluptuous, full-grown woman who should know better. With her hair tousled, her cheeks flushed and the robe accentuating every nuance of her body, she looked as if she'd just rolled out of bed with a lover. And Drew wanted that lover to be him. He'd never been tempted to fall into the raping and pillaging attributed to most pirates. Felicity sorely tested that.

She awkwardly reached past him to grab the decanter of wine, capturing his attention. He caught the bottle before she knocked it over, and refilled her goblet for her. She whispered her thanks while avoiding his gaze. Her pale throat contracted as she drank deeply.

Should he apologize? For what, he didn't know. Actually, he'd been on his best behavior, considering hers.

"Would you like something else? Tea, perhaps," he suggested.

"No. This is fine. Thank you."

The plate of food Solomon had brought was hardly touched. If she continued downing wine like one of his crew, she'd be ill again or dangerously drunk. It had been his experience that women of the prudish variety tended to become quite amorous when a bit of wine warmed their bellies. A repeat performance of her earlier exhibition would land her flat on her back. He was human after all, and barely that by some standards.

He didn't believe that a furious coupling was what she really had in mind when she began fanning his lust, though. Maybe she didn't realize what she was doing, much less inviting. The notion gave him the solution to his problem.

Solomon burst unceremoniously into the room with a huge tray laden with silver-topped dishes. He sat the tray down harder than necessary, making Felicity jump. The man glanced at her, then cut his gaze to Drew.

"Thank you, Solomon. I believe you've met Miss Kendall."

Solomon grunted a response. Felicity didn't even acknowledge his presence. Apparently, Solomon's usual disapproval had found another recipient this evening. Solomon stomped toward the door, forcing Drew to call him back. "You can take this," he called, lifting the tray of fruit and cheese.

Felicity retrieved the decanter of wine before Solomon marched back and snatched the tray away.

"Thank you," Drew said to Solomon's broad back. The man swiftly exited the room with a loud slam of the door.

"Solomon doesn't seem to be himself tonight. Things must not have gone as smoothly as he claimed while I was away."

"He doesn't like me. That's the problem." Felicity's voice sounded thick and an octave deeper than usual. Underneath her heavy lashes, the liquid brown of her eyes flared with surprise. She touched her lips and giggled. The slurred sound of her own voice seemed to amuse her.

He almost groaned when she licked her full lips, then lowered her gaze. Kissing her would be sheer ecstasy. His lips curled as he suppressed a wolfish grin. The thought of the hard, deep kiss it would require for his plan to be effective made it almost impossible not to smile. All he would have to do was bite hard at the bait she'd been naively dangling in front of him, and that would be the end of her girlish flirtations.

"You two didn't get on well?" he asked absently. He began serving their dinner from the silver dishes, his mind consumed with dessert, even if it would be only a nibble.

"No," she answered, drawing out the word. "And it's all your fault. You could have told me Solomon wasn't a slave when I accused you of . . . whatever I accused you of after I saw those papers."

"I've committed too many treacherous acts for you to keep track of, have I?"

She accepted a plateful of food. She sniffed it and wrinkled her nose. "That's what you want me to believe. Explain why you have papers claiming you purchased Solomon when you're just friends. What is this, anyway?" She scowled at the milky mound on her plate, blowing away a curl that had fallen into her face.

He doubted she realized she'd slurred the word *explain*.

"It's fish stew over rice. Try it. Solomon is an excellent cook."

She pushed the plate away in favor of her wineglass. "He probably poisoned it if he knew it was for me. It smells funny. Now answer my question."

"That would be the coconut milk. Our repasts are limited on the island." Drew took a bite of stew and swallowed. "You're safe. I served them from the same dish."

She brought a small spoonful of the milky soup to her lips, then swallowed without chewing. Her grimace revealed that she would have preferred to spit it out. If she'd had a couple of more glasses of wine, he wagered she would have.

"Things aren't always what they seem at first glance or taste, Felicity. If you weren't so eager to jump to conclusions, you might discover the truth once in a while."

She pushed away her plate, but this time with much more subtlety. "I can't take anything you say as the truth."

He didn't want her to pass out before he had the chance to kiss her. The imperative task would assure her continued chastity and had nothing to do with the anticipation dancing in the pit of his stomach. "If you eat at least half the food on your plate. I'll give you nothing but truthful answers for the rest of the evening."

She frowned. "How do I know that's the truth? So far you haven't answered any of my questions, truthful or otherwise."

"I swear on my honor as a nobleman and a gentleman."

She wagged her finger at him. "You've broken your promise already. You're neither of those things. You told me Lord Christian doesn't exist."

"Did I? Or was that another one of your assumptions? Lord Christian does exist. Or rather, he could have. At least the duke he claimed as his father does."

"You're purposely confusing me."

He shrugged, as if the information he was about to reveal held no importance. After all, the fact only ruined his life.

"The Duke of Foxmoor is my father. So, I'll retract the bit about being a gentleman and swear on the thread of noble blood coursing though my veins to tell nothing but the truth—at least for tonight."

"If your father is a duke, that makes you . . ."

"A bastard, but I believe you already assumed that." He held her gaze, refusing to let the sting of bitter memories weaken his stance. As he waited for scorn or pity to mar her lovely features, he cursed himself for laying himself open to her and her for believing him.

She did neither. Without the slightest indication he'd just revealed the demons under his bed, she warily ate her stew.

"Well, at least that's one thing in your favor. If you were raised an aristocrat, you'd be completely hopeless."

He began to breathe again. Perhaps Felicity didn't differ that much from her kindhearted father after all. "So there is still hope for my soul, Miss Kendall?

"Only if you answer my questions as you promised. Is Solomon your slave? And if he isn't, why do you have a paper saying he is?"

"Solomon's idea. The bill of sale you found while pillaging my belongings was all his doing."

"Oh, I see. You two are such good friends, Solomon decided to honor you by becoming your slave."

He took another bite of stew, fully enjoying her stir of temper. "Close, but not exactly." He wiped his mouth on a forest green napkin before sipping his wine. "Most people make assumptions, as you do. They decide a man's status before they have the facts. Solomon suggested we have documentation forged in the event a slave trader decided to slap him in chains and check his background later."

"I see." Her back stiffened.

He'd only been teasing when he baited her, but the sweep of her fair lashes against her cheek urged him to take back his words. In truth, he enjoyed her quick wit, even if it prompted her to jump to conclusions.

Avoiding his gaze, she intently spooned stew into her mouth even though she had almost emptied her dish. "And the child?"

Drew hesitated. Outright lying had become a way of life, but the silly promise he'd given Felicity weighed on him. He'd not really intended to be honest with her.

"A similar situation."

She brightened, but his simple explanation didn't seem to satisfy her. "So the little boy wasn't sold into slavery?"

"No." Drew played with the rice left on his plate. He'd drawn out the meal to encourage her to eat. When he wasn't forced to play the role of cultured Lord Christian, he had the table manners of a hound, devouring his food in a few bites, then completing his meal by tipping a mug of rum bottoms up. Of course when he was on his ship, the only time he was truly Drew Crawford, he usually dined alone.

"Well, what happened to the child?"

He glanced up to find Felicity alert with curiosity. His plan to sober her had met with rousing success, leaving him with the difficult task of distracting her from a forbidden subject.

"He's with his father. Did you notice the writing on the documents?"

"No. I was too stunned by their contents."

"You should have. You know the person who forged them."

She laid down her fork. "You forged them, or maybe even Solomon. You've scared me off assuming anything. For all I know, one of the wild men from your crew did the deed."

He rested his chin on his clasped hands and leered at

her. "I'm disappointed. I expected a better guess from my little spy."

"I've named the limited number of people we mutually know who would resort to forgery. Unless..." Her thoughtful expression turned to a scowl. "Samantha Linley would surely stoop to any depths for you."

The jealousy in her voice unexpectedly pleased him. "I doubt Samantha can even read. After the length of time you spent scouring the ledgers of the New England Trading Company, I can't believe you didn't recognize Richard Marley's script."

She dropped her spoon into her empty bowl with a clatter. "Master Marley? What else did he help you with?" She didn't have to say the rest. The question of Marley's death hung between them just as effectively unspoken.

His good humor faltered at the accuracy of her question. "You're jumping to conclusions again. Marley and Ben were like brothers. I know you don't think much of me, but are you so eager to think the worst of your father's childhood friend? Christ, Felicity, I thought you would understand why he did me the favor as much as anyone."

Anger punctuated each of his words, though its source was his own past deeds rather than her assumptions. He hated the reminder of his responsibility in Marley's death, but that was exactly what he needed. His fascination with Felicity had distracted him from the purpose of this voyage.

The softened slant of her warm brown eyes didn't banish his temper. "I do understand, and I would do the same under the circumstances." She hesitated only for a moment. "But you do believe Marley's death had something to do with you and your ... business dealings?"

He pushed away his plate. "Yes."

The creasing of her brow made him dread her next question. "Is my father in danger?"

Another reminder of his mission's importance loomed

in the anxiety permeating her breathless question. "Nothing will happen to Ben or you. I'll make sure of that."

She searched his features, her eyes moist and vulnerable. "You're going after El Diablo, aren't you? You weren't just running away from Barbados."

"It doesn't concern you, Felicity." His voice was gravel. God, did he actually see admiration in her expression? He knew he heard it in her question.

"You made a promise not to reveal my identity, and that includes any little secrets I spilled tonight due to too much wine. I won't have your meddling cause your father's death or Solomon's return to slavery."

She covered her hand with her mouth, her eyes wide with surprise. Mumbling the most blistering curse he could think of, he pushed himself from his chair. He had some French cognac stashed away somewhere and he needed it; he was babbling like a lovesick adolescent. Solomon would be furious if he knew Drew had revealed his status as a runaway slave. Drew might not have said the word *escaped*, but she would figure it out. Her shocked expression at his outburst told him she already had.

"Drew." She stood. "I won't tell anyone anything and I'll swear it on whatever you like."

Her tentative call halted his search. He turned to look at her over his shoulder. Her feet and ankles were bare. His imagination slid beneath the robe to continue the trek over her body. The anger making his blood churn more swiftly turned to lust with the force of a swollen river threatening to overrun its banks. He let the strength of his hunger simmer in his eyes. There was still the matter of the kiss. That would forever banish the hero-worshiping look that had temporally caught his heart in a vice.

"W-why are you looking at me like that?" Her eyes grew wide and frantic, like a hare snared in a trap.

He stalked toward her. "Why do you think?"

"Because you're a cad and think every woman was put

on earth for your pleasure." She squared her shoulders, but all that did was bring her lush breasts' sharp contours against the silk to prominence. How could a supposed Puritan have a body like that? In Drew's experience God had proven cruel, but not that cruel.

He stopped within a few inches of closing in on his quarry. If she wanted to push him away, she could. A flare in her eyes warned him that she had no intention of staving off his advance. The idea that her fiery disposition spread to other aspects of her nature griped him with a firm hand.

"Not every woman. Just you." Want and anger flashed in swift succession across her features, but Drew was too far gone to care what the anger might mean.

She backed away. "Don't. Don't tease me. You are supposed to be truthful tonight."

"I don't tease, Felicity. Do you?" He caught her by slipping his arms loosely around her waist. When she made no effort to push him away, just stared up at him and licked her lips in promise, Drew realized he'd miscalculated. A coaxing kiss or a gentle nibble on her shoulder would leave him with a much too eager woman. Drew's body was already confused about the game they were playing, and any more encouragement would be followed by an all-out mutiny. If he truly wanted to scare her off, he needed to take his pirate guise a step further. He just wished he didn't find the idea so appealing.

Without warning, he jerked her tightly against him and pressed his erection against the soft flesh of her abdomen. "See how honest I'm being right now?" He took advantage of her sharp inhalation to cover his mouth with hers. His kiss instantly demanded. He pushed his tongue into her mouth without the slightest whispery coaxing of his lips to soften the thrust. The unexpected brush of her tongue in return and the seeking hand that glided up his back incinerated Drew's plan, along with his last shred of conscious thought.

Her welcoming response to his raiding kiss softened his pressure on her lips. Instinctively, his body interpreted the subtle signals of her desire and gave in kind. He slid his hands lightly up her back. When he found his destination, his fingers tangling in the thick strands of her hair. He brushed the soft skin at her nape with his fingertips and swallowed a deep groan in anticipation of fulfilling a fantasy.

He grabbed fistfuls of the golden brown silk that had teased him from the moment he'd first gazed at her by candlelight. Gently he tugged, forcing her to tilt her head back.

He slid his mouth from hers to glide across her soft skin, stopping when he reached the hollow between her jaw and earlobe. He tasted her vulnerability with his tongue. Licking down the length of her neck, he hesitated at the base of her throat to inhale the intoxicating mixture of rose and sandalwood radiating from her heated skin. Lost in ravaging the spot with an openmouthed kiss, he heard her soft moan like a cannon explosion in his ear.

"Who are you?" he whispered between deep gulps of air. He felt as if he was drowning. His mind screamed: *This is Felicity Kendall. You're not supposed to be touching her like this.* But he couldn't shake the sensation that the woman in his arms bore no relation to the puritanical Miss Kendall. The women he held seduced like a siren whose moan proved more damaging than any song. Jagged rocks lay ahead, and all he could think of was steering straight for them.

He forced himself to loosen his grip so he could look into Felicity's face. Surely the reality of her image would banish the nymph back to the sea. She gazed up at him, panting for breath. Her heavy eyelids intensified the murky green shimmering behind the liquid brown of her irises. She licked her lips, wet and red from his rough kiss. He groaned and lowered his head at her invitation, knowing or otherwise.

"Felicity," he mumbled against her lips. This was the real Felicity, the woman who tempted and challenged him at every turn.

Her return kiss buckled his knees. Ever-increasing urgency made him light-headed. All his blood raged to one part of his body. He'd begun to ache with his need to be inside her. He thrust his tongue into her mouth, overpowering her teasing grazes.

He released her hair and raced his free hands down her back, drawing her closer with demanding pressure. He slid his palms over her bottom, then cupped her, tilting her hips so he could melt into her. The sensation demanded immediate action. If not for the barrier of their clothing, their encounter would have come to an abrupt and premature end.

A choked sound escaped her throat, muffled by their entwined mouths. He struggled for a grain of rational thought to tell him whether the sound was protest or encouragement. Her grip on his biceps and the fact that she didn't try to push him away persuaded him she meant the latter.

All he had to do was turn her a few inches, set her on the edge of the table, pull the tie of her robe and he could be inside her in the time it took to unlace his breeches. They wouldn't even have to unlock the maddening kiss fueling the urgency between them. He released her to contemplate the situation before lust and instinct ruled irrevocably. His fingers disagreed and roamed up her rib cage of their own volition. The moment he captured the weight of her full breasts, she arched into his touch.

Rational thinking appeared beyond either of them. He returned one hand to her lush bottom while his other continued its desperate groping. Her nipple burned through the thin silk and teased his palm with an unspoken promise. With another woman, her obvious arousal would be consent enough; with Felicity, he needed to hear her say she wanted him as he wanted her.

"Open your eyes and look at me. Is this what you want?" He guided her hand to the straining beast in his breeches. If that didn't scare her off, nothing would. With held breath, he stared into the hazy wonder in her eyes as she measured his length with the flat of her palm. Drew leaned his head back and let his eyes drift shut, reveling in her touch. He took that as a resounding yes.

Solomon's violent opening of the door forced Drew from drifting ecstasy with a violent shake. Drew turned his head to stare, stunned and blinking.

"You were supposed to keep the door locked," accused Solomon.

At the pressure of her hands pushing against his shoulders, Drew relinquished his bone-crushing hold. She continued to struggle in his arms, but he didn't let her go.

"Men who give a damn about their lives should learn to knock."

With one arm wrapped tightly around Felicity's waist, he forced her against him, shielding her from Solomon's gaze, even if she didn't want his protection. Solomon was one of the few men in the world he trusted, but still, Drew didn't want another man to see Felicity in her flimsy robe.

When her thrashing grew more desperate, he let her go only to shove her directly behind him. He faced Solomon, blocking the man's view. He let his impatient stare speak to the fact that he wanted Solomon to leave immediately.

"What?" he demanded, breaking the prolonged silence.

Solomon stared back, unmovable as a brick wall. "We are ready to set sail. I thought you would want to be on deck, *Captain*."

Drew gave up his battle stance and ran his fingers though his hair. The black satin ribbon holding it in place had come loose. He glanced over his shoulder at Felicity.

She stood a few steps away with her back to the door and her head bowed. Bloody hell. What had he done, or better yet, almost done?

He returned his attention to Solomon. "I'll be there shortly. Just give me a minute."

With a curt nod, Solomon retreated from the room, shutting the door behind him.

Drew moved behind Felicity. He reached out to lay his hands gently on her shoulders, but stopped. Instead, he balled them into fists and dropped them to his sides.

"Felicity," he said softly.

She turned to face him, then took a step back. The flush in her cheeks a few moments earlier faded. Her lips, still swollen and wet, were an inviting contrast to her pale skin. Unfortunately, the coldness in her gaze told him the invitation existed only in his imagination.

He searched his fogged memory, hoping he hadn't misinterpreted any of her other messages. "Are you all right?"

Her breathing sounded ragged. She responded with a silent nod and clutched the opening of her robe together with both hands. The way her fingers clenched the red silk disturbed its smooth beauty. She stared down at the floor as if she were ashamed.

Not for the first time, he sensed he should apologize, but felt too muddled to do so with any sincerity.

"I have to go," he said instead.

He turned and searched for the key he'd absently thrown down when he entered the cabin. Both keys rested among the dirty dishes from their meal. If Solomon hadn't stopped him, he was sure he would have been deflowering Felicity in a spray of broken dishes and spilled wine at this very moment. Almost simultaneously, the thought shamed and aroused him all over again. He dropped one key in his vest pocket and tore his gaze away from the table. After straightening his rumpled shirt, he glanced at Felicity.

Bloody hell. Was she crying? He cocked his head, inconspicuously trying to catch a glimpse of her face. Her cheeks remained dry. He didn't know what he would do if he'd made strong-willed Felicity Kendall cry.

He strode to the door, assuring himself he would apologize if necessary when they had both calmed down. Of course, that was assuming he could calm down. His heart still thumped against his chest and his unfulfilled arousal thrust painfully against his breeches.

He halted in his tracks with a sickening thought: What if he had frightened her rather than merely embarrassed her? That had been his intention in the beginning. Her passionate reaction to his advances had not made sense with what he knew of Felicity, but he'd been well beyond reasoning. He fished into his pocket and removed the only other key to the room besides the one lying on the table.

"Felicity," he called. When she looked up, he tossed the key in a shimmering arch. She caught it in one hand, while she managed to keep her stranglehold on her robe with the other. He wondered if she would ever cease to amaze him. "Lock the door behind me."

# Chapter Eight

A dark obstacle loomed over the hatchway, eclipsing the night sky. Drew didn't need the aid of a lantern to identify the barrier between himself and the fresh air he desperately needed to clear his head.

Ignoring the ladder leading down into the cabin, Solomon pounced from his perch to block Drew's path. "Would you explain what I just witnessed?"

"Has it been that long, Solomon? You need to get off the island more often."

Drew felt a sneer tug at his lips rather than the smile he intended. Irritation roiled through him, replacing the lust that had almost sucked him under. Actually, he should be thanking Solomon for interrupting his headlong decent into madness, but right now he wanted to punch something, and Solomon eagerly offered a target.

"I don't need to prove my manhood to every woman who crosses my path. I would never taint Marguerite's memory by mimicking your behavior."

Drew couldn't remain angry in the face of Solomon's

heated gaze. This was no good-natured lecture on Drew's excessive and sometimes dangerous romantic escapades. Solomon was serious, or he never would have mentioned Marguerite. His devotion to his deceased wife was nothing to make light of.

"I'm sorry I got you involved in this."

Instead of defusing the situation, Drew's comment brought Solomon a menacing step closer. "Since I am involved, I want to know what you were doing in there. I never would have agreed to bring Miss Kendall along if I thought you intended to abuse her."

"Abuse her? Hell, Solomon, you met her. I was only taming a shrew."

Solomon balled his hands into fists. "By forcing yourself on her? Have those rumors about El Diablo inspired you?"

A blow from one of Solomon's ready fists could not have done more damage. "I wasn't . . . forcing her to do anything. At least, that wasn't my intention. That woman makes me crazy."

Drew smoothed back his loose hair, wishing he hadn't lost his ribbon or his control in his dealings with Felicity. She'd wanted him just as much as he'd wanted her. Drew glanced at Solomon, who didn't appear any more convinced.

"I gave her my key to the cabin. She can lock herself in and me out if she wants."

Solomon relaxed his fighting stance, but worry lines pinched his features. "Felicity Kendall is trouble. Avery and Red have already questioned me about your mysterious guest. They won't tell the others yet, but if you don't get rid of her quickly, they'll begin to grumble. After all, you're the one who instigated the no-women-on-board rule."

Drew slapped Solomon's unyielding shoulder, relieved they were again on the same side. "I take full responsibility for anything that happens while Felicity's aboard the *Rap-*

*ture*. What choice did I have? I couldn't very well leave her on an uninhabited island."

Solomon shook his head and scowled. "No, we wouldn't want to scare any poor pirates who might happen by."

"She isn't *that* bad." Drew didn't know why, but he took Solomon's criticism of Felicity a little personally.

Solomon molded himself against the wall of the narrow companionway to let Drew pass. "Isn't that bad? She was ready to cart me back to Barbados in the name of freedom and turn you in with any information I would tell her—all for our own good. The woman is rash. She doesn't understand the ways of the world."

Drew reached for the ladder. Solomon's complaints echoed his own sense of foreboding.

His friend clutched the back of his shirt before he could escape. "Did she ask about Hugh?"

Drew's fingers tightened around the varnished slats. "No."

Anything else he might have added stuck in his throat. He never lied to Solomon, though Solomon knew he lied to everyone else. Felicity had not mentioned Hugh by name, so his answer didn't misrepresent the facts entirely. He never should have told Solomon she had seen the documents Marley had created.

"Good," said Solomon, letting go of him. "One more thing: Avery mentioned you spent most of the voyage from Barbados locked away in the great cabin. You mustn't let your attraction for Felicity show in front of the others. The crew has been too long in hiding and is eager for a fight. I don't want it over who will be the new captain."

"I can handle the crew." Drew climbed onto the main deck, eager to busy himself with doing just that. Commanding a band of half-civilized men was easier than handling one headstrong female.

If Solomon insisted on drowning her, Drew couldn't intelligently argue against it. Though he'd promised to take responsibility for Felicity's actions, he agreed with Solomon: Trouble accompanied her as faithfully as the moon rose over the Caribbean night. Despite knowing better, Drew's clandestine meeting with disaster in the form of Felicity Kendall tugged at him with more power than the strongest current in the sea.

Another lurch from the ship ground Felicity's knees into the wooden deck. Her search for a section of uncarpeted planks on which to kneel in prayer proved fruitful. A slow spasm tightened her lower back. Pain was a good sign.

Surely an hour or so of serious repentance would erase the giddy grin she'd had on her face upon waking that morning. Dashing Captain Crawford wanted her and wanted her badly.

He'd been successful in disguising more than just his identity, though. The self-centered swindler he played turned out to be as false as his name. His aid of runaway slaves revealed his true character. He might sway toward the wrong side of the law, but that proved easy to do with the unfair edicts issued by the crown.

She tried to focus on the screaming protest of her stiff joints, but her mood remained as cloudless and sunny as the warm day flooding through the open portholes. So she told herself the redemption of Drew's character didn't change the fact that their mutual lust went against everything she knew to be right.

She sighed. Why did his dishonorable intentions have to make her feel young and pretty again? After years of accustoming herself to being soiled, she could not wholeheartedly see the harm in feeling desirable, though the harsh voice in the back of her mind told her she should. She chased the voice away. After all, the real damage had already been done. She was no longer a virgin and would never have the opportunity to marry. Being in Drew's embrace reminded her of how much she'd given up. In the confines of Drew's cabin, all the reasons she should be chaste slipped away in favor of being truly alive. After all, he was a confessed rogue and she a vulnerable woman at his mercy. No one would expect her to emerge from the situation unravished.

A rattling sound at the door abruptly stopped her dangerous thoughts. She uncurled her abused limbs and got to her feet. On the other side of the door, a metal object scraped inside the lock as someone tried unsuccessfully to turn the latch. Drew must have forgotten he'd given her his key.

A glance at the neckline of her bodice confirmed the borrowed garment exposed more than it concealed. The lavender and raspberry brocade gown pushed her breasts up to her chin. The clothing did more than flatter her figure; the frivolous apparel rendered it almost impossible to remember why she was supposed to restrain her natural impulses. She found herself dashing to the door with a foolish grin on her face. If she could steal just a little more time in Drew's arms, she'd repent even harder tomorrow. It seemed a small indiscretion compared to a lifetime of loneliness.

Before her courage escaped her, she flung open the door, but found the companionway empty. Movement at the level of her waist caught her eye. She looked down into the wide-eyed face of a child.

"You're not a cabin boy. You're a wench." The small boy stomped past and into the cabin.

His curly black hair sprouted wildly about his head, forming a tangled halo. A scowl furrowed his brow, reminding her of Solomon despite the child's slender build.

"This place looks like pigs lived here." He pointed to the table that still held the remains of last night's dinner. "I hope you know the captain won't like this."

"Thank you for the warning. And who might you be?" She suspected she already knew his father.

"Do you know what a waggoner is? Or a quadrant?"

"I've seen a quadrant, though I don't know how to use one. I can't say I've ever heard of a waggoner." The fact that Drew had a child on board his ship surprised her almost as much as the child's hostile manner.

"I thought so. A waggoner is a book of maps, and you would be lost without them. Captain Drew just gave you my job because you're a girl."

Felicity knelt so they could be face to face. "He didn't give me your job, I promise. I'm glad you got here when you did. As you can see, I'm making a mess of things."

Her admission of failure seemed to appease him. "I'm Hugh. What's your name?"

"Felicity. It's very nice to meet you, Hugh. How did you come to be the cabin boy on this ship?"

"Hey, are you the one who didn't want me around here? My papa and Captain Drew said I couldn't be the cabin boy anymore because of grown-up things I didn't understand. Are you the captain's woman?"

After she caught her breath, she searched for an appropriate answer for a child. She didn't have one, and the boy's vocalization of her dark desires stunned her. "I'm not sure what you mean. I'm merely a guest."

Hugh narrowed his gaze, as if she were teasing him. Apparently, he didn't appreciate her discretion. "You know. He kisses you and takes your clothes off. Pirates love women. That's all they talk about."

The warm blush in Felicity's cheeks turned cold. "Pirates? You spend time in the company of pirates, do you?"

In a stance she'd seen Drew use, the boy folded his arms over his bare chest. "You're on a pirate ship, you know."

Drew was a pirate. The knowledge should have surprised her, but the revelation instantly filled in all the gaps left by his version of the truth.

Before Hugh figured out he had told her something he shouldn't, she quickly disguised her rampant interest behind a sweet smile. "Would you tell me what a cabin boy does on a pirate ship? I don't think I've ever met one before."

Hugh's small stature swelled an inch or two as he started talking about instruments and how Captain Drew liked his cabin tidied. He took her hand and led her over to a chair in front of the table. After instructing her to sit, he reverently brought out instruments and maps from a cabinet hung on the wall. He explained them carefully while instructing her not to touch.

"You never told me how you got your job, Hugh."

"I've always had it. I guess I didn't when I was a little baby." Turning the pages of a book of maps while pretending to figure out a course with a two-pronged device he had called a divider absorbed him.

"How long have you known Captain Drew?" She picked up a compass and examined it.

"That's not a toy," he warned. "I've known Captain Drew since before I was born. He and my papa were servants."

She put down the instrument. "Servants? Servants to whom?"

"A mean man, but they couldn't leave because they were 'dentured. But I don't think Papa was a servant. He was something worse, but I forgot what his job was called."

The word eluding Hugh came to her easily, but the servant part baffled her. She couldn't picture the commanding Captain Drew in any form of servitude.

"Indentured servant?" she said, surprised. That's what Drew had been. And Solomon a slave.

"That's it." He nodded, then continued with his imaginary navigation. "That was a long time ago. Papa says they would still be in that bad place if it wasn't for Captain Drew. That's why we have to forgive him his wild ways." He stopped and gazed up at her. His eyebrows knit, a serious contrast to his round, childish eyes and turned-up nose. "But we shouldn't act like he does."

"I see." She wondered what wild ways Drew had that even pirates had to justify. To think, she'd actually hoped to join the ranks of his romantic casualties.

"That's how I know you're his woman. He likes women, and especially pretty ones like you."

"I'm not his woman." She was torn between being flattered that Hugh considered her pretty enough to be one of Drew's women and furious that he had so many. Hugh's revelations did what her hours of prayer hadn't. She wouldn't continue to be willing prey.

Hugh stared at her, a worried expression pulling down the corners of his eyes. "Don't be mad. Did I do something to make you mad?"

She forced her tight lips into a smile. "I'm not mad."

"Captain Drew said women get mad for no good reason sometimes. That's why we're not supposed to have any on the ship." He paused, looking confused. "Are you Captain Drew's wife?"

"Oh . . . no!" She doubted her adamant denial would have convinced anyone but a child that she found the thought preposterous. The rush of yearning brought about by Hugh's simple but farfetched question flustered her. It wasn't that she wanted a rake like Drew for a husband; it was just that it had been years since anyone had thought of her as a possible bride to a man so desirable.

"Wives are different. Not like the women the crew sneak on the ship sometimes. But you're not like them, I can tell."

"Thank you."

"You're nice and pretty too. Pretty woman aren't nice sometimes." Hugh closed the book of maps.

"More words of wisdom from Captain Drew." She couldn't keep the sarcasm from her voice, even for Hugh.

He raised his wispy eyebrows. "But you're different, like

my Mama and Laura, or Captain Drew wouldn't have brought you onboard. You're the only one he's ever brought onboard. I just heard about the others. I didn't see them."

The clearing of a masculine throat caught both of their attentions. Hugh twisted in his seat. Felicity glanced over the boy's head. She had no idea how much Drew had heard, but his eyes glittered with amusement. As if his sudden appearance was not enough, his state of undress stole her breath.

He stood just inside the open doorway, the portrait of a pirate. Barefoot, bare-calved and bare-armed, he braced his hands on his hips, challenging everything and everyone. He still wore the same clothes from last night, minus the white shirt and boots. In addition to the multicolored vest and breeches reaching just below his knees, he had added a red sash at his waist, complete with the hilt of a vicious-looking short sword jutting above its wide band.

He looked more tanned than yesterday and his skin glowed with perspiration, as if he'd just been performing heavy labor. A thick muscle jumped in his right biceps, reminding her that she stared. When she glanced back to his face, she found him assessing her with the same intense regard. His humor had vanished. Their gazes held and her pulse quickened, as if he had touched her physically. She wondered if he was also recalling last night's encounter. There were reasons she should turn away from him, not let him see the effect he had on her, but she couldn't remember them at the moment.

Hugh's nervous babbling returned her to the present. "I was just putting your tools away, Captain Drew. You should have seen your room. Felicity made a big mess."

The man turned his attention toward Hugh. "You two seem to be becoming well acquainted."

Nodding his head in agreement, the boy smiled with strained enthusiasm. "She was asking me all sorts of questions and I was very helpful. She doesn't know anything about being on a pirate ship."

A muffled groan indicated Drew's displeasure at that information. "Hugh, you were asked to stay away from my cabin. You have other duties to perform, and my guess is those duties are being neglected."

"Anybody can untangle the berthing lines. I know why you and Papa don't want me in here, but Felicity isn't bad. She's nice."

Drew crossed his arms over his chest. "Perhaps Felicity wants her privacy."

Hugh glanced at her. She couldn't help but smile reassuringly in the face of his anxious expression. He turned to Drew with renewed confidence. "Oh, no. She likes me. We talked about all sorts of things."

Drew slammed the door shut, then strode toward them. He spoke to Hugh, while his gaze bored a hole through her. "I can only dare guess at the topics you two discussed."

She tried to think of something to add to the conversation, realizing all she had done was gape at Drew's bare arms since he'd entered the room. With his every movement, muscles rippled under his tanned skin. She wondered if she'd ever seen so much of a man's bare body. Erik had kept on his knee-length shirt during their brief encounter, but she doubted he looked anything like Drew.

She cleared her throat. "Hugh enlightened me on subjects I would never have imagined to broach. He's a lovely boy."

Drew grunted his response and returned his scrutiny to Hugh. "Regardless of your newfound friendship with our guest, you were told to stay away from my cabin. You disobeyed an order."

Hugh's bright features crumpled. "But I'm a lovely boy."

The child's glance toward her for conformation of his tentative statement melted Felicity's insides almost as effectively as Drew's presence. "It's really my fault. I let him in and then kept him when he wanted to leave."

"I see. Perhaps you're the one who should be punished." Drew's wicked grin emphasized the promise in his voice. Any discipline he doled out to her would be laced with more pleasure than pain.

Hugh leaped from his chair to stand next to Felicity. He squeezed the tips of her fingers. "He doesn't mean it."

"Hugh, leave us." Drew's stern command would make anyone question Hugh's reassurance. "I want to talk to Felicity alone."

The boy didn't seem half as startled as she. Drew was a pirate, she reminded herself. And the worst womanizer she'd ever had the misfortune to meet. She stiffened, tightly clasping her hands in front of her. From this point on, she'd be insensible to his charm.

Hugh paused beside Drew on his way out. "Are you going to tell Papa?"

Drew ruined his bloodthirsty pirate facade when he reached down and rubbed the boy's head. "You know I have to. We both promised after the last time."

Hugh's eyes glazed with the first signs of tears. "Yeah, but this isn't as bad as playing in the ammunition hold."

Drew glanced at Felicity. "I don't think your father would agree. Now get going before he finds you himself. I'll try to break it to him gently."

Hugh dragged himself to the door with his head down. Drew stopped him before he reached his destination. "It's very important that you tell no one about Felicity."

"Because she's your woman?" Hugh's whispered words held a conspiratorial tone.

Drew's gaze again drifted to her, but lingered several seconds too long. "Yes."

She held her breath, hoping the burning in her belly had not risen to her cheeks. Her fortress was breached with the first heavy blow. No one had ever claimed her as his.

Hugh seemed oblivious to the other secrets lurking in the room. "And you don't want anyone else to know because you don't want to share."

The child's assumption appalled her, but Drew seemed pleased he understood. "Right. Remember when Smythe and Red got in that fight last summer? You wouldn't want the same thing to happen to me."

Hugh shook his head, his eyes wide with understanding. "Red lost an eye and has to wear a patch now, and that yellow-haired girl didn't even have all her teeth."

Drew dropped to one knee and stuck out his hand. "It will be our secret, then."

After a vigorous shake, Hugh dashed from the room. When he stopped abruptly at the door, he almost fell over his feet. "Good-bye, Felicity." Hugh waved, then disappeared.

Drew stood, closed the door Hugh had left open, then strolled back to her. His movements were slow and purposeful. "Alone at last."

She gripped the chair in front of her for support. Her back went rigid with a combination of trepidation and anticipation. She wondered if he intended to continue their tryst from last night. Hugh had confirmed a moment before that Drew had no scruples. He didn't dance on the thin line between right and wrong; he crossed it. She should be appalled or at least frightened. Unfortunately, the only thing the pounding rhythm of her heart acknowledged was that he had called her his woman. How was she going to be able to resist him?

"You never mentioned you were a pirate."

He gently but firmly tugged the chair from her grasp and shoved it under the table.

"I never denied it."

Even his admission didn't make his deeds seem real. Who was the man who'd nursed her back to health and ruffled Hugh's hair? She tilted her chin defiantly. To her shame, it took all her willpower not to part her lips in invitation.

"I should have known. Your manner proclaims your profession loud and clear."

He seemed to be slowly leaning into her, but he abruptly straightened. "Are you talking about last night?"

He looked like kissing her had become the farthest thing from his thoughts. His disinterest insulted her. He was a womanizer and she was a woman. Apparently, she wasn't ready to return to the black-clad spinster just yet. She'd seen herself with new eyes and sworn he had too. "You could have been honest with me, as you promised."

"And that would have been better for you? You wouldn't have been offended when I declared my intention to prop you on the dinner table and have my way with you?"

An ember of dizzy heat burst in her chest and rushed to her limbs. Lord, but if he would only stop talking about it and . . .

Drew retreated to the far side of the table and rubbed his brow as if he had an intense headache. "I'm sorry; I don't want to offend you. I promise nothing like that will happen again. I only came here because I noticed the door open."

She should be grateful at his vow to be honorable, but his dismissal of the passion that almost persuaded her to toss aside years of rigorous repentance hurt. While she had lain awake last night wanting him, he'd been able to put her aside.

"All I want to know is why you got involved with an honest man like my father."

He began to put away the instruments Hugh had strung out all over the table. "It's a long story."

"I have time."

"Well, I don't. I'm trying to captain a ship, and since I'm a pirate other people want to keep me from doing that." He continued with his task, ignoring her.

She grabbed his bare arm with the intention of yanking him around to face her, not to mention give him a view of the cleavage even a Puritan minister couldn't help but notice. "Were you an indentured servant?"

He didn't budge at her hard tug on his arm. "If you insist on touching me, I'm going to have to take back my promise."

"Hugh told me you were an indentured servant and Solomon was a slave. Did you help him to escape?"

Her hand looked pale and small against the width of Drew's tanned arm, leaving her with a desire to see how it would compare against the broadness of his chest. She followed his gaze to the low-cut neckline of her dress. She could see clearly each of her full breasts, including the tips of her dark nipples. They hardened at his bold stare. Her depraved nature, a weakness she found impossible to control in Drew's presence, had always been her worst enemy. Even a pirate had more restraint than she.

He flicked his gaze back to her face. "I don't think you laced your bodice correctly."

"Oh, and you know all about how a women's dress should be fastened? Or should I say unfastened?" She hoped her show of anger would explain the tremble of desire that shook each breath. "Hugh knows more about the base appetites of men than I do."

He dragged his eyes away from her bodice. "Would you like me to teach you, love?"

She forced herself to meet his gaze despite his lewd offer. His smooth words mocked his passion of the night before, but that didn't stop her from wanting him to show her his skill. "You'll say anything to avoid my questions."

He circled her waist with one arm, pulling her snugly against himself. "Not true. I just think it would be more interesting if you answered mine."

Through their clothes, she could distinctly feel his body harden in places she shouldn't even know existed. Despite a nagging longing, she didn't have the courage to answer his question honestly. "Were you an indentured servant or weren't you?"

His abrupt release left her wishing she hadn't been so blunt. "I was. But I cut my service short. I found the life of an indentured servant nowhere near as enticing as the handbill promised."

His typically glib response to an event that had to have been painful aroused compassion in Felicity. She couldn't resist touching his cheek in a comforting gesture he didn't ask for and probably never would. "I can't see you voluntarily signing your life away for seven years. You must have been desperate."

He stiffened at her touch but didn't pull away. For once, he didn't meet her gaze directly. "At twelve, I was a little more humble. Nor was my servitude exactly voluntary. My mother died and my relatives couldn't afford me. It was better than starving."

She stroked a wild lock of hair from his forehead. "What about your father?"

He grabbed her hand and brought it to his lips. "What about him? I'm sure my departure suited him nicely. He had a legitimate son and didn't need his bastard around to further spoil the bloodline."

His tone remained light, but his tentative kisses across her knuckles warned Felicity she had wandered into territory far more dangerous than mere lust. And she'd thought *her* betrayal devastating. She slipped her free hand around the back of his neck and leaned into him.

"A ship sighted starboard," bellowed a voice from the deck above.

They jerked away from each other. Solomon sounded as if he were in the room with them.

"I wish I never got that bloody speaking-trumpet. It's supposed to only be used to yell at other ships, not to terrorize the captain." Drew's words didn't match his tone.

He sounded relieved by the interruption rather than annoyed. Avoiding Felicity's gaze, he escaped to a porthole that had already been cranked open. "Raise their colors and come about."

When he returned to the table, he ignored her completely. Straightening the mess left by Hugh suddenly seemed a task of life-or-death importance.

She suspected he'd revealed more of himself than he wanted. If she could force him to face his feelings, then maybe she could understand her own where he was concerned. "I know what it's like to be abandoned."

"Help me with this." He opened a wooden case. Shapes of the various instruments scattered on the table lay molded in red velvet. "Do you think me a monster? I wouldn't blame you for it if you did."

She matched the tools with their corresponding places in the case. "For being a pirate or a womanizer?" His entrance into her life made her unsure of everything she had believed to be true. At the moment, she couldn't muster the appropriate indignation for either offense.

He grinned, and she thought he might kiss her, but out of gratitude rather than passion. He glanced away without touching her. When he spoke, she realized he was giving her a much greater prize than a kiss. He honored her with a small glimpse into his heart. "I'm not the one my father betrayed. My mother suffered far more. She was merely a servant to him, but she thought he loved her. She never gave up hope that he'd somehow do the right thing by her and me. She died of a broken heart as much as the lung ailment that killed her."

"So that's why you have so many different women? You don't believe in love?" She wondered how much he would let her see of his secret self and intended to push as far as he'd let her.

"No." He answered the question succinctly and punctuated it by abruptly slamming the case closed. "I don't promise things I'm incapable of. The women I become involved with know that."

She searched his hooded eyes. She had pushed him too far, but it wasn't in her nature to stop at the first signs of resistance. "What about Laura? You must have cared for her to mention her to Hugh."

He searched the ceiling with his gaze. When he glanced back at her, it looked as if he wasn't going to answer. "Yes. I loved her. Too much, I guess."

"Oh." Her habit of probing in murky waters often got her into trouble, but she remembered too late to save her bruised feelings. He might want to avoid engaging his heart, but he wasn't invincible. Instead of being comforted by the fact he wasn't a complete cad, the tightness in her chest at hearing Drew's confession of love for another woman told her how lost she was.

After an agonizing moment, he came up behind her, encircling her with both arms. He pulled her against him and brushed her hair aside with his free hand. "All promises have been officially withdrawn, Miss Kendall," he whispered. Then he lightly kissed the back of her neck.

She melted against him. His disguises, though vastly different from her own, had been created to hide a broken heart. They both deserved to be healed, even if the effect would be fleeting. He might not care for her with the intensity he had for Laura, but for the moment she succeeded in capturing his full attention.

A metal object beat against the side of the ship made her jump. She tried to pull away from Drew's embrace, but he held her to him. He urged her closer with gentle yet demanding pressure until her backside fit into the groove of his hips.

A disjointed voice boomed near the window. "Ship on our starboard. She's following our course."

Seemingly lost in the act of smelling her hair, Drew ignored the voice. He cupped one of her breasts, weighing and massaging its heaviness in his palm. Felicity leaned into him lest she slide to the floor.

When he abruptly stopped and set her away from him with a curse, she wondered if she had done something wrong.

He turned her to face him. "I have to go. We're being pursued." He brushed his lips against her cheek as if he couldn't bear to stop touching her. "You distract me beyond endurance, sweeting, but I promise, we will finish this later."

He returned to the window. "What flag are they flying?"

"British," answered Solomon without the amplification of the speaking-cone.

Drew shook his head. "Solomon's probably leaning over the side of the ship, maybe even trying to look in the porthole. He doesn't trust me with you any more than I trust myself."

He turned back to the window. "Battle stations. I'll be right there." The boom of his voice warned Felicity that whatever frivolous roles he'd played in the past, he found this current game deadly serious. He strode to a trunk and flipped open the lid.

"Surely you don't mean to fight a British ship." She clasped her arms to keep the fear creeping up her spine at bay.

Beside the trunk, he stacked what looked to be flags folded into tight triangles. "Here we go. British." He held up the flag, though all she could glimpse of it was a fat red stripe. "We'll fly the other ship's colors and see if she leaves us alone."

"And if that doesn't work?"

"That could be a problem." He gathered the rest of the flags in his arms and dumped them in the trunk, then paused to grab a second flag to accompany the British one.

"Do you have a flag for every country?"

Colors clutched to his side, he strode to the desk and

yanked open the top drawer. "And then some. A pirate always has to be prepared."

From the drawer he pulled a brass-butted flintlock pistol.

She backed toward the far corner of the cabin. "You really are a pirate."

He closed the distance between them. "I think that's obvious. Felicity Kendall, I'd never expect you to cower in the face of a little adversity."

At his taunt, she managed to square her shoulders. "I never claimed to be courageous. Any intelligent woman would back away when confronted by an armed pirate."

After flipping the weapon around so he held the muzzle, he offered it to her. "Have I acted like that much of a bastard? For your protection, my lady. Do you know how to shoot?"

She eyed the pistol but refused to take it from him. "No."

He grabbed her wrist and wrapped her fingers around the cool brass. "Cock it, then squeeze the trigger. It's too difficult to reload, so make your shot count. Or you can club someone over the head with it. Just do your best. You always do."

She tried to quell her panic. The idea of physical violence against herself or anyone else made her queasy. "You don't expect me to fight? For all I know, that ship was sent for me by my father. He's probably worried sick."

Drew sprinted toward the door, grabbing the flags from the desk on his way. "Odds are they're here for me. Now stay in the cabin and be a good girl. Shoot anyone who bursts through that door who isn't Solomon, Hugh or me. Understand?"

"Don't go." She followed him to the door. Though she'd always prided herself on being a strong woman, she'd discovered her limit. Being left alone in the midst of a battle terrified her.

He put his hands on each of her arms and leaned down to kiss the top of her forehead. "Don't worry. You'll be safe."

To her utter surprise, her eyes shimmered with moisture. "What about you?"

"What? Be hurt and miss your probing questions regarding my past? Never."

"Please be careful, Drew," she whispered.

He stared at her mouth, but dropped his hands from her arms and turned away.

She stopped him with a tug at his elbow. "Send Hugh down. I'll look after him."

He hesitated. She sensed his struggle. It was the same one she'd been battling since he'd shown her his other side. At first she thought their mutual attraction mere lust; now she understood it to be something infinitely more dangerous. The idea of losing him before she figured out who he really was, or who she might be with him, sealed her fate. If he could trust her, she could trust him.

She blinked back the rush of emotion making her eyes tear. "Do you think I would do anything to harm Hugh?"

"No," he said without pause. "I know you wouldn't do anything to purposely hurt Hugh, but your good intentions can be dangerous. Look at the disaster that landed you here in the first place."

"I've made mistakes in the past. Many mistakes, but can't you see how you've affected me? You've changed me in ways I've yet to understand. I swear I won't do anything to hurt Hugh or Solomon . . . or you." She hadn't known she had felt this way until the words left her lips. But there they were, and their plain truth wouldn't allow them to be called back.

The fierce angle of his jaw appeared unmoved by her pledge, but she swore she saw a softening in his eyes. "I believe you told me in no uncertain terms you were out to harm me."

His answer hurt. She explained, "Things have changed. How can you blame me for not trusting you at first? You wear so many different masks, sometimes I don't know who I'm speaking with from one moment to the next. And it's obvious you have no idea what I'm all about."

He stared at her without blinking. "I'll send Hugh down. But promise me you won't do anything else to help."

She nodded in agreement. His words were a gift to both of them.

He shook his head as if to clear it. "I'm crazy," he mumbled to himself before heading to the door. He halted, turning to face her. "Felicity, Laura was my mother. Hugh nags to hear stories about mothers. I guess he's a little confused about women." His crooked smile made even his uncharacteristic blush disarming. "But so am I."

Without waiting for her response, he shut the door behind him and locked it. She had no idea when he'd taken one of the keys. In fact, she was barely conscious of her held breath. The cold ache she'd lived with for far too long thawed in a rush of warmth. She gave up her struggle and let her head follow the path her heart intended to travel.

# Chapter Nine

Avery Sneed dropped the last few feet from his perch high in the mainmast. "They don't know what the bloody hell they're doing," he said, and handed Drew the vellum telescope. "If they continue on their current course, they'll ram into our side. I say we take down their mainmast."

The telescope confirmed Avery's assumption about the merchant ship's crew. The Union Jack billowed proudly in the wind, while below men scrambled in panic. He couldn't read the name of the ship, but it looked naggingly familiar. He swung the scope in the direction of their standard.

Bloody hell! It was a Barbadian ship. As a rule, he avoided clashes with any vessels flying British colors and purposely veered from those also carrying the smaller Barbadian flag. Loyalty didn't account for his actions; meeting someone he knew and risking exposure did. If the other ship provoked an incident, Drew would be forced to fight, regardless of his preference. With Felicity on board, he wanted to avoid that possibility at all costs.

"Come about again. We'll try to lose them," he ordered, without taking his gaze from the other ship.

Avery repeated Drew's command. Throughout the ship, the crew echoed the orders in deep booming voices.

When Avery left to carry out his duties, Solomon took his place. "The men are restless. They've taken no booty since Marley's death and are eager for a fight."

"Are you questioning my command?" Drew lowered the telescope and gave Solomon a warning stare. His tone invited only one answer. His impatience to return to Felicity made him irritable.

Solomon clasped his hands behind his back, his expression placid. "I question your motives. I wonder how much Miss Kendall has swayed your judgment."

Drew tapped the telescope against the side of his leg. The scowl he directed at Solomon did nothing to dispel his friend's patient and unwavering gaze. The man was a muscle bound conscience who refused to be ignored.

Of course Felicity's presence on the ship swayed his judgment. He didn't want to risk a battle with her aboard, and it wasn't just because the slaying of British citizens would horrify her. He worried for her safety. At the moment, he couldn't afford to contemplate the other emotions attached to those concerns.

He avoided Solomon's question, choosing an argument he would find reasonable. "Since when are you bent on blood? Look at the way they sail. This wouldn't be a fight. It would be a slaughter."

Solomon shrugged. "Perhaps, but to run isn't our way. Running makes you a target. Have you forgotten the lesson I was taught on the subject?"

Drew contemplated the expanse of choppy sea separating their ship from the other vessel. Even if he wanted to, he couldn't forget Solomon's brush with slave-hunters years after his escape from slavery; Solomon's emotional scars remained too close to the surface. Escaping with

**Hugh had been the only thing keeping him alive after the** loss of his beloved wife Marguerite at the hands of the slavers. Not a day went by that Solomon didn't mourn her loss.

Drew's reluctance to attack a pursuing ship went against everything they both had done to survive. Conquer or be conquered. The motto took on more consequence when one had something to look forward to, and for the first time, Drew did. She awaited him in his cabin.

Solomon continued without waiting for Drew's answer. "Do I have to remind you what we are?" He lost his pretense of patience, balling his hands into fists. "We are pirates. We survive by being ruthless. If you show weakness we'll eventually be crushed. These seas are no place for the weak."

The *Rapture*'s change in direction thrust them forward. The tack did the same for the merchant ship following them.

"Raise our standard and let's see what that accomplishes," Drew said.

Solomon lifted his brows. "Does this mean you're ready to do battle? Once you reveal your hand, you must play it out."

Drew refused to think that far ahead. Once the other ship knew whom it was dealing with, perhaps it would turn tail and run. He would let it. "I'll do what I must."

After Solomon shouted the command to change the flags, he turned to Drew. "I'm relieved you've come to your senses. Your recent fame should ensure an uneventful surrender."

Drew sighed. "Since the bloody reputation was thrust upon me, I might as well use it to our advantage."

He swung his gaze from the other ship to the flag he'd designed unfurling in the wind. A white, devil-like skeleton complete with pointed ears and forked tail danced against a black background. In its right hand it held a sword with which it skewered a red, bleeding heart.

His personal standard had been a tribute to his escape from a Spanish prison off the coast of Hispañola. Stealing the heart of a señorita with keys to the prison won him the nickname. Her father had claimed only El Diablo himself could seduce his daughter and flee his hell. Through the years, the name had stuck.

The sound of a cannon, followed by a spray of water as the ball missed her target, was the other ship's answer to the raising of his standard. A second shot immediately followed, skidding off their bow and splintering wood in the process.

"What the bloody hell?" Drew blinked to clear the fury from his vision, then readjusted the telescope to survey the opposing crew. Merchant ships never fired on the better-manned and better-armed pirate vessels. Either he was being pursued by pirates using the British flag as subterfuge, or the captain of this particular vessel was a total incompetent. The rapid approach of the other ship, combined with the aid of the telescope, soon gave Drew his answer. The corpulent captain standing on the other deck came close enough to reach out and throttle. *Captain McCulla*.

"Captain!" Solomon's deep voice sliced through Drew's thoughts. He dropped the telescope but prevented the vellum tube from hitting the deck by catching it with his other hand. After his recovery, he glared at Solomon.

The man shrugged. "I wouldn't have shouted, but you didn't hear me the first time. I'm going below to check on the damage done by the shot."

Drew suspected Solomon meant to check on Hugh. He needn't bother; the shot had landed on the opposite end of the ship from where the boy hid. Felicity and Hugh were safe, but revealing they were together in his cabin had to be delayed. Drew couldn't afford another opponent just now.

"Don't bother. Hugh's safe. We've got more immediate problems. That's a New England Trading Company ship."

"Are you sure?" Solomon grabbed for the spyglass.

"I recognize the captain."

"Do you think Ben sent them after his daughter?" asked Solomon.

Drew hated the idea of Ben turning against him. Ben might not even realize he had Felicity, but if he did, his blind spot where his daughter was concerned might provoke him into doing something rash. Drew's own experience showed him how easy it was to overlook the unpredictable shrew behind those liquid brown eyes, especially if she was on your side. Yet if Drew could believe he had gained Felicity's loyalty, he had to trust her father. Ben had proved deserving of the gift over the years.

"No," he finally said. "Ben wouldn't send McCulla. Something's wrong. Let's come around beside her and see what Captain McCulla has to say for himself."

Solomon pointed to the swiftly approaching ship. "We're already too close. Their next shot will do irreparable damage."

"We'll tack around and approach on her leeward side. She's heeling enough to send her cannons underwater. McCulla probably won't think of that."

"I'll give Avery the orders. I need to go below." Solomon turned without waiting for Drew's reply.

Drew grabbed Solomon's arm. "He won't be there. He's in my cabin."

"With Felicity?" Solomon swung around.

"And a good thing I sent him there. That shot might have ripped right through the galley." Drew ignored his friend's scowl. "You can thank me later. Right now I believe you have orders to carry out."

Solomon's narrowed gaze promised he'd be doing more than thanking Drew after the battle. With his hands cupped around his mouth, Solomon bellowed orders that sent a dozen barefoot men scrambling.

Drew's swift sloop sailed circles around the bloated merchant vessel. He maneuvered out of cannons' range on the ship's windward side. Sailing around her stern brought him close enough to read her name without the aid of magnification. As Drew predicted, the wind filling the *Carolina*'s sails dragged her gunports below the waterline. Drew didn't bother to order his raised.

"Bring me that brass speaking-horn." Drew had watched the sailors directed by Captain McCulla scramble like scattering geese as they battled the strong wind and the maneuvering of Drew's vessel. The result placed them exactly where he wanted them: helpless.

Avery arrived with Drew's request almost instantly. Solomon raised a dark eyebrow. "I thought you hated that thing."

"The horn is to be used for calling to other vessels across the sea, not across the deck to harass the captain. It's a useful tool when handled properly, Mr. Quartermaster." The message Drew had was too important to be misinterpreted. He still hoped to disengage himself from this situation without bloodshed.

"*Lower your sails or we'll send you to hell.*" Drew's booming voice cut through the roar of waves and wind.

The men on the *Carolina* stared back at him. McCulla pushed aside his motionless crew and leaned over the rail. Drew stood close enough to see the veins bulging in his crimson neck.

"The bloody hell we will, you bastard," the other captain called. "We know all about your promises, Lord Christian Andrews—or should I call you by your true name, you spawn of the devil!" McCulla turned back to his crew and shouted orders no one seemed obliged to follow. After frantically waving his arms, he managed to send one man sprinting across the deck.

Drew tossed down the brass speaking-horn. He held a mask of fierceness in place while his insides slowly slid into his boots. McCulla's revelation was not good.

"If you know who I am, then you know my reputation. Lower your sails and there will be no need for a fight," he boomed in the harshest voice he could muster.

In answer to Drew's second request, the *Carolina* fired a cannon from her deck, shooting a hole though their mizzen topsail. A hunk of canvas fluttered to the deck like a wounded seagull—inconvenient, but not strategically important unless one factored in the uncontrolled fury it caused in Drew. McCulla whooped triumphantly, acting as if he had taken out their mainmast.

Drew's command was low and controlled. "Take down her sails and prepare to board."

Solomon nodded. His expression matched Drew's grim tone.

Within minutes, chain shot flew and hit its mark. Smoke from the cannons choked the air and watered Drew's eyes, but he didn't blink. He watched the mainmast of the *Carolina* topple, leaving her crew covered in a shroud of white sail. His well-trained men secured grappling hooks to the disabled vessel before the sailors could again see the blue of the sky.

He unsheathed the well-used cutlass Avery dutifully brought him. The leather grip had worn through to metal in places, but the blade was always honed to a deadly edge.

"Take as many prisoners as possible. I want the captain," he yelled above the excited voices of his men.

By the time he leaped onto the other vessel, McCulla had disappeared. Some swords clanked in futile struggle, but many men threw down their weapons as soon as the pirates swarmed their deck. Drew's crew quickly disarmed the few foolish enough to fight. He continued his search undisturbed by the one-sided battle. Not even the boldest of the *Carolina*'s crew seemed willing to engage him.

"Captain, we found him," called Avery.

Two of Drew's men dragged McCulla abovedeck and shoved him before Drew. The rest of McCulla's crew, a total of thirteen, were disarmed and herded into a circle.

"What the hell is this about, McCulla?" Drew demanded.

McCulla smelled as if he'd undertaken the voyage sealed in a cask of rum. "It's about the reward, El Diablo."

Liquor made McCulla bold when he should have cowered. Drew raised his cutlass and touched it to the man's throat. "What is this about, man?"

"Murderer," McCulla squealed as he tried to back away. "You'll murder me in cold blood just like you did Marley and his missus. I knew you weren't no duke's son."

McCulla didn't get far. Smythe, the one-eyed pirate who had pried him from his hiding place, pointed a wickedly sharp dagger at the center of McCulla's back. Drew waited for McCulla's retreat to bring the blade in contact with his flesh. It didn't take long. The captain jumped forward, howling as if he'd been run through.

"What do you think you know?" Drew wanted to learn what Ben and the others on Barbados knew, but feared giving away information McCulla didn't already have.

McCulla composed himself and lifted his trembling chin. "You ain't no better than me and never was. I know it was you who talked old Ben into taking away my command. And now we're all going hungry 'cause you murdered the hand that fed you."

Drew glanced over McCulla's motley crew. Despite their overgrown beards and rum-soaked eyes, Drew recognized a man or two, though they'd all seen better days. He returned his gaze to McCulla. At least he wasn't wholly responsible for the man's downfall. "You're out of work because you ran a ship loaded with sugar aground."

"You won't get away with this. Everyone knows about you, and there'll be others wanting the reward. And don't be expecting any help from Ben Kendall. The governor knows about him too," taunted McCulla. "How he helped you sell pirated goods."

"I needed someone as a front for my diabolical schemes. You idiot Barbadians conveniently found one for me," said Drew with more control. He pretended to examine his nails. "Of course, I didn't think anyone would believe simple old Ben could knowingly be a partner with pirates. I obviously underestimated your stupidity." If Drew kept McCulla talking, he might find a way to help Ben. Drew would never be able to set foot on Barbados again, but he had hope that Ben could still be redeemed.

McCulla smiled. "It'll all come out in the trial. For now, Ben's locked up and the governor seized his property. They gave me this ship to go after you, and they'll help anyone else who wants to bring you to justice."

"Excellent. That should tie up some of the governor's men, guarding Ben. Maybe hanging him will make them all satisfied and they won't waste time on me. That is, if they are satisfied hanging a man without proof." Drew called upon the acting ability he'd gained during his impersonation of Lord Christian to hide how badly McCulla's revelations shook him.

Though things looked bleak for Ben as well as himself, Drew wouldn't tip his hand to anyone—not even McCulla. Drew had bluffed his way out of far worse situations, though at the moment he couldn't recall how.

"You want proof? Well, I think a blooming duke is proof enough." The fool McCulla actually smiled. "The Duke of Foxmoor came to Barbados to pay you a visit. Thanks to Marley."

Drew's narrowed gaze was the only hint the blow hit its mark. Marley had wanted out of their scheme of selling pirated contraband as legal imports. At the time, Drew couldn't really blame the man. After all, he'd just married a young wife and, even at his advanced age, hoped to start a family. But never had he suspected Marley would turn him in. Well, maybe he'd suspected, but Ben had assured him Marley wouldn't. It looked as if they had both underestimated Marley's greed.

"That's right," continued McCulla, apparently encouraged. "Marley figured out you weren't who you said you were and wrote to the duke. You knew Marley was on to you and so you killed him and his wife. And you might have gotten away with it, if the duke hadn't shown up to see who had the nerve to sully his good name."

Solomon's gaze darted to Drew, but Drew had no answers for his friend's silent questions. That the Duke of Foxmoor, Drew's father, would travel all the way to Barbados to confront his illegitimate son seemed unlikely. He'd never given Drew the time of day when they resided on the same estate.

"Put the prisoners in our hold," Drew ordered. "The rest of you gather anything of value, we'll burn her when you're done."

Though McCulla deserved a flogging to be witnessed by his crew—the standard punishment for a captain who resisted a pirate attack—Drew didn't have the stomach for it at the moment. Too many things battled for priority in his mind. Both his father and Marley's betrayal multiplied the pain of discovering Ben's imprisonment. Did his vicious old sire want to destroy the only living evidence left of his indiscretion? Drew felt like a cornered animal. First he'd been framed for crimes he hadn't committed then his father had stepped down from a cloud to condemn him.

And of course there was Felicity. He'd made himself vulnerable to her, and when she found out about her father she would go for his throat.

Drew sheathed his sword. Solomon herded McCulla's crew—most of them too drunk to walk straight—to the other vessel. Feet apart, bare arms over his chest, Drew surveyed the scene with outward fierceness, but his mind tripped over one thought: How the hell was he going to tell Felicity Ben had been arrested?

"Cap'n?"

"What, Avery?" The irritating nature of Drew's thoughts was reflected in his curt reply.

The second mate never asked his question. A musket exploded, crumpling him. Drew dropped down beside Avery, scanning the deck for the source of the shot. Blood seeped just above the second mate's right hip. Drew quickly placed his hand over the softly fountaining wound.

"Get the surgeon!"

"We don't have one. Our last was shot taking a French frigate a few months ago." Solomon came to stand before Drew. In one of his fists, he held the collar of a copper-haired child; in the other, he gripped a musketoon. An acrid smell drifted from the weapon's short barrel.

"Tanner?" Drew recognized the skittish child he'd bribed a smile from with a piece of eight. Tanner's efforts to get away doubled at Drew's attention. The boy held back tears with a few loud sniffles.

McCulla lurched forward but was restrained by Smythe. "You little brat. You can't do anything right. You got the wrong one."

One of the crew hastily recruited to act as a physician came forward and began to rip the *Carolina*'s downed sails to make a bandage for Avery Sneed's wound. The sailor took Drew's place at the wounded man's side.

Drew crouched in front of Tanner. "Did McCulla order you to shoot me?"

McCulla erupted into a blustering string of denials.

"Shut up," commanded Drew. A blow from Smythe quieted the drunk captain when Drew's order hadn't.

Tanner shivered and kept his eyes downcast.

Drew reached out and raised the boy's chin. "I'm not going to hurt you, Tanner."

Solomon still held the boy by the collar, stopping him from squirming away from Drew's touch.

"He was hiding in some coiled rope," said Solomon.

"McCulla set him up as a marksman while he found a good hiding place." Drew gentled his voice. "Is that right, Tanner?"

Tanner avoided Drew's gaze despite all efforts to coax him out of his fear. Drew dropped his hand from Tanner's chin and rose to his full height. He reached out to ruffle the boy's hair, but Tanner flinched. Glancing at his blood-covered palm, Drew couldn't blame him.

McCulla had gone too far. He'd earned what Drew had once been reluctant to do. "Bring the rest of the prisoners over to our ship and leave them on deck while you flog the captain," Drew called.

"No!" cried Tanner, straining against Solomon's grip. The boy managed to connect his fist with Drew's thigh before Solomon pulled him away. "Don't hurt him. I thought you were nice to me, but you're nothing but a pirate like the ones who murdered my real mum and da."

"Let him go," said Drew. The boy flew at him, kicking and throwing punches. Drew blocked only the jabs aimed at his groin. Luckily, Tanner couldn't reach his face, though Drew deserved every blow.

When he realized his attack didn't wreak any damage, Tanner broke into hysterical tears. Drew had caused Ben's destruction, a crewman's injury, a boy's loss of innocence, and that was just today. Felicity's seduction remained to be completed. Tanner's paltry assault didn't do Drew justice.

When the jeers of his crew only enraged the boy all over again, Drew stopped the show. He hooked an arm around Tanner's middle and hauled him off his feet. "Take him to the hold with the other prisoners. Except for McCulla. Tie him to the mainmast. I'll deal with him myself after we tend to Avery."

McCulla's outrage fell on deaf ears. After all, he was the one who'd come after the bloodthirsty El Diablo. He was about to get what he'd wanted.

Solomon swung the frantic Tanner easily over his shoulder. The boy's kicking limbs didn't appear to faze him. "Aye, Captain. But don't you think the child would be more comfortable somewhere else?"

Drew moved the crewman tending Avery aside and gathered the unconscious second mate in his arms. "No. I think he'd rather be in the stench of the hold than anywhere near me."

He stepped over the gap between the two ships, careful not to jar Sneed's dead weight. Another unscheduled passenger would feel the same as Tanner if she had the slightest inkling of what had transpired this afternoon. Drew would have to do everything in his power to see that she never knew he was and always had been the infamous El Diablo.

# Chapter Ten

"I don't want to do this anymore. Teach me to read instead." The quill Hugh held stiffly in his hand drifted to a corner of the parchment to sketch a stick-figure animal.

"Hugh, don't. Paper is expensive." Felicity left her seat beside Hugh to stand directly behind him. A pattern of wrinkles on her silk skirt's front revealed the toll that appearing calm had taken on her nerves. Every clink, boom and scream coming from abovedeck had her gripping the delicate material tighter.

Hugh glanced at her over his shoulder. The battle raging around them didn't seem to bother him in the least. "You said you were going to teach me to read and write so I can keep Captain Drew's log."

"You have to learn your letters before you can read or write." She wrapped her hand around Hugh's, helping him to form the rest of the letters. After Hugh found pen and paper in an ornate box complete with sealing wax, she justified the use of Drew's precious writing paper for the noble purpose of teaching Hugh to write as well as creating a distraction. Of course, keeping busy soothed her own nerves and stopped her from running to the porthole every few minutes.

The unknown clanks and thuds seeping through the walls had brought her close to tears. The sudden unnerving silence worried her more. Visions of Drew lying in a puddle of his own blood grew with his extended absence. The not knowing was torture. Her stomach tied itself in knots as she imagined different forms of his demise.

She had badly misjudged him. If Drew survived and she still had the chance, she'd show herself to him in a different light. Perhaps she could find the trusting, vibrant young woman who had withered while hiding her shame. Perhaps she could open herself enough to trust a pirate with the heart of an angel. She had trusted an angel with the heart of a pirate once, and the reverse could be no worse.

All her years of pious repentance meant nothing to her now. For the first time since Erik, she wanted to take a chance on caring for a man. The irony in her choice of men didn't escape her. Reason had nothing to do with her desire for Drew, which made it all the more powerful. Would she have the courage to step out of the rigid role she'd forced herself into? Now that she realized how badly she wanted to, would she even have the chance?

A solid rap on the door startled her from her fretting, sending her into a full-blown panic. She rushed toward the bed. The pistol Drew had given her lay tucked beneath a pillow. She hadn't wanted to frighten Hugh with the weapon. When she noticed the trembling of her hands, she wondered why she bothered hiding it at all. Hugh with his nerves of steel would undoubtedly handle the weapon better than she.

Hugh exhibited none of her fears and got up to unlock the door.

"Hugh! No!" she screamed.

"Felicity . . . are you all right?" called a familiar voice from the other side.

The weapon forgotten, she rushed to wrestle the door's brass handle from Hugh's grasp. He opened the door in spite of her efforts, scowling in displeasure at her unwanted assistance.

Drew stepped into the cabin, and all of Felicity's fears conspired to squeeze her breath from her lungs. Drew's beautiful face was tight with pain. His bare arms and exotic vest were smeared with fresh blood.

"Are you hurt?" Drew dodged Hugh with the intention of placing his hands on Felicity's shoulders. He remembered the blood on his hands and stepped back. From arm's length, he examined her from head to toe. In that moment, not touching her was one of the hardest things he'd ever had to do. Not even when she tumbled out of the armoire had he seen her so pale.

Hugh tugged at the end of Drew's ruined vest. "I learned my letters. Want to see?"

She reached out and began to unbutton Drew's vest. "You need to sit down. Back in Boston, I doctored several parishioners and not one died." The tremor in her voice revealed she stretched the truth to comfort him. "Where is your wound?"

When her fingers grazed his bare skin, his sharp inhalation was audible. She froze for a second, then began to rid him of the vest more cautiously. She obviously thought she had hurt him. She had. Her frantic concern over his welfare combined with the flood of relief to find her safely in one piece overwhelmed him.

He wanted nothing more than to take her into his arms and prove to her how truly healthy he was. The look in her eyes told him she would respond favorably, but eventually she'd learn the truth. Before fate had trapped her in his armoire, he could have smiled and lied. The honesty they had shared changed everything. He deserved her hatred, not her concern. Guilt or something like it—he wasn't sure since he usually wasn't plagued with such an awful emotion—weighed him down like a suit of iron.

To stop her before her trembling fingers grazed his chest again, he grabbed her wrists. "I'm not injured." He let her go and turned away abruptly. He was more wounded than she knew.

Delivering McCulla's punishment had done little to return Drew's sense of control. He still reeled from his father's betrayal. Marley he could understand. The man was a realist to Ben's overoptimism. But Drew's own father . . .

To offer a reward for Drew's demise gave a new definition to the word betrayal. His father's actions wounded Drew in a way he'd no longer thought possible. And the only place he had to turn for comfort was Felicity. He knew he could lean on her and she wouldn't crumble.

"If you're not hurt, why are you covered in blood?" Felicity's voice held fear.

Drew forced himself to face her. "It's somebody else's." Despite his clipped words and hard stare, her compassionate gaze didn't falter. Were those actual tears making her eyes look so wet and inviting? All he had to do was open his arms and she'd be in them, doing whatever he wanted, whatever he needed.

But he had no right to find solace in her luscious body. Telling her of her father's imprisonment would accomplish what his weak morals alone could never master. Their seductive interludes would be nothing more than a vague memory or a forgotten dream. When she learned he was the infamous El Diablo, her feminine concern would be replaced by gratification at the sight of him drenched in blood, preferably his own.

"Did you kill somebody, Captain Drew?" Hugh's question reminded him that the boy was still in the cabin.

Drew strode past him to pour himself some brandy.

Hugh sat at the table drawing on something Drew hoped wasn't a map. "No, Hugh. I didn't kill anyone. Go find your father. He's worried about you."

"That wasn't much of a battle." Hugh sighed with obvious disappointment.

"Maybe next time. Now go." Drew gulped the brandy he splashed into the tankard, then refilled the container halfway to the top.

Hugh dashed from the cabin. Felicity quietly closed the door after him, then began moving about the room. Drew tried to ignore her as he swilled his brandy. He shouldn't have come here until his mind had cleared.

After seeing to Avery's comfort and McCulla's lashing, he'd convinced himself he needed to attend to Felicity's safety. A dozen bizarre accidents could have befallen her during the battle. And now that he'd seen her, he knew he had to tell her what had happened to Ben. The rift that would come between them already seemed like a stone wall stretching across the room.

He sank into a chair. The suit of iron guilt made it hard to stand—and Ben's fate pressed harder in Felicity's presence. He clutched his tankard as if it were a lifeline.

Felicity appeared beside him holding a basin of water floating a clean white cloth.

"What's that?" he mumbled between gulps of brandy.

She set the basin on the table. "Despite your present appearance, I know you've seen soap and water before. Would you be so kind as to remove your vest?"

"I told you, I'm fine."

She picked up the cloth and squeezed out the excess water. "I'd like to see that for myself. You could be stunned and not realize you're hurt. That happens, you know."

Drew sat up and shrugged off the vest to prove to her he was intact, physically anyway. "I've met the wrong end of a sword more than once. If all this blood were mine, I'd know it."

She rubbed a small piece of soap against the washcloth until foam appeared. Her movements were stiff, as if she struggled for control. She circled behind him and began to gently wipe the blood from his upper arm.

"Don't do this," he snapped. The strong scent of rose and sandalwood crept from the soapy water, reminding him of the moment he'd found Felicity draped in the ruby-silk robe. He should yell at her for even thinking of dousing him with the fragrant lather, but alluding to the scent would give the memory too much power. It was like a bruise too painful to touch.

She continued cleaning his arm with long, gentle strokes. "I want to help you. I need to make up for the way I've treated you. I want you to know—"

"You're wiping another man's blood from my body. I'm no saint. Anything I've gotten from you, I deserved." He pinched the bridge of his nose to keep from saying more until he found the right words. When he brought away his hand, he realized his fingers were still covered in blood.

She rinsed the cloth in the basin, then dabbed away the smudges left by his touch. "Hear me out, Drew. I misjudged you from the very first moment we met. I only saw exactly what you wanted everyone to see."

He leered up at her. All he had to do to make her hate him was be himself. Apparently that was enough for his own father. "And you know better, sweeting? I've lured many a good woman into my bed on the ruse of letting her save my black soul. Is that what you had in mind?"

She threw down the rag, sending water splashing over the edge of the basin. "Certainly not."

To get a better view, he leaned back in his chair. Her angry eyes shone like sunlit moss. How could he have ever found her fiery features cold?

While she silently fumed, he used his cupped hands to pour water over his chest and arms.

"You're making a mess." She grabbed the cloth and

wiped away the pink streaks left by his hurried effort.

He brushed her hand away. "It's a ship, Felicity. A little water isn't going to hurt anything."

She persisted despite his not-so-gentle hints to leave him alone. He noted the tilt of her chin, a sign he'd come to interpret as a prelude to battle. When he was drunk enough to deliver his news, the row they'd have was sure to rival anything in the past.

She dried him with quick, rough strokes. "I know what you're doing. You're not going to stop me from saying what I want to say."

He almost laughed. "Has anyone ever accomplished that feat, Miss Kendall?"

She looked him over. When she appeared satisfied, she placed the soiled rag in the pink-tinged water. After sitting down beside him, she focused all her attention on his face. The intensity of her gaze pulled him to her. He met her smoky eyes, something he'd been trying to avoid since entering the cabin.

"As I said, I misjudged you." She held up her hand when he tried to interrupt. "It doesn't matter what name you're using or who you're pretending to be. There is a man underneath all that who didn't deserve the horrible accusations I made."

He laughed, though the irony of her words left him with the feeling he'd swallowed an anchor rather than anything resembling amusement. "Oh, there are a few things I could say to change your mind."

She smiled and shook her head. It was a closemouthed grin, a gesture of confidence. "You've said things that should have irrevocably condemned you in my mind, but nothing has. And I have tried to persuade myself. I hate to be wrong."

"Felicity, you're not wrong. Trust your first instinct."

"I am trusting my instincts, and it's the first time I've truly done so in years." She gently placed her hand over his clenched one. "Children don't lie. They aren't clouded with notions of how people should be. The way Hugh looks at you . . ."

He couldn't stand another moment of her regaling him with praise for his good nature. "Felicity, your father's in jail. The Barbadian government believes he's my accomplice."

When she snatched her hand away from his, an Atlantic wind blew through his hollow chest. He hadn't meant to say it so bluntly, but now that it was out in the open, he was glad. Let her hate him for what he'd done to her father. Maybe her animosity would relieve some of his own self-loathing at the thought of Ben rotting in a jail cell while Drew tried to seduce his only daughter.

She flattened her palm against her chest. "I don't understand. How could you know this?"

"The ship we just took was the *Carolina*. She brought the news."

"That can't be." Her features wavered between disbelief and horror. "Surely no one would believe my father a pirate."

He topped off the brandy in the tankard and pushed it her way. "Drink. It gets worse." To his surprise, she took a large swig and hardly grimaced before she swallowed another. "All your father's ships have been seized. Captain McCulla was lucky enough to gain use of one in order to hunt me down. They believe Ben and I had something to do with Marley's death."

"That's ridiculous. A pirate killed Marley." She shook her head, as if trying to clear it. "My father would never do anything to break the law."

He'd not tell her of Ben's involvement in their scheme to sell pirated goods. At least he could spare her that. As sharp as she was, Drew found it amazing that she didn't know how heavily in debt her father had been when he fled Boston. The fact that she'd ignored the man's obvious faults spoke to her capacity for love. Not that Drew had experienced that kind of unconditional sentiment, or ever would. Still, it made the world seem less cruel to know it existed.

"My father came to Barbados and is offering a reward for my capture." No need to tell her of Marley's involvement. She'd never believe Drew hadn't killed him. Drew wouldn't believe it himself.

"How could he do that to you? What is your crime? Oh. Being his son."

Drew abruptly stood and paced the room. The look of compassion on her face proved harder to digest than he'd anticipated. That she soothed his soul with the very words he'd longed to hear didn't help. He strode back to her, leaned one hand on her chair and braced the other against the table. "I'm a pirate. Remember? Perhaps on your arrival in Barbados you missed some of my associates' heads rotting on spikes."

"But he's your father. And why is my father being accused? This isn't right."

The tremor in her voice forced him to straighten abruptly. If she started crying, he'd have no choice but to leave the room. He couldn't take much more of these emotions ravaging his sanity. His heroic sacrifice, giving up Felicity's seduction in order to tell her the truth about her father, should have freed him from his guilt. It hadn't. Her unhappiness made him even more miserable. Knowing he had inadvertently caused it cut him until he felt as if he would actually bleed.

Drew sat back in his chair and gulped brandy from the bottle. He needed fortification in order to stick this out. Leaving Felicity alone to face her hurt was not an option. To his dismay, his lowness had limits. With any luck, the brandy's heat would burn away the demons of emotion. He'd rather be stinking drunk than feel like this. But first he had to explain to her why he was such a complete and utter fiend.

"Knowing Ben, he tried to defend me. Since the Duke of Foxmoor can't set his hands on me, Ben gets to be the sacrificial lamb. I suspect they're hoping I'll come to his rescue."

Felicity's watery gaze hardened. "Your father wants you dead, doesn't he?"

"It appears so." He rubbed his forehead to avoid looking into her eyes.

She stood. Her angry footsteps told him she'd taken up pacing where he left off. "Those aristocrats think they can always have their way even if they trample good men in the process. If it weren't for their greed, my father would never have had to leave Boston in the first place. I won't stand for it anymore."

His neck ached from watching her stomp circles around the room. He got up and leaned against the table with his arms folded across his chest. "What in the hell do you intend to do about it? Have you forgotten I'm not exactly innocent in all this? Don't doubt for a minute I'm a pirate."

As she swung around to face him, her skirts swirled about her trim silk-clad ankles. "You were driven to it. Your father abandoned you. What were you supposed to do, starve? Or worse, stay an indentured servant? Anyone who cared to know you would realize that would never suit you. I don't blame you for escaping."

Drew tried to maintain his relaxed stance. Playing the callous bastard worthy of her hatred grew harder when she appeared not to know her role. She should be railing at him, not defending him. Though he suspected her tirade had more to do with salving his hurt feelings over his father's cruelty than defending his choice to become a pirate. God bless the female heart.

"Of course I agree with you about my being driven to a

life of crime. Even I'm convinced by your passionate defense of the good man gone bad, but I don't follow the rest. The only reason Ben is in jail is because they can't get their hands on me."

She stopped directly in front of him. Her touch on his cheek forced him to look into her eyes. "We both know the New England Trading Company barely broke even until you came along. If my father was a pauper, no one would have looked at him twice."

He laid his hand on top of hers and turned his face toward her palm. He shouldn't touch her, but her initiation of the contact made it impossible not to respond. "I gained that money illegally, Felicity. I used your father's business as a front for selling stolen goods on Barbados."

He should have told her more, but he couldn't let her know of his connection with El Diablo. Money might be a strong enough motivator for Barbados's current governor, a man infamous for corruption, to seize Ben's ships, but the population's terror of El Diablo was an infinitely more powerful reason to arrest Ben. Especially since El Diablo was accused of killing two of their citizens in their own home.

Felicity tucked a lock of hair behind his ear, forgiving him for things for which he hadn't asked forgiveness.

"I realize the company's wealth came from your stolen goods, but my father didn't. He's an honest man. He won't survive in prison."

It took everything in Drew's power not to draw her into his arms, quenching his hunger and her fears. He recognized the vulnerability behind her bravado. He captured her hand and brought it to his mouth, turning their joined hands to press his lips against her palm. The callous bastard be damned. He had to reassure her that her father would be fine, even if he wasn't sure himself.

"I won't let Ben stay in jail."

"If we go to Barbados and confront this Duke of Fox-whatever, they'll have to let my father go. You are his son, after all. That can't be a crime."

He flicked his tongue against her palm, then whispered against her bare wrist. "It's the Duke of Foxmoor . . . and I think impersonating his legitimate son might be a crime. I know piracy is."

The taste of her undid his good intentions to make her hate him. He swore he heard her moan softly before she pulled her wrist away and stepped back. Without hesitation, he let her go. Thank God she had the sense to pull away. He tried to remember how he had come to be licking her palm in the first place. His response to her nearness had taken over his common sense. If she touched him again, he feared he'd be lost.

Felicity folded her arms over her chest and drew a shaky breath. "I'll have to go back alone, then. The first step is to unite the merchant class in my father's defense. Common citizens have strength in numbers. When the duke realizes he's accused a well-respected member of the community—"

Drew pushed away from the table and stood before her. "Slow down, my little hurricane. I know Barbados would never be the same if you unleashed your fury upon its poor souls, but I have to handle this without your help."

She touched his shoulders lightly. He tried not to flinch at the contact on his bare skin. As if she sensed his unease, she let her hands glide down his arms to grip his hands. Not better. The draw of her palms along his skin sent a shiver he clamped down on his jaw to suppress.

"I can't sit idly by and watch my father's life destroyed at the whim of some self-centered aristocrat."

To break the skin-to-skin contact, he pulled her against his chest, careful to keep his hands on the thick layers of her corseted waist.

"Felicity, I don't want to have to rescue two Kendalls. Please, do it my way."

His brotherly hug might have worked if she hadn't leaned her curves into him in all the right places. He set her away from him with teeth-jarring abruptness.

She blinked in surprise. "You have a plan?"

He tried to think of something to say to satisfy her, but all he could do was stare at her parted lips. Her breath came in gusts of sweet scent that fogged his thinking. He had to take care of this woman, protect her. If he couldn't save her from himself, he'd save her from being snared in the web her father had.

"Trust me," he whispered, close enough so she could feel the brush of his words on her wet lips.

The urge to devour her held him in place. He feared it wouldn't be a simple kiss, but an all-out assault. His body wound tight and his control teetered on a fine thread stretched taut. A damning chant taunted him, reminding him of what he'd caused her father and binding him from moving. If Felicity had any sense of self-preservation, she'd stop staring at him through doelike eyes and remove herself to the other side of the room.

"I trust you, Drew." The opportunity she had asked for came, and she surprised herself by having the courage to grasp it. Unfortunately, it was her father's life at risk instead of her immortal soul. If not for Drew's deception, her father wouldn't be in prison at all; but her father had made a habit of trusting scoundrels, and at least Drew intended to right his wrong. Common sense dictated that she keep up her guard against him, but common sense had never assured her with the same determination she saw in Drew's eyes. She slid her hand under his hair to cup the back of his neck. "I trust you," she repeated with more conviction.

At her breathless declaration, Drew tensed and balled his hands into fists at his sides. She knew what he thought. Saw his battle in every hard line of his body. If she wanted

162

him to stop, if she had lost her nerve, she should say so now.

She forced her conscience to contemplate the question, though her heart already knew the answer. No, she didn't want him to stop. If she let this opportunity pass, she might never have another. The entirety of her adult life had been filled with regret. She had no intention of adding more. She wanted him to incinerate the barrier between the woman she forced herself to be and the woman she really was.

Before either of them came to their senses, she stood on her tiptoes and kissed him full on the mouth.

Instantly, he pulled her against him in an almost painful grip. His kiss mirrored her sense of urgency. There was no teasing build-up to the penetrating thrust of his tongue or the hard press of his lips. With shaking hands, she explored the contours of his tight, muscled chest. She dragged her fingertips through a patch of burnished hair, then slid to the smooth skin covering his ribs. Freely touching him was an intoxicant in and of itself. Though she dearly wanted to, she lost her nerve before she dared to go lower, and slipped her arms tentatively around his waist.

He wrenched his mouth from hers. His breath singed her when he spoke. "I won't play cat-and-mouse with you anymore, Felicity. I told you we would finish this, and finish it we will if I stay in this cabin a moment longer."

She traced wet kisses across his collarbone. The taste of his skin shattered any choice she had in the matter. "Stay," she said, then bit him lightly.

He swept her up in his arms and carried her to the bed. He dropped her roughly and was on her before she had a chance to protest or even catch her breath. She wondered if she should tell him she wasn't a virgin; then he was kissing her, and nothing else seemed to matter. The dreaded discovery of her tainted past had hinged on con-

163

demnation by a godly man. Drew's plundering kisses proved he wasn't that, if she'd ever had any doubt.

He alternately licked and kissed his way across her jaw, then followed the curve of her neck. Without ceasing his trek, he yanked down her bodice and continued his wet path over the swell of her breast. She gasped, both eager and mortified. She didn't know a grown man would want to do such a thing. Her eyes squeezed shut against the lush sensation. He drew her nipple into his mouth, sending a rush of liquid heat straight to her sex. She pushed against his unyielding shoulders, shocked by his boldness as well as her own reaction. But the drugging pleasure swept away her objections along with all rational thought.

She forced her eyes open to keep herself from being completely carried away by her dark desires. Late afternoon sunlight flickered through the oval windows lining the cabin, illuminating the slick trail where Drew's kisses had branded her. His dark hair fanned against her pale skin and his free hand possessively gripped her other breast, rubbing his thumb distractedly over the strained pink nipple. His closed eyelids fluttered with ecstasy.

When she realized he was enjoying this as much as she was, she had to remind herself to breathe. Without warning he pinched the nipple he toyed with, sending shards of erotic pleasure splintering down to her toes. Her sex tightened unbearably. She arched her back off the bed. Her fingers entwined in his tangled hair as she held him to her. "Please."

"Please what, sweeting?" he said, his voice husky.

She wasn't exactly sure if she was begging him to stop or to continue. Her heartbeat roared in her ears. She let her head fall back and struggled to find the right words. In an attempt to show him, she rotated her hips, brazenly rubbing against the leg he had positioned between her knees. It was her undoing.

"I want to feel you inside me." An urge desperate and

primal drove her past any inhibitions she'd ever had.

He jerked up his head and stared into her eyes. To her surprise, his obvious shock didn't shame her. Not when his eyes dilated with hunger.

"As you wish," he said, with a roughness she hadn't heard in his voice before. The sound alone was a new kind of seduction.

Slowly, he moved over her. Their coupling would be a closeness she could understand. He would share her hunger instead of making her the feast. Not that she didn't like it, or her breasts didn't ache at his sudden retreat, but she needed him to be as swept away as she.

He grabbed the hem of her dress and pushed it, along with her underskirts, up to her hips. All the last-minute tugs of conscience were forgotten when he touched the back of her knee and nudged her legs farther apart. She moaned when he dragged his fingers up the inside of her thigh. In equal proportions, she feared he'd touch the center of her desire and that he wouldn't. No one had ever told her men and woman did things like this, touching and kissing in secret places.

When he reached the apex of her thighs, he ran his fingers through her curls, then circled her with his index finger. She rocked her hips and called out his name on a desperate breath. She soon learned his grazing caress wasn't enough. It was only just another step in her descent into madness. For a moment, she wondered if he was purposely torturing her for all the trouble she'd caused him.

"Easy, sweeting. The longer I take, the better you'll like it." He slipped a single finger inside her.

A flood of liquid warmth dampened her thighs at his touch. He cursed, then quickly withdrew his finger. Her cheeks and breasts burned with embarrassment over her uncontrollable response.

He must have noticed her discomfort because he nuzzled her ear and whispered, "You feel too good. I don't want to prove myself inadequate in this. Though I fear you might outmatch me once again."

He kissed her hard on the mouth and reentered her. The fullness of two fingers had her convulsively clutching him, each grip sending out stronger spasms of pleasure. He moved in and out, simulating a rhythm she longed for him to duplicate with his body. Her world narrowed to the feel of his tongue in her mouth and the fingers he slid inside her. Without a will of her own, she matched his rhythm with her hips. She grasped his shoulders, urging him deeper inside.

When he pulled away, she struggled to her elbows, not caring that her legs spread and her sex pulsed in his full view. He sat on his knees, his gaze fixed upon her bare breasts, before dropping lower.

Blindly he yanked at the strings of his breeches. His stare touched her physically. She didn't move to cover herself, but watched his muscles flex while he tugged at the lacing. His breathing came heavy, and for the first time in their acquaintance he appeared completely unmasked. Raw with need and want.

When he finally managed to undo the ties on each side of his waistband, a triangular flap fell forward, exposing him. Her slight intake of breath probably warned him he'd made a tactical error. She raised her heavy gaze up to his face, then back down to the violent jut of his sex. She'd never seen a man's privates before. With Erik, it had been dark and they were both fully dressed. There'd been no coaxing touches, and little kissing. He took her before she had a chance to change her mind. And she certainly would have if she had seen this.

Drew lifted her chin back to his face. "Lay back and let me love you. All will be fine. I promise."

He placed his hands on her shoulders and tried to gently persuade her to lie flat on her back. The softness of his words eased some of her fears, but not completely. Her slight anxiety added an element of danger to her already heightened arousal. There was no turning back now; her body craved him despite her fear. Before he could lower her to the bed, she wrapped her fingers around his rigid flesh, testing to see if he was as unyielding as he appeared. He jerked at her touch.

"Did I hurt you?" He was as hot as a flame, but the way the muscles in his stomach tightened and his breathing quickened told her she hadn't. Her touch was as torturing to him as his slow exploration had been to her. She slid her hand up his length and was rewarded by his soft groan.

Abruptly, he grabbed her wrist. "Let go or this will be over before we start."

She smiled and allowed him to guide her down to the bed. Her anxiety faded to a demanding anticipation.

He kissed her deeply, then pulled away to position himself between her legs. On braced arms, he slid across her swollen flesh without entering her.

She pushed his breeches down to his thighs and kneaded his taut flanks. Her fingers dug into him, pulling him to her as she pushed up with her hips. She had been waiting for this too long to draw it out any longer. For most of her adult life, she'd held herself in a prison of her own making and the moment he took her, she'd be free.

He shifted his weight to his knees so he could grab both of her wrists and stretch her arms above her head. "You are making it awfully hard to give you a pleasurable experience."

"Make love to me," she demanded. "I'm ready."

"I don't want to hurt you, Felicity. The slower we go, the easier it will be."

She met his gaze. "I'm not a virgin."

He blinked. "What?"

She closed her eyes to block out his startled expression. She hadn't meant to say it, but she could tell he held back, and she refused to have less than his uncontrolled lust.

Drew had made her want him from the moment he'd first held her gaze in his powerful grip and she deserved all that his penetrating stares had promised. She needed him to be as weak in his hunger as she was in hers.

He released her wrists and moved away from her, forcing her to open her eyes. He sat on his heels and studied her. His chest rose and fell with each breath. She dropped her gaze lower. Her confession hadn't cooled his desire in the least. In fact, he seemed to swell under her direct gaze. A drop of moisture clung to his tip, assuring her that she wasn't the only one who revealed her need so openly.

A glimpse of his face found him watching her with such single-minded intensity, his breath quickening through his parted lips, she suspected her gawking had aroused him as much as her touch. The madness that had gotten them this far surged within Felicity. As if he could somehow control her by his stare, she rotated her hips. His gaze dropped to her sex and his release of breath was audible.

He crawled between her thighs, his face close to hers. "Ah . . . Would you care to elaborate? Quickly?"

She let her hands glide across his tensed flanks to the tight muscles in the backs of his thighs. In her coaxing exploration, her fingers accidentally brushed him, and he sucked in his breath. His gaze shuttered and he no longer appeared capable of simple speech, much less having a lengthy discussion about her past.

"Please. No questions. Just make love to me."

He remained poised above her. The muscles in his arms strained with tension. She had the unsettling realization that this might well be the last time she was ever this close to another human being. Surely he wouldn't deny her this because she had slipped and revealed her worst secret. She turned her head and kissed the inside of his elbow with her open mouth. "I need you."

"You're full of surprises, Felicity Kendall. And I have to say this is one of the better ones." He dropped his head and watched as he rubbed the length of his erection against her wet passage. She arched against him and he gritted his teeth. "I need you too."

He braced his weight on his hands. "Guide me," he said, in a tone that didn't reflect his teasing of mere seconds before.

She reached between them and gripped him. His eyes were closed, but he moved to her slight pressure as if she controlled his body as easily as her own. The first blunt touch against her sensitized opening sent waves of ecstasy to wash away her fears. But then he pushed forward, taking control and stretching her with a sharp jolt. As if sensing her discomfort, he paused until the invading pressure was eased by pleasure and her body pulsed in invitation. She gripped his forearms, urging him to continue. This was nothing like her first time. If Drew didn't slide deeper, she'd be digging her nails into his skin. Instead of surging into her, he withdrew slightly and pushed forward again, stretching her slowly to accommodate him. She rocked her hips, wishing he'd hurry, but he retreated again.

"This will be better if you let me lead." He leaned down and licked a path from the hollow under her jaw to her ear. "Surrender to me, Felicity," he whispered.

With great effort, she forced herself to relax and breathe while she waited for him to fill her. Each small thrust of his hips was torture. It must have been for him as well, because a fine sheen shone on his shoulders and beaded his upper lip. She gripped the sheets to keep from grinding her hips into his.

When she knew she couldn't stand another second of his slow, shallow strokes, he surged to fill her completely, then stilled. But his sweet torture wasn't over. While he stayed snug against her, he moved in a way that pressed a sensitized knot deep inside her. She gasped and rolled her hips against the new assault.

"Like that?" he asked with a satisfied smirk in his voice.

"No." But another gasp and a soft moan gave her away. "I don't believe you." His voice deepened, and she sensed he was ready for more as desperately as she.

Finally, he moved again. His rhythm began in slow, coaxing strokes, then quickly grew harder and faster. Each thrust compounded in urgency. He wrapped his arm underneath her knee, forcing it back in his attempt to be deeper inside her. Her hips matched his escalating rhythm while her arms clutched him to her. Lost to the demands of her body, she felt as if she were being sucked down a dark tunnel. Then, without warning, all her coiled need unfurled in spasms of pleasure so intense she had to bite down against crying out. She stiffened and arched against him. In the end, she couldn't control the sigh of release torn from her throat. He thrust deep within her and stayed, letting her battle the waves coursing through her.

When she had barely caught her breath, he rose up on his elbows and moved again. After only a few deep strokes, his whole body tensed. A fierce intake of breath told her he'd succumbed to his own violent undoing. His head sagged and his face lay hidden in the fall of his hair. She brushed back the heavy strands, wanting to see the loss of control she'd felt. He turned his face away, but she still glimpsed the intensity of his release in the harsh line of his jaw. Slowly, he lowered himself on top of her. Chest to chest, she could feel his heart race unsteadily.

He rolled to his side, pulling her into his arms. They lay with their heads on the same pillow, face to face. In the entirety of her life, Felicity had never felt closer to another human being. She gazed into his eyes and saw the depths of his soul. And for once, she kept hers open as well, letting him see all there was to see. Unlike her first foray into intimacy, the aftermath of this encounter would be worth the all-encompassing peace she felt at that very moment. If she didn't know better, she might call it love.

\* \* \*

It took all Drew's strength to pull his drenched skin away from Felicity's. The full moon peered from its vantage point high in the sky, shone through the porthole, revealing it was well after midnight. Drew hadn't left the cabin since walking in to deliver the news that he was sure would drive Felicity away from him forever. As usual, she had surprised him.

He moved a tangle of her hair to kiss her pale, moon-bathed shoulder. Her dress remained twisted around her waist. He suddenly realized he still wore his boots, and his breeches were shoved below his knees. Next time, he'd undress her and kiss every inch of her, including the sweet fruit hidden by those lush nether curls that matched the ones gripped in his fist. He wondered if she'd balk at the idea. He nuzzled her ear with a grin. Probably not. Her passion matched his own.

He eased off the bed and straightened his breeches. After he rummaged in the wardrobe on the far wall for a clean shirt, he paused to gawk at Felicity. She burrowed deeper into the soft bed. After a second round of lovemaking, she was undoubtedly exhausted. She probably wouldn't awaken till noon.

A quick stab of sensation brought back the moment he'd first pushed into her tight body, and it had him aroused all over again. He closed his eyes and pictured the second time, the way they had laid on the sides, face to face. Still slick with sweat, they'd started exploring each other. Not passionate at first, just testing the new boundaries of their intimacy. Drew touched the tip of her nose, the fleshy part of her earlobe, and then grazed the swell on the underside of her breast. In return, she'd traced his lips with her fingertip, then, coaxed by his tongue, stuck her finger into his mouth. He'd sucked the digit until she threw her leg over his hip and let him slide into her, each of them grasping and rocking, wrenching all the ecstasy they could from each other.

171

He shook his head to clear the vision. He had prisoners in the hold, he reminded himself sternly. Prisoners who knew who he was. His father had not only betrayed him but also assumed he was a cold-blooded murderer. Ben was in jail. Drew stopped his hasty lacing of his shirt. Ben would not be pleased with Drew's behavior this evening. That damn guilt started tightening his chest again.

He bent over to tuck his breeches into his boots. Blood finally rushed to his head, the smart one. The ramifications of what he'd just done pushed themselves through the satisfied haze of quenched lust. He glanced at Felicity, making sure she hadn't disappeared. She looked like a cat who'd just gotten cream for the first time. Even in her sleep she grinned.

Her happiness did little to ease a swift stab of regret, though. Surely, she wasn't in love with him. She had hated him up until . . . He wasn't exactly sure when their relationship shifted—but it had. They understood each other. Felicity was a grown woman, not a girl. She knew what happened between them had nothing to do with deeper feelings. His desperate need to convince himself sounded weak in his own ears. How would it sound to her?

If he was honest with himself, he would admit he'd wanted to seduce her the night of the Linleys' party. Better than usual, his conscience had put up the pretense of a struggle, but it knew it always fell back before his desire. Unfortunately, there were a gaggle of other emotions besides lust attached to his relationship with Felicity. Emotions he couldn't afford to think about. Not at the moment.

Felicity's unexpected reaction to his advances hadn't helped him do the right thing, either. At least she hadn't been a virgin. He wouldn't have her deflowering to add to his list of crimes.

He stilled at the realization. As silently as a creature of the night, he strode to the bed to gaze down into her face.

Her innocent features didn't give him any answers to the thousand questions crowding his mind. As curious as he was, he'd honored her request not to be interrogated. But that was in the heat of the moment. Now that his head had cleared, he'd like a few explanations. Not that he minded her lack of chastity; in fact, it was a trait he cheered the abandonment of in the fairer sex. Nothing in her manner, however—in bed or out—spoke of a string of lovers. Her raw passion held no hint of artifice or experience. The man who had gotten to her before him had undoubtedly meant something to Miss Kendall.

It seemed Felicity had a few secrets of her own, and as much as the knowledge should have brought him relief, it unexpectedly made Drew see green.

# Chapter Eleven

The cabin door banged open and interrupted Felicity's passionate embrace of Drew's pillow. Her gaze jerked up to find Hugh skipping into the cabin. Solomon followed, his hands occupied with a tray. Warmth spread to Felicity's cheeks. She couldn't have felt any guiltier if an *A* had been embroidered on her low-cut bodice. She loosened her grip on the pillow she held to her face and pretended to fluff it.

Hugh regarded her quizzically, while Solomon avoided eye contact altogether.

"Why were you smelling that pillow?" asked Hugh in a combination of innocence and accusation that could only be believable in a child.

"Don't be silly. I was only making the bed." She glanced at the rumpled sheets and wished she had concocted something else to cover her shameful fondling of Drew's pillow.

When she'd awoken to late morning sun pushing through the portholes, Drew had disappeared and their night together seemed no more than a dream. Yet the satisfied ache in her muscles, along with the heady fragrance of their erotic encounter, assured her every whispered word and frantic caress had been real. His scent on the pillow had rekindled the details and made her heart pound.

Hugh tried to yank the pillow she clutched to her chest away from her. "I'll help you make the bed."

She held the damning evidence above her head while she blocked his advance and his view. "That won't be necessary, Hugh. My, what a feast you brought. Why don't you help your father set the table?"

Hugh followed her suggestion without the slightest hint he noticed her discomposure. Solomon's stiff movements as he banged the silver dishes told her any attempt to keep him from noticing the enormous four-poster bed's tangled bedclothes would be in vain.

"My apologies for startling you. The captain thought you might be sleeping and didn't wish you disturbed when I left your breakfast."

She forced herself to look serene, if not innocent, when she strode toward the table. Her swollen lips and stubble-burned cheeks prevented any hope of that. "So much food and such elegant serving dishes. Do you two plan to join me?"

"Miss Kendall, I must say, in our short acquaintance, I've never seen you so cheerful." Solomon's dry tone deflated her smile. "Sleep well, did you?"

Hugh interrupted, saving her from choking out an answer. "I already ate. We stole those dishes. I helped. Will you teach me some more writing?" Hugh turned to his father, holding a tattered piece of parchment in his outstretched hand. "Look at what I wrote, Papa."

Solomon pulled his attention away from the stiff performance of his duties to glance at the paper his son waved in his face. Felicity swallowed hard, forcing herself to stand straighter. Obviously Solomon suspected what went on last night and didn't approve. She shouldn't be surprised by his censure, nor should she expect to escape the consequences of her indiscretion. Try as she might, she didn't care. Her body still tingled from Drew's thorough attentions. A real smile crept to her face.

Solomon scanned his son's work. His gaze met Felicity's over the sheet of paper. He was not smiling, but the cool look of judgment had left his dark eyes. "Thank you for teaching Hugh. I would be grateful if you'd continue. Perhaps—that's if you don't mind—I could join in on the lessons?"

She felt her smile widen until her cheeks hurt. Solomon's minor concession might well be the keys to a kingdom. Everything seemed so much more wonderful today. "I would love to. You're welcome to watch, but you've no need to worry over my capabilities as a teacher. My education exceeds that of most women, or men, for that matter."

Solomon continued picking up the dishes left from dinner two days past. "You didn't even get a proper meal yesterday. The captain put me in charge of feeding you and I've been neglectful. I made a tray for you last night, but—"

She interrupted before he went any further. "I understand, Solomon. No need for apologies." After draping her rose-colored skirts over the cushioned seat, she lifted the silver cover from a plate steaming with poached eggs. Hunger pangs thudded against her ribs.

"I'm famished. Thank you both for the feast."

Solomon relaxed visibly. "Those are real chicken eggs. Drew said to give you the best we had. There's bread and smoked fish as well."

"Thank you," Felicity said through a mouth full of food. Usually she had better manners, but she seemed to be doing many things out of character these days. "Please sit. I'll begin Hugh's lesson as soon as I've finished eating."

Hugh plopped down in the seat next to her. "Can I have

another piece of paper? I want to draw an octopus. I've seen one before. Have you? The one I saw was dead and smelled like—"

"Hugh, let Miss Kendall finish her breakfast." Solomon picked up the tray laden with dirty dishes. "I have some duties to attend to first, but please start the lesson without me. I'll have to catch up anyway."

She stopped devouring the eggs long enough to answer. "You haven't missed much. I just went through the basics."

Solomon squared his already broad shoulders. The tension she noticed before returned. "I don't know the basics, Miss Kendall. I was hoping you could teach me with Hugh."

She tried to blink away her surprise, sure she'd misunderstood. "But you're the quartermaster. Doesn't that involve keeping records?"

"I have my own system that serves me quite well." His words were delivered with such finality, she fully expected him to stalk from the cabin. Instead, he stayed where he was. "Still, I'd like to learn to read and write properly."

She felt like a fool. A runaway slave wouldn't have had much opportunity to learn to read and write. Obviously, his request had come at great personal cost. Solomon wore his pride like a shield. "Of course. It would encourage Hugh if you participated in his lessons."

Solomon nodded, then turned to leave.

"Solomon," she called out. "Hurry back. I don't know how much time we have before we reach Barbados, but we'll need every moment to get you two reading and writing."

He paused at the door. "We're not going to Barbados. To the best of my knowledge, we don't have a specific destination. We should have all the time we need."

"What?" She slowly lowered her forkful of food.

"Is something wrong, Miss Kendall?"

"I thought . . . It's just that I thought . . ." She wondered if the chill settling around her heart showed in her eyes. The hint of Drew's possible betrayal pricked like a thorn. She hid the unexpected slice of pain behind a rush of bravado. "I assumed taking me home was the captain's first order of business. I'm sure he's as eager to have me out of his hair as you are."

Solomon's raised eyebrows signaled his skepticism. "We both know that's not true. At least the part about the captain wanting to be rid of you."

Drew might want her, but had he lied to obtain her? Her rediscovery of her buried sexuality had been all-consuming. It hadn't occurred to her that Drew might deceive her just to make use of her body. Of course, she knew their liaison was purely physical. Unlike with Erik, whom she thought loved her, would marry her, she expected no such promises from Drew. Knowing this she assumed would protect her from the devastation of being rejected. Suddenly she realized there where far worse things than a broken heart. Instead of just gambling with her own future, had she gambled with her father's as well?

She pushed away the plate of food, her appetite evaporated with the sting of reality. "I can't eat. I'm worried about my father. I need to return to Barbados immediately."

Solomon relaxed his stance, rattling the dishes on the tray. "We'll see to getting you back as soon as possible. I'll talk to the captain." He turned to go.

She stopped him before he reached the door. "You're anxious to be rid of me. Aren't you, Solomon?"

Solomon shook his head. "It's not for myself that I'm concerned. I am grateful for your interest in educating Hugh. My fear is for the crew—and that the captain is too anxious to keep you."

Before Felicity could recover from his remark or question him further, Solomon left the room. She recognized compassion in the man's eyes when she'd mentioned her father. He'd even offered to speak to Drew on her behalf. But was he friend or foe?

Hugh tugged on her arm. "Can I draw?"

Felicity tried to shake off her troubled thoughts so she could focus on the child. "First I want you to recite the letters we learned yesterday."

After the letter *C*, Hugh's recitation fell on deaf ears despite Felicity's best efforts to pay attention. She glanced out the window and guessed it to be close to noon. Drew would come soon. She would not listen to the dark voice warning her that he was just like Erik, was only using her for his own ends. The way Drew had made love to her should be proof enough of the two men's vast differences. Drew had asked for her trust and she willingly gave it, and so much more. He would not promise to help her father, ravish her, then forget about the whole thing. Would he?

A moan slipped from Avery Sneed's slack lips. Drew stilled his careful ministrations until the unconscious man relaxed. Again, Drew started to pull the blood-soaked bandages from the wound, wincing himself when the cloth stuck unmercifully.

"How is he?" asked a deep, melodic voice somewhere behind him.

Solomon's silent approach startled Drew, but years of living by nothing but his wits had trained him not to show any outward reaction. He continued with his task, as if Solomon had not just appeared out of nowhere. "I didn't think our lanky Mr. Sneed could look any more gaunt, but I was wrong."

In the faint glimmer of sunlight seeping from the deck above, Avery Sneed resembled a corpse. With the added glow of a lantern, Drew could see that Avery struggled to take shallow breaths. Each slight shudder of his thin chest gave Drew hope. Most captains would have resigned themselves to his death. A gut wound was almost always fatal.

179

Their lack of a qualified surgeon lessened the man's chances even more.

Solomon silently stood over Drew as he worked. The quartermaster had a way of tempering Drew's streak of stubbornness with common sense. He knew by Solomon's patient stance what the man wished to say: Tending Avery Sneed was a futile endeavor. In this case, Drew didn't think he would appreciate his friend's dependable rationality.

"Shouldn't you be instructing the navigator on our next course, Captain?"

"I came to check on Avery after I questioned the prisoners. The boy you assigned to take the surgeon's place didn't know what the hell he was doing."

"And you do?" Solomon moved closer, examining the wound himself.

In the small airless room, the quartermaster's unyielding presence suffocated Drew. The cabin used to store supplies was hardly suitable as a sickroom, but it was all they had for privacy, and at least it was quiet. Drew would have used his own cabin, but Felicity occupied it. Surely, Solomon had something to say about that too. Drew forced his thoughts away from Felicity and what had happened yesterday. He'd already badly neglected his obligations as captain because of his weakness for her. Felicity and the change in their relationship would have to wait.

Drew glanced at Solomon. "If you insist on hovering over me, you can put yourself to use. Hand me the brandy on the crate beside you."

Solomon passed Drew the bottle. "Has Miss Kendall driven you to drink before noon?"

Drew ignored him and poured the amber liquid over Avery's wound. The wounded man no longer had the strength to even whimper.

"Drew—," began Solomon.

"Don't say it. I know his chances aren't good and we've lost plenty of crewmen before, but Avery's been with us

180

longer than most. If he isn't going to get the benefit of a bloody surgeon, then I'm going to try to keep him alive as long as possible."

He left out the part about his guilt over Avery's injury. He'd been so concerned with not hurting the men of the *Carolina*, he hadn't ensured the safety of his own crew. If Felicity wasn't on the ship, he would have acted differently. Why, was something he was not ready to think about right now.

Solomon picked up the bundle of clean bandages sitting next to the brandy and gave them to Drew one by one. "I still need to know the course you wish to take. Did the prisoners give any clues to El Diablo's location?"

"Well, that's bloody unlikely since I'm El Diablo and they know it," snapped Drew. As soon as he placed the clean strip of cloth over Avery's wound, red devoured white.

"I meant the impostor, the man responsible for Marley's death."

"No. They thought I was insane, asking where they saw me last. It seems the bloody bastard has disappeared." Drew thought to apologize for his outburst, but he was already doing too many things out of character—like apologizing and snapping at Solomon. "I haven't slept much," he added, a concession to his conscience.

"I didn't think you'd slept at all."

Drew waited for the rest. Thankfully, it didn't come. "You can tell the navigator to plot a course for the Bahamas. If the bastard isn't hiding out there, someone else will know about him."

Solomon angled Avery so Drew could wrap the dressing around his thin chest. "The Bahamas are overrun with other pirates. Do you really think it's one of the Brethren who's impersonating you?"

A member of the Brethren—the name by which the loosely knit brotherhood of pirates referred to themselves—

was a definite possibility for the source of his troubles. Of course, a more logical source came to mind, but Drew refused to consider it. His noble father might be a lot of things, but not a murderer of old men and women. "Who else? Nobody becomes a pirate for the fraternity."

While Drew added a second bandage, Solomon held Avery in a sitting position. "But why kill Marley?"

"Why not? Marley was advertising his windfall loud enough. He was an easy target. And with flotillas of His Majesty's ships scouring the trade routes, new sources of revenue have to be found."

Solomon gently guided Avery back to the table. "No. Marley's murder was personal. They wanted to point the finger at you. Someone knows about your connection with the New England Trading Company. I know it seems extreme and complicated but your father—"

"No." Leave it to Solomon to read the fears Drew wouldn't even admit to himself. "He's a bloody duke. They don't have to murder people. They can just snub them out of existence."

Drew tied the ends of the bandage and continued. "Perhaps Marley spoke of Lord Christian's connection to El Diablo to someone besides my father. I suspect Marley was killed for either money or revenge. Spreading rumors that El Diablo committed the murders was a logical solution to hide the crimes. And I think our culprit has to be a pirate—or at least have the heart of one."

Drew had long ago eliminated any of the pampered planters on Barbados from his list of suspects. Philip Linley might be put out with Drew for bedding his wife, but the man wasn't a killer of innocent women.

Drew immersed his bloodstained hands in a bucket of salt water. "Maybe I'm wrong and the impostor's not a pirate. But whoever he is, he needed a pirate crew to carry out the deeds he wanted done, and the Bahamas would be the best place to find one. I'll see to the navigation myself."

Solomon blocked Drew's exit. "Have you considered the culprit may be a certain Spaniard after revenge? They don't like it when you escape from their prisons or seduce their daughters."

Drew grinned for the first time since leaving Felicity's arms late last night. "I'm well aware of that possibility, Mr. Quartermaster. That's why I'll do the navigation. And I'm steering us as far away from the Spanish Main as possible."

Solomon finally stepped aside to let Drew brush by. "What of the men we took from the *Carolina*? We can't keep them in the hold indefinitely."

"We'll drop them off in Nassau. There's a semblance of civilization in New Providence since Woodes Rogers became governor. From there, they can find a ship back to Barbados. The longer it takes them to spread word of our acquaintance, the better it will be for Ben."

Solomon stopped him before he slipped through the door. "And Miss Kendall; are you going to drop her off in Nassau as well?"

"I can't leave her there. It's still overrun with the worst dregs of humanity. It will take Rogers more than a few hangings to clean that place up entirely."

He hadn't been fast enough to escape Solomon's probing questions about Felicity. Drew leaned against the doorjamb, bracing himself for an argument on a subject he wasn't entirely clear on himself.

Solomon didn't disappoint him. "We're still close to Antigua. You could leave her there. It's a British colony. She'll have no trouble finding her way to Barbados with coin enough to get her there. We could also find her a trustworthy companion."

"And lose two days? I don't have time to waste. I have to find a pirate for the British to hang before they decide Ben will do."

There it was. Drew didn't want to think about it, much less admit it out loud, but there it was: He wasn't going to let Felicity go. She'd worked her way under his skin, and the joining of their bodies only made his desire for her stronger. He didn't know if the same unnavigable current pulled her to him as it had him to her, but there could be no other explanation for the change in her, or his desire to keep her close and safe—even against his better judgment.

Solomon shook his head. "I think you're making a mistake. Miss Kendall seemed eager to return to Barbados."

"Of course she wants to go back to Barbados. She thinks she can help Ben. But we both know she'd only end up causing trouble. It's better for everyone involved if we keep her with us until this is over."

By the frown hardening Solomon's face, Drew expected him to comment on the trouble Felicity was likely to cause onboard, but the man said nothing. Drew had thought of it himself. But the only reasonable thing was to hold on to her.

His justifications eased the tension in his gut when he thought of sending Felicity away, either back to Barbados or Boston. He owed it to Ben to keep her safe, and knowing her propensity for rash action, that would best be accomplished by keeping careful watch over her. Ben might not be overwhelmed with gratitude regarding Drew's seduction of his daughter, but Drew couldn't think of that part right now.

He turned to leave, weary of a subject that had plagued him since his blood had cooled and he'd realized what he'd done. His lack of regret for bedding Felicity worried him almost as much as his urgent desire to do so again.

Solomon followed him out into the companionway. "When I spoke to Miss Kendall this morning, she seemed distressed to learn we weren't returning to Barbados. She tried to hide it, but she was momentarily at a loss for words. I'm sure that doesn't happen often."

Drew swung around to face Solomon, hoping he could

hide his distress better than Felicity. "You talked to her this morning? What did you tell her?"

Solomon shrugged. "Nothing, really. I certainly didn't reveal you're the infamous El Diablo whose name is a curse on every God-fearing man's lips."

Drew rubbed his forehead. "Just try not to say much to her. She has a way of getting information you don't intend to give her."

"I'll manage. And you?"

Drew reached for the ladder. "I told you I can handle Felicity, and I will."

"I can see that."

"Try to force some water down Avery. I'll check on his dressing again this afternoon, then I need to get some sleep."

"Aye, Captain," Solomon said.

As Drew climbed up the steps leading to the main deck, the quartermaster called one last piece of advice: "If you plan on getting any sleep at all today, I would avoid using your cabin."

Felicity, Drew thought. He couldn't think about her right now.

# Chapter Twelve

In the dim passage leading to his cabin, a shadow moved. Drew blinked, unsure of what he saw. The sun's last rays, dancing brilliantly against the water before sinking into the sea, had left his vision spotty. Stepping into the darkness temporarily blinded him. Still, he swore someone watched him from the shadows. Solomon had been with him on the upper deck only moments before. Hugh was supposed to be splicing rope with another crewman. No one else should have been in this companionway.

Drew shook off the premonition of danger, a reaction to too many years of being an outlaw. On his ship, he was safe.

The fading sun spilled a shaft of muted light through the open hatch. It struck metal. A figure emerged from the shadows, pointing a pistol at his chest.

A flash of instinct urged Drew to lunge at his assailant. Grabbing just beyond the glimmer of metal rewarded him with the feel of bones and skin. His opponent appeared too stunned to react. Drew yanked the man's arm above his head, forcing the weapon out of range. In the same instant, Drew used his body to slam his attacker against the ship's inner hull, pinning him with his weight. Full contact revealed his mistake. A soft feminine grunt escaped with an exhalation of breath.

"Felicity?"

"Drew." Relief punctuated her voice and the sudden slump of her body against his.

Every curve she possessed tormented his raw nerves. Vivid details of their lovemaking flooded his senses. His body grew taut, reacting with much too much enthusiasm to her nearness.

"I thought one of the prisoners escaped," he murmured close to her mouth. Before he could think better of it, he kissed her. He lost himself in the softness of her lips. His reasons for avoiding his cabin all day suddenly seemed unimportant. The smell and taste of her overcame any point in reasoning. He tore his mouth away from hers, looking for a place to support both their weights.

The red glow of early dusk poured through the open hatch and banished his wayward thoughts. Anyone could glance from abovedeck and see him on the verge of devouring Felicity whole. He slowly woke from his drugged lust. Had she been pointing a gun at him?

He had one hand on Felicity's breast and the other low on her back, pressing her against his arousal. Peeling her off him was almost painful. Felicity's arms had been draped around him. With his withdrawal, they fell to her sides.

He grabbed the pistol dangling from her limp hand. "What the hell is this?"

Felicity's hooded gaze narrowed. Lips that were still slightly parted and wet from his kisses pursed. "I'm angry with you."

Drew stepped back and guided her into the privacy of his cabin. "Obviously. You can tell me about it inside. You know you're not to leave the cabin."

She sidestepped his touch, entering the room of her own accord. Her sudden distance cooled everything like a dousing of winter rain. "Oh, yes, for my own safety. Well, it's not so safe inside your cabin, either."

"And what's that supposed to mean?" he asked. But he knew full well what she meant. He teetered between anger and self-recrimination. Anger seemed the better way to fall. "I was the one who was almost shot. What is my crime? Not being a saint? I believe that makes two of us."

Felicity whirled around to face him. "You promised to help my father."

"And I intend to. What were you doing outside, anyway? I thought we understood each other." Drew was relieved that her first attack was something he had an excuse for. His reason for bedding a vulnerable woman under his care was something he had yet to justify, even to himself.

"By going back on your word the moment you've gotten what you want. If that's your idea of helping my father, then we don't understand each other at all." Her voice cracked. Just as quickly as she had faced him moments before, she turned around, showing Drew her back.

The thudding sound of his own heart echoed in his ears. A combination of foolishness and overconfidence had mistakenly led him to believe he could remain detached after he'd seduced Felicity. What he'd expected her reaction to be, he couldn't say. Or rather, he hadn't bothered to take into consideration. The soft purple fog of dusk drifted through the windows, providing Drew with the illusion of cover in which to watch Felicity. His anger at her leaving his cabin slipped in the face of his own unscrupulous behavior.

He'd pacified distraught lovers before, but with Felicity he was at a loss. A pretty bouquet of half-truths and outright lies whispered against her neck would enrage her. The truth was he wanted to give her more than that, but he had nothing to offer. An apology for taking advantage of the situation didn't seem appropriate—especially since he wasn't sorry.

"Nothing has changed." He stepped toward her with the intention of placing a brotherly pat on her rounded shoulder, nothing more. Though he hadn't expected hysterics from her, he assured himself he could deal with this. Realizing she wasn't that much different from other women gave him a shaky boost of confidence. Maybe now he could put his own feelings in perspective.

His fingers barely grazed her before she shrugged off his touch, stepping away. With her spine stiff, she turned to face him again, a picture of composure. He was thankful for the fading light that shielded him from her gaze, which experience warned would be cold and cutting.

"Then why, pray tell, are we not returning to Barbados to arrange my father's release?"

"I won't be much use to Ben dead, and that's exactly what I would be if I stepped foot on Barbados. Or is that what you had in mind?"

Her balled fists indicated he'd nicked her composure again. "How dare you? I'm not the one who has gone back on her word. I've no need to defend myself."

"Nor do I, but you've already condemned me. May I ask what offense has warranted my execution—not going to Barbados or ravishing you?" Drew retrieved the pistol from his waistband and held it out to her.

Blue twilight had overtaken the room. Felicity had to move closer to see what he held. "I wasn't going to shoot you. I went to find you and took the pistol for protection. You told me your ship was dangerous."

"You knew bloody damn well you weren't supposed to leave the cabin, so why did you?" He felt the anger creeping up his neck all over again and found it a welcome relief to being on the defensive.

She lifted her chin, letting him know she was not about

to be intimidated by his show of temper. "Because you were avoiding me. As you are now."

"I had things to do, but I'm here now, and I'll explain if you let me."

With a curt nod, she settled in a chair at the table.

He had no idea what explanation he would give. The truth in her accusation struck him hard. All day he'd told himself he was too busy, but the reality was, he was afraid to face her. That she could see through him so easily scared him more than he'd ever admit.

He pulled out the chair beside her but was too anxious to sit. Instead, he leaned his hip against the table and crossed his arms over his chest. While he thought of what to say, he gazed at Felicity.

She had arranged her hair in a tight knot and wore the same gown as she had the day before. Though it was probably the most demure of the gowns in the trunk, if he lit a candle he'd be able to see a good portion of her pale breasts. Leering at her wasn't likely to help his cause. Besides, darkness was better for confessions and lying. With Felicity, a little of both was his best line of defense.

"Freeing Ben involves capturing the man who killed Marley. If I return to Barbados without someone for them to arrest, Ben could stay in jail for the rest of his life or hang right beside me."

She patted the knot imprisoning her hair. "My father could already be hanged by the time you accomplish that feat. Besides, you said everyone knows you aren't really related to the Duke of Foxmoor. Why should they believe you, even if you do manage to capture El Diablo? They all know you're a charlatan."

A derogatory name he'd used to describe himself, sometimes with pride, rankled from Felicity's lips. Her obvious lack of confidence in his abilities didn't sit well either. Nor did the fact that his plan didn't sound any better to him than it did to her. But he had no other solution. If he tried to break Ben out of jail, he'd no doubt be captured. He was sure the Barbadians were planning for just such an attempt. As vague as it might sound, finding out who killed Marley might give Drew a clue as to his next step. But he wasn't about to share his doubts with Felicity.

"Since you're keeping record of the facts, I *am* related to the Duke of Foxmoor. On all other counts, you are correct. I've already been condemned, as has Ben, by association to me. If I can give the Barbadians Marley's killer, they can at least stop blaming us for something we didn't do." He could also tell her that Ben knew of the consequences of their association, and if Drew was captured during a pirate raid, he'd never expect Ben to expose himself to come to his rescue. As much as that was the way of his business, Drew found it difficult swallowing that excuse, and he knew Ben would never desert him.

"But you're still a—" began Felicity.

Drew held up his hand. "I know what I am, but being a fraudulent aristocrat is better than a murdering pirate. Everyone will assume I tricked Ben as I did everyone else."

She made a disgusted sound in the back of her throat. "At least convincing people of your devious nature shouldn't be hard to do."

"This is about more than my plans to help Ben." Drew knelt before her. He needed to look into her eyes. She acted as if she didn't care if he lived or died, so long as he made sure her father was safe. No doubt his day-long abandonment had hurt her. Women needed to be reassured after they'd been made love to even in the best of circumstances, which his liaison with Felicity certainly was not. Any self-respecting lover of women knew that proper etiquette on the day after was crucial. He usually sent a gift at the very least.

He lifted Felicity's hands from her lap and held them. "Are you angry with me for seducing you? I know you were vulnerable after the news about your father. You needed a comforting shoulder to cry on, and I suppose I had other ideas."

Felicity tried to yank her hands away, but he held them tight. "You didn't seduce me. I seduced you, and don't lump me in with all your other women. You've no right to assume you know what I'm about."

"You're jealous. Felicity, I've known many women in my life, but you're different than—" The shake of her head gave him an excuse to stop babbling. He feared he was about to confess something to her he'd barely admitted to himself.

"Spare me your honey-coated promises." Her tone made it clear she found nothing sweet in anything he said. "We both were in full control of our senses. I don't expect anything from you other than your honesty in dealing with my father's predicament."

He dropped her hands and stood, which took more effort than he'd expected. Her chilly composure broadsided him. Well, he'd not been in control of anything when he'd made love to Felicity. He was out of his mind with lust and continued to do bizarre things every time he found himself in her presence. She didn't appear plagued with the same affliction. His concern over having a fawning female on his hands hadn't left room for him to consider his own rejection. Or maybe it had, and that was the real reason he'd stayed away from his cabin. Leave it to Felicity to use such a vulnerable part of his anatomy against him. Now he had a good idea how a few of his clinging mistresses felt when he discarded them.

If this was the way Miss Kendall wanted to play, he could do it better. "So, how is it you came to be in such control of your faculties in the bedchamber, love?"

Felicity studied her hands in the darkened room. Cracking her icy demeanor gave him only a moment's satisfaction. He really wasn't much of a gentleman, though he did know enough not to bring up a lady's past. Whatever Felicity's previous experience with men, he was sure it was limited, and his mention of something she obviously went to great efforts to hide probably embarrassed her deeply. It was an underhanded maneuver carried out in an attempt to salve his own wounded pride.

"I'm sorry. I shouldn't have said that."

Drew went to light a lantern, but the tremor in Felicity's voice stopped him. "I suppose you deserve to know. Most men would expect an explanation."

"Not necessarily. I only asked because I was surprised." He gently placed his hand on her shoulder in silent support. Her deception might have been a good thing or he'd have had her in his bed sooner. Dealing with the aftermath earlier in their relationship would have been worse than this. She'd have shot him for sure.

She exhaled loudly before she began to speak. "It happened only once, when I was much younger. My mother died shortly before I discovered men—or should I say, they discovered me? I had no one to talk to about such things. I was raised in the Puritan church, and all the woman I knew were of the same mind."

"Not a place for a girl burgeoning to womanhood to ask for guidance in matters of the heart."

"The matrons had much advice to give—all of it condemning everything about me. They thought me too headstrong."

He straightened, with exaggerated surprise. "No!"

Felicity smiled, almost laughed. "Yes. They were right, though. I fell in love with the most handsome man I'd ever seen. Impulsively and foolishly, I gave myself to him. He broke my heart and stole money from my father."

"Handsome, was he? What did he look like?" Drew stalked around to face her. He stopped himself from asking if the bastard was more appealing than he. He didn't like this turn of events.

"Erik was blond, blue-eyed, tall. He looked like an angel."

Drew wished he'd never started this bloody conversation. "Surely those are the exaggerated perceptions of a giddy young girl. Blond men have an tendency to look effeminate, weak."

"He didn't, but that doesn't matter. He made me feel like a grown woman, and I was eager to be one in every way. I was a fool."

"No. You were innocent and he was a bastard. Where is he now?" If he was anywhere in the vicinity, Drew had a mind to pay a call on the fop. He'd see how his blue eyes looked rimmed in black.

"I don't know. He left Boston shortly afterward. He promised to marry me but said he wanted to prove himself to my father first."

"Thank God the scoundrel left before you were stuck with him. You were lucky."

"No, I wasn't. He worked for my father, and later Master Marley discovered he'd been embezzling from the company. He used me to disguise his deeds."

Drew reached down and took her hand. This time she gave it willingly. "Don't worry, sweeting. Not much got past Marley. Your angel had to have been very sly. It wasn't your fault."

"You fooled Marley."

"But I'm a tricky devil. A master of deception." Of course, he hadn't fooled Marley, but revealing that now wouldn't improve Felicity's mood.

Despite his self-restraint, or rather his need for self-preservation, Felicity continued to frown. "That's what I'm afraid of."

Instantly, he understood. He massaged her palm with his thumb. "I'm not like him. I admit I love women, but I don't use them to carry out my evil schemes. I can do that all on my own." At least he could be honest about that.

One exception came to mind, but in that case, he hadn't actually consummated the relationship. He could not have done that to the little señorita who helped him escape from prison, even if he had had the strength, which he had not. It infuriated him that any man would use Felicity so callously. After he found Marley's killer, he knew who was next on his list.

She kept her head bowed and spoke to their joined hands. "That's the real reason I forced the captain of the *Queen Elizabeth* to take me to Barbados. My brother's marrying, and I can never do that."

"You can marry. There is no reason you can't. Of course, it wouldn't hurt to curb that sharp tongue of yours until you get to know a man."

"No, Drew. The church was pressuring me to marry when I left. I hoped my age would make them leave me alone. I'd be an outcast when my new husband found out my secret." She pulled her hand away and dropped it in her lap.

"No decent man would do that." He wanted to touch her, comfort her the only way he knew how, but that wasn't what she needed from him right now.

"You don't know what they do. They are very strict. They'd burn you at the stake."

He shifted. Though the idea of another man possessing Felicity irritated him, for her sake he felt compelled to make suggestions he found unappealing. "Find a man who isn't a Puritan."

"Most men expect their wives to be virgins and younger than twenty-nine. I gave up the idea of having a husband years ago." Her heavy sigh wounded him more than he thought possible.

Even in the dark, Drew could see how much her confession hurt her, but what could he say? He wasn't looking for a wife and probably never would be. His romantic entanglements never became this complex. Another man would claim her without hesitation if he glimpsed the passionate woman behind her stiff demeanor. Selfish as he was, he found that thought unbearably disturbing. Instead of comforting words he didn't have, he lifted Felicity's chin and pressed his lips lightly against hers.

She accepted the chaste kiss, but sat back, ending it before it began. "This is pointless. It's my father I'm concerned about." After a moment of silence, she said, "You won't tell him my secret, will you?"

He bolted from his relaxed position. "Christ, no. He'd have me hanged."

She giggled. He hadn't realized she was capable of it. "I suppose I can trust you on that count. The whole thing wouldn't cast you in a good light if you told, would it?"

"No. Not much of the truth does." He leaned back against the table.

"Why do you always paint yourself as such a wicked character?" She angled her head, studying him. "Look at what you did for Solomon and his son."

"Now I'm not so bad? A minute ago I was a charlatan, a man who went back on his word to a beautiful woman."

He couldn't tell if Felicity blushed, but he suspected she did. She said, "Don't waste your compliments on me. I know I'm not most men's ideal. I'm too tall and too . . . what did you say earlier? Sharp-tongued."

"I'll be glad to take that back or, rather, change it to sharp-witted. I suppose some men are intimidated by a woman who can out-think them." No doubt her misconceptions about her value came from the same page of the Puritan doctrine that shamed her about her incredible sexuality. If he couldn't marry her, he could wipe away any doubts about her mistaken assumptions forever. "And I didn't say you were pretty. I said you were beautiful."

Speaking from his heart left Drew's throat dry. Felicity's searching gaze touched him physically. She was a magnet pulling all the secrets from his soul. He had sins too weighty to be drawn out, so he gave what he could.

"Felicity, I swear to you, I will do everything in my power to secure Ben's release. If I take the ship back to Barbados right now, it will only make matters worse. Please try and see that."

The longest minutes of his life passed while she considered his plea. He felt like the boy who'd cried wolf too many times. Now that he desperately wanted to be believed, he worried his years of duplicity had left him completely uncredible. Perhaps it had been so long since he was sincere, he no longer sounded authentic when he tried.

Finally, Felicity sighed. "I guess I don't have much of a choice."

That was not the answer he'd been hoping for. He needed her trust. "Dare I agree? You'll prove me wrong. You've shown me you'll create a choice when none is available. I'm asking for your trust and support in this."

She dropped her gaze from his, clearly showing her hesitation. "Will you promise to keep me abreast of your plans? I don't like being kept in the dark like a child."

He'd already altered his life too much for her. Maybe if he'd not tried to present himself as halfway civilized, he wouldn't be asked to behave like a suckling pup now. "I'll keep you informed. But don't jump to conclusions if I'm not down here every hour on the hour updating you on our progress. I am running a ship, you know."

He got up to light the candles ensconced in glass globes on either side of the bed. He still grappled with the reason he agreed to her every time he intended to say no. The glow of the flickering light sparkled in Felicity's eyes. When she looked at him that way, he no longer cared who had given in to whom. He returned to take her hands in his, gently prompting her to stand. "Trust me, then?"

She tilted her head to meet his gaze. "Yes."

"But you said that before. Why should I believe you?"

"You know a secret I've told no other. Doesn't that

prove something?" Her lips parted slightly, as if she wanted a kiss.

He recognized the invitation but held back. "One other person knows. I don't imagine you favor him with your trust—or anything else, for that matter." Drew stopped short of asking her if she had loved the scoundrel, almost breaking his own rules. Matters of the heart were to be avoided at all costs during seduction. After pressing his lips against Felicity's knuckles, he turned her hands over and kissed the center of each palm. "But let's never speak of it again, sweeting."

He guided her into the pool of light cast by the globes and reached for the pins holding back her hair. Instead, he found a wooden handle protruding from the tight coil. One simple tug unfurled her wild mane. When he realized he held a tool for splicing ropes, he lifted a questioning gaze. The piece had come from abovedeck.

"Hugh left it. I needed something to hold up my hair."

He tossed the wooden fid over his shoulder, already lost in the midst of Felicity's tangled locks.

"May I kiss you?"

"Please." Her eyes fluttered shut, brushing her slightly flushed cheeks with her lashes. As he watched her mouth, she licked her parted lips in further invitation.

Her yielding tempted him beyond belief, but he forced himself to savor the treat. He allowed his halfhearted struggle for control to be swept away by the tide of desire. The pull of her yanked him under, and nothing else mattered. Lust flooded his lungs and limbs with the burn of dense saltwater.

Before he finished, he planned to worship every inch of her, obliterating thoughts of any other lover. With soft kisses, he teased each corner of her mouth, then moved to lightly suck her lower lip. A squeak of pleasure escaped from the back of her throat.

He trailed his mouth down her neck until his lips

pressed against the throbbing of her pulse. The brush of his tongue quickened the rhythm. Blood pooled in his groin, making him demandingly hard sooner than he wanted. His pulse pounded a warning and he forced himself to set her at arm's length. "I want to undress you."

Briefly, her green-brown eyes wavered between shyness and anticipation. Then a slow smile crept to her wet lips and she appeared to find her courage.

"Do as you like with me, *sweeting*."

She echoed his usual endearment boldly, as if he were something she would like to eat, and raised her arms in invitation. If he wanted to keep his composure, he dared not think the innuendo intentional. He slipped behind her to attack her laces with shaky fingers. While he eased her dress past her shoulders, he couldn't resist kissing the skin he revealed. He was truly lost and intended to take her with him.

"Open your eyes," he whispered huskily.

A nude woman with half-hooded eyes stared back at Felicity from the mirror. Her wet and swollen lips parted with her desperate gulps for breath. Pink nipples strained against the paleness of her rounded breasts. Lord, she had never even seen herself unclothed before. The sight shocked her. She lowered her gaze and stared at her toes. But curiosity tempted her to sneak a second glance.

Slender ankles widened into long legs, then curved hips. Her rounded tummy dipped into a slight waist. But her full breasts captured her attention, especially with Drew's rough hands slipping beneath them. Long brownish blonde waves fell over his arms and teased the swell of her bottom. She watched Drew nuzzle the curve of her shoulder and forgot to breathe.

"See? Beautiful," he murmured.

She couldn't look away, though a voice struggled up from somewhere to tell her she should. Drew's fingers closed around one nipple and sent a jolt of fire straight to her sex. A rush of wet heat flooded her, and she dropped her gaze to see if the evidence of her desire glistened on her thighs. His followed.

She leaned her head on Drew's shoulder and closed her eyes before her knees buckled.

Apparently, Drew was in no mood to give quarter. "Lean on me, but watch. I want you to see me touching you."

Through heavy eyelids, she obeyed. He moved one hand down to caress her belly, while he kneaded her breast with the other. The contrast of his tanned hands gliding across her pale flesh transfixed her gaze on his deliberate movements.

When his fingers grazed her hipbone, she shut her eyes.

"Drew," she whispered, turning her head into the folds of his shirt.

His hands stilled. After a moment, she opened her eyes and peeked again. She met Drew's bright gaze in the mirror. His stare physically touched her with the same intensity his hands caressed her body. Booted feet braced on each side of her bare ones. He was still fully dressed, but through his snug black breeches, she could feel the taut muscles in his thighs. The heat of his unyielding erection burned her fevered skin. His gaze melded with hers before he continued.

"Better," he murmured in between pressing kisses along her shoulder. His fingers entwined in the dark curls at the apex of her legs, then slid farther down. Gingerly, he probed her swollen flesh. His index finger grazed the place were her passion pulsed. Her knees grew weak and she began to tremble.

The gentle pressure turned to dizzying circles as Drew found a rhythm that forced her to moan.

"Drew," she pleaded again.

"Part your legs for me, sweeting."

"I can't," she answered. She was in serious danger of losing her balance and her sanity. "I'll fall."

He abandoned the nipple he'd been teasing to wrap his arm around her waist.

"Go ahead. I've got you."

She leaned into his solid body. Timidly she stepped her legs farther apart. The things she'd done in the shelter of a bed partially dressed were a different matter standing stark naked in front of a mirror. His finger slipped inside her. This time, Drew was the one who moaned.

His invasion deepened, then retreated, increasing the sweet torture with each movement.

It was too much. "Drew, take off your clothes."

"Not yet." His sudden withdrawal left her aching and empty.

When he carried her to the bed, she happily assumed he'd changed his mind. After laying her down so her legs dangled off the edge, he dropped to his knees, draping her limbs over his shoulders.

She struggled to sit up. "What are you doing?"

He smiled wickedly. "Let me kiss you where no one has kissed you before." His grin drooped slightly. "Or had he?"

A tentative shake of her head returned the possessive gleam to his blue-green eyes. Compelled by the insistence in his gaze and the desire to please him, she lay back, shaking and panicked. He rewarded her cooperation with a kiss on the inside of her thigh that sent a tingling jolt to the pit of her belly. When his lips touched her, Felicity shuddered and forgot all her objections. And when he caressed her with his tongue, she would have threatened his life if he stopped.

The room swirled in a dizzying array of colors. She arched her back off the bed, then tilted her hips, writhing to get closer to the unbearable pleasure. He lifted her buttocks off the bed, kneading her with his strong hands. She struggled to raise her head before she lost all touch of where or who she was.

In the mirror's reflection, Drew's dark, tousled head pressed between her pale thighs. Her own eyes were heavy and glazed, staring back at her with wanton abandon. The picture was her undoing. She collapsed as the tight coil deep inside her began to unravel. Her moans sounded like screams in her own ears. She convulsed to the tips of her toes.

After she caught her breath, Drew kissed her lightly in the center of her stomach before he stood.

She reached out to him, too limp to do anything else at the moment. "Don't go."

He yanked his white cambric shirt furiously over his head. A ripping sound didn't stop his enthusiasm in removing it. "At this moment, I couldn't be dragged from your side, sweeting."

The shirt stuck at Drew's wrist, where he seemed to have forgotten to undo the ties. A rippling of his muscles and another tear of cloth freed him from the tangled mess. He discarded his boots and breeches just as quickly.

He rose to his full height. His long, lean body glistened with a sheen of perspiration.

"Wait. I want to look at you." She wanted to forever capture the image in her mind or else she might someday believe their encounter only a vivid dream.

"I can't wait." He covered her body with his own, drinking deeply from her mouth like a man dying of thirst.

The taste of herself on his lips sent a forbidden rush of excitement coursing through Felicity. She touched him everywhere she could, her hands roaming and anxious. His skin felt like fire. She explored every cut and bulge of his sinewy back, arms and buttocks. A feral noise escaped from his throat and he put a sudden stop to her exploration by wrapping his arms around her and rolling over onto his back.

Instinctively, she sat up with her legs straddling his hips. Oh, but she liked this. She braced her hands on his chest, tilting her hips against the rigid heat pressing into her moist center.

"I'm at your mercy," he said in a strained voice. His eyes looked drugged. He stared at her a moment longer before he gave in to the weight of his eyelids.

His reaction banished her awkwardness at the strange position and made her bold. She raised herself on her knees and guided the joining for which they both longed. Her wet opening, slick from a combination of her own lust and his kisses, welcomed the invasion. His moan in response told her that he experienced the first rush of pleasure with the same intensity she did. The moment she settled fully against him, he clutched her hips and led her to a pace she didn't mind following. Their bodies ground in a maddening rhythm until she felt the familiar tightening. The sensation urged her faster and harder. He stilled his movements, letting her wild abandon have its rein. In moments, she pulsed around him, gripping him with her release.

Before the last spasm had wracked her body, he was moving again. His fingers dug into her hips with painful force, but she didn't cry out. She stared in fascination at his undoing. When she held him in her body, there was nothing he could hide from her. She braced herself on his chest as he drove into her, watching him for the signs that he had relinquished every last bit of control. He thrust deeply, then tensed, a strangled moan on his lips.

After his rapid breathing grew more normal, he opened his eyes and grinned at her. She caressed his face, thinking he looked vulnerable and boyish. His heart appeared in his eyes, or perhaps it was only her imagining what she wanted to see.

He pulled her into his arms and snuggled her against

his chest, kissing the top of her head. "You are beautiful, love. Don't ever doubt it again."

Felicity closed her eyes, letting herself believe his casual endearment genuine. In the morning she could awaken to reality. Or, if she was lucky, she could make this moment last until El Diablo was captured and her father freed. After that, Drew would fade into a distant memory like all girlish fantasies. She buried her face against his shoulder to hide the sudden wetness clinging to her eyelashes.

# Chapter Thirteen

" 'For a whore is a deep ditch; and a strange woman is a narrow pit,' " said Solomon, stumbling over all the words with more than two letters.

"Excuse me?" Felicity shook off her hazy daydream.

He stared hard at the leather-bound book resting on the table and repeated the sentence cautiously.

With a sigh of relief, she leaned over and read the passage herself. He'd recited from the *King James Bible*, not made a personal observation. She let her high spirits distract her from pondering the truth in the statement or the source from which it came.

"Wonderful! You weren't honest with me, Solomon. You couldn't have possibly come this far by just picking things up."

"Actually, Miss Kendall, the captain tried to teach me to read and write when we were much younger. I was too proud to learn then. Perhaps I remember some of his instruction, though Drew was never much of a scholar."

"I can't say I'm surprised." Felicity laughed. She knew

she must be blushing. She did so every time Drew was near or his name was mentioned. Glancing in the large gilded mirror would show how much of her happiness reflected in her face, but she dared not look in its direction. To recall the things they'd done in front of that mirror in the last few days would make her cheeks match the shade of her rose-hued dress. Drew had shown her ways of making love she hadn't known existed.

"You are a good teacher and an intelligent woman." Solomon paused. "I only wonder why you make such foolish choices."

Felicity pretended to study the book instead of acknowledging Solomon's comment. She'd rather assume Solomon referred to her entrapment in the armoire than any current mistakes he found her making. The dire words of the Holy Bible wouldn't ruin her mood, and neither would Solomon's ambiguous comment.

"Here. Let's switch to the Gospels. I'm tired of Proverbs."

Without further discussion, he did as she asked. His dry rendition of the gospel according to Saint Matthew encouraged her to go back to her daydreaming.

She would never agree the days and nights spent with Drew were a mistake. Even if Solomon had bluntly referred to her intimacy with Drew, she would neither deny nor defend it. The rational and moral reasons against their alliance were obvious. Yet she had never been happier.

Her father's imprisonment always loomed in the background, but she had come to believe Drew would set things right. And when Drew touched her, she forgot everything else in the world. Linked in passion, they had no past . . . and no future. She tried to stop the unpleasant thought before it came, but it was too powerful to call back.

Her existence would return to its prior drabness when Drew sailed out of her life forever. His absence would leave a gaping hole where her heart resided. In all his kindness to her, he'd never mentioned any feelings beyond lust. Drew was not the kind of man to settle down; nor was she the type of woman to live on the run. After the scandal of her father's incarceration, they'd be forced to return to Boston and live a quiet life in seclusion. Drew, on the other hand, would always be one step ahead of the law. He was as free as the wind that powered his ship, and just as elusive.

Knowing what she was to lose couldn't make her regret her love for Drew. She could no longer deny the truth from herself. Every moment with him strengthened the emotion.

Hugh bounded into the room, interrupting Solomon's dry reading and halting her slip into melancholy.

"My turn yet? I want to read out of the book too," demanded Hugh.

"We're going to do something better. I'm going to teach you a song today that will help you remember your letters."

"Songs are for women. I can read out of the book. Let me try!" Hugh crossed his arms over his bare chest. Despite Solomon's efforts to dress the child like a little gentleman, he always looked like a wild savage before noon.

"Hugh, do not question Miss Kendall. She's doing us both a great service." Solomon's deep-timbred voice took on a sternness that reverberated against the walls without him even having to raise it.

"I'm sorry." Hugh hung his head for a respectable half a second before perking back up. "Can you teach me how to be a doctor instead? Then I can help Mr. Sneed. He's sick."

"You're a physician?" Shock and something else mingled on Solomon's drawn brow.

She got to her feet and fluffed her skirts. "No, I'm not a physician. I've had experience with—,"

"You are so. You told Captain Drew you helped sick people all the time and no one ever died. I heard you," insisted Hugh.

"Calm down, son." Solomon fixed Felicity with a serious stare. "Were you a nurse or a healer of some sort?"

"Well, I consider myself a midwife and an able nurse, but I'm certainly not qualified to train Hugh as a physician." That she stumbled over her title as midwife, even to Solomon, aggravated her.

The matrons of her church had been outraged when she, an unmarried woman, showed an interest in the skill. She'd become attached to the notion after she realized she would never have children of her own. Despite their objections, Felicity assisted midwives who were not of the Puritan faith and in situations where no one else would help. She had even gone so far as to deliver a child by herself, sworn to secrecy by the unwed mother. It galled her, admittedly much more after her own fall from grace, that women always took the blame for men's pleasures.

With her conviction bolstered, she met Solomon's direct gaze. "Actually, I'm an excellent midwife. I never lost a mother or a child."

Solomon stared through her, lost in secret thought. She doubted he had heard her.

"I don't need a midwife, but do you think you could help a man with a musket wound in his midsection?"

"I'd have to see the patient to give an opinion."

"Seeing the patient is out of the question. You can tell me what to do and I'll render the treatment." The way Solomon stiffened warned her that any trust she'd gained from him during their lesson was slipping.

"I could tell you the wrong thing and make it worse. I can't suggest a treatment without seeing the injury. Bring him to me blindfolded." Felicity wasn't about to give up when she could finally be of some use.

"He's unconscious. I think moving him would kill him."

Hugh tugged on Solomon's coat. "Papa, you can't let Mr. Sneed die. He's teaching me to throw dice, and no one else will play with me."

Solomon ignored his son. A struggle showed in every strained line of his face. He was seriously considering letting her treat one of Drew's crew. If she succeeded, Drew would be grateful. He'd remember her for that if nothing else. She'd be more than just one of the many women who passed through his life.

"You can't let one of your men die without at least giving me the chance to save him."

Solomon picked up the Bible, the only book they could find on the ship, and walked toward the door. "I'll speak to the captain. The final decision will have to be his."

"No." She blocked Solomon's way. "He'll say no. If the man dies he'll blame himself."

Solomon jammed his hands into the pockets of the embroidered long coat he always wore, despite the heat, to his lessons. He started to speak, then stopped.

Up until now, she'd never seen Solomon unnerved.

He studied her as if trying to make a decision. "If I take you, you must promise to obey my every instruction without argument."

She pressed her hand over her heart. "You have my word."

"We will see the patient. You will evaluate his injuries; then you will tell me how to proceed from the safety of your cabin. Understood?"

"Can I come too?" asked Hugh.

"Absolutely not." Solomon spoke more harshly than she'd ever seen him address his son. The strain of disobeying Drew's orders must have caused the outburst. "I have a more important job for you, Hugh." Solomon instantly softened his tone. "You'll be the lookout. This is a secret mission, and no one else can know."

Hugh straightened and shoved out his bony rib cage. "Aye, sir."

Solomon turned to Felicity. "Wait here. I'll make sure the area is clear. And put one of Drew's coats over your dress or you'll stand out like a lit candle."

Solomon exited the room with Hugh. She paced, fearing the quartermaster would change his mind before he returned. If she could not give Drew her love, at least she could give him the life of a crewman. She just hoped nothing went wrong.

The stench of rotting flesh smacked Felicity full in the face when she entered the small cabin. A brass lantern hung from the ceiling, casting a dull yellow glow. Shafts of sunlight the size of pinheads punctured the crevices in the planks above. Solomon followed on her heels. He crowded her into the room and shut the door behind them.

Felicity approached the makeshift bed. "He needs fresh air and sunlight. The wound is infected." The bed was nothing more than boards balanced by crates. Blankets padded the hard surface and a clean sheet covered the patient.

"Hurry," said Solomon. "If the sea picks up, I'll have to lash him back in his hammock and you won't be able to examine him at all."

A quick glance at the injured man's face startled her with recognition. At closer inspection, she placed him as her father's driver from Barbados. The man was one of Drew's crew, and a trusted member at that if he knew of Drew's double life. Her mission's success took on new importance, strumming her already taut nerves in a discordant jangle.

She took a deep breath and lifted the sheet of heavy canvas. Avery's midsection was wrapped several times with a clean bandage. She rolled up the sleeves of Drew's borrowed jacket another turn and began to remove the bandage. Without a word, Solomon lifted the patient while she unwrapped the dressing. When she came to the last layer, she realized why the bandage had been so snug. "Has he been bleeding like this since his injury?"

"It stopped for a day or so, then started again. The bandage cut the flow considerably."

"I'm sure it did. It cut off his circulation and caused the wound to fester."

With the last layer of cloth removed, she discovered the wound to be not nearly so large as she feared. Luckily, the musket ball had penetrated his side, rather than his stomach. It was possible the shot had missed any delicate and irreparable organs. If she could stop the bleeding, he might have a chance. Though her experience with musket wounds was nonexistent, she believed Avery could survive the infection.

"Where's the musket ball?"

"What musket ball?"

"The one you removed from the wound. A piece might have broken off and could be causing the infection. There's no wound on his back so . . ." Her voice drifted off at Solomon's perplexed expression.

"Our surgeon was killed. I don't think anyone thought to remove the musket ball."

"Did your surgeon leave any of his instruments?"

"They're in that bag." Solomon pointed to an unopened leather case tucked in a shadowed corner.

"Has anyone bothered to use it?" She seized the bag and began examining its contents. A handful of instruments lay scattered in the bottom, and fewer medicines in moldy bottles lined the sides. The lack of supplies and implements really didn't matter anyway; she wouldn't know what to do with them if she had them. She pulled out a sharp object that looked useful for cutting and another appropriate for probing.

"I'll have to remove the musket ball if he's to have any chance at all."

"We have an agreement. You are to tell me what is wrong with the patient and I am to render the treatment."

"I don't know how to remove a musket ball, nor have I ever seen it done." She patted the wound with a brandy-soaked cloth, cleaning away the dried blood.

Solomon watched her over her shoulder. "What if you make it worse?"

After cleaning the excess blood and puss from the wound, she poured brandy over the instruments. "If I do nothing, he'll bleed to death."

"This won't do. You're likely to be discovered if you stay. You need to get back to your cabin without further delay."

She turned to him, shoving the instruments in his direction. "Fine. You do it, but it must be done."

He jumped back and stared at the instruments as if she had just shoved a severed limb in his direction.

"Do it then, but be quick about it."

She didn't bother to tell Solomon how ridiculous his request was. Be quick about it? She had no idea what she was doing.

With her eyes closed and instruments poised above the patient, she paused to pray. Certainly the Lord had every right to turn a deaf ear to her request, considering her recent behavior, but surely Avery shouldn't be made to suffer for her lack of morality.

"What are you doing?" Solomon's hiss rattled her concentration. "You're praying, aren't you?"

"A prayer can't hurt." As ready as she would ever likely to be, she gripped the surgical knife until her fingertips turned white.

"I'm not reassured." Solomon moved so close she could feel his breath on her neck.

The wound had begun to close on the edges, but the new skin was puffy and red. To probe for the shot, she would have to widen the opening. A surprisingly steady hand lowered the instrument to make her first incision.

After carefully cutting the skin away, she gingerly inserted the long metal instrument with the flattened spoon on the end. Perspiration formed above her lip. Accidentally disturbing some vital organ terrified her, so her probes were purposely shallow. With no hint of success, she removed the instrument and breathed again.

An exhalation of air whooshed against her neck. Solomon must have been holding his breath too. "Try it again. You didn't go deep enough."

She glanced over her shoulder. He looked as nervous as she felt. She nodded and turned back to Avery, encouraged by Solomon's support. Avery, on the other hand, was not as agreeable. He moaned. When she tried to reinsert the instrument, he reached for her.

She jumped back. "Good Lord!"

Solomon grabbed Avery's arms and pinned him to the table. "Hold still, Sneed. We need to get the ball from your side. Be a man about it, sailor."

Avery Sneed thrashed more violently.

"Good work." To stay out of his reach, Felicity backed against the hull.

Solomon didn't appear offended by her sarcasm. In fact, his eyes shone with excitement. "This is the most active he's been since his injury. I think he might be coming around."

"Wouldn't you, if someone was sticking a blunt object in your side?" She still had to finish the job, and Avery's return to consciousness could make her lose her nerve.

When Avery was secured, she returned to his side. She touched the man's fevered face, then bent to whisper in his ear. "Avery, go back to sleep. When you wake up this will all be over."

"He's not supposed to know you're here," interrupted Solomon.

To her relief, Avery calmed instantly. He probably had

just used all the fight he had left. "If he remembers, which I doubt he will, tell him he dreamed it. Now, let's get this over with."

She still held the spoonlike instrument in her right hand and returned to work without further delay. Drew would not believe Avery Sneed dreamed his encounter with a woman, but hopefully things would turn out well and she could tell him the truth herself. If she couldn't tell him she loved him, she wanted to do something for him no one else could. Forcing her mind away from the distraction Drew always became when she thought of him, she focused all her attention on the difficult task at hand. She ignored Avery's quiet moans and prodded deeper into the wound. After a few moments, her efforts were rewarded.

"I feel something."

"You do?" Solomon sounded surprised at her minor success.

With all the concentration she possessed, she carefully scooped the round object from the wound. Her fingers ached from the strain of holding the spoon so tightly, but she feared her hand would shake if she loosened her grip. Just as she almost had the shot out, the door banged against the wall. She froze, holding her breath.

Hugh stood in the doorway. "Captain's looking for you! Captain's looking for you!"

Without letting go of Avery's arms, Solomon motioned Hugh into the room with a jerk of his head. "Get in here and shut the door."

Carefully, she guided the instrument out of the wound before there were any more interruptions. The spoon came up full of red muck, but closer inspection revealed the dull metal of a musket ball. She thrust the spoon in Solomon's direction. "I did it!"

Solomon let go of Avery and picked up the blood-covered shot. He held the round object between his thumb and forefinger. After examining the ball carefully, he grinned. "It's whole. My God, Felicity, you did do it."

Solomon grabbed Felicity and hugged her. As if regretting his impulse, he released her instantly. He stepped back as far as the tight quarters would allow.

Hugh pulled on his father's coattails. "Papa, Captain Drew is looking for you. He almost went to Felicity's cabin, but I told him you were in the riggings fixing a tangled line."

Solomon's smile sagged. "He knows I hate heights. Now I'll actually have to climb one of those things so he can see me jump out."

Hugh shrugged, obviously unconcerned with his father's dilemma. "I want to hold the musket ball."

"No, Hugh, it's dirty. Go on, Solomon, I have to clean and stitch the wound. I don't want Drew to find us before I've finished."

Solomon wiped his brow with a handkerchief he pulled from his pocket. "I don't want him to find out at all. I'll occupy him with something so I can return you to the cabin without his suspecting anything. Hugh, sit by the door and keep a look out."

Her care of Avery Sneed must have finally earned Solomon's trust if he agreed to leave her without an argument.

"Don't even think about leaving this room without me. Wait here if you finish before I get back," he added before he and Hugh, who was still begging to hold the musket ball, left the room.

In the surgeon's bag she found some curved needles specifically designed for her purpose and got to work. By the time she had Avery bandaged again, it seemed as if an hour had passed. She admired her work, then forced some brandy down the man's throat for good measure. The dressing no longer needed to be so tight or thick to keep the white cloth from turning red. With nothing else to be done, she sat down to wait.

Unfortunately, patience was a skill she'd never mastered.

After a few more moments of struggling with her will to stay put, she crept to the portal and quietly opened it. A peek wouldn't hurt. She could send Hugh to see what was keeping Solomon. Glancing down both sides of the dim passageway revealed that Hugh had deserted her. She stepped out into the empty corridor.

To the right was the way she had come. The left faded into darkness. A couple of steps in that direction showed a small opening that angled into a crease. By the way the walls met, she must be at the bow of the ship. Sacks of supplies and a few crates littered the cramped space. No wonder Solomon was anxious about bringing her here. Drew's cabin resided at the stern, the opposite end of the vessel.

Felicity heard a noise somewhere abovedeck and tiptoed back the few feet she had traveled. Safely inside Avery's sickroom, she almost had the door completely shut, the last bit of evidence of her dull yet forbidden adventure, when she heard a disturbing noise. A child's muffled cry echoed somewhere in the passageway.

# Chapter Fourteen

Felicity followed the soft whimpers back into the triangular storage area she had just left. The child's cries originated from inside something, but the strange echo kept her from finding the source. She rolled a heavy sack off a stack of supplies, fearing Hugh might be trapped underneath. The bag of grain landed with a loud thump, which increased the boy's hysterics.

"It's all right, Hugh. Where are you?"

Silence greeted her question. Something was terribly wrong. Had he lost consciousness? Removing a musket ball from a grown man was one thing; tending a frightened, hurt child was another. Frantically she scoured the dim storage area for a clue to Hugh's location. Until she hit her toe on the heavy, metal ring protruding from a grate, the hold had gone unnoticed. With a shout of pain, she grabbed her injured foot.

"Shut up. I hear a woman," said a man's muffled voice.

She stopped hopping. The voice came from the hold. Hugh's cries began again, but were stopped short by the distinctive sound of a slap. The grate in the floor, secured with the heavy lock that had tripped her, separated her from the bodies that went with the voices. Solomon would be furious, and so would Drew for that matter, if she let one of the crewmen see her. Yet she couldn't let Hugh continue to be hurt by the mysterious man. She had no choice.

She knelt to peer into the darkness beyond the grate. "Unhand that child at once or I'll bring the captain."

"I don't need the bloody whore of a pirate to tell me how to take care of my son. If you brought us some rum give it over; if you ain't, you can save that trap of yours for that murdering bastard," said the man out of the darkness. His slur was followed by a couple of male snickers.

The outrage! No wonder Drew didn't want her around his crew. The man was undoubtedly being imprisoned for insubordination. That would explain his obvious disdain for Drew, but it did not excuse his treatment of Hugh.

Felicity recovered from her momentary loss of words with a vengeance. "Give me that child right now or I promise you whatever fate Drew has for you will increase in severity tenfold."

A grimy face appeared on the other side of the grate. "Sure, love. Just open her up and I'll hand the lad to you." He lifted a child until his red head almost hit the crossed metal holding them in. The boy blinked at her from a tear-stained, freckled face.

He wasn't Hugh. The man had called the child his son. Regardless of their relation, she was determined to get the child away from him. But she wasn't stupid; she wouldn't unlock the grate even if she had the key. If Solomon would not see to it, she would tell Drew. Surely he didn't realize the crewman's son had been locked up with him.

"I'll have someone release your son, but if you lay another hand on him, I'll see that your punishment is doubled."

"I already got fifteen lashes, but I know he ain't done with me." The prisoner lowered the boy and grumbled. "Stupid slut, you going to have your devil lover kill me twice?"

"I don't want to die," whimpered the boy. His voice sounded weak. He needed immediate care.

"You won't die, little boy. I won't let that happen." Felicity leaned closer to the grate. The child had disappeared into the darkness, swallowed by the shadows of at least a dozen men.

"El Diablo lets his whore run his ship? I bloody doubt it," said the same man. A few of the men agreed in mumbled curses. The rest seemed to have succumbed to the gloom.

For some reason, she recognized his voice, though she was sure she hadn't made the acquaintance of anyone so horrible. "Who are you?"

"Harold McCulla, former captain of the *Carolina*. And who might you be? Show me your tits and maybe I'll remember you. You remind me of a wench I fondled at the Hare and the Hound back on Barbados."

His name brought a flood of clarity. The boy must be Tanner, though his red, swollen face hardly resembled the happy ragtag boy she'd met at the docks. These were the men from the ship Drew had captured. Everything started to make more sense. She'd been so upset over the news of her father, she'd not even thought of the men onboard. This dingy hole was a proper home for McCulla, but Tanner would have to be placed elsewhere.

"My name is Felicity Kendall, Mr. McCulla. After my father's reputation has been cleared, I can assure you that you will no longer bear the title of captain. I'll see to other accommodations for your son." She got to her feet, dismissing McCulla and his vulgarity.

She turned to leave, but McCulla's burst of laughter stopped her. "I should have recognized that snippy tone.

Looks like you sold your pa out for a roll with the devil himself. I heard the ladies lifted their skirts at a wink from El Diablo, but Kendall's pinch-faced daughter—why bother?"

She stomped back to the grate. "El Diablo's not on this ship, so stop frightening your child and your crew."

"Well, the captain sure ain't 'Lord Christian.' You're not stupid enough to think you're humping some fancy lord, are you? Nope, you're nothing but El Diablo's whore, and a traitor to your own father," goaded McCulla.

"You're a drunkard. That's why they took command of your ship away from you in the first place. You're probably drunk now."

"This is the first time I've been sober in ten years, and I can't say I like it much. I can tell you the honest truth, though, and I'll enjoy that. Your father's going to hang while you're slutting around with the one who caused it. Maybe you're the one who's drunk to think El Diablo's not going to kill you when he's through with you. Just like he killed Marley and his missus."

Felicity swallowed hard. McCulla's horrible accusations made her heart race. "You don't know what you're talking about."

McCulla's slow smile did nothing to remove her unease. "He likes to cozy up to his victims first. Uses 'em for all they're worth before he does them in. That's what happened to Marley once El Diablo figured out he was on to him."

Felicity stiffened, refusing to let this fool see her tremble. He unnerved her with his obscenities, nothing more. "You're a liar. You're just trying to cover up for your own traitorous behavior. You deserted the only man in Barbados who didn't openly scorn you."

McCulla's blessed silence assured her she'd finally gained the upper hand. But before she reached the light that marked the companionway, the captured drunk's words reached out and stopped her as effectively as a tug on her skirt.

"The real Duke of Foxmoor is on Barbados right now. Said Marley wrote him about a pirate passing himself off as one of his kin. I might not be as smart as you or your back-stabbing lover, but I don't have to be to know who killed him."

She straightened and backed away. The sensation that had begun as a nagging dread in her belly spread up her spine. Doubt turned to cold fear, making her slightly dizzy. There was an explanation. McCulla's bitterness at being captured prompted him to goad her. To lie.

"And it wouldn't be much of a feat to guess who's gonna be next," yelled McCulla at her back.

She forced herself not to run. To calmly shake off the sensation of betrayal. This time it would be different. Erik and Drew were nothing alike. They were not both good-for-nothing liars. If McCulla was to be believed, Drew was infinitely worse. Diabolical, in fact. Even as she tried to remember the reasons she should trust Drew, memories of another deception chilled her to the bone.

Solomon slipped into the dim cabin and shut the door. "Felicity, are you all right?"

"I'm fine." Her voice sounded strange and distant to her own ears. She sat quietly on a crate in a shadowed corner. The fingers of her right hand dug into the back of her palm as they lay clasped in her lap.

Solomon's eyebrows knitted and he frowned. He glanced at Avery Sneed, who still lay unconscious. "Has Avery gotten worse?"

She concentrated on speaking calmly and evenly. "I checked the bandage only a moment ago. The bleeding seems to have stopped."

"Let's go, then." Solomon appeared to be scrutinizing her stiff movements, yet thankfully he withheld any comment. "To distract Drew, I had to convince him he'd made a mistake in his navigation. I wondered if your patience would hold out that long. I must say I'm surprised."

She had no idea if it had been mere minutes or an eternity since Solomon had first left. A thick fog had descended around her. No matter how many times her heart assured her her sense of disorientation would soon dissipate, her head argued that what the lifting mist would reveal would be worse. Had she been speeding blindly toward a precipice from the moment Drew entered her life?

She had gone over every one of McCulla's words. Everything coming from his filthy mouth could be dismissed if not for the reason Drew's father unexpectedly arrived on Barbados. Drew had mentioned he'd found out about his charade but failed to say how.

Solomon turned. "Are you sure you're all right? You're pale."

"I'm fine," she said too quickly. "Maybe just a little queasy. There was a lot of blood."

"Can you make it to the cabin? We have to hurry."

Calling up a weak smile, she nodded. He started back down the corridor. She followed swiftly to keep him from questioning her further. Her composure hung by a gossamer thread.

She tried to remember every last detail of the handbill she'd seen concerning El Diablo at the Linleys' party. That particular part of McCulla's tale didn't make sense. How could Drew be El Diablo? Drew had not been the man in the drawing, or surely she would have noticed a resemblance. At the time, she would have been more than eager to point out any similarities. She had detested Drew's fictitious Lord Christian from the moment he opened his arrogant mouth. The silly powder on his face and hair had rendered the Drew she had come to know unrecognizable. With that thought, her buoying hope sank.

A vague image of the crude sketch resurrected itself. The eyes were different. Wild dark hair and a crooked Roman nose might be similar, but the rough look men attain while at sea might account for the similarities. Struggling to remember El Diablo's face as it was portrayed in the drawing faded the image rather than clarifying it. She just wasn't sure.

The door closed behind her, and she couldn't recall the words she'd just spoken to Solomon. Grateful to finally be alone, she paced the room, giving her anxiety free rein.

She wanted to believe Drew incapable of the duplicity McCulla insinuated, but years of cynicism had grown too powerful to be ignored. If only she had one thing to hold on to, one small clue to sway her in Drew's favor, she would stamp out her doubts and trust him unconditionally. He had brought light to her forgotten heart. She could not stand to be thrust back into darkness.

Looking for anything to ease her mind, she opened the cabinet where Drew kept his navigational instruments. She unrolled a few maps and peeked through cases holding the devices Hugh had shown her, but found nothing to reassure her. Pulling open several drawers garnered the same results.

Something she'd heard about El Diablo back on Barbados congealed in her mind. A flag. El Diablo had a distinctive flag. Of its own accord, her gaze drifted to the trunk where Drew held his bounty of colors. Without bothering to put away the maps and instruments she'd disturbed, she drifted to the trunk and knelt in front of it. A lock she hadn't remembered there before dangled from the lid's latch, taunting her gullibility. For the first time since her mistake with Erik, she planned to prove that disjointed voice wrong.

The key would be too hard to find. Instead, she hunted for an object small enough to fit into the lock. Hairpins would have done the trick if she had any. She'd perfected her talent as a lockpick early in her childhood. The idea of a locked door or chest had always tormented her curiosity.

The long pick she used to hold her hair might be slender enough to squeeze past the lock. She retrieved the wooden fid from her belongings. The tool narrowly fit. In a matter of minutes, she sprang the lock.

She flung open the lid and unfurled three flags in a frenzy. Her gaze barely passed over the Union Jack's red cross. She registered the standard of Portugal with merely a glance. The third flag's country she couldn't recall, but the blue background and yellow cross posed no apparent threat to Drew's character—unless she considered how easily Drew changed allegiances; but she could ignore that. She had thus far.

When she brought the fourth flag out of the trunk, she paused before revealing what lay inside its folds. Even in its tight triangle shape, she could see this flag was different from the others. The background was solid black. A portion of what looked to be a heart dripped red. She tried to convince herself that the shape only looked like a heart and the drops blood because of her state of mind. That she would find evidence against Drew in this form was too ironic to be believed.

If she put the flag away and confronted Drew with McCulla's lies, the next time she picked up this particular flag, she'd find nothing but a red sun spitting sparks or some other strange design she hadn't expected. Would a person in love, if she were capable of such an emotion, insist on evidence that her lover was not a cold-blooded murderer?

As much as Felicity wanted to be that trusting, confident woman, she wasn't. Not yet. Doubt still had a foothold and picked that moment to sprout dark tendrils to wrap around her heart.

Felicity closed her eyes and unfurled the flag with a hard

flick of her wrists. Never in her life had she longed to be more wrong. When she opened her eyes, the image on the flag danced in triumph. The white skeleton with pointed tail and ears skewered a bleeding heart with the longest, sharpest sword Felicity had ever seen.

She clutched the flag to her chest and closed her eyes. The devil had hit his mark again.

# Chapter Fifteen

The rattle of a key in the door jerked Felicity out of her waking nightmare. A quick glance around the room revealed open drawers and scattered instruments. Unfurled flags lay stretched out around her like fallen soldiers in crisp uniforms. Whoever opened the door would instantly recognize something was amiss. For her own protection, she should hide what she'd discovered. Her soul might be ravaged as thoroughly as the room, but that would be her secret alone. She forced herself to stand, and realized she still clutched the damning flag.

Drew entered with a dinner tray balanced on his arm, and any sort of halfway intelligent plan evaporated with her breath. He looked like the man she had fallen in love with, and only her fiercest inner voice could stop her from going to him. She needed him more than ever, but the man she thought she could depend on above all others had turned out to be her worst enemy.

His bewildered assessment of the damage to his cabin provided the chance for her to swipe her tear-stained face with the flag she held. She stopped, forgetting that what she held was more than mere cloth and thread. It was her worst fears materialized, about herself and Drew. She glanced up at him hoping to see the devil-like skeleton beneath the handsome rouge's facade, but all looking at him did was make her heart beat faster than its already frenzied staccato. How dare his presence make her feel anything at all! Blessed anger began to pump through her veins.

He set down the tray on the pedestal table. "Lose something?"

His cool sarcasm hardened her. He wore simple black breeches and a white linen shirt opened loosely at the neck. A black ribbon that tied back his hair gave him a deceptively civilized look. His every movement radiated arrogant confidence. She'd been blinded by her own wretched loneliness, or she might have seen how truly he resembled Lord Christian in manner if not in appearance.

The fear and revulsion she should feel would not come. With her illusions shattered, she should see what the artist in Barbados had captured in his sketch: dark, soulless eyes with no remorse. If she looked into Drew's eyes, she might see the monster lurking inside the man. She knew better than to commit that mistake. Passion-filled eyes, the color of tropical seas, would haunt her dreams forever.

Drew strolled around the room, shutting drawers. "I've been through hurricanes that have caused less damage. Since the seas have been remarkably calm, I can only surmise you're displeased with me."

For the first time in her life, Felicity was afraid to speak. It didn't worry her what Drew might do once she exposed him. Her anxiety arose from the poison that would spill out once she opened her mouth. Hurt and betrayal and rage consumed her. She didn't know if she could ever stop the tirade once it started.

He must have read the rush of turbulent emotions on

her face because his puzzled gaze softened and he abruptly strode toward her. She put out her hand to stop him.

"Don't come near me!"

Her own voice, strained and raspy, grated on her frazzled nerves. It must have had the same effect on Drew, because all pretense of calm dropped. He held out his palms to her and shrugged his shoulders; his brows rose slightly in confusion.

She found the edge of the flag and let it unfurl. Words were too painful to speak. Thoughts of her own safety escaped her. If he cut her down at that very moment, it would come as a relief.

Before she could stop herself, she met Drew's gaze. His eyes mirrored the agony ripping her apart. She let the flag drop to the carpet, unable to hold it a moment longer.

"You lying bastard!" She whirled away from him, wrapping her arms around herself for comfort. Her closed eyes could not block out the image of his wounded gaze. The look was deception wielded by an artist. His show of pain represented a ruse to persuade her to forget what she knew to be true. Heaven help her but it was working.

She waited for Drew to come to her, to touch her shoulders in an act of compassion. She would shrug off his attempt, proving to him and herself that she would no longer be his pawn. The pressure of his touch never came. She hadn't believed she could feel any worse. She was wrong.

Obviously, he didn't intend to carry the game further than his token look of hurt at her accusation. The anguish she thought she glimpsed might have been an expression used out of habit. Surprise was curiously absent from his display. Perhaps he'd expected her to discover him. Perhaps he'd intended to kill her all along.

When she turned to bravely face that possibility, ready and willing for a fight, she didn't imagine anything so ruthless. He stood where she'd left him, staring at the flag crumpled on the floor.

He looked up at her with wide eyes and damp lashes. "Felicity, what can I say to make you—"

"Don't bother saying anything. I talked to McCulla. I know everything." She found the strength to stare at him coldly. He wouldn't know how much he hurt her or how close she came to falling into his arms in spite of everything.

The moment of vulnerability left Drew's wet gaze. His features hardened. "I won't deny I'm El Diablo. The Spanish gave me the name five years ago. How the hell was I supposed to know it would bloody stick?"

She heard the anger under his words. Let him be angry. She could bear his cool aloofness and his anger, but not his mock concern.

"You lived up to the name, didn't you? Will you kill me once you've tired of me? McCulla wanted to know."

Drew didn't answer, but for the first time in their acquaintance he looked truly murderous. She stepped back with the realization that despite her emotional devastation, she had no desire to die after all. The crimes he'd committed against her thus far were nothing in comparison to those of which he was capable.

He stalked her, backing her into the wall. Anguish over her broken heart hadn't left room for her to consider that he could actually stop the organ from beating altogether. The furious set of his jaw rapidly changed her mind.

"How would you like it done, love? After all we've been to each other, it seems too ordinary to just skewer you with a cutlass or slit your throat. I know; perhaps I should strangle you with my bare hands." He wrapped his fingers around her neck. "Isn't this much more intimate? And I won't be bothered with any blood in my cabin."

His rough fingers covered her neck, his touch mockingly gentle. Her traitorous body interpreted the contact as a prelude to something more sensual than strangulation. Damn him for touching her with a lover's caress rather than a murderer's grip. His hold slackened and his hands slid down to her shoulders. He caressed the hollow of her neck with his thumb.

"For one moment . . . did you think I could ever hurt you?"

Of all the treacherous things the chameleon could do, he'd turned the shade that left her most vulnerable. The soft pleading in his eyes was more dangerous to her than his callused hands around her neck.

Her arms came up between them, violently breaking his embrace. "Is that the look you gave Beatrice Marley before you sliced her open? I won't shut my eyes in a pretty swoon while you do your dirty work. I'll curse you until I've taken my very last breath."

Drew looked at her as if seeing her for the first time. Without another word, he strode to the door. Before he reached his destination, he abruptly turned to face her again. Self-preservation sharpened her instincts. He wouldn't take her by surprise.

His tight jaw pulsed with suppressed violence. "Don't worry that I'll kill you, love, though you are sorely tempting me. I don't care for men, and I've nothing else in which to spill my lust. You've served your purpose too well to destroy just yet."

She wished he had strangled her. On pure impulse, she rushed him, but he caught her wrists before her nails could draw blood. His show of superior strength fanned her outrage. She kicked him in the shin and anywhere else she could reach. He tried to dodge her onslaught by holding her away from him, but her aching toe told her she'd gotten him at least once.

The fruitless struggle brought her quickly back to her senses. Her violent outburst plainly displayed the ravaged soul she had desperately wanted to hide. He had taken away even her pride. She gave up with a defeated sob, yanking herself free of his grip.

She turned her back on him as tears rolled down her face. "Get out. I never want to see you again."

"This is my cabin. I'm afraid you'll have to see me again," he said in a thin, brittle voice.

She struggled to remain on her feet. Pain consumed her. He had to be out of the room before sorrow overtook her. Tomorrow she would be stronger, but not today. "Then leave me alone. I know who you are. I know what you are."

Drew said nothing, but she could still feel him standing behind her. She had to say something, anything, to make him leave. "Your game is over and we're all losers. Richard Marley and his poor wife, and God knows how many others died by your hands. If my father joins your list of victims, I swear I'll find a way to send you to hell."

"I'm already well acquainted with hell. I'm the devil, remember?"

She heard his departure but waited for the lock to click before she fell to her knees. Each sob burned her already swollen eyes and bruised her aching chest, but still she could not stop. After today, she'd force herself to act with all the strength she possessed. Her wretched tenacity would get her out of bed in the morning, even though she wanted to go to sleep forever. That same unyielding will would allow her to destroy a man she still loved any way she could.

The cabin door's thick wood muffled Felicity's sobs. Drew rested the back of his head against the sturdy portal, unsure whether the noise came from inside his own head or from the other side of the door. For the rest of his life, he would hear her broken cries in the darkness of his mind. If he moved away from the room, maybe he could block out the sound, but he had nowhere to go. He could not let anyone see him like this. The tears Felicity freely wept were trapped inside him. Recriminations ate him alive.

He'd wanted to comfort her, wrap his arms around her, but she made it plain she loathed the touch of a murderer. She had been correct in laying the blame for Marley and Beatrice's deaths squarely at his feet. He might not have killed them by his own hand, but if not for their association with him, they'd be alive today.

Drew walked away from the cabin, unable to bear being so close to Felicity without holding her. An orange haze filled the companionway, signaling late afternoon would soon give way to evening. He braced his back against the hull and waited. Dusk would allow him to hide in the shadows abovedeck.

When Felicity had believed him to be the man who'd murdered a man he'd once called a friend and a helpless woman in cold blood, he'd been beyond hurt and bloody well furious. In truth, Drew should have killed Marley once he'd revealed to Ben his plan to turn Drew in to save himself from possible exposure. But Ben had told Drew in confidence, and even if he hadn't, Drew doubted he'd have been able to do in Marley, and certainly not his wife. That act in itself had been the first nail in his coffin. A pirate who shied away from ruthlessness didn't survive.

Now, Drew had committed an even graver error: He'd left himself open to the opinion of a woman. After they'd made love, he would lie in bed surrounded by darkness and Felicity, and things he thought he'd forgotten had been pulled from him like rotten teeth. Throbbing memories of his childhood and of his family, to his surprise not all heartbreaking, evaporated in the sweet heat of the cabin. How could she see him as the fiend described by McCulla? But her accusations strayed too close to the truth. He'd finally been forced to see himself through her eyes.

The games he'd been playing had cost too many innocent lives. If Ben's name was added to the growing list, it would be as good as killing his friend with his own hands.

He'd repaid the man's kindness by dragging him along to spit in the face of England, society in general and even the devil. And as if that wasn't enough, Drew had taken Felicity to his bed while running from the hangman's noose.

Now his sire was calling in his due, and Marley, Beatrice and possibly Ben were forced to pay with their lives. Thus far, Felicity only had to sacrifice her heart. Though it physically sickened him for her to believe him a ruthless killer, he couldn't blame her. The overwhelming evidence almost convinced him he was the one and only El Diablo.

He pushed himself away from the hull in disgust. His phantom persona couldn't take the blame for the disastrous end to Drew's relationship with Felicity. She had seen through him from the very beginning. He had kept things from her; not actually lied, but never told her the whole truth about anything. That was the way he had always lived.

Drew emerged on deck to find a waning moon struggling through a veil of dark clouds. Night promised to be swift and black. He strode across the deck, not doubting his face looked as menacing as the sky. Felicity deserved better than the half-truths he'd doled out. He'd smiled and only told her what he wanted her to hear. Somehow, he'd expected her to find out in the end, but he hadn't anticipated the knowledge would rip him apart.

He should have apologized or at least taken his due like a man, but instead he'd acted like the bastard he was and always would be.

He'd lashed out at her for forcing him to care about what she thought. Her belief in McCulla's tale left him feeling betrayed. The disgust in her eyes stopped him from defending himself. At least if he had tried, she might not despise him now.

Let her hate him. She'd still be close to him, but as his prisoner. He had told her he was already acquainted with hell, but the word he'd tossed around flippantly was about to take on new meaning.

His aimless wandering returned him to the door of his cabin. He braced his hands on either side of the portal. Having Felicity in his bed every night and not being able to touch her would be torture. The days would be worse. He'd have to avoid his cabin altogether. Felicity would skewer him with venomous glares or slap him with verbal accusations.

He fought the urge to fling open the door and promise anything that would make her look at him again through sleepy, sated eyes. That seemed like a lifetime ago. Even if he gave in to his weak impulse, nothing he could say or do would bring her back to him. He walked away from the cabin in no particular direction.

Sometime before dawn, Felicity heard Drew's footsteps. She had retreated to bed, hoping the pretense of sleep would ease her emotional turmoil. It hadn't. Drew's approach proved that. She cursed her racing heart, willing herself to breathe deeply and her body to relax. Feigning sleep would forestall a confrontation for which she was not yet prepared.

He sank down on her side of the bed. Earlier, she had scooted to the edge of the large mattress. In the event he wished to sleep in his own bed, she thought the distance easier for both of them. Apparently, he had other ideas. His closeness stole her breath.

Behind the shelter of her closed eyes, she could feel his gaze on her, hear his breathing. Each second seemed an eternity. He just sat, nothing else. If his intention was to sleep, an expanse of empty bed loomed on her other side. His purpose in the room had everything to do with her. Had he decided to smother her while she slept?

She pictured her demise, hoping to dispel the deep desire to have him touch her. She had forced herself to imagine every brutal crime Drew had ever committed in an attempt to make herself stop mourning her lost love. For the second time in her life, the man who had stolen her heart didn't exist.

In Drew's case, she'd been unsuccessful in convincing herself of that. Too late, she realized she'd never really loved Erik. She had used him as an excuse to stretch the bounds of her sheltered life. His advances had met a willing partner.

If she weren't so busy testing her wings, she might have noticed Erik was a scoundrel before he left Boston with her father's money. Though Drew's reputation made her first lover look like a saint, in the deepest recesses of her heart she could not see Drew for what he was. God help her but she still loved him.

He picked up a lock of her hair. Instead of preparing for the attack she should expect, she lay perfectly still, fearing he'd stop if he knew her awake. He gingerly replaced the strand, then leaned so close, she could feel his breath on her cheek. If he kissed her, she'd throw her arms around him and remember to hate him all the more in the morning.

With his arms braced on either side of her, he hovered as close as he could without actually touching her. After a moment, she realized he was smelling her hair.

"Please forgive me," he whispered in the tangles next to her ear.

In that moment, Felicity knew she would. She'd forgive him anything and in the process lose every ounce of respect for herself. When he was near, she didn't even care.

He straightened but lingered beside her a moment longer before standing. She clutched the sheet under her fingers to keep from reaching out to him. Until she heard the door close, she didn't realize he'd left the room.

She flung back the covers and swung her feet to the floor. "Drew!" The cabin's dark silence forced her to consider whether Drew's presence was just a desperate dream.

No, he'd been no dream. His essence lingered in the cabin as clearly as the warmth left over from the hot day. But he was gone now, and she couldn't go chasing him around the ship in her nightclothes, or anything else for that matter. She retreated under the covers and recalled his caress and his plea. Fortunately, her father's face obliterated the softening creeping through her limbs and around her heart. To hold Drew within her body again, she might be able to turn her back on everything she believed, but she could not turn her back on her father.

When Drew was out of sight, her loyalties were without question. If her father was to have any chance at all, they must remain that way. She must get off Drew's ship. No matter the risk to herself or to Drew, she had to set things right. She had to let the authorities know the truth. Her father wasn't going to take the blame for Drew's deeds.

The next time temptation came to her in the night with soft whispers, she knew she would relent. The cost of her weakness would be her soul and her father's life. She might be willing to sacrifice the first, but the latter would surely destroy her. More danger threatened her in the confines of these four walls than did on the rest of the ship.

# Chapter Sixteen

The pretty barmaid set a bottle of rum on the scarred table and winked at Drew. She reminded him of Felicity. Not because the slender blonde resembled Felicity in the slightest; it was just that she was female. Actually, every damn thing conjured images of Felicity.

He should have stayed away from her room last night. The pain of being physically near her, yet knowing she despised him, haunted him all day. Their arrival in New Providence should have turned his thoughts to the business at hand. But instead of studying the scarred faces that roamed the cobblestone streets, he found himself distracted.

He uncorked the bottle. After filling a battered tankard for Solomon and then himself, Drew drank deeply. The cheap rum burned his throat and made his eyes water. He had to get a hold on himself.

Forcing a smile, he glanced at the barmaid. She must be new to the island. Though the front two were seriously bucked, she had all her teeth, and her skin glowed with a slight tan instead of bruises. Women didn't stay pretty long on New Providence.

Between his thumb and index finger, he held up a gold doubloon. He turned the coin until it caught the light pouring in from the large glassless windows cut in the tavern's front. "I'm looking for a man who looks like me. He calls himself El Diablo. Have you seen him?"

She reached for the coin, purposely caressing Drew's fingers in the process. He moved his hand and let her have the coin.

A seductive smile curled her lips. "No. I can't say I've seen anyone as handsome as you, love."

Her mouth was thin and even more so when she grinned, nothing like Felicity's full . . .

"Surely you've heard of a pirate using that name. I've been told he has a king's ransom on his head."

"If you're after the reward, you best be quick. His Majesty's men came 'round not but an hour ago asking the same thing. Those Redcoats drove away the business, they did. Could be fortunate for you, though. With my customers scared off, I haven't a thing to do for the rest of the afternoon."

"Nothing would please me more, but I fear I have a matter to settle with El Diablo that takes priority over my own pleasures."

The lie rolled smoothly off his tongue, rewarding him with the barmaid's promise to save any new information for his ears alone. The urgency to find the man who had killed Marley was real enough, but he had no desire to rise to her offer. Felicity had temporarily soured him on all other women. If only he could handle her with the ease with which he had enlisted the barmaid's loyalty. Felicity would serve him his tongue on toast if he dared attempt to sway her with honeyed lies.

Solomon toyed with his untouched tankard of rum. "That wasn't wise. Calling attention to the fact that you hold a remarkable likeness to El Diablo cannot be healthy. The woman could tell the British about you for the reward you were thoughtful enough to mention."

Drew shrugged. "We don't have time for subtleties."

Solomon's brow furrowed. "I could have made inquiries without you. You should have stayed aboard the ship."

"No. I couldn't." He'd rather be chased by a platoon of Redcoats than stay on his ship a moment longer. Felicity's animosity had started to seep through the walls.

To Drew's relief, Solomon had ignored his dark mood through their search of New Providence's crowded waterfront. Admitting he was upset would be akin to acknowledging how much he'd come to care for Felicity. He hoped his other unwanted conclusion was more mental flogging brought on by his rift with Felicity, rather than the only solution to his problem.

"The Redcoats are scouring the Caribbean for El Diablo and you're tossing pilfered doubloons like they were a mere pittance. You couldn't make it any more obvious that you're a pirate." Solomon kept his voice low and calm, but his dark stare bored a hole through Drew.

"They're Spanish doubloons. The British would probably congratulate me."

Drew poured himself more rum. The pressure of Solomon's hand on his arm stopped him from bringing the tankard to his lips.

"What the hell are you doing?"

Solomon removed his hand when Drew lowered the mug. "I was about to ask you the same thing. Or rather, what did *she* do?"

Drew had been dreading that question. Solomon was too smart not to figure out that Felicity was at the root of his foul temper. "If you're going to rub your infernal good sense in my face, the least you could do is let me get drunk first."

"Do you want to die, Drew? Stumble drunk from this

establishment and someone will likely slit your throat for tossing around gold coins faster than the British can hang you."

Drew lowered his gaze and massaged his forehead. His strained nerves could not stand a confrontation with his closest ally. "Felicity knows everything."

"I don't doubt our Miss Kendall believes she knows everything, but we both suspected that from the beginning."

Drew looked down at his full tankard of rum with longing. Solomon was going to force him to say it.

"Somehow she left my cabin and talked to McCulla, and she knows I'm El Diablo. Should I tell you you were right about her now, or can we save it for a time when I'm feeling less inept?"

"I took Felicity from the cabin." Solomon curled his hand around the tankard. Though Solomon didn't drink, Drew thought Felicity might have driven him to it. "She saved Avery Sneed's life. If you need to blame someone, blame me. Don't punish her."

Drew shook his head. Convincing Solomon to ignore his orders proved Felicity's abilities had no end. He was even defending her. Drew certainly couldn't blame Solomon for withering under her demands. If she remained in her current state of mind, he was as good as hanged.

"Your punishment for disobeying an order is to deal with Felicity for the rest of our journey. I know it's harsh, but there's no choice. She detests me."

Solomon's expression hardened into a threat. "Felicity Kendall isn't like your other women. You can't use her, then toss her aside without a second thought."

"I'm the one who's been tossed aside." Drew leaned back in his chair. "She thinks I killed Marley and Beatrice. She's convinced I seduced her to gain her cooperation."

"What did she say when you told her the truth?" asked Solomon.

Drew scanned the room, making Solomon wait for his answer. It seemed the British had indeed turned the Fatted Pig, a place known for the availability of every excess known to man, into a dusty tomb. Two well-worn pirates, one missing an arm, the other a piece of his nose, occupied a table in front of one of the large windows, capturing the breeze from the bay. Solomon and he were the only other patrons besides the men he had posted at the door and the long bar at the back. The delay didn't help him come up with a decent response to Solomon's question.

He had acted like a complete ass. The fact that it was for her own good didn't ease either Felicity's or his own suffering. "I didn't say anything. I let her believe the worst."

Solomon leaned forward. "Do not underestimate Miss Kendall. You need to explain yourself to her."

Drew had bungled the chance to explain things. An attempt to do so now would be met with fierce rebukes. She'd never believe another word from him as long as he lived. "No. You were right about Felicity from the beginning. I never should have brought her onboard."

Solomon shook his head. "I was wrong about Felicity but right about you. Miss Kendall demands to be treated with honesty. She likes to make her own choices. When given the opportunity and the correct information, she is fair."

"She found that bloody flag. What could I say to that?"

Drew should have realized the flag would cause him nothing but grief. All the other pirates who'd created a name for themselves had a personal standard that struck fear in the hearts of their victims before a shot had to be fired. When details of Drew's flag had begun to be whispered among the Caribbean ports, Drew had actually been thrilled. After years of being a bastard without name or family, he'd finally reached a level of status that set him apart from the unwanted child he'd been. No one would look upon him with scorn ever again—fear maybe, but not scorn. Unfortunately, the devil was finally calling in his due for fulfilling Drew's secret desire, and it was time to pay in full.

"Felicity is a fighter. She doesn't always choose the easiest path. It's obvious she cares for you, and you owe her a chance to make up her own mind." Solomon's words brought Drew out of his dangerous thoughts.

Drew shook his head. "It's better that she hates me. Too many people have suffered because of their association with me."

"It is obvious that making her your enemy is not better for you, and I doubt it has proven to be so for her. Your distraction could cost you your life. Have you considered what would happen to her and the rest of us if you were captured or killed?"

Drew tipped back his wooden chair, balancing it on two legs. He hoped he looked relaxed. Solomon's question gave him the chance to finally say out loud the idea he'd struggled with since he'd cooled from his confrontation with Felicity. Both Felicity and Ben, not to mention Solomon and his crew, would be a hell of a lot better off if he were captured. He was the one the British really wanted, whether he was Marley's killer or not.

"I think we should consider a plan to exchange me for Ben."

Solomon looked absolutely incredulous for the first time in their acquaintance. He blinked several times before his eyes narrowed. "And then what?"

Drew had trouble meeting his gaze and stared down at his tankard instead. The *and then what* was something he'd rather not think about. He shrugged. "You take Felicity and Ben somewhere safe. You can join them. I think Hugh would be better off in the company of a woman rather than a gang of pirates anyway."

"You're serious?" Solomon continued to stare, forcing Drew to meet his gaze.

"I see no other way."

"So, you just sacrifice yourself for all of us? That's not the way it works. Ben knew what he was getting himself into when he decided to sell our stolen goods. The Piracy Act is clear that merchants who deal in pirate contraband are to be treated as pirates. If the roles were reversed, would you expect Ben to turn himself in to save you?"

Drew might have been able to accept this reasoning if Felicity wasn't involved. "If my father hadn't come to Barbados, I doubt Ben would have been arrested. I don't know why I ever thought pretending to be his legitimate son was a good idea."

Actually, Drew did know why. He'd wanted recognition even if he had to steal it, as he'd had to steal every ounce of pleasure he'd ever gotten out of life. He'd had to steal his very survival. Maybe giving it up so easily wasn't such a good idea after all.

"I won't let you turn yourself in. Let's continue with our plan to find Marley's killer. Perhaps the man still has some of Marley's goods with him. We'll pay off some magistrate and have him arrested. Then the Barbadians can hang him and let Ben go."

Drew shook his head. Solomon's plan was weak at best. "That's not going to satisfy my father."

"I don't give a damn if it does or not. As angry as Felicity is with you at the moment, I don't think she wants you to sacrifice yourself, and I know Ben wouldn't. Let's wait and see what happens. They're holding Ben in hopes of attracting you. If all else fails, we'll try to sneak him out of jail."

Drew took a deep breath, the first he'd been able to draw since the idea of turning himself in had taken root. Solomon was right; now was not the time to give up. Not yet.

243

Despite the unbearable state of affairs between him and Felicity, he hoped Solomon was right about her as well. "I would most dearly relish getting my hands on Marley's killer, and I suppose I should try to make peace with Felicity. I couldn't saddle you with her in her current state."

"I'm afraid Miss Kendall proves unmanageable in any state."

Drew picked up his tankard, toasted his friend, then drained its contents. The rum's bite cleared his head. Drew innocently shrugged in the face of Solomon's displeasure.

"Time to start acting like a pirate instead of a lovesick swain."

Drew stood, then snatched his weatherbeaten hat from the equally worn table and plopped it on his head. He forced its wide curving brim to angle across his face. "Shall we go?"

Solomon stood. "Are we going back to the ship so you can straighten things out with Miss Kendall?"

"Not yet. Marley's killer didn't vanish into thin air. We'll ask around the docks, then wait for nightfall. Even the Royal Navy can't keep a pirate from rum and wenches once the moon is out."

Drew paused at the open door and scanned the room a final time. The barmaid waved from where she leaned on the back bar.

Solomon caught the exchange and glared at Drew. "You will speak with Felicity?"

Drew smiled at the woman, then nodded to his men guarding the bar. They knew to follow discreetly.

He returned his attention to Solomon. "As soon as we get back." Drew would have to ensure this excursion lasted until dawn. "Hopefully Felicity will have calmed down by then." Drew doubted it, but it didn't hurt to believe in the impossible. It had gotten him this far.

Solomon looked skeptical. "What if she hasn't calmed down?"

Drew stepped into the sunlight. "I give you my word as a former scoundrel, I will speak with Felicity no later than tomorrow morning."

Solomon followed him out the door. "Former scoundrel? Miss Kendall has made you see the error of your ways?"

The heavy smell of the sea drifted on a warm tropical breeze. Drew turned and headed in that direction. "If I stay alive that long."

On Felicity's third try, the lock clicked open. She pushed the door wide, hesitating on the threshold of freedom. The dark companionway reminded her that she still had a long way to go on an uncertain path. Even then, she could not consider herself free. Drew's betrayal would always hold her heart prisoner. She found her courage and stepped out. The chance for escape might not present itself again.

She paused her climb to the upper deck on a rung close to the top. A soft breeze blew through the riggings and a gentle splashing echoed against the silent ship. She hauled herself through the hatch and crept out onto the open deck.

Longboats full of men had left the ship throughout the day. Since she had no idea how many crewed Drew's vessel, she'd given up trying to keep track of who might be left onboard. The one thing she was sure of was Drew's absence.

An agonizing stab of loss pierced her with renewed force. At first, she'd been excited to discover they were in port. It was the chance she'd prayed for. When Hugh had arrived later in the afternoon and informed her of Drew and Solomon's absence, she knew with sickening certainty that nightfall would bring her best chance for a successful escape.

Even as she darted across the deck, sliding behind a thick

mast, she felt the pull to stay. She blamed it on fear of the unknown and slipped off her dress.

A peek around the mast brought the guard strolling the deck into view. He was whistling. She wished she shared his confidence.

After he passed, she slid to the other side of the mast and received her first glimpse of their destination. Dots of light clustered along the shore. The glow signaled a heavy population on the island. Her hopes of finding an established government, British if she were lucky, and someone who would help her, increased.

She pulled off her underskirts, then her shoes. In spite of her shivers, the sultry night warmed her skin. Wearing only a thigh-length chemise would be practical for swimming the distance to the shore. The length more than doubled the pond where she had learned to swim as a child. Sheer determination would have to keep her from drowning.

She rolled her shoes in her discarded clothes and secured the bundle around her waist with a wide sash. She waited for the guard to repeat his pacing in the other direction before creeping to the railing. Guilt plagued her despite her carefully considered decision to leave the prisoners in the hold. Her difficulty with the sturdy latch on the door confirmed she would not stand a chance at picking the thick lock securing McCulla and his men. McCulla could rot in the filthy hold for all she cared, but the child and the other men didn't deserve their fate.

Leaving them and going to shore on her own ensured her best chance of success. If all went well, she would find help for the others. She swung her leg over the railing and stared down at the long drop to the water.

The distance to the shore seemed to have increased. Suddenly, it appeared five times the length she had ever swum before instead of only double. She lifted her other leg over the railing. A quick glance at the guard showed he had circled the bow and was headed her way. It was now or never.

She let go of her death grip on the railing and jumped away from the ship. Instead of the hard, icy shock she'd expected, the warmth of the water embraced her. She swam underneath the surface until her lungs felt as if they would burst.

When she came up to catch her breath, she tasted salt. Despite the drenched bundle on her back, she floated easily. The warmth and the salt buoyed her above the surface. Treading water, she turned to look back at the ship. The guard leaned over the railing with a lantern in his hand. After a moment, he moved away.

Dark clouds drifted across the sky. The moon illuminated lighter patches of mist, painting them pearl gray. She memorized Drew's ship in the unearthly incandescence. The guard paced across the deck again with his lantern held over the railing. He appeared to scan the water below. Silently, Felicity glided farther from the spill of light. She needed to find her way to shore, but she hesitated a little longer.

The guard's pass brought the red lettering hugging the ship's side into view. Curiosity held her despite the burning that had begun in her legs from keeping herself in place.

She blinked and quickly reread the swirling script before the name was again swallowed in shadows. Drew's treachery took a final and fatal stab. The irony of it forced her to choke down a sob. She had never been anything more to him than a game. One he had played a thousand times before. She swam toward the lights on shore, the bold red script of the *Rapture* emblazoned in her mind.

Concentrating on each stroke that took her farther from Drew's floating den of debauchery kept her buoyant while her heart sank. She paused to note her progress and to catch her breath. The glow of civilization seemed just as

247

distant as when she began. She glanced back at the *Rapture*. The vessel blended into the night with only an occasional twinkle from a dim lantern to hint at its existence. Panic fluttered in her chest as she gazed at the expanse of murky sea separating her from her past and her future. She wouldn't die like this, wouldn't let Drew win. Strengthening her resolve, she pulled herself through the water.

Just as her arms grew too heavy to lift, her toe hit something solid. She lowered her feet and stood in waist-deep water. Voices and laughter carried over the soft murmur of waves lapping against the beach. The commotion came from the rows of planked buildings facing the shore. Light spilled through open windows where men amused themselves in drinking and carousing. She didn't have to see herself to know her chemise hung transparently against her skin. Fortunately, the men were too consumed to notice anything as subtle as a shadow wading out of the darkness.

She darted to a palm tree at the far end of the beach, away from the taverns. A yank on the bundle tied around her waist spilled her clothes to the fine white sand. The sopping wet clothes would at least cover her decently, and with any luck, she could dry in the shadows until morning. Hopefully, she'd find the officials of the island before breakfast.

Her struggles to straighten the twisted material of her bodice were interrupted by the sound of male voices moving in her direction. She forced her arms in the sleeves and pulled the dress up over her breasts without lacing it.

Three men stumbled across the beach to one of the dozen small boats lining the shore. To her relief, the men lifted one of the launches and grappled with lugging it to the water while they argued among themselves.

Hurriedly, she pulled on her stockings. After she was fully dressed, she leaned down to look for her shoes. At least she still possessed her own sensible boots. They were the only remnants left of the orderly and prudent life she had abandoned so readily. In retrospect, the years of lonely recriminations seemed a small price to pay. The penalty for being a fool multiplied tenfold the second time around.

Even so, she knew if she ever saw Drew again, she'd succumb to his charm as easily as she had before she knew the depth of his depravity. Saving her soul was almost as important as arranging her father's release from prison. The first might be hopeless, but the second would be accomplished no matter what she had to do.

She located one boot and yanked it on. To find its mate, she got on her hands and knees, brushing her fingers across the powdery sand in wide arches.

"What have we here?" leered a drunken voice. "A randy bastard he was who tumbled ya and didn't help you find your drawers. You won't get that kind of treatment from me, lass."

She jerked her gaze to find a bearded sailor swaying on the balls of his feet. A gold ring dangled from one ear and a red scarf covered his head. Lank strands of hair hung down his back. Cold fear squeezed the breath from her lungs. She stood up, backing away.

He slowly stalked her as if he were coaxing a scared animal to come out of hiding. "Come on, lass. I ain't going to hurt you. I got money. Gold coin." He reached into a pouch hanging at his waist and jingled metal.

Her usual bravado escaped her. This man was a real pirate, and he thought she was a harlot to be purchased.

"Sir, you've made a mistake. I've been held hostage. I'm trying to find help—"

"Don't worry, lass. Bertie will help ya." The pirate grinned, then took a giant step toward her. Felicity scrambled backward, stumbled over the hem of her unlaced dress and fell on her rump in the sand. Bile rose in her throat.

The pirate laughed. "Got you now. You're a feisty one. I like it when you girls play coy."

One of the men carrying the launch yelled in their direction. "Hey, Bertie—you pissing a river? Getcher arse back over here and help us."

When the pirate turned to answer, Felicity scrambled to her feet and ran. Terror made her quick, but not quick enough. An arm yanked her off the ground before she got far.

"Bloody hell. Now I'll have to share you," he said near her ear.

His breath smelled of strong spirits, his body of salt and filth. She struggled unsuccessfully to smash an elbow into his stomach. Despite her frantic struggles, he carried her easily to his friends.

The light from the taverns grew brighter on the open beach and his companions stared wide-eyed at her breasts. She looked down. Her worst fears were confirmed. Her gown had shifted in the struggle, exposing pink nipples against mounds of white flesh.

"Christ. Look at those. I want a feel," said his companion.

The pirate pulled her against him, gripping her bare breast with his other hand. "I found her, so I get her first."

His erection dug into her bottom. She swallowed hard to keep from vomiting. In desperation, she brought her one booted heel down on his toe.

The man yelped. He loosened his grip but didn't let her go. "She's got some life left in her."

"Yeah, but is she worth a flogging? Captain told us to go back to the ship so Roger and Niles can come ashore," said a second man. They all carried swords. Their filthy, scarred faces proved they used them often.

Her captor hoisted her back against him. "Captain wouldn't want me to miss out on a piece like this. Bet he'd want a go himself. I might take her to him and get on his good side."

"Gives us a reason to swig another ale," said the man who still leered at her breasts. "I might get a chance with that señorita at the Bloody Boar. She had an itch to mount my bowsprit, I can tell you that."

All the men except the speaker laughed. Felicity struggled not to listen to their conversation or picture what they intended to do to her. She would die before she let that happen. Her captor lifted her with one arm wrapped painfully around her rib cage and dragged her in the direction of the taverns.

A second man shoved his friend, sending him staggering. "The only thing she had an itch from was the bugger who had her before you."

Instead of exhausting herself with useless struggles, Felicity remained still in spite of her growing hysteria. Her captor squeezed her to near unconsciousness. She took shallow breaths, willing herself not to panic. The drift of their conversation wasn't helping her stay calm. She tried to block out their argument over their individual sexual prowess but found the task impossible.

"My bowsprit is bigger than all yours. But we'll let our little lass be the judge." Her captor leaned down and bit her lightly on the shoulder. When she jerked away, he laughed and squeezed her tighter.

She blinked back tears. After surviving the last month in the bed of the most notorious pirate in the Caribbean, she'd escaped only to land in the arms of these drunken savages. She doubted her current captor would care, but it was the only idea she had at the moment.

"Have you heard of El Diablo? I was waiting for him when you found me." Her voice sounded like a strained whisper. She wondered if the men heard her at all.

Her captor stopped abruptly. "That's the one the British are looking for. You know him?"

She was afraid to hope. "I've been on his ship this last month. He'll be furious when he finds me missing."

"I don't want any trouble with the likes of him, Bertie," said one of his friends.

"Won't be no trouble, but there might be a big reward." Her captor shifted her weight onto his hip. "Where can we find him, lass?"

"He's . . ." As far as she knew, Drew was in one of the taverns. The idea of revealing any information that might cause his capture constricted her throat.

Her dilemma was solved by an outburst from the sensible one of the four. "Oh, no, Bertie, you're not getting us in on this one. Let the whore go."

"You always were a scared one. Run on back to the ship. The rest of us will get the reward and the bastard's whore to boot. We'll be famous as El Diablo himself."

The other two men looked at one another and hesitated. Thankfully, the sensible one wanted to get rid of her as badly as Bertie wanted to keep her.

"You're drunk. And even if you weren't, what makes you think you got a chance against El Diablo? He'd feed you to the sharks."

She intended to tell them Drew was an actual cannibal, but the words stuck in her throat when the sensible one tried to yank her from her captor's arms. Suddenly, she became the object in a tug-of-war.

"Let go of her, you black-hearted bastard, or I'll knock you senseless," said Bertie. The other man didn't heed the warning, and Bertie followed through on his threat. In the erupting fray, Felicity found herself thrust to the ground.

She pushed herself up, spitting out sand. If she was hurt, she didn't have time to notice. She yanked up her bodice, grabbed the hem of her skirt and ran faster than she imagined possible.

The sailor named Bertie called after her, but she didn't dare look back. Nothing could stop her flight. A roaring sounded in her ears and she wasn't sure if it was the rush of wind or the beating of her heart. Sand turned to cobblestone and bit into her bare foot, but she refused to slow down.

The voices grew louder. She feared the pirates were behind her. A group of men loitered in the street, but they looked no better than the men chasing her, so she shoved past them. Someone yelled at her to stop. The voice had a crisp English accent. She stopped so abruptly, she slid forward before she caught her balance.

Instead of a rescuer, she found a white stallion rearing above her. A shove to the ground cut short her scream as the breath was knocked from her lungs. Pain exploded down her side. She struggled to remain conscious. She lost. Darkness enveloped her.

# Chapter Seventeen

Drew emerged from the *Rapture*'s lowest deck in a barely controlled rage. His crew scrambled about the main deck in preparation to set sail, while Solomon stood in the center of the activity, calmly giving orders. Drew forced himself not to shout, but to walk to where Solomon stood without attracting the attention of his men.

Drew motioned Solomon aside. "Don't let the prisoners leave the ship yet."

Solomon sent a sailor standing near them on a task before he turned his attention to Drew. "The skiff taking them to shore left shortly after our return. You said you wanted to be out of the harbor within the hour." Solomon's gaze narrowed. "What's wrong?"

Drew forced himself to speak slowly and calmly, though he was sure nothing in his expression hid his anger. "Felicity's not in my cabin."

Solomon stiffened, but Drew had the distinct impression his irritation was directed toward him rather than Felicity. "You shouldn't have left things the way they were between you two. Did you remember to lock her in when we left the ship?"

Drew wanted to lash out at Solomon, or anyone along for that matter, but he restrained himself. He unballed his fists and flexed his hands. "Do you think I would take the chance of letting her loose in her present state of mind?"

"Hugh probably let her out to see to Avery. I'll check there first."

Drew nodded. "I'll take over on deck. We'll move the ship to the other side of the island when the crew return with the launch. We can't leave New Providence until I find Felicity."

Damn Felicity. She'd left them in a dangerously vulnerable position. Pink dawn had already turned to a clear, bright morning, ensuring the *Rapture* would be easy to spot once someone started to look. Anchoring at the edge of the bay protected them from discovery as long as no one knew El Diablo lingered in the harbor. Once McCulla and his men found an ear to bend, every Redcoat on the island would be looking for his ship. And then there were the other pirates. For the size of the reward his father was offering, many of them would see their own mothers dangle at the end of a noose.

Drew had intended to be under full sail before McCulla stumbled into his first tavern—his most likely destination since Drew had supplied his prisoners with coin to see them safely home. Drew chose to believe his extravagant gesture reflected Ben's wishes rather than a foolish attempt to redeem himself in Felicity's eyes. A lot of bloody good it did him now.

He'd wring her pretty white neck in earnest when he found her. The dangers awaiting her if she'd left the ship were too numerous to consider. He paced the deck, checking inside coils of rope and anywhere else that might provide a clever hiding place.

The minute he had met the quiet emptiness of his cabin,

a sick sensation in the pit of his stomach told him she was gone. Luckily, overwhelming fury soon followed. Believing Felicity had disobeyed him was easier to accept than . . . He'd not stopped Solomon in his quest to locate Felicity belowdeck because Drew wanted his intuition to be wrong. Just as he wanted his other realization to be a misguided, overemotional conclusion brought on by lack of sleep. He was in love with Felicity.

Having never been in love before, he hadn't recognized the strange and decidedly consuming emotion. But the devouring fear that engulfed him when he discovered her gone showed him the truth. His chest tightened with every breath. Even the risk he put himself in—more importantly, the peril he subjected Solomon; Hugh and the rest of his crew to—could not make him change his course. He would not leave the island without her.

Solomon returned on deck with a tight jaw and a bleary-eyed crewman. The discreet shake of Solomon's head came as no surprise. "Mr. O'Neil was on watch last night . . . I thought you might want to question him."

O'Neil had the body of a man and the freckled face of a boy. He went from looking sleepy to looking nervous. "Did I do something wrong, Captain?"

Drew feared one of his reassuring smiles might turn into a grimace. The best he could do was try not to scowl. "No, not at all." This pup was no match for Felicity on a mission. "I just need to know if anyone left the ship last night."

The crewman glanced at Solomon, then back at Drew. "Most everybody left to go to the island except for the cook and Hugh. I thought they all had leave, sir."

Drew shook his head. "Something else. I'm looking for anything unusual you might have noticed."

The young sailor studied his feet for a moment, then lifted his gaze. "I heard a splash—like a dolphin jumping through the water. Thought maybe it was begging for a free meal. I looked but didn't see anything. I only heard it once."

"Thank you. That's what I needed." Drew turned away and stared at the island. The bloody shore had to be at least a mile from the ship. The idea of Felicity reaching land scared him even more than her drowning. The inviting white sand disguised a nest of rapists, cutthroats and thieves.

Drew stepped toward the railing and gripped the sleek wood. He addressed Solomon. "You'll lead a group of men to shore. I'll stay onboard and move the *Rapture* to the other side of the island."

The quartermaster sighed. "I'm glad to see you're being sensible about this. I thought you might insist on going—"

"If I were sensible, we would leave her." Drew squeezed the railing until his hands cramped. "Don't take any men to New Providence who had direct contact with the prisoners."

"What should I tell the crewmen I take?"

Drew's gaze never wavered from the island. "I don't care. Just find her."

Solomon moved away to carry out Drew's orders.

"Wait." Drew called Solomon back. He didn't want to think it, much less say it, but he had to know what happened to her. "Search the harbor first. The water is clear enough that you should be able to see the bottom."

Solomon leaned on the railing, inches from Drew. "Felicity wouldn't jump only to drown. She knew she could make it."

That was exactly what Drew feared most. At least drowning would have been quick. Knowing the hell she would endure if she fell into the hands of a real pirate almost made him wish they would find her embraced by the warmth of turquoise water.

*   *   *

The longboat carrying Solomon and the search party rounded the jagged rock marking the deserted cove on New Providence's north side. Drew steadied the spyglass. Felicity wasn't with them. Solomon still had two more hours of daylight. Drew lowered the telescope and wrapped his arms tightly in front of him to steady himself against the blackness threatening to overtake him.

Solomon wouldn't have returned until nightfall unless he'd found Felicity or her body. Drew lifted the spyglass again. He searched the bottom of the boat.

Hugh tugged on the back of Drew's shirt. "Did they bring Felicity back?"

The angle of the telescope didn't allow him to see below the men's knees. "I don't know."

"I want to see," whined Hugh as he grabbed for the leather tube.

"No. Go belowdeck." Drew couldn't breathe. He'd promised himself he'd never feel this way again. His mother's death had been beyond endurance. He had been a child alone in the world. A man wasn't supposed to be consumed by this kind of suffocating grief.

"I need my papa," Hugh wailed in a dry, sharp imitation of anguish.

Drew closed his eyes and groped for patience for Hugh and strength for himself. Hugh's tantrum stemmed from his fear for his father and Felicity. Every man on board knew Drew had sent their fellow crewmen to the island to search for a woman. They also were acutely aware of the peril it put them all in. Though the grumbling ceased at his approach, Drew suspected Hugh had heard all the rumors and speculation.

Drew forced himself to deal with the matter at hand instead of succumbing to his spiraling mood. Felicity might not be dead, and Hugh could not remain on deck squalling like a hungry seal.

He bent down and clasped the boy's small shoulders.

"Do as I asked. I'll send your father down as soon as he returns. That's an order."

Hugh curled his lower lip and puffed out his cheeks, but he did stop making that awful noise. Without warning, he threw his arms around Drew as far as they could reach. "I'm sorry. Did Felicity drown?"

Drew wanted to return Hugh's embrace. He wanted to hold him and keep him safe forever. Fifty suspicious stares burning into his back stopped him.

He gently peeled Hugh off him, then stood. Drew managed a crooked smile. "Let's pray she hasn't."

Hugh turned with real tears in his eyes and ran below.

A loose tackle, banging against the mast in the breeze, counted out the minutes it took the longboat to reach the ship. The crew grew silent. It seemed they held their breath with Drew as the men from the launch climbed onboard. Solomon's bleak expression confirmed Drew's worst fears.

Solomon paused in front of Drew. "Let's go below." He headed in the direction of Drew's cabin without waiting for a response.

Drew followed in a daze. It took all his strength to keep his features harsh and his stride angry. He was the captain, and if he wanted to stay the captain, he'd better not show his weakness.

When they reached his cabin, Drew closed the door behind him, wishing Solomon had chosen a different location. He had avoided the cabin since he found Felicity missing. Her presence overpowered the room. He couldn't believe her fierce spirit had been wiped out. He still felt her. She couldn't be dead.

As if reading his mind, Solomon tossed a black shoe on the table. "We found this in the surf. Do you know if it belonged to Felicity?"

Drew picked up the soggy leather boot. He'd hated her in black. Why hadn't he thrown the damn boots overboard

Cheryl Howe

with the rest of her puritanical garb, or tied Felicity to the
bed to keep her from leaving him, or sent her back to
Barbados the moment he found her?

"Drew."

Startled, Drew realized he clutched the wet shoe to his
chest. This was worse than his mother's death. He had
been a boy and could have done nothing to mend her broken heart. But Felicity—he had caused her death. Cold
fingers of grief reached into his chest and squeezed his
heart. It took all his concentration to listen to what Solomon was saying.

"She's not dead."

Drew's blood began to pump again. "Then where is
she?"

Solomon reached in the pocket of his jacket and pulled
out a folded square of parchment. "Your friend at the Fatted Pig gave me this. Some other men came by asking
about El Diablo, and the barmaid figured out who you
were. She's quite impressed."

Drew took the tattered note and opened it. A blond curl
drifted to the floor like a feather. He picked it up, rubbing
the hair between his fingers. He wasn't sure if he wanted
to laugh with relief or roar with rage.

" 'I have something you want. Come to the Fatted Pig
an hour before dawn. Alone and unarmed. Bring enough
coin to keep me from gutting your lady or turning you in
for the ransom.' "

When Drew finished reading the note out loud, he
crumpled the missive in his fist. He entwined the lock of
hair around his finger and rubbed the pad of his thumb
across the silken strand.

Solomon braced his hands on his hips. "You're not going."

Drew dropped the crushed ransom note to the floor. He
strode to a huge chest and yanked open the lid. A pile of
clothes littered the floor before he found what he searched

for. He brought the smaller chest to the table in the center of the room and dumped its contents, sending gold and silver coins cascading in a glittering waterfall.

Drew sat down and began to sort through the booty. "What's the value on my head these days?"

Solomon planted his hands on the table and brought his face close to Drew's. "You don't have that much."

"I might not need it at all." He reached for the lock of hair he'd tucked in the pocket of his breeches. "If a hair on her head has been touched, beyond this strand, I'll kill them."

"By yourself and without a weapon?"

"I'll have a weapon and so will you. I'm not stupid." Drew looked up from his stacks of coin, waiting for Solomon's argument. He could be walking into a trap, probably was—but his choices were limited.

Solomon sat down across from Drew. "Are you going to give them all this? It's all you have."

"It doesn't matter anymore. It wasn't worth it after all."

The unexpected truth in Drew's confession left his throat raw. A life of piracy had brought him riches and power, or so he'd thought. He had accepted his ill-gotten gains as proper payment for the injustices that had been handed to him and every man like him born without privilege or rank. But like everything else in his life, that had been just another excuse to do as he liked.

He had consciously chosen a crooked path. In fact, he'd reveled in his own wickedness. But he'd be damned if Felicity would pay for that. She'd given him her heart and he'd given her a wooden, theatrical prop and called it himself. When he got her back he'd give her anything she wanted. He'd even try to retrieve the young man who still possessed values and morality.

It was the man he might've been if he'd not ventured to Barbados. If she wanted never to see him again, he'd give her that too. Hell, he'd gladly make her an honest woman and provide her a house full of brats. He'd even leave piracy, but only after one more lawless act.

Drew raked the treasure back into the chest without counting any more.

Solomon scrambled to save the coins he had just carefully stacked. "Wait. I can't count as fast as you."

"We won't need it. I've a better idea."

Drew slammed the lid closed. He wouldn't mind handing over every last guinea he had to have Felicity safe, but a dead man wouldn't have need of treasure. Drew fed on his lust for revenge, longing for dawn.

# Chapter Eighteen

Through the Fatted Pig's two large windows, Felicity watched the night turn light blue, then pink. The rising sun gave the world shape. She had preferred the muted shadows. Morning would make it easier for the soldiers guarding her to kill Drew. They said they wanted him alive, but she didn't believe that. Their heavy arsenal of weapons told her as much.

No matter how many times she insisted Drew would not come for her, dread tickled her belly, telling her he would. She meant nothing to him, so why should he risk his life and, more importantly, his gold to rescue her? Her death, conveniently carried out by faceless strangers, would solve his problems nicely.

Her gaze drifted from the deserted street to the man with the musket across his knees crouched by the door. Another quick glance over her shoulder brought a jaunty salute from Admiral Meldrick. He'd traded his white uniform for what he apparently took to be the clothes of a ruffian. His crisp fawn breeches and linen shirt tied with an elaborate cravat still spoke loudly of civilization, a thing sorely lacking on New Providence. Though Meldrick's authority had surely saved her from a fate worse than death, she still wished she hadn't been forced into the position of bait. The butterflies in her stomach rose to her mouth with the sour flavor of fear.

She clasped her hands in her lap and waited. The men at the table beside her seemed absorbed in their card game, unconcerned that a notorious pirate might burst through the door any minute. Both men were dressed in well-worn canvas breeches and linen shirts with faded blue checks. The brilliant red sash each man sported around his waist, a standard for pirates on the island, stood out against the drabness like a beacon. Clean-shaven faces and neat hair gave away the fact that they were British officers.

She shifted in her roughly crafted chair, knocking the uneven legs against the planked floor. Drew was late. She'd told them he wouldn't come.

It hadn't been her idea to set the trap for Drew, but she had gone along with the scheme. In the first place, she doubted he would rescue her, and her cooperation seemed to appease Admiral Meldrick. She suspected he'd have gladly let the brutes who chased her into the street keep her if Bertie hadn't started babbling about El Diablo. Apparently Bertie had a price on his neck as well and had felt compelled to distract the admiral from himself.

Without warning, the bright blue door swung open. The startled marksman moved sideways to keep from being hit. Felicity glanced behind her in time to see Admiral Meldrick duck behind the bar.

Drew strutted into the room as if he was an honored guest. His presence consumed everyone's attention. He wore snug black breeches tucked into knee-length boots. His white linen shirt hung open at the neck. Missing from his waist was a sash and, more importantly, the weapons that were usually secured by the cloth. That fact did not lessen the aura of danger surrounding him. His wind-tousled hair fell loosely around his shoulders and his eyes narrowed in feral aggression.

The two men next to her shot to their feet in a shower of cards. Obviously they'd not expected Drew to come either, much less make such a dashing entrance. The man on her right fumbled for his pistol and pointed it at Drew.

Felicity gripped the bottom of her seat to keep from leaping out of it. Why had he come? She fought a dangerous combination of hope and fear. Her emotions were too tangled at the moment to know what any of it meant.

Drew stalked toward them, apparently unconcerned by the threat. Not once did his gaze stray in her direction. "Sorry I'm late. I was detained by some friends of yours. I convinced them I could find my way here on my own."

"That's far enough. Move your hands away from your body," said the one holding the pistol.

Drew obeyed. "Release the woman. You have your prize."

"Search him," said the higher-ranking soldier to the man next to him. The other soldier hesitated. His raised eyebrows showed he thought the request the ravings of a madman.

The officer used both hands to steady the weapon. "That's an order. I'm aimed at his heart."

The soldier inched toward Drew.

"Mistress Kendall is under our protection now." The officer holding the pistol squared his shoulder in a confident stance. "I won't subject her to any more of your brutality, Mr. Crawford."

Felicity glanced down at the modest gown hiding her feet. The tight pull of her prudish bun and the high neck of her borrowed dress made her feel a fraud. Fortunately, Drew ignored her. If she had to look into his eyes, she would give herself away. They would all realize she was still in love with him.

"Are you going to hang me on New Providence?" said Drew matter-of-factly.

She jerked up her head. She couldn't bear to watch Drew hang. The man ordered to search Drew squatted as he patted the length of his leg. Without a weapon, Drew would never have a chance to escape. She blinked away the tears threatening to run down her cheeks. What had she done?

"No, Mr. Crawford. It seems you've made one of His Majesty's favorite noblemen angry with your escapades. He's on Barbados and wants to see you hang properly. You'll have a trial, but—"

The man's words were cut off by the sound of a thud near the window. She didn't see the blow that sent the marksman beside the door sliding to the floor. The bulk of a pirate looming outside the window gave no doubt of its source. Before the officer holding the pistol could react to the new threat, a streak of metal imbedded itself in his chest. He looked down at the protruding handle of a dagger, then fell to the sandy floor.

Drew swiftly brought up his knee, smashing it into the chin of the man searching him. Solomon, followed by Drew's crew, spilled through the windows and door. British soldiers adorned in bright red coats leaped from behind the bar.

Felicity jumped from her chair. She turned in a full circle while the battle erupted all around her. With the cutlass retrieved from the downed man at his feet, Drew engaged two soldiers at once. Swinging cutlasses and screaming men made it hard to follow the tide of the melée.

Felicity knelt to pick up the pistol dropped by the man with the dagger in his chest, who thankfully remained facedown. Before she could decide whether she should roll him over and check for signs of life, the table beside her exploded under the weight of a body being tossed onto it, sending her to her feet. She darted out of the way of the red-haired giant who leaped on the fallen soldier, and gripped the pistol until her knuckles turned white.

As swiftly as it began, the clash quieted. Felicity frantically searched for Drew. To her relief, the men littering the floor mostly wore red coats.

"Felicity."

Her softly spoken name sounded above the soft moans and angry curses. She spun to find Drew walking toward her. He reached out to her with his right hand, the lowered cutlass in his left dripping blood. Solomon yelled something and the pirates hurried through the door.

With his arm still outstretched, Drew stepped closer to Felicity. "We must leave now. There are more British in the area."

The door of the tavern swung shut when the last pirate dashed out. Drew stayed, his back to the door.

Felicity dropped her gaze, afraid she'd weaken if she looked too long into his eyes. "Get out of here."

Drew moved purposefully toward her, looking as if he intended to throw her over his shoulder and carry her out. And God help her, she wanted him to go. She glanced up at him and forced herself to see the killer she knew him to be instead of the man she feared she still loved. In the breadth of Felicity's exhalation, everything she thought she believed in fell away. She knew she had no choice but to act and act now. She raised the pistol and fired. The shot flew over Drew's shoulder. The force of the blast startled her. She staggered, unbalanced by the noise and her own actions. Acrid smoke rising from the pistol burned her nostrils. She blinked hard to orient herself.

Solomon swung open the door. "We're saddled and ready to go. More soldiers are on their way from the harbor."

Drew stared at her, the understanding of her seeming betrayal dawning on his features. Without a word, he turned and ran to join Solomon. A sob caught in her throat. She couldn't have explained her actions even if he'd given her the chance. She didn't understand herself. At that moment, all she could think about was killing the man aiming the musket at Drew's back.

The door again swung closed. The marksman slid to the floor, clutching the hole in his belly made by Felicity's shot.

The ship heeled violently leeward. Water rushed over the sailors' feet as they scrambled to keep from being swept overboard. Drew held the wheel steady, yelling orders above the rush of wind. Cold rain stung his cheeks and he squinted to protect his eyes. The British became little more than a speck on their stern, but he'd not slacken their sails, even in the face of the storm. The *Rapture* sliced through the turbulent waves with the grace of a gull in flight.

Soaring with the wind lessened the heaviness in his chest. He didn't want to stop or slow down. If he did, he feared he'd sink under the weight of Felicity's betrayal. Had she orchestrated the trap or was she just a willing participant? The muscles of his jaw tightened at the thought of either possibility.

He'd recognized the British trick the moment he encountered the soldiers lurking on the outskirts of town. The patrol of seamen there instead of the well-trained, redcoated marines could only mean that the British were undermanned or the ground troops were involved in something more important. Drew wasn't that lucky. It had to be a trap.

Fear had been his first sensation when he realized who held Felicity, but not for himself. She would undoubtedly trust the demons in uniform and babble on about her father and his innocence, unknowingly giving the British enough evidence to hang Ben with a clear conscience. Being the fool that he was, it had not occurred to him that she'd hand him over to prove her point.

The trap had not concerned him. What choice had she really had once the British got their hands on her? He could have freed her, and they could have been on their way without too much damage done. It was the way she'd stared through him as she leveled the pistol that severed his heart. The ball had missed him, but the shot had found its mark.

Sails strained against another powerful gust, forcing Drew to give the order to release the tension on the sheet or risk tearing his foresail. The ship's leeward side emerged from the water, but Drew maintained their speed.

He should hate Felicity. He should see her for the conniving women she was. Even Samantha Linley would be impressed. Unfortunately, his heart still beat faster at the thought of Felicity Kendall. And with each throb, the knife there twisted.

Solomon staggered up beside Drew and shouted something that was lost in the roar of the waves. Drew shook his head. Solomon raised his voice to the pitch of a kettledrum. "The navigator wants to know where in the hell you're going."

"Just hell in general. Care to join me?"

Solomon shook his head and pointed to the small cabin used for navigation. Drew signaled to one of the men on deck to take the helm, before following Solomon into the shelter.

Pulling off his hat and canvas jacket left Solomon relatively dry, while Drew stood dripping water onto the floor. "I've been to hell. It was a sugar plantation on Barbados and, as I remember, it was your idea to leave."

Drew peeled off his shirt, and Solomon tossed him a dry piece of cloth. He squeezed excess water from his hair and dried off his upper body. When he felt relatively dry, he approached the large desk covered with maps. The navigator stepped away.

"Go below and get some rest." Drew took the compass from the tired man.

He waited for the navigator to leave before he spoke. "That plantation wasn't really hell, just one of her many settlements, my friend. The real place exists only in the darkest parts of one's own heart."

Drew lifted the top map, glancing beneath it. When he didn't find what he searched for, he bent down and rifled through a chest below the table.

He stood and unfurled a map on top of the others. "This is the place."

Solomon glanced over his shoulder. "The Orient. That's on the other side of the world."

"Exactly."

"What about Felicity?"

Drew picked up a divider. He swung the points of the instrument across the map. "It's been my experience that when your loved one points a gun at your heart, it's a signal her affection has waned."

Solomon ignored the map, scrutinizing Drew instead. "The British could have coerced her."

Drew studied the map in hopes of diverting Solomon's interest away from himself. He felt like an open wound and he feared it showed.

"They could have, and she could have aimed for my knees."

Solomon folded his arms over his chest. "Your bruised manhood is no reason to leave her in danger."

Drew put down the instrument and faced Solomon. "You weren't there. The little witch fired a pistol at my heart at two paces. Thank God I neglected to teach her to aim."

Felicity had hit her mark just the same, but he'd not taught her that. Some twisted irony must be at work, bringing him low by the same method he'd used so many times in his favor. Every woman whose affection he'd innocently toyed with had received revenge through his weakness for a female who wanted to kill him. As bad as Felicity wanted it, he'd be damned if he'd appease her with his life. Wasn't the destruction of his newfound heart enough?

Solomon finally glanced at the map. "Maybe she missed you on purpose."

"Don't worry about Felicity. They're likely to make her governor of Barbados by the time this is over."

"What of Ben? You're abandoning him too?"

"I feel for Benjamin, but Felicity is his flesh and blood. I didn't have anything to do with it."

"Miss Kendall's rejection must have wounded you deeply to make you turn your back on Ben. I don't think I've ever seen you like this." Solomon pointed to a spot on the map. "I've always wanted to visit China. I think it would be good for Hugh to see the world."

Drew glared at Solomon's downcast face. He picked up the weights holding down the map, letting it curl up on Solomon's nose. "Ben's in much better care with Felicity as his protector. She'll secure his release in a week with stories about me that will make Blackbeard look like a suckling babe."

The portal leading from the deck tentatively creaked open. Drew expected to see Hugh, who'd been ordered belowdeck, but instead a white-faced Avery Sneed stumbled into the room. "Heard we were engaging the British. I'm ready for duty, Captain."

"Sorry, Avery, but we've outrun them." Drew stepped toward the man with the intention of helping him back to his hammock.

The second mate clutched his side and wavered on his feet but straightened at Drew's approach. "No need for your assistance, Captain. I'm as strong as I ever was."

"Back to your quarters, Mr. Sneed." Solomon barked the order. He motioned Avery through the door with a wave of his hand, making no move to help him. "You'll have the helm tonight, and with the impending British threat, we don't have room for mistakes."

Avery nodded. He limped from the room with his head held high and his back straight. Drew stood in the open portal, watching him go. The rain had stopped, but the strong winds shoved at the wounded man's thin form. When he disappeared belowdeck without falling flat on his face, Drew closed the door.

"Do you see? She can even raise the dead—and they call *me* El Diablo."

"Felicity means well, despite her tactics. She's not a killer. You're mistaken about what happened."

Drew stepped around Solomon to return to the navigation desk. Solomon hadn't experienced the sensation caused by having the woman you love aim a pistol at your heart. Drew had almost been disappointed when she missed. Maybe then he could have hated her and not felt as if he'd left a vital organ behind.

For his own sake, he changed the subject. "You're not going to let Avery return to duty tonight. That's an order if it has to be."

"I traded some of your brandy for laudanum in New Providence. I'll slip some in his grog," Solomon said.

"You're getting crafty, Solomon. Learning tricks from me?"

Solomon laced his hands behind his back. "No. Felicity gave me the idea. After treating Avery, she thought having a sedative on board would be useful."

"All of those uses no doubt had something to do with my demise." Drew rolled up the map of the Orient and tossed it back into the trunk.

Solomon's eyes widened in exaggerated surprise. "We're not going to China after all?"

Drew pulled a map from the bottom of the stack and placed it on top. "We'll skirt the islands close to Barbados to make sure I'm right about Ben's safety. At least I'll have a clear conscience when I retreat in disgrace."

"We can also make sure Felicity stays out of trouble."

Drew laughed, surprised he still could. "Solomon, Felicity doesn't find trouble. She creates it."

Admiral Meldrick looked down his hooked nose at Felicity. "Miss Kendall, do you have any idea of the trouble you're in?"

She lifted her tired gaze. "But I don't know where he would go."

The British admiral slapped his riding crop across his gloved palm. "He didn't take you to an island where he might have a home or to anyplace where he feels safe?"

"I've already answered that."

"Answer it again." He brought the riding crop across the table in a loud whack.

She had stopped jumping at the sound two hours earlier. Her elbow propped on the table kept her head from drooping. "I'm tired. I don't know anything else to tell you."

He picked up a lantern and held it close to her face. "You've told us nothing. You know we can have your father tortured before he hangs."

She glared at him in spite of the light hurting her weary eyes. "I've had an awful day, and I would like to rest now."

Behind her, a soldier shifted his feet in the powdery sand accumulated on the planked floor. She could feel the other soldiers' unease as well. Admiral Meldrick must have sensed it too because he returned the lantern to the table and paced away from her.

She'd not been allowed to leave the tavern since the skirmish that morning. Meldrick had been furious at the debacle. Many British were wounded, but only two had died—the man who had been skewered with the dagger and the marksman Felicity had shot. The young man lingered for an hour before he finally succumbed to his wounds. It was an hour she would relive in her nightmares.

Admiral Meldrick paced back to her, the pleasant smile curving his lips an indication that he'd calmed down, or that he was going to eat her whole.

"Excuse my temper, Miss Kendall. The Duke of Foxmoor chose me for this mission and you've made me look a fool. The duke is a powerful man. He's promised me his favor for bringing him El Diablo's head. He could help you too and, more importantly, your father."

She stared through him without answering or acknowledging she'd heard. He'd said nothing new. He asked the same questions and made the same threats repeatedly. Anything else she might do or say in her near delirious condition would only cause her father and herself more harm.

Admiral Meldrick strained to maintain his grin. The lines on his face grew frightening. "I want you to think. Did Andrew Crawford mention a home or friends in the area?"

She'd considered telling them of Drew's island, since she didn't have any idea of its location. Even if she wanted to, she couldn't tell the British how to get there, but the secluded inlet was Hugh and Solomon's hiding place as well. She couldn't risk inadvertently condemning them to a life of slavery. Bringing herself to think of the well-mannered Solomon as a pirate proved as difficult as convincing herself Drew was a killer.

She rocked her head back and forth in the cradle of her hand. "No. I don't know who his friends are," she whispered.

Admiral Meldrick's riding crop smashed across the table. "Have you forgotten, at least five witnesses saw you murder one of His Majesty's men?"

"I was aiming at El Diablo. I missed. I told you that already."

The lie stuck in her throat every time she told it. Admitting to her crime would not bring the marksman back. Lying might keep her father and herself alive. Obviously, Admiral Meldrick didn't believe her; he shook his wigged head and paced in the other direction.

Running into the British soldiers had not been a blessing after all. Everything Drew had said about the treatment she would receive from King George's representatives had turned out to be true. With each passing moment, she dug herself deeper into a hole that would bury her father, and it appeared she would be going under with him.

Her choice to save Drew had been a reaction, not a thought-out plan. Knowing the consequences of what she'd done and having to live with the man's death on her conscience didn't make her regret saving Drew's life. He thought she'd betrayed him. Even that was as it should be. Yet despite her resolve and the redemption of her soul, she'd wanted to take Drew's hand when he'd offered it to her. She fought back tears. Through her exhaustion burned the ache in her chest.

A commotion outside the tavern warranted only a slight lifting of her head. She'd not eaten since before she'd found Drew's flag and had slept only for a few short hours. The weight of her head seemed immense. Holding it up with her tired neck represented a colossal task.

She glanced toward the door. Captain McCulla entered the room, propelled by two soldiers. Felicity found the strength to sit straight. A headache started at the top of her neck and wrapped around to her eyes. Her resolve to remain quiet didn't stop things from getting worse. Surely she was being punished.

"This man claims he was El Diablo's prisoner." The soldier holding up McCulla's right side adjusted his grip.

The red-faced captain had turned crimson and his head

wobbled on his neck. He was falling-down drunk.

Admiral Meldrick sauntered regally toward McCulla. He stopped short and waved his riding crop in the air. "Good heavens, but this man's foul. This had better not be a waste of my time, because it certainly is an affront to my senses."

"Aye, sir. I got information for you. That bloody bastard El Diablo is right in this very harbor waiting to be plucked," slurred McCulla. "I can take you to him."

Admiral Meldrick covered his mouth and nose with a lace-trimmed handkerchief. The gold fringe on his immaculate white uniform shimmered with his movement. "Your information appears to be at least a day old. A vessel in my fleet gave the ruffians in question a merry chase only to return empty-handed less than an hour ago. If you can tell me where El Diablo can be found—and I assure you it's nowhere near New Providence—I'll be glad to entertain further discussion on the matter. If not, be gone."

McCulla wiped the back of his hand across his mouth. "If you provide a bottle of rum, milord, I can tell you everything about the thievin' bastard, including his real name."

Disgust appeared undisguised on Meldrick's face. "Remove this drunkard from my sight." The admiral pivoted on his heel, dismissing McCulla.

"Wait. I can tell you about his ship, about his crew—" When he spotted Felicity, McCulla swallowed his sentence. He lifted his arm and pointed at her. "That's his whore, right there. She helped him with everything. She's probably spying for him so he can come back and slit your throats in the night."

"Indeed." Meldrick's gaze swung to Felicity, then back to McCulla. "Lovers, you say?"

Felicity knew better than to speak.

McCulla licked his dry lips. "She had the run of the bleedin' ship. They planned to let her da take their punishment while they rutted like animals. You should 'ave seen the way he had her dressed, not all prim and proper like she is now."

Meldrick smiled. "Get Mr. McCulla a bottle of the libation of his choice."

All traces of Felicity's exhaustion were swept away by fear.

Meldrick dropped his handkerchief to the floor, carefully placing his knee on the cloth so as not to soil his crisp white breeches. He knelt beside Felicity and gently took her hand. "You failed to mention you were Andrew Crawford's lover. Is that why you ventured from Boston to Barbados in the first place?"

She started to speak, but the admiral held up his other hand. "Don't bother to deny it, Miss Kendall. Your cheeks have turned a most delightful shade of red."

She yanked her hand from his grasp. "My father had nothing to do with my relationship with Mr. Crawford." She lifted her chin, refusing to quail under the triumphant glow in his eyes.

Admiral Meldrick stood. "I'm afraid you've lost your credibility. I almost believed you were aiming at El Diablo when you pulled that trigger, but not now. Not only will I see to the prompt execution of your father on our return to Barbados, but you'll be swinging right next to him."

Bile rose in the back of her throat. If she had to speak, she would have choked. Instead, she glared at Admiral Meldrick. He looked exceedingly pleased.

"What do you suppose our El Diablo will do now?" he asked. Not waiting for an answer, he strutted to the table where McCulla greedily gulped down rum, and the two men began to converse as if they were childhood chums.

Drew would not come for her this time. She and her father would die.

# Chapter Nineteen

Felicity jerked back from the stench rising from the darkness at the bottom of the stone steps. The guard escorting her into the Barbados gaol gingerly touched her elbow. She yanked it away and continued her descent on her own. She didn't deserve his care. In the luxury of the British vessel that brought her back to the island, she'd almost been able to forget her status as a prisoner. Entering the tomb that incarcerated her father altered her false sense of ease.

Convincing Admiral Meldrick to allow her to see her father had been too easy. His congeniality had raised Felicity's suspicions—especially considering the dire pronouncement he'd made earlier about obtaining her death. But the royal treatment she'd received on their voyage back to Barbados on the HMS *Warwick* had brought an understanding: it was not too late to save her neck or her father's. During several nights' meals with the admiral, not a word was mentioned regarding her impending trial. She'd come to understand that Meldrick found the idea of hanging a woman almost as appalling as she did. He fully expected her to eventually condemn Drew and save them both a lot of unpleasantness.

Through their dinner conversations, she'd learned of the warships accompanying them. Admiral Meldrick bragged of El Diablo's inevitable crushing defeat if he attempted a rescue. On their last night at sea, with no sign of Drew or the *Rapture*, Meldrick's jovial mood turned sour. However, he had perked up when she'd insisted upon seeing her father as soon as they docked. The condition of her father's imprisonment explained Admiral Meldrick's response.

She deserved to be in this dungeon alongside her father. Then she might rid herself of her loyalty to a killer. Not that she wanted to hurt Solomon and Hugh, but if she told the British of their island . . . The thought fell away unfinished. She wouldn't reveal information that could lead— even inadvertently—to the capture of Drew or his crew. Therefore, she and her father would die.

She fought back tears. While sacrificing her own life would be just penance, her father didn't deserve to be kept like an animal or have his life taken from him. He'd never harmed another human being in his life. Yet his own daughter didn't have the strength of character to save him. Not if it meant sacrificing Drew.

Light pierced the darkness through small windows located high in the stone walls. Cells lined each side of the passageway. A dank must seeped from the floor and the walls, making it hard to breathe. Prisoners leaned against the stone, silently watching them. An occasional rattled chain or the steady drip of water were the only sounds penetrating the hollow stillness of despair.

In one of the cells, thin arms and legs protruded from a bundle of tattered clothing. What was once a man lay huddled in the corner, shrinking from a shaft of sunlight touching the dirt floor.

Felicity hesitated until the guard propelled her onward.

When she realized the man wasn't her father, she let out a sigh of relief. The feeling only lasted for a moment. The third cell she came to held the man she sought.

Her father staggered to the bars separating them, his eyes wide with disbelief. He reached out to her, but had only enough room to push his fingers through the metal. "Felicity?"

She interpreted the smile lighting his sunken features to mean he'd not heard of her exploits or her fate.

She hooked her fingers through his. "Father, I've been so worried about you." Her voice came out low and husky, but she managed to gulp back her sob.

"I must say the same, daughter." His filthy clothes, probably the ones he'd been wearing when he was arrested, swallowed him. The cream of his stockings had turned sooty gray. Tufts of white hair sprang like horns from the sides of his balding head. Despite all this, he smiled at her. "I suspected you got yourself on Lord Christian's ship, but—"

"You know that's not who he is. He's an awful man. Truly awful." This time she choked on her words. She'd not meant to bring up her relationship with Drew, but her heartache spilled from her like a child confessing her nightmares in the hope her father could banish them forever.

He squeezed her fingers. "What's this about, Felicity? Drew wouldn't mistreat you. He wouldn't mistreat a woman—"

She pulled her hand away. "I think Beatrice Marley would disagree. He's the one they call El Diablo. Surely you know that. That's why you're here."

His smile faded, revealing the gauntness in his drooping cheeks. All her memories of her father centered around his rounded, smiling face and his laughter. He'd been just like that on her arrival in Barbados, but she'd not appreciated him. Instead, she'd noticed only his failings, as she perceived them. She'd condemned her father, believing him to be a fool. With the impending demise of her own short, painful life, she finally realized she too was a fool.

She wrapped her fingers over his, regretting making him frown. The truth would not change their fate. If condemning Drew upset him, she'd hold her tongue even if she choked on it.

Her father attempted to smile again, but the effort merely wobbled his lips. "Don't be sad for me. I knew the possible consequences of my actions, and now I'm paying for them. But I don't blame Drew, and neither should you. For once in your life, Felicity, try to see with your heart and not your eyes."

"I did see with my heart and believed all of Drew's lies." Leaning her forehead against the cool metal bars hid the tears in her eyes. She had no right to cry for herself when her father remained in this place. "I actually convinced myself I loved him." Her confession burned her throat. She lifted her head to look into her father's face. She owed him the truth. "God forgive me, but I still do."

"I see." Her father's direct gaze warned her that he understood far more about her relationship with Drew than she intended to tell him. "Perhaps Drew has a few things to answer for in that respect, but I can assure you his goal wasn't to intentionally hurt you."

She squeezed the bars of her father's cage, anger filling her now instead of sorrow. The fact that her father could still defend Drew proved the man's seduction of him had been more thorough than her own. "You've always softened your heart to fools, and now you've extended your blind kindness to murderers. Drew used me. He used you. He murdered your dearest friend, his innocent bride, and still you can't see what he is. I should have shot him while I had the chance."

Her father's eyes narrowed, the warm brown hardening into an expression she'd never seen before. "Your mother made me promise to let you have more freedom than other girls because of your strong spirit. I've done that, but this time you've gone too far. I assure you, if you do anything to bring about Drew's capture, I will go to my grave with a rift between us that will never be healed."

"How can you take his—"

"Do you think me such a simpleton that I didn't know Drew was not who he claimed to be?"

She tried to convince herself she misunderstood what he was saying, but his chilling revelation seeped past her anger. "You knew he was a pirate all along?"

Her father sighed. "Yes. Marley and I were traveling the same course we'd been on in Boston. Without royal influence or noble blood, we didn't have a chance in trade as honest businessmen—even in England's remotest colonies. Drew changed our fate or we would have lost everything, including the house your mother left your brother."

She blinked, realizing her eyes had been wide with surprise. "But it was Mother's wish for the house to be Jonathan's when he came of age."

Her father lowered his gaze. "Legally, the house was mine. I'm ashamed to say I put up your home as collateral to obtain the money it took for Marley and me to start over again in Barbados. I swear I planned to make the money back twofold and give Jonathan his inheritance. With Drew's help, I was able to do that."

Felicity stepped back from the bars separating them. She questioned whether she'd ever known her father at all. "And you sought out a reputed killer to ensure your financial success? I don't understand. I never would have thought you would profit on other people's misery for any reason."

"For once, daughter, hear me out before you condemn me. I found Drew half-conscious after he washed up on a beach on the other side of the island." He raised his hand to stop her when she opened her mouth to interrupt. "I'd been contemplating my financial woes and walking aimlessly. The young man looked in worse shape than I was. I thanked God for that which I did still possess and took him home to nurse him back to health."

"When will you learn not to take in every stray dog you see loitering in the streets? If this hasn't taught you your lesson, I don't know what will."

"Let me finish and we'll see who will learn the lesson!"

Felicity bit her lip to keep it from trembling. In all her life, her father had never raised his voice to her.

"The skin around the lad's ankles and wrists had been rubbed raw. He looked as if he hadn't eaten in weeks. When he came to his senses, he told me he'd been captured by the Spanish. He'd escaped from a prison on a small island on the Spanish Main, but his crew hadn't been so fortunate. They were hanged on their capture."

She noticed the guard lurking at the end of the corridor and lowered her voice to a whisper. "You let an escaped prisoner stay in your home?"

"He was a runaway indentured servant who'd turned to piracy out of necessity. You must understand, I was close to debtors' prison at the time. I sympathized with his plight, knowing I might soon meet a similar fate. You and your brother would have been turned out on the streets."

She gripped the bars. "And you trusted him, knowing he was a thief?"

"Yes. And if you could listen to the truth you know in your heart, you wouldn't be swayed by falsehoods spread by others. I know Drew is a good man, even if he's confused about himself."

The guard shuffled toward her. "Just a few more minutes," she pleaded. He nodded and disappeared into a dark corner of the prison.

She turned back to her father. "I found El Diablo's flag in Drew's cabin."

Her father dismissed her damning statement with a wave

of his hand. "That flag was used for intimidation. As was the character. El Diablo was as much a fiction as Lord Christian. Lord Christian was Drew's identity on this island, El Diablo off. Drew was ruthless, yes, and he was a pirate. But women and children had nothing to fear—"

"Then who killed Marley and his wife? Did you not know that the Duke of Foxmoor claims Marley wrote to him about Drew's impersonation of Lord Christian?" Felicity heard the desperate emotion in her voice, but whether she hoped to convince her father or herself, she didn't know.

"Marley shouldn't have been so greedy. He was fine selling pirated goods until merchants started hanging beside the pirates they bought from. Marley thought he could disassociate himself from Drew and wring some money for his silence from the duke as well. I thought I'd talked him out of his scheme, but . . ." Her father lowered his gaze.

Felicity stared hard into her father's downcast face. "You truly knew about this?" She wanted to ask if he was involved in the murders but stopped herself. If that were the case, everything she ever knew to be true would be turned upside down. "Please tell me you didn't know Drew planned to kill Marley and his wife."

Her father raised his gaze, and again he was so unlike the amiable man she'd grown up with she pulled away from the bars. "I'm only going to say this one more time: Drew didn't kill Marley, and he'd never, never murder a woman."

"How can you be so sure?" She wanted him to give her something solid to sway her in Drew's favor and never make her doubt him or herself again.

"Because I know the man. Apparently you don't."

She couldn't meet her father's steady gaze. "No, I suppose I don't."

Through the bars, he touched the tip of her nose. "I'm sorry you ever became involved in this. Drew had no right to . . ."

He thankfully let his words drift off. Felicity had the urge to tell him Drew's advances hadn't been uninvited, if only to erase the worry from his features, but to do that she'd have to explain more than she dared reveal, especially to her father.

He cleared his throat. "Your heart will heal, daughter. It's the rest of you I'm worried about. That's why both Drew and I wanted you to leave Barbados as soon as you arrived. I have some money hidden. Leave now and go back to Boston."

"I can't." She'd not planned to tell her father of their shared fate, but she'd not expected his confessed involvement in Drew's deeds. "I left Drew only to run into the British. They used me as bait to lure him into a trap, but I shot one of their soldiers and Drew escaped. Our trial is set for a week from tomorrow, with the execution taking place immediately afterward."

Her father slammed the palm of his hand against the bars, making her jump. "I feared your strong-headedness would be the death of you. You should have stayed with Drew. He would have protected you."

If she had stayed, Drew would have absorbed her body and soul. Even now, she craved him. "I can't trust him, and I still don't know how you can."

"Drew might be a pirate, but he's not a heartless killer. I'm not saying men didn't die in the taking of ships, but he did not seek to kill. He did what he did to survive."

The guard had inched his way back to their side of the corridor.

Her father continued in a whisper. "You've been with him? If he has such a flagrant disregard for life, why didn't he kill you? You certainly haven't made things easy for him—on any count."

Her lungs seized with the sensation of stepping out into a frigid Boston morning. She stared at her father, searching for the truth.

"You haven't answered me," she said. "Who do you think killed Marley?"

Her father slumped, and for the first time since she'd arrived he looked truly defeated. "I don't know. Marley told someone else about Drew perhaps, someone who didn't mind spilling a little blood to fatten his pockets."

She recalled the dinner party at the Linleys' home and searched her memory for a slip by Drew to convince her father of his guilt, but even as she did so, an uneasy sensation turned in her stomach.

Her confusion must have shown on her face, because her father spoke again. "Use that sharp mind of yours, and you'll find the truth. If Drew killed Marley and Beatrice, why didn't he kill me too, and sail away without a trace? He could have, you know."

The guard hesitantly tapped her on the shoulder. "Miss Kendall, Admiral Meldrick is waiting to see you. I'm sorry, but we have to go."

She remembered the young man from the tavern in New Providence. He was little more than a boy and always looked nervous in her presence. She nodded and blinked back tears she didn't have to feign. She turned back to her father, pressing her palms flat against the bars. "I'm sorry, Father. I've caused you so much trouble."

Her father wiped his cheek with his sleeve and touched her fingertips with his own. "Nay, daughter, I've caused my own trouble, but I can't bear to see you punished for something you're not a part of. If Drew can come for you, he will. Don't let your pride get the better of your common sense. Promise me you'll go with him without a fuss."

She lowered her head and whispered, "No, he won't come. He thinks I betrayed him." Her gaze snapped up to meet his. "Besides, I won't leave without you."

The young soldier shifted. "Please, Miss Kendall. You're going to get me punished."

Her father leaned against the bars, as if trying to kiss

her cheek. "Do whatever you can to save yourself. Drew won't blame you for that. Go, daughter. May God be with you," he whispered.

She tore herself away from the bars and turned to the young man hovering behind her. Blindly, she followed him from her father's cell. But before she reached the steps, she turned to look at him one last time.

Her father smiled and waved, but she could see the tears on his cheeks shimmering in the single shaft of light piercing his cell. She turned away and let the tears wrench free from her tight chest, oblivious to the awkward comforts of the soldier beside her. He gently guided her up the moss-covered steps with a hand on her elbow.

When she emerged from the underground prison, the bright tropical sun stung her bleary eyes. Life bustled in the busy street, contrasting the bleakness in her soul. The smell of sewage and trash standing too long in the heat caused her to feel even more wretched.

How could she have known so little about her father? Instead of helping him, she'd been undermining him in her attempt to destroy Drew.

In a wave, the gnawing feeling of unease that had begun in the pit of her stomach overtook her. Her knees grew weak and for the first time in her life she thought she might actually faint.

She stumbled over to some shade provided by an over-hanging balcony and rested against the two-story building's cobalt blue wall. Blaming her condition on the heat, she sent her frantic escort in search of a fan.

She clutched her midsection, willing her turbulent thoughts to calm. Everything she knew about Drew pointed to the man her father claimed him to be. Too, nothing he'd ever done hinted that he would kill Marley and his wife in cold blood. Believing Drew hadn't been responsible for the Marleys' deaths salved her sense of being betrayed. At the same instant, his innocence brought home the consequences of her mistake.

Her eagerness to accept the worst in Drew had almost cost him his life and still could. He had never shown her anything but gentleness, yet it had been easier for her to believe McCulla's lies than her own heart.

Drew must hate her. Would he have told her the truth if she stayed?

She'd never know the answer to that, but it didn't change what she had to do now. Fear of letting herself be vulnerable to Drew had caused her to destroy the only chance at love she would ever have. Rectifying the havoc she had wreaked was all she could give him. To do that, she had only one resource available to her: the truth. She wiped the tears from her face and stepped from the shade.

The young soldier caught up with her before she moved too far down the street. She refused to accept the embroidered fan and fringed umbrella he tried to shove into her hands.

"I'm fine. I need to see the Duke of Foxmoor. Do you know where he is?"

"You need to rest, mistress. You looked pale as a ghost back there." The soldier ignored her protests. He opened the umbrella and held it over her head.

"Just take me to the duke. I've remembered something about El Diablo I think he'll be anxious to hear."

The soldier sighed. "I'm glad to hear that. I didn't want to be a part of hanging a woman, but I have to follow orders."

She stopped, realizing she didn't know where she was going. "Do you know where he is, then? I'll only speak with the Duke of Foxmoor."

The soldier relaxed visibly for the first time since he escorted her from the *Warwick* to the prison. "His Lordship is staying at the Linley plantation. That's where we're to meet Admiral Meldrick."

She took the umbrella from the soldier and stepped out of the way so he could lead her to the plantation. Admiral Meldrick had expected her visit with her father to break her will. Bringing her directly to the duke after her ordeal at the prison was Meldrick's plan to still play the hero. He'd be in for a surprise he wouldn't like, but she was gambling with her life that the duke would feel differently.

# Chapter Twenty

Drew ripped the broadsheet from the stone wall and crumpled it in his fist. With the westerly winds at his back, the voyage from St. Lucia to Barbados would take no more than three days. His instinct to inch his way closer to Barbados and Felicity had proven correct. At the time, he'd hoped to find a clue as to the Marleys' killer. Instead, he'd meet his death. It might have been the course he'd been traveling all along.

In the pocket of his long velvet coat, he stuffed the handbill announcing the trial of El Diablo's accomplices. The coat's lining of pistols and daggers were useless against the weapons the British held. Watching Ben hang would have been difficult. Drew had seen friends die before, and Ben had freely chosen the wrong side of the law. With Felicity, he could make no such justification.

Up until he spotted the announcement of the trial, Drew believed he might still save Ben. The British had imprisoned him for the real purpose of bringing back El Diablo. If they hanged their bait, what good would he be? But now they had something that would bring their prize in on his knees. He'd never allow Felicity to be hanged. Somehow they must have discovered that. The bastards had hardly given him enough time to deliver himself to them. This time, Solomon wouldn't be able to persuade him to be patient. The hourglass had already been overturned, and too many grains of sand had accumulated on the wrong side.

He signaled to the group of men he led on this search of St. Lucia's taverns. They'd visited only a few, but there was no need to continue. Both the British and his father would receive exactly what they wanted. He sent a crewman to alert Solomon and the others of their imminent departure, while he went to ready the ship.

He shifted the brim of his tricorn to cover his face. The unbearable heat of midafternoon left the cobblestoned streets virtually deserted. Even so, he couldn't afford to be noticed. Getting captured before he could barter with his life would ruin any hope of saving Felicity and Ben. In all his years as a pirate, his life had never seemed more valuable.

He strode back to the docks, sweltering under the weight of his coat. A tickle of fear fluttered his insides, but his determination to make things right was stronger. Ironically, he'd spent a lifetime struggling to survive only to give up without a fight. Despite everything, he still loved Felicity. He had no qualms about sacrificing himself for her safety. The choice was simple: There wasn't any choice. Time was running out and he had only one card left to play.

Felicity paused in the shadows of the Linleys' cool marble foyer in desperate need to calm herself. An unexpected surge of anger shook her at the idea of coming face-to-face with Drew's father. This was the man who'd badly mistreated Drew and had caused her own father to be thrown in jail. She must be humble, play on the man's sympathies, if he had any. Surely he didn't realize the man who called himself Lord Christian by day and El Diablo by night truly was his son—the one he'd abandoned all those years ago. If so, they were all doomed.

With what she hoped was a tight grip on her emotions, she entered the crimson and gold drawing room of Linley Hall. Philip Linley and Admiral Meldrick fawned over a man equal in flamboyance to the decor. The vermilion satin of his trousers stood out like a bloodstain on the cream brocade chair on which he sat. When he rose, surely his breeches would leave a permanent mark. All three men eyed her as if they'd been delivered their main course.

She stood straight in her plain brown dress, despite feeling like a smudge on the gilded wall covering. The splendor that had once awed her left her with a sense of isolation and doom. Perhaps the Duke of Foxmoor had retired from the afternoon heat, and the man staring at her behind a powdered mask of malice was only a traveling companion. He exuded status but was much too young to be Drew's father.

Admiral Meldrick stood, greeting her with a warm smile. He acted as if she were the guest of honor instead of a prisoner summoned for interrogation. She had no intention of being put on the defensive even if they did succeed in intimidating her.

She ignored the grinning admiral and directed her request to the hostile stranger. "I'll speak only to the Duke of Foxmoor."

The white-faced man leaned back in his chair. He curved his lips in a ghoulish imitation of a smile. His makeup cracked at the corners of his mouth and around his eyes. He was not as young as Felicity had first thought. A tall white wig and the red bow painted on his lips made him look like the exaggerated sketches of aristocrats in the *Boston Gazette*. He didn't wear a coat and his silk vest embroidered with tiny purple flowers accentuated his thin frame.

Though he carried himself with the bearing of someone who had possessed the title king all his life, he appeared to be only a little younger than Drew. The man opened his Cupid's mouth, confirming Felicity's worst fears.

"How convenient. I've been wanting to speak with you as well. Miss Kendall, is it? Jarrod Andrews, the Duke of Foxmoor, at your service."

Admiral Meldrick walked toward her. "Did you enjoy your visit with your father, Miss Kendall?"

He touched her lower back, giving her a gentle nudge. She stepped away from him, marching into the room of her own accord. "No, I didn't."

Jarrod Andrews relaxed in the overstuffed chair as if it were a throne. Philip Linley had pulled a stiff wooden-backed seat up to the duke's. Linley sat on its edge, appearing to follow the duke's movements with every nerve in his body.

She stopped in front of Jarrod Andrews, directly meeting his gaze. "I expected someone older."

Linley's posture stiffened. "Miss Kendall, though I know you were born in the colonies I expected you would have been taught how to address your betters. His lordship inherited the title from his father a few years ago and should be addressed as 'Your Grace.' "

His thorough reprimand assured her Master Linley would not be an ally. Neither man hovering near the duke would likely sing any praises for Andrew Crawford. So, the duke was Drew's brother, not his father. This could be to her advantage. The legitimate son might not know about his illegitimate brother.

But the permanent sneer on the duke's face warned that he did know and would like nothing more than to wipe his brother's existence from the face of the earth. The prospect of Drew's body hanged from a gibbet in the center of Bridgetown no doubt pleased Philip Linley just as much. Unfortunately, Felicity's only hope lay with the duke, and that prospect seemed bleak at best.

She squared her shoulders, trying to appear more confident than she felt. "Excuse me, Master Linley. If my manner displeases you, then perhaps you should leave the room. I have some important information for His Grace that does not concern you."

Admiral Meldrick swept between her and the two seated men. "We all know how distraught you must be, dear lady. Neither His Grace nor myself want to see a woman hang for the deeds of a fiend. Please speak openly."

She refused to allow Meldrick to remain in center stage. "Your Grace, I've been told capturing Andrew Crawford is of dire consequence to you because he impersonated a member of your highly respected family."

The *Your Grace* left a bitter taste in her mouth, but alienating the duke would not save Drew's life. "If we could speak privately, I might be able to shed some light on the matter."

The duke lost his nauseating grin and his face again was veiled with ice. Even his dark eyes were devoid of emotion or life. "Is it true you were the pirate's mistress?"

She dropped her facade and glared at him. Even if she could remain humble, it wouldn't save Drew. Jarrod Andrews would not help her no matter how many *Your Graces* she spat at him. Nor would he care if a bastard brother were hanged—but he just might give a damn if the whole world knew he had pirates in his family, on the right side of the blanket or not.

Admiral Meldrick jumped to her defense before she could think of a reply caustic enough for the duke's question. "Your Grace, I'm sure Miss Kendall did not voluntarily lie with a brute like El Diablo. The poor lady had no choice, and no one here could blame her for it." Meldrick turned toward her. "Tell us where we can find the swine so we may repay him for the brutality imposed on your delicate person."

Philip Linley slammed his hand on a low table, rattling the teapot. "Good God, Meldrick, she's as guilty as her father. Drew Crawford could seduce cream from a cat. I doubt he had any trouble with Ben's spinster daughter."

Felicity swung her barely controlled fury in Linley's direction. "Should we add the wife of a prominent plantation owner to the list?"

Linley shot to his feet, his face as red as the crimson material covering the seat of his chair. "You little slut!"

The duke quieted Linley simply by raising his hand. "Do calm down. I see living in these unbearable conditions has turned the residents of Barbados as wild as its shrubbery."

Linley sat down with his head lowered. The duke stopped Meldrick from again taking control of the conversation with another showing of his noble palm. He pointed to a chair, leaving Meldrick, a mere admiral, with no choice but to obey.

"I don't care if Miss Kendall claims Andrew Crawford tied her down and raped her while holding a cutlass to her throat." The duke directed his chilling stare at her. "My patience has run thin. Tell me where I can find El Diablo."

"Finding Andrew Crawford will not solve your problems." Revealing she had no intention of handing them Drew's head on a platter would not serve her cause. The promise of information was what held their attention.

"Need I remind you, in addition to the impending threat of hanging, the scoundrel has caused irreparable damage to your reputation whether he touched you or not? No man of honor would put a lady he cherished in that position," said Meldrick. His patronizing tone was becoming strained.

She wanted to laugh. These men held up her virtue for public speculation and she didn't care. Drew had cherished her, but she'd thrown it in his face. Years of being a slave to her private shame had left her too insecure to recognize his love. She wouldn't be a pariah for losing her virginity before marriage; she'd be hanged for not saying she was raped. "You're wrong, Admiral Meldrick," she said. "Andrew Crawford is an honorable man. I was no innocent, and I took him to my bed willingly."

"Good God! The man really is Satan incarnate," exploded Philip Linley.

If Admiral Meldrick had his riding crop, she guessed he'd have rapped it on anything nearby. Instead, he screeched over Linley's ravings: "You were not brought here to make a desperate plea for your lover. We are giving you a chance to save your neck!"

The duke appeared unmoved. She disregarded the other men. They'd already convicted Drew.

She addressed the duke. "Drew didn't commit the crimes of which he is accused."

The duke didn't blink, nor did he move a muscle. "Eliminating piracy in the Caribbean is not my concern. Finding the man putting a smudge on my family name is."

Felicity smiled sweetly at the duke, but she had no doubt triumph sparkled in her eyes. He knew Drew carried his blood. She'd stake her life on it.

"No doubt you would be appalled by the idea of the Andrews name being publicly linked with piracy, as would the rest of your esteemed family. I see your father has passed away. Do you have any siblings, perhaps a brother?"

Admiral Meldrick beat his fist on his thigh. "Miss Kendall, the Duke of Foxmoor's lineage has no bearing—"

Jarrod Andrews, Duke of Foxmoor, showed his teeth. She guessed it was his attempt at a placating smile. "I believe we are making Miss Kendall nervous. Perhaps more progress would be made if I spoke with her in private, as she first suggested."

A word from the duke proved as good as King George's himself, at least on Barbados. Philip Linley and Admiral

Meldrick promptly removed themselves without a grumble.

Felicity stood before the seated demigod, feeling like the fly before the spider. She reminded herself of her earlier victory and sat down in a chair vacated by one of the men, not waiting for an invitation. The duke stood.

After raking her with his gaze, he sneered and showed her his back as he paced the room. He matched Drew's height, but Jarrod Andrews appeared slight, where Drew looked lean and sinewy. He strode toward her, then stopped with his hands behind him, his feet braced apart. The gesture created as forbidding a figure as Drew in his pirate guise.

He tried to bore a hole through her with his stare, but she retaliated by mirroring his steady glare.

"Well, here we are. Alone at last. Tell me, my little colonial, what do you think you know?" The dark brown of the duke's eyes absorbed the light, making them appear black. Though of an entirely different hue, Drew's eyes also turned dark when he became angry or passionate. She suspected the duke possessed a full mouth much like his brother's, but his constant sneer and the ridiculous color he painted his lips made it impossible to tell for sure. Their relationship would be obvious once it was brought to light.

She tilted her head in an exaggerated show of studying him. "You know, Your Grace, your resemblance to your brother is striking."

He gave no outward sign that her jab pierced him. In fact, he remained rigid. "You speak gibberish, Miss Kendall. You're wasting my time."

She arranged her skirts, refusing to appear flustered. After a moment, she glanced up at him and smiled brightly. "Congratulations. You have a brother. Stir any memories?"

"No."

"I'm sure it's easy enough to check. Drew's mother was a servant at your father's country estate. She lived in the village near your home. And there is the resemblance. You both must look like your father."

The duke returned to his makeshift throne. He leaned back and, to Felicity's frustration, appeared completely relaxed. "I grew up in London. A lovely tale, though. I might even find it amusing if it were not at my deceased father's expense."

His dark eyes remained intense, directing a piercing stare at Felicity. She struggled not to fidget. "I know the truth. A truth you obviously don't want revealed. Take back your reward, release my father and your relationship to El Diablo will stay our little secret." She thought she saw his jaw twitch and held her breath.

He brought a lace handkerchief from his sleeve and dabbed at his nose. "This *will* stay our secret, I can assure you of that."

The promise in his calm tone couldn't have been more threatening if he had armed troops flanking him ready to carry out whatever mischief he had in mind. The duke didn't need a visible show of force. He was a force all on his own. For the first time, Felicity realized just how powerless she was in this situation. And she'd thought she had grown up in an unfair environment, persecuted for merely wanting to be young and alive.

Drew's life had been much harder. He'd been condemned for even being born. What chance did he ever have against the absolute authority of men like the duke? She studied the man in question, looking for the bluff behind his threat or any signs that his powdered arrogance hid a trace of compassion. Every muscle in the duke's face had tightened. He looked ready to strangle her. She should say nothing. Confrontation would only bring the duke's vengeance down upon Drew that much harder. As much as she wished she could, she found it impossible to hold her tongue. How could the man be so cruel?

"Perhaps you can get away with killing your brother, but

my father is well liked. And if I follow in his wake, some-one on the island is going to speak up. There is only so much destruction you can wreak without calling attention to yourself, *Your Grace*." She didn't have to add the sarcasm in addressing him as his title warranted, but she couldn't help herself.

"I don't know if you have the more vivid imagination or your pirate. You'll tell no one of this nonsense because no one will believe you." His tone gave no indication that her words disturbed him, but he shifted slightly.

"There is the resemblance—and your last name is An-drews, his first name is Andrew. I'm sure it will be enough to stir curiosity once I bring it to people's attention. Per-haps I already have. I'm sure you've noticed how easily rumors spread on Barbados."

He tilted his head as if to study her. "How is it you came to be scooped up by Admiral Meldrick again, Miss Kendall? Did El Diablo spit you out like so much gristle?" He let his gaze drift over her. "Yes, I can see that. And yet you still feel compelled to defend him. Plain women are so loyal."

She blinked, momentarily losing her train of thought. As hard as it must have been for Drew surviving on his own, he was fortunate not to have been taken to the bosom of this family of vipers.

The duke cleared his throat in the face of her momen-tary discomfort, but she swore she saw him smile behind the hand he used to politely cover his mouth. "Whether or not Drew Crawford is related to me won't change the fact he is a pirate and will be hanged for his crimes. I had nothing to do with that. And as for you, Miss Kendall, things would go so much more easily for both you and your father if you'd put your considerable energies into bringing the fiend who kidnapped you to justice rather than making up tales no one wants to hear."

The Duke of Foxmoor was giving her a clear choice. If

her father had not been thrown in jail without real proof of any crimes, she might not believe the duke could wave a hand and have all the charges dropped. Judging by the events that had transpired since the duke's arrival, he could proclaim himself King of Barbados without opposition.

"Shall I assume by this blessed moment of silence that we understand each other?"

An image of Drew and her father swinging from a scaffold chilled her, but not enough to cool her fury. As long as she drew breath, she'd not let Drew's family continue to persecute him. "You'll have to catch him first."

"That's why we have you, my dear. To make sure I don't miss a visit from a long-lost relative. You'll be my guest until your execution, of course. But not to worry; if your lover doesn't come to your rescue in time, I'll make sure you see him in hell."

Being Jarrod Andrews's guest at the Linley plantation involved three days in a locked room no bigger than Felicity's cabin on board the *Queen Elizabeth*. The windowless closet, tucked beneath an eave of the roof, held only a bare cot and a chamber pot. During the heat of the day, she could do little more than lie still for fear of swooning. A servant girl brought her stale bread, bland soup and water with a touch of rum once a day.

She assumed the rations were the same given to the slaves, and she suspected the girl gave her the food out of the kindness of her heart rather than on instructions from her master. Despite her miserable accommodations, Felicity didn't feel mistreated as much as forgotten. Her father's conditions were much worse. Even the mean comfort of her cot fed her guilt.

When the message to meet the Duke of Foxmoor in front of the house arrived, she was too excited to leave her room to be concerned. Escaping appeared an impossibility behind the locked door. Despite telling herself otherwise,

THE PIRATE AND THE PURITAN

hope that Drew would rescue them still fluttered to life at the slightest opportunity.

Sweet fresh air engulfed her as she was ushered through the servants' door in the back of the house. With a burst of energy, she rushed around to the front yard. She halted on the edge of the wide gravel drive. A carriage of gilt and polished mahogany winked in the noonday sun. Jarrod Andrews, the Duke of Foxmoor, stood by the conveyance, challenging the coach's splendor with his own. He glanced at her and frowned.

She cautiously approached him. Whatever he had in mind, it wasn't for her benefit. She had to keep up her guard if she wanted to out fox him.

He put a lace handkerchief over his nose and directed her into the coach. She tried to match his haughty demeanor despite the fact that her appearance warranted his action. To her surprise, he offered her his hand to assist her into the carriage. She took it and daintily lifted her skirts, as if she wore a gown of pink satin rather than filthy brown rags. Her skin crawled at the contact with his warm gloved palm. She forced herself not to wipe her hand against the plush velvet upholstery.

During the coach ride to Bridgetown, they continued their mutual silence. For once, her healthy curiosity abdicated to common sense. Even if she asked where he planned to take her, she feared he'd only tell her a frighteningly twisted version of the truth. She couldn't afford to lose her wits. Each day of her confinement had been a test of will. She knew the duke hoped time would break her spirit and force her to condemn Drew.

The Duke of Foxmoor gave no outward sign that he still expected her cooperation. He alternated between ignoring her and studying her with humorous speculation. When they stopped in front of the prison, she assumed he'd grown tired of waiting for Drew's attempted rescue and planned to put her in a cell next to her father. She had no opposition to the arrangement. If she were closer to her father, it would be easier for Drew to rescue them both.

After the duke made his exit with the help of his footman, Felicity stepped down from the coach. Her father stood in the street outside the prison. He blinked and squinted as his eyes adjusted to the light, but otherwise he appeared unharmed. When she ran to his side, the guards by the prison doors showed no interest in stopping her. She hugged him, forcing herself not to grimace at the ripe scent he'd gained during his incarceration.

"Are you ill?" She stood away from him and looked him over, trying to discern the cause of his release.

He breathed deeply and rubbed his deflated belly. "I'm fine. I never noticed how sweet the Barbados breeze is before."

She turned to find the duke tilting his head in mock admiration of their reunion. "Touching. It warms my heart to be the instrument that unites a father with his child."

Foxmoor's obviously happy mood ruined her pleasure at seeing her father released. Something was very wrong. "I don't understand."

The duke shrugged. "You're free to go. You both claimed your innocence and I have decided to believe you. There's no further reason to hold either one of you."

A chill settled around Felicity's heart. "If you kill us, El Diablo will hunt you down. . . ."

He laughed. "You seem to think highly of your value as a bedmate. Maybe you're right. At least your champion is willing to trade his life for yours, but he won't be hunting anyone down ever again."

Before she could ask him to explain, a regiment of boots hitting cobblestones forced her attention in the direction of the docks. A group of soldiers marched toward them. Red coats flanked a prisoner who stumbled to keep up with the soldiers' lively gait. As they neared, Felicity recognized

Drew. Chains on his hands and feet awkwardly shortened his stride.

She would have run to him if her father had not stopped her.

· The duke laughed again. "Let her go, old man. I can't wait to see Miss Kendall grovel for her lover's release. It will be so romantic."

Her father whispered near her ear. "Keep your temper under control. Don't make it worse for Drew."

She nodded. Her father released his grip on her arm slowly, as if he expected her to change her mind at any minute and bolt for Drew. She stood straight, swallowing the lump in her throat.

Despite his chains, Drew looked every bit the dangerous pirate. His hair was loose and windblown—the set of his jaw defiant. He stared straight ahead. She didn't avert her gaze from him on the chance he might look her way. She had to find a way to tell him how sorry she was, even if it was only in a pleading glance.

Admiral Meldrick himself, mounted atop a white stallion as crisp as his uniform, led the brigade of soldiers needed to escort one prisoner. "Here he is, Your Grace. Walked right up on the beach like his note promised."

Drew's rebellious glance swung to the duke. Felicity wondered if he found it any easier to take once he realized that his father wasn't the one who betrayed him. His fierce expression gave nothing away, but Felicity swore she saw something in the depths of his eyes flare with recognition as he gazed upon his brother—and worse, understanding.

The duke looked Drew over with obvious disdain. "Doesn't seem very repentant, does he?"

Drew was the same height as his brother, but Drew appeared to loom over the thinner man. Chains rattled as Drew strained against them to lean toward his accuser.

The duke stepped back, then straightened, as if he'd

caught himself in the telling act. "Do you have your prisoner under control, Meldrick?"

Meldrick dismounted, then pushed aside the soldier standing next to Drew. Felicity had not noticed the shackle around Drew's neck until Meldrick yanked the chain connected to it. Drew jerked forward but didn't drop his gaze. Meldrick yanked again. "Lower your eyes before your betters, swine, or I'll have you whipped."

Felicity closed her eyes. She wanted to intervene but feared anything she said would encourage the duke to carry out Meldrick's threat. The sound of Drew's deep voice made her swiftly open her eyes.

"Do what you want. You're going to kill me anyway."

"No!" she called out before she could stop herself.

Drew didn't acknowledge her outburst, but he tensed visibly.

The duke appeared to notice Drew's reaction, because he stepped forward and smiled. "Looks as if your whore doesn't want to have you tortured before your execution, so why don't you behave?"

Drew relaxed against his bonds but still stared indignantly at the duke. "She means nothing to me."

"Of course not. But you seem to have won her over. Some women enjoy being brutalized. Perhaps we should arrange a display with the soldiers to see if my theory holds true." The Duke of Foxmoor clasped his hands behind his back and smiled pleasantly.

Felicity's father nudged her behind him. She watched over his shoulder but remained silent. Despite his chains and being outnumbered twenty to one, Drew's thinly veiled fury would surely erupt if anyone laid a hand on her. But the duke probably counted on that. She wasn't prepared to watch Drew die. As long as she drew breath, that time would never come.

Admiral Meldrick cleared his throat. "I don't think we need to threaten Mistress—"

"Shut up. I'm in charge here," interrupted the duke.

Drew lowered his gaze and hung his head. The display confirmed her theory concerning the Duke of Foxmoor's power. She didn't think his threat idle, and by his submission, neither did Drew.

"Now that we all understand each other, you may show the prisoner his cell. I want his written confession by dusk." The duke waved a lace handkerchief in the air as if he were swatting flies, dismissing everyone.

Meldrick shoved Drew in the direction of the gaol. He didn't look up again. The duke disappeared into his carriage as Drew descended into the darkness.

With an arm around her shoulders, her father guided her away from the prison. "What shall we do?"

"Get him out, of course, but first I need to enlist someone's help."

# *Chapter Twenty-one*

When the faint glow from a torch reached the dirt floor of his cell, Drew didn't glance up to see who approached. He'd stopped reacting, stopped thinking, stopped eating and stopped sleeping. Though the hour hovered between dusk and dawn, he felt no compulsion to close his eyes.

After he'd given his statement, denying any relation to the Duke of Foxmoor and his family, Drew as he knew himself stopped existing. His father was no doubt celebrating in his heavenly mansion. Drew would have laughed if he still had the will. Funny that he would think that his father went to heaven, and funnier still that Drew had experienced the news of his passing as an unexpected blow.

To his utter surprise, Drew wasn't any wiser than his mother. Tucked away in a place he hadn't known existed had been an ember of hope that he'd someday know the man whose likeness he bore. Drew should thank his brother for snuffing that useless spark completely, along with every other hope he'd been foolish enough to have.

Once he'd confessed to all the crimes attributed to El

Diablo—even the ones he hadn't committed—and exonerated Felicity and Ben of any association to his evil deeds, his life had no other purpose. His death would provide those he cared about, with release from their associations with him.

"Be as quiet as possible. I'll be back for you in an hour. Are you sure you want me to lock you in the cell with him?" said a voice Drew didn't recognize or have any interest in.

"I'll be perfectly safe, but I don't want you to get into trouble. I can find my own way out. If you leave me the key, you won't have to come back."

Drew jerked up his head at the sound of the voice that rang in his nightmares. In every horrid dream, she told him to go when all he wanted to do was stay in her arms forever. But this was no dream; it was worse.

An adolescent soldier in a red coat shook his head at Felicity. "No, ma'am. I'll be more than in trouble if you let your husband go. I told you I felt bad watching you cry after you visited your pa, but I'm not ready to die because you're being mistreated."

She touched the arm of the young man opening the cell door. "Thank you for helping me. I promise no one will know I was here."

Drew stood. The easy exchange between them made him furious. He had no idea he could still feel anything so strong.

He moved toward her before he remembered he was chained to the wall. The soldier's eyes widened when Drew accidentally rattled his bonds. The young man unlocked the cell door and ushered Felicity inside while keeping the metal grate between them. After the cell was securely locked once again, the soldier hurried away, taking the light with him.

Felicity stayed in the shadows, just outside his reach. He didn't realize he'd said her name until she rushed to him.

"I'm here." She touched his face and rubbed her thumb over his mouth. "Have they hurt you?"

He parted his lips, brushing her thumb with his tongue. She tasted warm and clean. He raised his arms to wrap them around her, wanting her molded against him. The chain binding his hands to his feet stopped him. The reminder brought him instantly to his senses.

He jerked his head away from her touch. "What in the hell are you doing here?"

She let her hands drop to her sides. "I don't blame you for being angry—"

"Answer my question. Your British friends have already gotten my confession. What else do they want?"

She winced at his accusation. "I talked that young soldier into letting me see you. I told him we were married and we had to keep it a secret."

He balled his hands into fists. She was determined to ruin the one good thing he'd ever done in his life.

"Are you crazy, or just that damned vindictive? I told them you and your father weren't involved, and now you go and tell them we're married? Christ!"

"He won't tell anyone. I had to see you."

"What did you do to gain such undying devotion? Threaten him with a pistol, perhaps?"

She tried to touch him. "Please. Just listen to me."

He jerked away, but the shackles that bit into his skin reminded him that his options for movement were limited. Feigned detachment provided his only means of escape, a talent he'd all but lost since meeting Felicity. He leaned against the wall he was bound to, hating her seeing him chained like an animal.

"Why? So you can gloat?"

"I didn't try to shoot you. I swear. I shot the marksman behind you. That's why the British wanted to hang me as your accomplice."

"It doesn't matter now." Oh, but it did. She hadn't tried

to kill him! She had saved him! The idea might make him think he had something to live for. He had to do everything he could to keep the dangerous thought at bay.

"Get out. I don't want you here."

She inched toward him. "I can't leave. I'm locked in until the soldier comes back. I came here to tell you something, and I won't leave until I do."

"So tell me."

She moved a little closer. In the dim light that drifted from the night sky outside the stone jail, she met his hard glare with pleading in her soft brown eyes. "I love you."

He tried to shut out the sincerity in her wet gaze by closing his eyes. In spite of his efforts, warmth spread through his chest. It was happening. He wanted to live. "Felicity . . . don't."

When he felt her lean against him, he opened his eyes. Her hands rested on his shoulders; then she kissed his cheek. He meant to tell her to stop, but his words came out as a moan. She found his mouth with her own. The soft brush of her tentative kiss broke his restraint. He took her with his tongue as he longed to do with his body.

He pulled his mouth away from the intoxicating pleasure to kiss the vulnerable skin under her jaw. "I've missed you."

Her hips were within his restricted grasp. He pulled her roughly to him and pressed himself into her lush contours. The sensation teased. He had to have more. "I want you."

She responded to his abandon with her own urgency. She unlaced the top of his shirt and slid her fingers over his skin. "You don't know how many times I dreamed of touching you again."

He grabbed the material of her skirt and balled handfuls of the cloth in his fist until he had it raised enough to caress her bare thigh. She yanked her skirts higher, holding them so he could touch her with both his hands. He cupped her round bottom and bent his knees, rocking against the apex of her thighs in sweet torture. Her welcoming heat radiated through his clothes. It was his last coherent thought.

In one swift motion, he lifted her and swung her until her back rested against the stone wall. The part of his mind he was no longer in control over straddled the thick chain attaching him to the wall, while maintaining his balance with his limited movements. He held her against the wall with his weight and attacked the tie on his breeches.

The restraints on his wrists and ankles were no match for his blind lust. He slid his forearms under her thighs, spreading and supporting her. He bent his knees and surged into her. She arched against him, and he covered her gasp of surprise at his rough entry with an equally penetrating kiss. He withdrew and thrust again.

She pulled her mouth away. "I love you."

"Say it again," he said as he thrust harder.

She repeated the words he'd never thought to hear from her. He buried himself inside her. A wave of pleasure too strong to fight broke over him. His fierce release almost drove him to his knees. After catching his breath, he collapsed against her, then showered soft kisses over her face, half in apology for his loss of control and half just to ensure himself she wasn't a dream. He tasted the salt of her silent tears.

"Have I hurt you?" He eased his hold and let her feet slide to the floor. Even in the semidarkness, the impression of the chain attached to his wrist was visible on the inside of her thigh.

She followed his gaze. "It doesn't matter. That's not why I'm crying."

He moved his hands away from her. Her skirts fell over the welts, and he kissed the top of her head instead of kissing the marks he'd left on her skin. That, he didn't trust himself to do. He had treated her like a whore, without the least care for her feelings.

"Why are you crying, then?" His voice sounded too harsh even to his own ears.

She laughed softly, breathlessly. "Because I thought I would never get to touch you like that again."

"I think I did most of the touching and the taking."

"But I loved every minute of it. I love everything about you."

He pulled away from her and began awkwardly trying to tie the cords of his breeches. The chains made the job he had accomplished when driven by blind lust seem a feat of magic. "Not everything."

She brushed his hands aside and finished fastening his breeches. "Everything might be an exaggeration." She moved her hands to his chest and looked up into his face. "But I won't doubt you again. I swear."

He studied her trusting, upturned face and realized the enormity of his mistake. He would give her the world if he had it, but the only thing he could give her would hurt her. Unfortunately for both of them, his death was the one thing that could save her.

"My execution will keep you from being disappointed, because deception is the only thing I've ever excelled at."

She balled the front of his shirt in her fists. "I won't let that happen. I'm already planning to get you out of here. All I need from you is to tell me how I can find Solomon."

He wrapped his fingers around her arms and set her away from him as far as he could. He pushed until the metal cut his skin. "I don't want you to do anything. Do you understand?"

She shook her head, trying to touch his face. He stopped her by shoving her with enough force to cause her to stumble. It was all clear to him now. He wasn't making a noble sacrifice by giving up his life. He was being a coward.

Yet, wasn't it better to be a coward if it saved one's life— or, in this case, the life of someone who meant more to Drew than he'd ever thought possible. Drew was never one to quibble over tactics if it got the job done. The job was to keep Felicity safe.

The look of desperation and determination that pursed her lips frightened him more than his initial introduction to his filthy cell. With no other escape, he turned away and faced the wall. He had to stop her, but experience had proven that stopping Felicity required an act of God . . . or the Devil.

She touched his shoulder. "I love you. I don't want to live without you."

He turned to face her, mustering up all his acting ability. "But I don't love you. Surely you know that."

She pressed her hand to her mouth and stepped back. Her face drained of glowing loyalty, but he couldn't say his success pleased him. "I-I never thought . . . my father said . . ." She swallowed hard, and to only his slight surprise, squared her shoulders. "You exchanged your life for mine, and I'm not going to let you die."

Truly, she was unbelievable. No wonder he'd fallen so completely under her spell.

"Actually, I did it for Ben—but I guess you did sway my decision a little. Two for one. That's a pretty good bargain."

She cocked her head and studied him. He forced himself to meet her steady gaze to prevent her from figuring him out.

"You said you missed me."

He seized on the note of doubt in her voice. "I believe I said I wanted you. You've always been an eager mount, maybe too eager." He shook his head and sighed. "If I ever kept a woman permanently, she'd have to be a virgin first. Sorry."

She tucked strands of her wild mane back into her bun. Her chin quivered. "I don't believe you."

"That's wise. But I think we both agree it's highly unlikely I'd settle down with one woman, virgin or not. I think I'd rather hang."

When he thought he couldn't take another moment of her hurt stare, she whirled away from him and strode to the far side of the cell. "I don't need to hear any more of this."

He couldn't move to comfort her, which was just as well. That he'd attacked her most vulnerable spot had been intentional. He had no choice; her life was at stake. As far as he knew, she was crying. The words he'd chosen were especially cruel. They had to be. He leaned against the wall and waited. Her silence unnerved him.

"What are you doing over there?"

"Waiting to be let out," she said from the shadows.

She didn't sound as if she'd been crying. She sounded angry. He realized he would never see her again, and he hated the way things had to be left between them.

"I'm sure I'm not capable of loving *any*one, Felicity," he said.

"Shut up."

He took her advice. If he kept babbling, he might end up confessing his love—and that he could never do. He slid to the floor and waited.

He was rescued from the tortured silence in half the time promised. The young soldier was out of breath when he unlocked the door. "Soldiers are coming. I have to get you out of here."

Felicity slipped through the door the moment he swung it open. She kept her back straight and her gaze away from Drew's. Her composure belied what had passed between them.

Drew was a wreck. During the time she'd stood in the darkness of his cell, remote yet painfully near, he'd felt as if he'd been made to chew on his own heart. It was as tough and rancid as weevil-infested biscuits. Watching her leave made him physically ill. His stomach burned.

313

"You haven't seen the last of me, love."

He looked up to see her staring at him from the other side of the bars.

Her eyes seethed with anger, but she smiled sweetly. "I'll be at your execution."

The tangible pain of a boot connecting with Drew's ribs distracted him from the emotional agony of Felicity's parting words. Success had never tasted so bitter. A few more blows delivered by his other unexpected visitors that night would soon bring him to sweet oblivion, a place where Felicity's hatred could no longer hurt him.

As abruptly as it had begun, the beating stopped. Drew blinked away the trickle of blood blurring his vision in time to see the soldiers' black boots backing away from him. There were three of them. At first, instinct had urged him defend himself. The restriction of his chains had rendered the action ineffective, and only amused his attackers. Submitting to the beating had not been so bad after he realized it lessened the pain in his heart.

A disjointed voice floated somewhere above him. "I wanted him docile, not dead."

Drew recognized the man's nasal twang. Hatred gave him the strength to lift his head off the ground.

"Very good. You're conscious." The Duke of Foxmoor turned to the soldiers. "Leave us. I wish to speak to the prisoner in private."

"He's a dangerous one, Your Grace. I don't think—"

The duke stopped the soldier's warning with a wave of his hand, then strutted closer to Drew. "You doubt my ability to handle this cur? I would have beaten him myself, but I had no wish to soil my hands with his blood. Get out."

The soldiers shuffled from the cell without further argument.

Drew raised himself onto his elbows to get his first unguarded look at his younger brother. That he'd never seen him before this morning was not by chance. He'd steered clear of his father's estate even if other boys from the village cut across the wooded acres and fished in its streams. To all except his illegitimate son, his father had been a kind overseer, a paternal landlord.

Watching his brother parade around the dirty cell with a lace handkerchief covering his nose had Drew wondering what kind of man his father really had been. Apparently the old duke hadn't had much in the way of fathering skills; neither of his sons seemed to have turned out well. If it weren't for the resemblance in height, Drew would doubt they shared blood. On his worst day, Lord Christian didn't swing his hips or dangle his wrists. If Drew had thought he appeared half as effeminate as the man in his cell, he'd have never taken on the role of fop, much less worn makeup.

"What are you looking at? Sit up." The heightened pitch of the duke's voice revealed his nervousness.

Drew struggled to comply, stopping midway when the cell spun. The soldiers had delivered several blows to his head before Drew dropped to the ground and wisely shielded his face with his arms.

The duke leaned over him. "You're not so threatening, are you, El Diablo? I must say, you surprised me when you escaped from that Spanish prison, so I was expecting someone a little more flamboyant. Why did you keep throwing our father's name around, anyway? After ignoring you in his own backyard, did you really think he'd aid you from halfway around the world?"

Drew lifted his head from where it hung between his braced arms. Apparently, his brother didn't share his desire not to know what the competition had been up to over the years. Probably because he didn't see Drew as competition at all. "I don't recall using the Andrews name during that particular adventure, but I'm glad you're keeping careful record, brother."

The duke's cocky grin drooped on one side at Drew's appellation. "Oh, but you did claim to be a child of my father's. A bastard, no less. Apparently the Spaniard thought that was enough to garner payment of a ransom. But alas, it wasn't."

Drew sat up on his knees, testing his ability to stay conscious before he used the wall to help him stand. The duke watched him with a satisfied smirk on his face. No doubt he thought the knowledge that his father would leave Drew in a rat-infested torture chamber to die would come as some sort of striking blow. Drew remembered making the claim now, but it had only been to stall for time. The hope of a ransom had saved Drew from immediate execution, and in the end, he had escaped.

"Why are you here?" Drew was ready to cut the confrontation short. "As you can see, I won't be escaping this time."

"No. And you turned yourself in to save a woman." His brother made a tsk-tsk sound that had Drew thinking of desperate ways to slip from his shackles. "I wish our father had lived to see this. He'd never have believed it. When he heard of your pirate escapades, I fear he thought you an idealized hero in some tragic epic. He always loved untamed things. How I'd relish him knowing I was the instrument that brought you down."

"You didn't do much. Were you always such a tattler? Probably hid behind your mother's skirts." Drew paused as casually as he could manage, considering his circumstances. "That's right; you were sickly, weren't you? Could never go out and play with the other children."

"I was the heir. The only offspring my father had that mattered. My mother thought I needed sheltering." The duke squared his shoulders. "But she was wrong. I killed Marley and his wife, you know."

Drew placed his hands flat against the moss-covered wall behind him and tried to appear relaxed instead of on the verge of fainting. "I don't believe you." He wasn't sure if he did or not. His head spun, and he desperately needed to lie down, but he suspected his answer would be the most upsetting to his brother.

"Who else would have committed the crimes?" The duke stepped closer and pulled off his tall white wig. Hair the same color and texture as Drew's fell around his brother's shoulders, and even Drew was forced to see the resemblance. "Came to give Marley his reward for the information he'd so thoughtfully provided. With the help of some hired ruffians, of course. His pretty young wife saw our approach from the window and ran down to greet us. At first she thought I was you. She was all ablush that you came strolling up to her front door in the dead of night. Did you bed her?"

"No." Drew wanted to close his eyes against the duke's words, but he didn't want to reveal how much his brother's ruthless acts shook him.

"I did. A shame to kill her, but there was no way around it. Marley, on the other hand, brought his fate upon himself. You don't blackmail a duke. It's not done."

Drew watched his brother in silence, recognizing his cold detachment as something Drew had once cultivated in himself. But even at his worst moments, he'd had limits. Apparently, the Duke of Foxmoor had none.

"You look at me as if you wish to say something. Speak, dear *brother*." He said the word with ill-disguised contempt. "That's why I've come tonight." The duke strode closer. "I decided to offer the reward for Marley's murder instead of doing away with you myself when that dear, sweet Beatrice mistook us, even momentarily. I posed for the drawing." The duke stuck out his jaw and angled his face for Drew's inspection. "I think I might be the more menacing pirate. From what I see, you don't live up to your reputation."

"Why didn't you just kill me?" Drew tried to keep his shoulders rounded, though a strong desire to reach for his brother had broken through his pain-fogged brain. "Why go to all this trouble?"

"Do you think I came all this way just to *kill* you? Do you think I care about you that much? Hardly. If you had died in that prison, as you were supposed to, you would have saved all of us a lot of trouble." His brother's direct gaze challenged Drew to argue.

"I never wanted anything from you or our father."

The duke hooked his thumbs in the pockets of his embroidered jacket. "Well, believe it or not, he wanted something from you."

Drew straightened before he could stop himself, his interest rattling his chains.

The duke nodded in acknowledgment of Drew's reaction, then he paced to the other side of the cell. "No, I don't think I'll tell you." He paced back again. "The reason I didn't kill you was because our father acknowledged you in his will."

Drew didn't have the strength to hide his surprise.

"Oh, yes. And he was still alive to receive that little ransom note from the Spanish. Wanted to send the money and bring you back to the bosom of the family to recover. I couldn't have that. And not just for myself. I wouldn't let him insult my mother's memory like that."

Drew took a step toward his brother, all restraint swept away by an awful realization. "You killed him, didn't you?"

"Not precisely, no. Our father was an accomplished horseman. Did you know that?"

Drew nodded, despite himself. He'd often seen his father ride through the village on his latest mount. How many years had it taken Drew to stop holding his breath with the hope the duke would finally pause to speak to him?

"Look at you! Please don't tell me you actually loved the pompous ass. I assure you, he wasn't worth the maudlin expression. Be glad I loosened the stitching on his saddle and dug a trench under his favorite jump. He'd just gotten a new stallion—a mean animal that was supposedly untamable. Everyone told Father he'd break his neck on the bloody thing. I just made sure he did."

The duke sagged for a moment, then stood straighter as he took a deep breath and let it out again. "It felt good to get that off my chest." He rubbed the velvet lapel of his jacket, which would have covered his heart if he had one. "There was speculation about his death, of course. Everyone knew we didn't get on, but luckily no one but me knew about the ransom letter. The old man thought I would somehow be pleased to know I had an older brother. As if I didn't already know."

The duke paced in front of Drew, rambling on as if he were talking to himself in a mirror. "Well, that old bugger got the last laugh, because I didn't know he'd left you money, and even referred to you as Andrew Crawford Andrews in his will. I mean, really, what kind of noble name is that, Andrew Andrews? It might have been clever of your mother to name you Andrew in the event anyone in the village missed the fact she was my father's whore, but I'm sorry—if all that came to light in London . . . Well, we just wouldn't want that, would we?"

His brother paused to stare at Drew, waiting for him to rise to the slur against his mother. Let his brother think what he wanted. He had no right to know how Drew's mother, against reason, loved his father and the child they'd created together.

"So you see," his brother continued with a slight smirk, "I couldn't kill you outright without bringing undue attention to myself. I certainly had no intention of taking you home and welcoming you into the family. Actually, if Marley hadn't brought your existence to light, you might have escaped with me thinking you died in that Spaniard's prison. I'm so glad that didn't happen, aren't you?"

"I don't want my father's money. I have plenty of my own." Drew's head was slowly clearing. The room no longer spun, but what came into clarity was entirely more unsettling.

"Less than before, I imagine. That was an added benefit of seizing the New England Trading Company's assets. Of course, the ships and goods had to be divided among the governor and a few wronged citizens besides myself, but I made out nicely."

Drew studied the moss that crept up the wet stone of his prison while his brother's words washed over him. His brother's confession didn't really matter. Even if he told someone about the duke's involvement in Marley and Beatrice's murder or even his father's, no one would believe him. Drew was an outlaw, after all. He had committed enough acts of piracy on his own to warrant his hanging. Felicity's involvement in his life had made the end to his games inevitable. His life meant nothing without her in it, and having her in it would be her death warrant.

Drew leaned against the wall and crossed his ankles. "Congratulations."

"Thank you." The duke sighed. "Well, I feel as if I've just been to the confessional. I suppose I should be on my way and let you rot in peace." He yanked his wig back on and tucked his hair beneath it. Rows of tight white curls adorned with a burgundy-colored ribbon provided the bloodthirsty fiend with an effeminate air that covered his tracks as well as his title. Drew could now see why Lord Christian's disguise worked so well. And he'd thought himself clever!

The duke bowed at the waist. "I can honestly say it was a pleasure to meet you."

Drew tried to keep the bloodlust out of his eyes and maintain his relaxed stance. Let him out of his chains and he would rip out the duke's liver and make him eat it. In light of his brother's list of victims, Drew had no doubt Felicity was in serious danger.

Drew suspected his brother read his thoughts, because the main stepped outside the cell and closed the door. He took the torch from its holder on the stone wall.

"One more thing." The man's genuine smile set Drew on edge. "Felicity is going to have a terrible accident shortly after your execution. You told her too much."

Drew lunged, but his chains brought him up ridiculously short of reaching the duke. His brother's laugh drifted over the rattle as he walked away.

Drew eased back against the wall. A cold fury cleared his vision, allowing him to see through the pitch-black gloom. He'd have his chance with the Duke of Foxmoor after all. Being the martyr was no longer an option. His prison rations remained in a dark corner of the cell, untouched. The runny gruel and moldy bread had looked too revolting to eat before, but things had changed. He needed his strength.

A large rat challenged him over the bread and lost. Drew picked off the largest sections of spongy green from the damp loaf. He swallowed the first bite before he gave in to the urge to spit it out.

Without examining the contents too closely, he took a gulp from the bowl. He winced and took another long swallow. After he forced down the rest of the food, he'd sleep. And tomorrow he'd find a way out of here.

# Chapter Twenty-two

"Where are all the guards?" whispered Felicity.

"I don't know. Maybe we've finally had some luck."

In the inky darkness, she heard Solomon's shrug in his tone rather than witnessing it with her own eyes. She stared down into the void at the bottom of the steps. After the first two, the rest disappeared into nothing.

"Or maybe they're all down there."

A map of the jail, procured from one of its former inmates, had revealed the back entrance. The thick oval door stood off the main street so pedestrians wouldn't be bothered by the flow of dead prisoners. Not many survived the Barbados gaol's harsh conditions. Even fewer escaped. The wooden door, reinforced with steel bands, was supposed to be locked and guarded.

Solomon touched her shoulder. "It's too late to change your mind. He's to be executed tomorrow."

To distract from her sudden rush of fear, she checked the contents of the sack slung over her shoulder. "I'm just making sure I have everything." She readjusted her breeches. The increased freedom of wearing men's cloth-ing boosted her confidence. She could do this. She had to do this.

When Solomon showed up on her father's doorstep shortly after Drew's arrest, he'd wanted her help only as an informant. She'd had other ideas.

Being part of the escape plan kept her from thinking about her last meeting with Drew. She could still pretend she was a part of his life, and that the hurtful words he'd said didn't exist. She turned to Solomon. "I'm ready."

Without a word, he nudged her forward. She gingerly descended the first step. One. Two. She placed her hand against the cold stone, using the wall as a guide. There were twenty-three steps in all and she had to count every one of them.

Concentrating on getting down the windowless stairwell without breaking her neck didn't stop her anxiety over see-ing Drew again. After her initial devastation ebbed, she'd realized his cruelty at their last meeting had sprung from a desire to keep her from helping him. It was obvious. Unfortunately, his declaration about not loving her sounded too close to the truth. Her father had tried to warn her. Drew's reputation with women alone should have convinced her she'd never be more to him than a passing fancy. His words only confirmed what she already knew.

*Twelve*. She forcibly pushed away the thought and fo-cused on the steps. When her fingers brushed something slimy, she fought the urge to wipe her hand on her breeches. Touch had to double for eyesight.

Despite his lack of feelings for her, she still loved Drew and would do anything to see him safe. *Eighteen*. She couldn't let her personal heartbreak foil the plan. He had never promised her anything but lust. Even she was slightly surprised that she'd expected more. Perhaps her love for

Drew had grown so strong that she found it hard to believe the intensity was not returned.

*Twenty-three.* She stepped down onto the soft dirt floor. Cells lined the walls. Muted moonlight drifted through the high windows. Gray clouds with dark bellies shut out the stars, keeping her from seeing more than a few inches in front of her. She had to strain to make out the cells. Drew was supposed to be in the last one.

She counted the cells and stopped at Drew's. From her bag, she removed the long, sturdy file she'd selected for picking the heavy latch. If it hadn't been for her extraordinary talent for opening locks—a skill that could not be bested in speed by even the most experienced cutthroats in Drew's crew—she'd have been forced to wait on the *Rapture.* She wanted to be the one to set Drew free. Her rescue would show him his words hadn't destroyed her. He meant as little to her as she did to him. Only she herself had to know her heart was permanently shattered.

She laid her hand against the cell's face, feeling for the lock. The slight pressure pushed open the iron gate.

She froze. It should have been locked. The small fear that lay curled in her belly got up and stretched. She crept inside the cell. Empty chains lay in a heap against the wall.

She pursed her lips to silence her anguished cry. They could not be too late. It was unthinkable. He hadn't been in the cell long enough to die of starvation or disease. Solomon's informant had said they'd seen him—She didn't complete her thought.

A hand clamped over her mouth a second before she was shoved to the ground. The file flew from her grasp, landing on the dirt floor out of her reach. Her assailant fell on top of her. She tried not to panic as she fought for a chance to free herself. Squirming in her captor's grasp, she reached for the long, sharp file. Her fingertips grazed its tip. If she could grab it, she could use it as a weapon.

Her assailant groped her body, stilling his movements

when he touched her hips. The fierce grip he had on her loosened. He lifted his weight and rolled her over.

She recognized the opportunity and acted swiftly. Mustering all the strength she possessed, she yanked up her knee between his bent legs.

He rolled off her with a familiar grunt. "Felicity." He groaned. "It's me."

She scrambled to her feet, pushing strands of hair out of her face to assure herself it was indeed Drew.

"You scared me."

Drew curled into a ball on his side. "I guess—" he paused to catch his breath—"you're still mad."

"Yes, but I only kneed you because I didn't know it was you." She stood over him, straightening the oversized jacket that had twisted in their struggle. Being in his company brought the sharp sting of his rejection back in a rush.

He grunted as he slid to his knees.

She put her finger to her lips. "Shh. We have to be quiet."

"I think I'm going to be sick. Do you know how bad it hurts a man when you knee him in the groin?"

"Yes." She held herself stiffly. Running to his side would only remind them both of how foolish she'd been in declaring her love. "I wouldn't have put so much force into it if I knew it was you. Now hurry."

He finally got to his feet, but had to bend over his knees for a few seconds before straightening. "What the hell are you doing here, anyway?"

"I'm here to rescue you."

"I think you emasculated me instead."

She choked down a terse rejoinder. Curtailing his virility, even temporarily, wouldn't hurt him. She should have kneed him in the beginning instead of falling in love with him.

"How did you get out of your chains?"

325

With a jerk of his head, he directed her attention to a dark corner in the cell. "I had the key."

Her gaze focused on a crumpled figure, blood running from his mouth. A tray of food lay scattered around him, as if he'd been surprised while delivering Drew's last meal. Immediately, she looked away. Turning her back to Drew, she tried to hide her revulsion. She really was in over her head this time. Having another death on her conscience was more than she could bear. If the British caught them, no one would be spared.

"Let's go. The others are waiting."

He grabbed her arm and turned her around. "He's not dead. Just resting."

She tried to pull away, but he brought her closer by wrapping his arms around her waist. "We have to hurry."

"It's all right. Sam took care of the guards at the back door." He leaned forward and had the audacity to try to kiss her. Really, he thought too highly of himself as a womanizer.

"Sam?" She turned her face to the side, avoiding mouth-to-mouth contact at all costs. When she realized who Sam was, she also learned he could hurt her more than he already had. "Samantha Linley!"

"Be quiet. Sam's having an affair with the officer in charge of the prison. They're upstairs right now. You met him at the Linleys' party. He makes sure the back door is unlocked and unguarded for their meetings."

Felicity stared at Drew, too shocked to speak. Was this a common occurrence for him? Did he expect her to take up with one of his crew after he was done with her? "It's amazing she finds the time."

"They meet on Tuesdays when Philip is engaged elsewhere. She made special arrangements for tonight, but we have to hurry." He tried to push her toward the cell door, but she stepped out of his reach.

"I didn't realize you two were still so close, but I suppose

326

I should have after our last conversation." Her throat tightened. She swallowed down the emotion.

He turned and grabbed her shoulders, holding her in front of him. God, but it looked like he intended to try and kiss her again. She tried to jerk from his grasp but he held her still. "I'm not exactly sure why Sam helped me, but I think it might have something to do with her feeling a little trapped herself. Though, I wasn't too surprised when she stopped by my cell on the way to see her soldier. Sam thrives on stirring her husband's temper. She brought me some food and told me when the back door would be unlocked. Nothing more." He squeezed Felicity's arms and lowered his voice. "Things were done with Sam and I before I ever met you, but even when we were together, neither of us had any illusions about love."

Felicity shoved him hard. She had no wish for him to stare so earnestly into her eyes and tell her of his shortcomings again. "I have no desire to hear about your relationship with—" He stopped her by putting a finger over his lips. "Shh. Don't want to wake up the others." He paused. "Or maybe we do?"

He reached down and scooped up a handful of keys. "We'll let the others go, too." He pulled a few keys off the ring and tossed them to her.

She scrambled to catch them. "They are killers and God knows what else. Besides, we don't have time."

He grabbed her arm and pulled her from the cell. "It'll give us more time. It will be a diversion."

She didn't want to do it. Damn him. How could he go from woman to woman so callously? Linley? And why had he accepted Samantha's help to escape and not her own? "No. I won't release them."

He strode to the nearest cell and tried different keys in the lock. "Oh? So your father was a killer, was he?"

She scooped up the file from the dirt. By the time he found the right key, she could open all the locks. Let him free all the prisoners. Let him sleep with whomever he pleased. All she wanted to do was get out of there and then remove herself from his company . . . permanently.

She shoved Drew aside. The nearest prisoner stood by the door, not asking questions, just eager to be released. She sprung the lock in seconds.

Drew squeezed her shoulder and whispered much too closely to her ear, "I knew there was a reason I liked you so much."

Tears sprung to her eyes, but she distracted herself and him by quickly opening the rest of the cells. He might like her, but he'd never love her. Apparently, he liked Samantha Linley also, and who knew how many others. He probably didn't even notice who filled his bed. It was a wonder he kept the names straight.

When she stumbled, Drew pulled her down the long corridor and up the stairs. The freed prisoners, even the bundle of clothes that sprouted legs and a shaggy head, followed without having to be told. Felicity wanted to jerk away from Drew. His touch was torture. Unfortunately, she couldn't navigate the stone steps with his speed unless he helped her. She wondered if Samantha melted at Drew's slightest caress as she did. Damn him for being such a thorough lover!

At the top of the stairs, Solomon held the door open for them. "A cart's waiting."

Drew hauled Felicity up the last steps and into the alleyway.

Solomon closed the door behind them and they all rushed to climb into the bed of the wagon. Unruffled as usual, Solomon didn't even blink at the extra ten passengers. After the last man had climbed aboard, Drew lifted Felicity onto the cart.

"Stay here," he said, then sprinted around the cart to talk to Solomon, who held the reins of the two nervous horses.

Felicity sat up on her knees so she could see over the bodies crowded around her. Solomon's stance warned her he wasn't happy with whatever Drew was telling him. Both he and Solomon swung their gazes in her direction, giving her the distinct impression their argument had something to do with her.

A light flared, then steadied in a window above them. Wooden shutters were closed against the night, but the lantern light seeped through the slats, throwing more attention on them than they needed. Solomon jumped into the driver's seat and Drew sprinted back to her. Felicity slid against the man next to her, making room for Drew. Apparently, whatever they had been discussing wasn't as urgent as their immediate need to be away from the prison.

Drew pushed Felicity's head down while he tried to draw the tarpaulin over her. "Obey Solomon. I'll see you on the ship."

She grabbed his wrist, preventing him from covering her with the dirty canvas. "No. Come with us."

The shutters from above swung open, banging against the building. Both their gazes jerked to the window. A man hung over the edge. With the light at his back, they couldn't see his face, but blond hair hung around broad, naked shoulders. "Bloody hell!" his curse echoed in the alley.

Drew used the moment of surprise to wrench free from her grasp and step back. "Go, Solomon."

"Get in the cart," Solomon's hoarse words sounded as desperate as Felicity felt.

Drew took a few more steps away from them. Felicity reached out her hand to him. "Please. Get in the cart." Instead of the shrill demand she had intended, her voice sounded weak with fear.

He shook his head and continued walking backward, watching her as if he were trying to memorize her features. A shaft of moonlight fell on his face, and she realized his left eye was blackened and his lip cut. He'd been beaten since she last saw him.

"I lied in the prison. I do love you." A grin tugged at the corner of his mouth that wasn't swollen. "I hope I get the chance to make you believe that. If not . . ." He let the sentence he suddenly seemed unable to complete drift off. "Either way, I'll make sure you're safe." He tore his gaze away from hers. "Go, Solomon!" he said through gritted teeth, then turned and ran down the cobblestone alley.

She sat on her knees, too stunned to do anything but watch him go. To turn to Solomon and demand he do something meant she'd have to take her eyes off Drew. That he'd said he loved her only gripped her heart with the renewed force of pain. Hearing those words wasn't worth watching him run away.

The door to the prison banged open, forcing Felicity to dart her gaze in the direction of the sound. The slap of reins against horseflesh, followed by wheels crunching sand on cobblestone, drifted over her in unnaturally slowed time. She could no longer see Drew, and hoped neither did the half-dressed man now standing in the middle of the alley.

He paid no attention to her or the cart pulling away, but kept his gaze on the place where Drew's white shirt had last been visible in the thick night. After a few half-hearted paces while pulling a red coat over his bare shoulders, he turned again to the cart.

Felicity fell back on her heels when a wheel hit a rut in the cobblestone. The urge to slip off the cart, while she still could, had her gripping the wooden side in indecision. The soldier turned back to the prison and Felicity knew he would sound an alarm. Why did Drew run away on foot? He'd surely be captured unless she could stop the soldier from alerting the others.

Before Felicity could do anything, Samantha Linley slid through the open door. Her dark hair swayed around her shoulders and the silk of her cream-colored gown caught the light from the window. She blocked the soldier's way and kept him standing in the alley with a deep, long kiss. Perhaps she would gain Drew only a few more minutes, but that might make all the difference.

Darkness enveloped the cart as it drew farther from the prison. Only the couple's shady silhouette remained visible until they abruptly parted. Samantha rushed in the direction of the cart. At first Felicity feared she was coming after them; then she thought she might be trying to warn them. When it came to Drew's life, Felicity would take any ally she could, even one as questionable as Samantha Linley.

Samantha abruptly darted between two buildings lining the alley, a space barely visible in the dark, and Felicity spotted the glint of metal off the unlit lantern on Samantha's waiting carriage. A flash of insight tightened Felicity's chest. Was that how Drew planned to escape—hide in Samantha Linley's carriage?

The wooden cart driven by Solomon careened around the corner and onto Broad Street. Felicity slipped under the canvas tarp not wanting to be spotted on Barbados's main thoroughfare. She huddled against the other prisoners, her heart still pounding in her ears. The urge to peek from underneath her cover to see if Samantha's carriage pulled into the street tempted her. Knowing that Drew's best chance for escape lay with Samantha Linley, filled Felicity with a stomach-churning combination of hope and dread.

He'd said he loved her before he left, and everything in her wanted to believe him. When her habitual doubts tried to raise a damning chorus, all she had to do to snuff them out was recall the look on his face before he disappeared down the alley. He'd sacrificed himself for her safety more than once, and if he wanted to try to prove to her that he truly loved her, she'd give him all the time he needed. And though it was the hardest thing Felicity had ever had to do, she stayed hidden because Drew asked her to, and she trusted her heart while knowing full well there was a strong possibility she'd never see him again.

# Chapter Twenty-three

Felicity trained the spyglass on the crowd surrounding the scaffold. The soft roar reaching her on the deck of the newly painted *Rapture* confirmed they were eager for a hanging. She hoped they would be disappointed.

When her father tried to wrestle the telescope from her, she slapped away his fingers and scowled. Drew's continued absence tried her sanity. Her father would just have to wait.

He rubbed his knuckles and returned her glare. Time in gaol had roughened his soft temperament. "Give it here, daughter. I'm just as anxious as you to know what's going on."

Grudgingly, she handed over the leather tube. They were all on edge. "We should do something. Perhaps I should go down to the dock to—"

Solomon's baritone voice was as firm as his solid presence behind them. "No one leaves the ship until the captain's return."

As hard as she tried, Felicity had been unable to pry any

information from Solomon after they'd returned to the ship. Her pleas for answers regarding Drew's disappearance were met with monosyllabic grunts, though she suspected he knew much more than he let on. The only explanation she received was that Drew had had unfinished business.

Scanning the growing crowd from the deck of the *Rapture* only increased Felicity's fear. What had been so important that he had had to leave her? He said he loved her and wanted to make her believe it. Being by her side in the flesh would have been plenty; he didn't need to run off on some mysterious errand. She feared he'd left to save them from being caught with Barbados's most-wanted fugitive, wanted to get back to the ship on his own. Had he failed? Why was there a crowd around the scaffold if he'd escaped?

With her naked eye, she could barely distinguish the wooden scaffold from the blur of people gathering for El Diablo's hanging. The excited buzz wafting over the distance seemed to promise the entertainment would take place as scheduled. "I can't bear this. Do you know for sure that he wasn't recaptured, Solomon?"

Solomon's tone held the familiar calm that at the moment tempted Felicity to shake him. "A good strategist does not waver from his plans at the first tingle of doubt. All will be well."

Having Drew in her life however briefly was a gift. Discovering that he truly loved her had been a miracle. But she'd gladly give up the latter just to know he was safe.

"I see something!" Her father's voice held all the panic Felicity felt.

She yanked the spyglass away from him, raising it to her eye before he could grab it back. Immediately, she spotted Drew, and her worst fears tightened her throat like a noose. Watching Drew hang would kill her as well. "There he is!" She pointed with her free hand. "They're leading him to the scaffold. Solomon, please, do something."

"May I see the telescope, Miss Kendall?"

She didn't respond. Her gaze remained riveted on the scene below. A blindfolded man, flanked by a guard, was led in chains to the scaffold. The dark, shoulder-length hair teased by the trade winds told her more than she wanted to know. As if that weren't proof enough, Drew wore the same stained clothes he'd had on at his capture and their escape last night.

She trained the glass on his face, trying desperately to hold back tears that would blur her vision. Below the black swath covering his eyes, his cheek swelled red and purple, and a cut from his lip oozed fresh blood. Something had gone terribly wrong after Drew had left them last night.

"Give me the telescope." Solomon's words were a command.

Felicity slapped the tube in the quartermaster's waiting palm, hoping he'd finally do something once he saw with his own eyes the seriousness of the situation. "We have to act now. I won't let him hang."

"Did you notice the condemned man's guard?"

"There was only one by his side, but I'm sure there are more soldiers around. We'll need every man if we want to take Drew by force. Perhaps we should fire a cannon into the crowd."

Ideas ran through her head like shooting stars, but all were just as fleeting. The odds were against them, but she would not give up. She would forfeit her own life before she would watch Drew die.

Her father gently touched her arm. "Solomon will handle this. He won't let anything happen to Drew."

Solomon took her shaking hand and wrapped it around the telescope. "Drastic measures will not be necessary. Take another look at the man beside the prisoner."

She lifted the telescope to her right eye and closed her left. The blindfolded prisoner had reached the scaffold. He appeared to be babbling. Faint jeers from the crowd drifted toward them on the wind. They appeared to be laughing at what he was saying. She hated to take her eyes off Drew even for a moment but forced herself to look at the guard.

He was impossibly thin. Sandy hair fell limply across his pale face. He bore all his weight on his left leg, as if his right side pained him. He shifted and grimaced. Recognition hit her in a wave. In all the turmoil of the past weeks, she'd forgotten to ask if her patient had recovered. Apparently, he had. "Avery Sneed," she said to herself as much as to Solomon and her father.

"I don't think Mr. Sneed would be escorting our captain to the hangman's noose. Do you?"

Solomon sounded as if he'd moved away. When she turned to find him, her movements were blocked by a solid chest. Strong arms encircled her waist, closing the distance between them with a squeeze that robbed her of her breath.

"I'd have Avery whipped with the cat-o'-nine-tails if he ever even thought about it."

She squirmed, trying to look into her captor's face. An oversized tricorn that sporting a mauve plume covered the top of his painted face, but she'd recognize the voice anywhere. She tore off his hat and long white wig in one swift motion.

Sea-green eyes sparkled down at her with amusement. "I take it you don't like my borrowed clothes? Sorry; I had to loan out the ones I had on."

She wrapped her fingers in his hair and pulled him down for a deep kiss. "You scared the bloody hell out of me." She kissed him again. "Who's being hanged?" she asked when she finally let him go.

Drew kissed her back, quick and hard. When he lifted his head, he laughed in deep, melodic tones. "I hate to tell you this, sweeting, but you now have more paint on your face than I do."

"I don't give a damn!" She pulled him down for another kiss to prove it. "Now, answer my question."

Drew wiped paint from the tip of her nose and answered, "El Diablo. Who taught you how to curse like that?"

"The Devil," she whispered against his lips. Her hands played in his hair.

"What else did he teach you? Perhaps we should go to my cabin so you can show me."

She put her palms against Drew's chest to push him away from her. "We should leave before that crowd realizes there isn't going to be a hanging."

Drew rested his hand on her shoulder. "There will be a hanging. But we should still make a hasty departure. Solomon!" Drew turned away from her. "Are all the men accounted for besides Avery? He'll lie low for a few days, then meet us in the Bahamas."

"Aye, Captain. I'll be glad to see the last of Barbados." Felicity heard the relief in Solomon's voice and wondered if he had been as worried as she.

Her father brought the spyglass to his eye, scanning the shore. "I think they're going to hang that man, Drew. I don't want to see an innocent killed."

Drew retrieved the wig and hat from where it had landed on the deck. "You won't. My brother is getting nothing less than he deserves. He killed Marley and Beatrice. And my father." Felicity caught the edge of anger in his voice, but suspected the hurt and betrayal that went deeper. She slid her hand into his. "I'm so sorry. Did he hate you so much?"

Drew shrugged. "I don't think he cared about anyone else enough to actually hate them. We all just got in his way. My father recognized me in his will, and my brother didn't want that. Marley met his fate because he tried to blackmail the Duke of Foxmoor." Drew glanced across the water to the distant shore. The expanse was too great to see what transpired with the naked eye, but she suspected Drew could easily picture his brother's demise. "I've discovered there are worse things than being a pirate."

Felicity turned to face him. "So, you switched places with him. Did Samantha help you?"

Drew met her gaze with a slight rise of his eyebrows. "Samantha? I didn't know you two were on a first-name basis." He kissed Felicity's forehead, she guessed to reassure her for something she no longer needed reassurance about. "I didn't want her further involved. I know my way around the Linley plantation very well on my own. That's where Solomon and I spent some miserable years toiling in the fields. We still have a few friends there who were eager to help."

"Precisely why I'm more than ready to leave," Solomon interrupted. "I haven't let Hugh on deck since we've been in Carlisle Bay. Shall we raise anchor?"

"Absolutely. Sam told me the duke has a valet and secretary who travel with him, but everyone is used to his long disappearances. I left Linley Hall in disguise before most of the staff awoke, but I imagine someone will become suspicious before the day is out."

"What if they discover they hanged the wrong man?"

Drew smiled. "They won't. They'll be happier believing the Duke of Foxmoor drowned than admit they hanged him in place of a notorious pirate. Just to be sure, some witnesses will come forward with some of the clothes he left on shore when he went for a swim." Drew hooked his arm through Felicity's and started dragging her toward the companionway that led below. "I need to talk to you. Solomon, get us out of here."

"Aye, Captain." Solomon eagerly disappeared to follow Drew's orders.

Before Felicity could dreamily follow Drew below, her father blocked their path. The way he dropped his gaze and cleared his throat burst her bubble of happiness. "I know Felicity is a grown woman, but she's still my daughter."

"Hold on, Ben. Let me talk to Felicity in private, and I'm sure we can straighten out everything."

Felicity pulled away from Drew. If she followed him below, she'd surely lose her head. She didn't doubt he loved her—his actions had proved that—but how that love would be viewed by society hadn't occurred to her until now. She might have broken free of the strict moral shame she'd been subjected to for most of her life, but the look on her father's face told her that loving Drew on Drew's terms would be harder than she expected. Even so, she'd not go back to her former life. Being condemned as a fallen woman would be worth it to spend her life with Drew.

"It's all right, Father. I love him. I want to be with him."

Drew grinned at her as if he hadn't expected her to defend him. "That's good to hear."

"At what price?" Her father hooked his arm with hers and tried to pull her away. He looked at Drew. "We survived this, but the life you lead is too dangerous for Felicity. And what if there is a child?"

Drew's gaze swung to Felicity. When she shook her head no, he seemed to relax. Unfortunately, her father brought to light consequences she hadn't fully considered. She untangled herself from her father's grasp. "Let us speak in private."

"I can settle this. Of course, I preferred to do it in private so I didn't have to make a fool of myself in front of the crew." Drew dropped to one knee. He glanced at her father. "Am I doing this right?"

Her father nodded, the grin on his face telling her he realized what Felicity could hardly believe. Drew took her hands in his. A few sailors had stopped what they were doing to gape openly.

"You're ruining your bloodthirsty reputation, Drew. You'd better get up before your crew thinks you've gone mad." Felicity's voice sounded calm, though her insides were jangling uncontrollably.

"That's all right. We'll have to get a new crew when they find out I'm leaving piracy. All except for Solomon and Hugh, of course. Will you mind being a boring merchant's wife?"

"Boring sounds wonderful to me. But what about you?"

Drew glanced at Ben. "Can I get up now?"

Ben nodded, but continued to stare at them both with a grin on his face.

Drew stood and pulled Felicity against him. "I'm afraid you're going to have to provide all my excitement from now on. New Orleans doesn't have much in the way to offer for entertainment, but it's a young city. And more importantly, it's not British. A good place for all of us to start over." Drew wrapped his arm around her waist and urged her against him. "Fortunately, keeping me in a constant state of . . ." Drew glanced at her father, then cleared his throat. "Keeping me entertained seems to be a specialty of yours."

Her father's cheeks flushed. He bowed politely. "I'll leave you two alone now."

The sails unfurled in a protesting flap before they caught the wind and pushed the *Rapture* away from Barbados.

"Are you sure about this, Drew? As much as I love you, it's hard for me to imagine you as the domestic sort. And for you to settle down with one woman . . ." She let her sentence go unfinished and shoved on his shoulders so she could gaze into his eyes. If she witnessed a hint of regret there, she'd have to find the courage to let him go.

He didn't relinquish his tight embrace. "Oh, no. You're not getting away from me this time. You've ruined my taste for other women. No one has ever seen through me as effectively as you have. Nor loved me despite it."

The honesty she glimpsed in his sincere gaze left her mouth dry. She touched his lips with her fingers. "How could I not love you? You've done the same for me."

He grabbed her hand and kissed the center of her palm. "So, are we settled? It will be Monsieur and Madame." He paused. "There's one problem. When we reach New Orleans, who shall we be?"

"All I want is to be your wife and for you to be yourself."

Drew took her arm and dragged her into the relative privacy of the companionway in front of his cabin. Alone at last, he kissed her with slow, possessive adoration. When he pulled away, they both had trouble breathing. "I'm counting on you to help me figure out exactly who that is. In the meantime, I'll discover the rest of what you've been hiding, my passionate little Puritan."

She reached down and toyed with the top button of his breeches. "Let's start now. I think I have a few freckles you've missed."

He dipped down and swept her up in his arms. After he wrestled the portal to his cabin open, he grinned wickedly, then nipped her shoulder through her clothing. "Freckles suit you. If I have my way—and I will—that's all you'll be wearing for a very long time."

She buried her face in the crook of his neck. This time, she believed every word.

# AFTER THE ASHES
# CHERYL HOWE

A stagecoach robbery is the spark that sets fire to Lorelei Sullivan's plan for the future. She and her brother moved to New Mexico Territory to escape the past, to ranch, but Corey has destroyed all hope of that. Lawmen now want him—and Lorelei won't see the boy hang.

Yet defying the law places her between two men she can't trust: her sibling and Christopher Braddock, who is her brother's one shot at redemption—a hard, silent man who lights a fire inside her. And as his kiss fans the flames of desire, Lorelei wonders whether she will be consumed by this inferno or rise reborn from its ashes.

-----------------------------------------------

# MOONBOW
## IN THE
# *Mist*

# DIA HUNTER

Leaning out to peek at a flat boat poling up the Cumberland River, Naomi Romans falls flat on her face. Cradled in Shaw Larson's strong arms and staring up into the river peddler's pretty yellow-green eyes, Naomi finds everything changed . . . even herself. The fall brought her memories *back*. She isn't Naomi; she is Prima Powell, the missing daughter of a New York millionaire. Bedeviled by a pair of raccoons, befuddled by two years of lost memories, and bedazzled by Shaw's gentlest touch, Naomi is certain: she is the girl who went stumbling off so long to find moonbows in the mist . . . and now she's found something even better.

___4891-4                                        $5.50 US/$6.50 CAN

**Dorchester Publishing Co., Inc.**
**P.O. Box 6640**
**Wayne, PA 19087-8640**

Please add $2.50 for shipping and handling for the first book and $.75 for each book thereafter. NY, NYC, and PA residents, please add appropriate sales tax. No cash, stamps, or C.O.D.s. All orders shipped within 6 weeks via postal service book rate. Canadian orders require $2.50 extra postage and must be paid in U.S. dollars through a U.S. banking facility.

Name_____

Address_____

City_____ State_____ Zip_____

I have enclosed $_____ in payment for the checked book(s).
Payment <u>must</u> accompany all orders. ❑ Please send a free catalog.
**CHECK OUT OUR WEBSITE! www.dorchesterpub.com**